Also by Margaret Duckett

Straight Up and Down Please.
And Now a Triangle.

To

Almina

Do it Again Please

Margaret Duckett

With my best wishes,

Margaret Duckett

PENQUITE PRESS
SHINGAY

Do it Again Please
Copyright © Margaret Duckett 2002

ISBN 0 9540367 2 7

First Published 2002 by
Penquite Press
Shingay Herts

Printed in Great Britain for Penquite Press

4

Although the names of some of the shows are
factual, the events and characters are purely fictitious
Any resemblance of these characters to any person,
living or dead, is co-incidental

To Bill who is always there for me.

List of Abbreviations

KC	Kennel Club
CC	Challenge Certificate
Ch	Champion (3 CCs)
BIS	Best in Show
RBIS	Reserve Best in Show
BP	Best Puppy
BOB	Best of Breed
RBOB	Reserve Best of Breed
BOS	Best Opposite Sex

CHAPTER ONE

Caroline Amery stopped outside the imposing shop window with a beating heart. Yes, this was the right place; she read the name of Branscombe, Hedges and Carruthers, Solicitors on the shining, glass shop front. Taking a deep breath and straightening the jacket of her one and only suit, she opened the door.

"Good morning, can I help you?" A young, smartly dressed woman sat at a desk and, immediately Caroline felt that her best suit was dowdy and her hair was a mess. Summoning up her courage she said, "Yes, I'm Mrs Amery, Mrs Caroline Amery, you wrote to me asking me to come and see you."

"I see. Can you tell me who wrote to you, in other words, who is dealing with this matter?"

"Yes, it was a Mr Carruthers."

"Right, well, if you would like to take a seat, I will inform him that you are here."

Caroline sat down, she was so nervous that she could hardly think straight. She had been so surprised when she had received the letter from the solicitors last week, she didn't even know that Aunt Ellen had died. She felt guilty about that. All the way up in the train to Banbury she had thought about Aunt Ellen, her mother's sister, not that she had many memories of her at all. Aunt Ellen had married a major in the army and, all the time that Caroline was growing up, she had been abroad. Ellen had always corresponded regularly with her sister and she, Caroline, had always received lovely, unusual presents from Aunt Ellen and Uncle Charles for her birthday and at Christmas. Apart from that, the only time that she could remember actually seeing and talking to Aunt Ellen was when Caroline and her mother had attended Charles' funeral.

When her Uncle Charles had retired from the army, he and Aunt Ellen had bought a house in the country near Banbury. It was a fairly substantial house built in red brick and with a large garden, both had impressed Caroline very much at the time of the funeral. She had also thought that Aunt Ellen was very slender and beautifully dressed, she wore perfume, jewellery and high heels and seemed the complete opposite of her mother. There weren't any children around and

Caroline's mother had told her that they had had one little boy but he had died from malaria when they were abroad. It had all been very sad especially as there had never been any more children.

Her mother had sent a wedding invitation to Aunt Ellen when Caroline had married Dennis but Aunt Ellen had not been well enough to attend, but had sent a handsome cheque. Similarly, when her mother had died she had informed Aunt Ellen, but, although she sent a beautiful wreath, she again had not been well enough to come. Since then, Caroline had dutifully sent her Aunt a card on her birthday and a card with a little present at Christmas. Her Aunt had always thanked her and enclosed a small cheque for her and Dennis but apart from that she...

"Mrs. Amery, would you like to come this way please."

Mr Carruthers turned out to be the complete antithesis of what she had imagined, he was young, smartly dressed in a dark grey suit and had a lovely smile. He stood up to shake hands with her, "Do sit down Mrs Amery, it's a pleasure to meet you."

"Thank you."

"Would you like some coffee?"

"No thank you."

"I hope that your journey was comfortable?"

"Oh, yes, yes very."

"Did you travel by car?"

"No, no by train."

"Oh, I see, well, if we can get on with the preliminaries. Have you brought identification, birth certificate etc.?"

"Yes, they're all in my handbag," she pulled out a brown envelope and handed it to him.

"Did you know your Aunt well?"

"No, not very well. She lived abroad a lot."

"Yes, so I understand. She was your mother's sister I believe?"

"Yes, that's right, her younger sister. My mother died two years ago."

"Oh, I'm sorry, so this is a double loss for you."

"Er, yes."

Caroline's heart was beating so hard that she could hardly speak. Just what had Aunt Ellen left her. It must be something nice surely. She wished he'd get to the point. Aunt Ellen had gone into a nursing home quite recently so Mr Carruthers was now telling her, in fact, only a month before she died. He had been in the process of putting the house up for sale at the time. However, two days before she had gone into the nursing home, she had asked him to go to see her and she had made a new will. Caroline uncrossed her legs and then re-crossed them, the suspense was killing her, she wished he'd get to the point, just what had Aunt Ellen left her!

Mr Carruthers opened the file in front of him and took out some papers, "Now Mrs Amery, I shall read out the will."

Caroline had her hands so tightly clasped together that her fingers were white, the blood drained from her face as the solicitor started reading the will. Aunt Ellen had left several thousand pounds to the Great Ormond Street Hospital for Sick Children! Oh God, what had she left her! There were several other big bequests, one to the Red Cross and one to Medecin sans Frontieres, then there were several small amounts to people that she did not know. She looked at the solicitor's face willing him to tell her what she had got, that's if there was anything left by now! Just then he looked up and smiled at her, "Now, Mrs Amery, your Aunt, Mrs Ellen Cartwright, wanted you to have the house and its' entire contents together with a bequest of £80,000 for its' maintenance, with the proviso that you......."
She heard no more, tears welled in her eyes and she gasped for breath. She rummaged in her handbag for a tissue.

Mr Carruthers stopped reading, "Are you alright Mrs Amery, can I get you a glass of water or something?"

"No, no th- thank you. It's just a shock that's all. I hardly knew her. I didn't think that... The whole house you said."

"Yes, that is correct. It is yours outright, there is no mortgage outstanding or loans made against the property. It...."
Caroline stopped listening, that great big house and £80,000, her mind was blank, she couldn't believe it.

"How much is it worth then, the house?"

"Difficult to say Mrs Amery, that is not my field of knowledge. I can tell you that it is in excellent condition and in a very sought after area."

"Can I go and see it?"

"Yes, of course, I have the keys and would be happy to show you round at any time."

"Today?"

"I'm sorry, not today, I'm due in court. Perhaps we could arrange a time though suitable to us both."

"Right, well I'll go home and tell Dennis, that's my husband, and I'll be in touch. He'll want to see it too."

"Certainly Mrs Amery and may I take this opportunity to congratulate you on your good fortune. I hope that you and your husband will be very happy there."

"Oh, we shan't live there, I'll sell it."

"But, Mrs Amery, didn't you understand the terms of the will?"

"What terms?"

"As stated in the will and as I read out to you, you receive the house and its' contents together with the stipulated sum of money, only if you live there for the next five years. Mrs Cartwright seemed to think that, by then, you would have fallen as much in love with the house as she had."

"What did you say, five years?"

"Those are quite clearly the terms of the will."

"But what about Dennis's job? What about our house now?"

"I presume that you mean your present living accommodation. Well, you could sell it."

"So, if I don't live here, I don't get anything?"

"I'm afraid that is the case Mrs Amery, but let me assure you that it is a lovely house and this is a very pleasant part of England. Do you have a family because there are some excellent schools in the area."

"No, Dennis and I didn't have any children."

"I see. Well, if you wouldn't mind waiting a moment, I'll just get these photocopied."

When he re-entered the office, Caroline stood up, her legs were shaking and she smiled weakly and pulled her suit jacket straight, "Well, thank you Mr Carruthers. It's been a bit of a shock all round. I shall have to talk to Dennis. Can I ring you?"

"Certainly Mrs Amery, at any time. I do understand."

Tightly clutching her handbag, she slowly made her way out of the office smiling briefly at the receptionist and saying goodbye. She walked along the unfamiliar High Street until she found a public house. Going up to the bar she ordered a large brandy and a cup of coffee. The licensee looked at her white face and offered to bring the drink over to her if she would like to sit down. She suddenly felt very tired and cold, she shivered in her one and only suit and wished she had brought her comfortable old fleece that she wore to dog shows. Having got some strength and warmth from the brandy and coffee, she ordered another coffee and a sandwich. About half an hour later and somewhat fortified, she made her way back to the station.

Dennis got out of the car and let himself in at the front door, he could hear the radio playing in the kitchen and knew that she must be home. Good, he was hungry and wouldn't have to get himself anything, he had thought about stopping at the fish and chip shop on the way but felt guilty about leaving the dogs any longer. Poor devils' had been shut in for most of the day.

"I'm home."

Caroline was putting two plates of salad on the kitchen table. Blast, he wished he'd stopped now at the chip shop.

"Well, what did you get? Some earrings or a brooch or something?"

She looked up at him and he realised that something wasn't right, "What's the matter Caroline? Didn't you get to see the solicitor?"

"Oh yes. I saw him alright."

"Well, didn't your Aunt leave you anything at all?"

"Sit down, it's only tinned pilchards and salad, you can have some bread and butter if you want."

"Yes, please."

"You start your salad and I'll tell you all about it. I'll just cut the bread."

She had to go through the events of the day twice before Dennis fully realised the implications of the will. The salad sat on his plate almost untouched.

"But, I can't give up my job. What about the darts club?"

"For goodness sake Dennis. The darts club's the least of our worries."

"Yeah, but what about my job?"

"Well, I've been thinking, you could apply for a transfer. After all they must have a branch of the insurance company up there. I'm sure that you could easily get a transfer."

"Hey, hold on, you're not seriously considering going up there to live are you?"

"What, haven't you got it through your thick head yet. The house must be worth several hundred thousand and we get £80,000 as well. You won't get money like that from working for the insurance, will you, not ever. You know that! We'd be well off for the first time in our lives. Anyway, I've got a stinking headache and I'm going to take a couple of Aspirin and go to bed."

"OK. I'll be up soon. I want to watch the football on the tele."

Having taken the dogs for their walk, Dennis locked up, made himself another cup of coffee and sat down in the kitchen with their three Cumbrian terriers.

He sat there mulling over the terms of the will and what it meant for them, while he stroked the head of one of the dogs. Looking down he said, "D'you know Patsy, life's a bugger." Getting up, he switched off the light, put the dogs in the kitchen and made his way upstairs.

CHAPTER TWO

As the plane landed with a bump and the noise of the reverse thrust of the engines made her ears hurt, Fiona gave a deep sigh, turning to Simon she smiled and let go of his hand. She really did not enjoy flying, well certainly not the take-offs and the landings anyway. She had endeavoured to think of nice things, like making love to Simon, or the way the dogs greeted her in the mornings, or the flowers in the woods, they all helped to take her mind off the landing, but she still felt very nervous and tense.

It had been a wonderful trip to Germany, it was their first overseas appointment to judge Cumbrian terriers and they had both been very well received. They both had some beautiful dogs to go over and they had been applauded for their final choices. The hospitality of their German hosts had been second to none and they both felt that they had been a success and that it might lead on to further appointments. It was the first break that they had had since getting back together after their separation and they had decided to make it their honeymoon: the one that they had not had when they got married due to pressure of work at the kennels. After leaving their German hosts they had travelled to a small hotel in Bavaria; the views had been spectacular from the bedroom windows, the food and service excellent and they had been able to walk and talk and resolve all the little worries that had upset them in the past.

The plane was just taxiing into place on the runway and people were beginning to fold up magazines and gather their possessions as Fiona thought about those wonderful few days. Each night Simon had undressed her and had quietly kissed every inch of her body, she had then responded by kissing his body until neither of them could resist the force of their love any longer and he would enter her and the rhythm of their moving against each other would reach an elating, shouting, laughing climax. One night, after they had made love once and dozed off in each other's arms, Simon suddenly opened his eyes and leapt from the bed and began rummaging in Fiona's Vanity bag,

"What ever are you doing now?"

"Looking for something you bought, I've had a bloody good idea. Ah, got it."

He pulled a small glass bottle containing some pinkish liquid from the bag, "Yes, here it is."

"That's that expensive skin lotion isn't it that I bought today. It's got a gorgeous scent."

"Good."

Simon came back to the bed, "Come on, stand up."

"What are you going to do?"

"You'll see, come on stand up and turn your back towards me."

She complied and he told her to close her eyes. She started as his hands touched the tops of her shoulders, slid down one side of her arms and up the other side and back to her shoulders. They then gently slid down to her breasts. He circled them several times pulling at the nipples. The scent of the lotion on his hands wafted up to her nostrils, "Oh Simon, that's lovely."

"You're telling me kid."

She could feel his arousement as he continued to put the lotion on his hands and slide them down her belly. He then knelt and slid his hands down and over her thighs, her calves and, gently lifting each foot, he caressed her toes, the soles of her feet and her heels.

"Turn around now my lovely girl."

He kissed her and held the kiss as his hands moved over her back, pushing her breasts against his chest and her belly against his. His hands slid over her buttocks and then down and between her thighs, she moaned and moved her legs apart......

"Fee, are we getting off this plane or not."

Startled, she realised that Simon was standing up in the aisle and the plane was almost empty of passengers, the air hostesses were looking in her direction and smiling. She blushed furiously and hurriedly got up, "It's all your fault."

"Mine. How d'you make that out?"

"I'll tell you later."

They passed through Customs and caught the bus to the car park.

"Here she is, waiting patiently. Soon be home. Are you looking forward to seeing the dogs Fee?"

"Now I am, but I must admit I hadn't given them a thought for the last few days."

He looked at her and grinned, "No, I had other things on my mind too."

As they got to the cottage and the car came to a halt near the kitchen door, Fiona suddenly thought of Sally, her very first Cumbrian terrier who had died some months ago. Tears came into her eyes at the knowledge that she wouldn't be there to greet her, she quickly turned to Simon, "Simon..."

"I know Fee, I know, come on. Let's go in, Ruth will be making us a cup of tea for sure."

As he spoke the door opened and Ruth's smiling face appeared, "Ah, here you are. Did you have a good flight? How was the holiday? Everything's fine here."

As Simon had thought, the kitchen was full of the smell of cake and the kettle was just coming to the boil. Ruth was a kennelmaid in a million and they were damned lucky to have found her. They paid her well over the going rate but she was worth every penny.

Towards evening, after Ruth had gone back to her family and Fiona had unpacked their suitcases, they walked round the kennels, greeting their own dogs and checking on the boarders. There had apparently been no problems while they had been away and the dogs all looked fit and well. As Fiona turned towards the woods, Simon took her hand and together they walked up to the little spot, marked with a plaque, where Sally lay, "I still miss her so much."

"Yes, I know you do. So do I; I often think I see her running around the place."

"Yes, I still call her sometimes, when I'm busy and not thinking."

" Do you know Fee, I think the light's beginning to go already, we've passed the longest day." He turned and held out his hand, "Come on, I'll make you a cup of tea or shall we have a beer?"

As they lay cuddled up in their own bed that night she said, "Heavens Simon, I've just had a horrible thought. It's Natalie and Paul's wedding in a fortnight's time."

Simon turned over, punched his pillow and groaned, "Don't remind me."

The following week seemed to fly past, there were a couple of matings booked for their stud dogs, two of the boarders were going home and three were coming in. Fiona was busy in the kennels when a familiar voice called out to her, "Is that you in there Fiona?"

"Yes, hello Natalie. How are you. Nearly ready for the big day?"

"Oh, don't mention it. I've come to see you to get away from it all."

Fiona looked at her sharply. Was there something wrong? Had she found out about her and Paul's past relationship? She quickly looked at Natalie's smiling face, no she looked just the same as always, well definitely slimmer than when she had first met her but apart from that, she looked her usual pleasant, homely self.

"How's Paul?" she asked trying to make her voice sound perfectly normal.

"Oh, busy as ever. He's trying to clear his workload ready for our honeymoon. I've told him that, if anybody else's finances are in a ruinous state, they must find another accountant."

"So, is everything ready for the big day?"

"Just about, I think. Candida and Jason are flying in on Thursday. The marquee has already been erected on the lawn so, even if it rains between now and the wedding, the ground will be dry. Most of the guests have replied and - one of the reasons I came over Fiona - would you please come round tomorrow and tell me quite honestly, if you like the dress I've chosen. I really would appreciate your opinion. It's so difficult at my age."

"Nonsense, you always look smart. I've always thought that you have very good dress sense, you know what suits you."

"Yes, I know. Mothery things! I want to look... attractive for Paul."

They chattered on while Fiona finished the kennel work and they then went down to the cottage for a cup of tea. While Fiona was pouring the milk into the cups Natalie suddenly looked at her and said, "Fiona, tell me, do you think I'm making a mistake in marrying Paul?"

Fiona spilled some of the milk onto the table and had to mop it up, she then quickly picked up the teapot and poured the amber liquid into the cups. She always liked to use cups not mugs for Natalie, "Good heavens Natalie, what a question. Are you having last minute doubts then?"

"Yes and no. No, I love Paul and he makes me very happy. We get on well and he fits very well into my circle of friends but....."

"But what?"

"Oh, I don't know really. He's been a bachelor for a long time, perhaps he won't like living with me all of the time and then there's his work. You know how much time he spends on it and I would like him to spend more time with me. My dear Richard left me well provided for and.... well, to be honest, all the time he was ill I hardly did anything but look after him and now I should like Paul and I to travel, I should like to have weekend parties, entertain our friends, show the dogs, I should like us to do all sorts of things together now."

"Have you spoken to him about this?"

"Only vaguely."

"And?"

"Well, he said yes, that would be very nice."

"Natalie, I think that you are worrying unnecessarily. The only thing I would say is that, with all the plans that you have mentioned, how are you going to fit in dogs and the dog-showing?"

Natalie gave a deep sigh, "Oh dear, you're going to think ill of me Fiona but, to tell the truth, although I love the dogs and I have enjoyed the showing and making new friends, especially you and Simon; and meeting old ones like Audrey, I want to do so much more now that I have a companion in Paul."

"And what does Paul think about that?"

"I haven't told him."

Fiona quietly sipped her tea; poor Natalie obviously didn't have a clue what a scheming, ruthless sod Paul was in his endeavours to get on in the dog world. She quietly suspected that part of Natalie's attraction was her old friendships with some of the hierarchy in the dog world and the Kennel Club. Should she say something? Best not, for one thing, she very much doubted whether Natalie would believe her, as always in the dog world, there was no written proof, and for another it would totally destroy the hold she had over Paul.

Thanks to him, she and Simon were now on the list for some CC wins and they would certainly be down for future championship show judging appointments, all this would crash if she even hinted what Paul was really like, why he wanted to marry her!

"Would you like another cup of tea Natalie?"

"No thanks, I really must be getting back. So you'll come over tomorrow morning will you Fiona?"

"Yes, I'm looking forward to seeing your dress and your going-away outfit, you are going to model them for me aren't you?"

As Natalie's car disappeared down the drive, Fiona sighed. What a mess! What a pity that Natalie hadn't seen through him; not that she herself had. Too much was at stake now for her and Simon to say anything to Natalie, she would just have to put a brave face on it. Perhaps it would be a perfect marriage.

That evening, as Simon came in from locking up the kennels he looked at Fiona, "You're looking pensive, anything wrong?"

"No, I've got to go over to Natalie's tomorrow to give my opinion of the dress that she is getting married in and her going-away outfit."

"God, rather you than me."

"Do you think that Paul will give up showing now?"

"God, the thought never crossed my mind, I doubt it, he's fiddled and crawled bloody hard to achieve his success. He won't give up without a struggle. Why?"

"Oh, just something that Natalie said."

"Mind you, with all her connections, he hardly needs to show does he. Right, now do you want a hot drink or a cold one?"

Putting her gloomy thoughts out of her mind she smiled, "A hot one please. Are we going to enter Windsor Champ Show? I've got to send it off tomorrow."

"Yes, you know how the system works. We aren't going to get the CC there but we've got to be seen; probably get a first. Never mind we will be able to make Stream up next year for sure."

She smiled, Simon had no idea of her 'arrangement' with Paul. He thought that the 'Simfell' kennels was back at the top again because they were back together and entertaining. It would be a good thing though to have the New Year's party again this time. She enjoyed those, she'd speak to Simon about it..

CHAPTER THREE

"Here's a cup of tea Dennis. Come on, sit up, we've got to get cracking, we've a lot to do today."

"Aw, it's Saturday."

"I know. It's also the day that we arranged to get the keys from the solicitors, so come on."

She put the hot mug of tea into Dennis's unwilling hand and hurried out of the room saying, "I'll have my shower now and you can have yours when you've finished your tea."

Dennis sighed and sipped the hot tea. For the past couple of days she'd done nothing but talk about her aunt's house. It was all absolutely ridiculous, they were perfectly happy where they were. She'd been thrilled to bits when she'd seen this new development going up and they'd managed to get one of the semi-detached houses. They'd been here about ten years now and it had suited them right from the start. It was easy for him to get to work, Caroline had a little part-time job at the local florist's shop, which she said that she enjoyed. The dogs had a nice bit of garden to run around in and there was a big park nearby where, if he took the pooper scoopers, nobody objected to the dogs having a good run. Their neighbours were alright too, Arthur and Madge were getting on now and you hardly ever heard them. He often did a bit of tidying up or decorating for them in the house or the garden if they wanted any help and Caroline did some shopping for them if they didn't feel up to it. On the other side of them, Julie and Ray were good friends, they often went out for a drink together and they took it in turns to do Christmas dinner for each other. They also looked after the dogs if they went to a dog show. He usually managed to get out of going but, sometimes, just to keep Caroline sweet, he went with her. Most important of all, The White Horse was only just around the corner. No, as much as it would be very nice to have the money, moving was out of the question, they'd be absolutely miserable up there on their own. He was only going up there today so that he could show her how absolutely stupid the whole idea was.

"Shower's free."

"Right."

Dennis saw her come out of the solicitor's office with a big smile on her face. He reached out and turned the ignition key.

"Oh Dennis, he says that it is a lovely house and he is sure that we will fall in love with it."

"Where do I go from here or didn't he tell you how to get to it?"

"Of course he did. Go along here until we come to signs for the ring-road, take the ring-road west until you see signs for Hawderfield. When you get to Hawderfield, take the signs for Merring. The house is on the right. It's called, 'Little Owls', isn't that lovely."

"I'm hungry, I suppose he didn't tell you if there was a pub nearby?"

They had driven several miles without any sign of a pub when Caroline suddenly grabbed his arm and said, "There it is. Look, see the name, 'Little Owls'."

Dennis turned the car into a wide, gravelled drive bordered with large shrubs and trees and brought the car to a halt in front of a fairly large red-brick house. The front door had a stained glass panel in the middle of it with smaller panels of stained glass on either side. There were large rounded bay windows to the left and to the right of the front door.

"Blimey, it's big enough to run a B&B," Dennis murmured as he looked at the imposing front.

Caroline turned the key in the front door and they entered the silent house. The only sound as they walked from room to room downstairs was the ticking of a grandfather clock in the large hall. Their feet made no sound on the deep-pile carpets and Dennis felt that he should whisper if he wanted to say something. A lot of the furniture and ornaments were obviously foreign, picked up no doubt on her Aunt and Uncle's various tours abroad with the army. The curtains were made of beautiful, heavy materials, the carpets were obviously of top quality; the overall feeling was one of quiet respect. The kitchen on the other hand was large, light, airy and full of the latest in white goods. The crockery in the big dresser was exquisite and Caroline let out her breath in a long sigh, "Oh Dennis, just look at that. Surely this wasn't their every day crockery."

Upstairs everything was very similar in quality except that each of the four large bedrooms had a matching pastel theme, a different colour for each room and all were light and airy. The master bedroom had a modern, en-suite bathroom and shower while two of the others had wash-basins in them. The bedrooms at the back of the house looked out onto the garden, Dennis wandered over and looked out, "Good lord, look at the size of this garden, you can't even see the end of it."

Joining him Caroline said, "Oh Dennis, look it's got a lovely patio and a fishpond with a fountain! I only remember it as big."

"I wouldn't like to have to mow the darn thing."

"Don't be silly, we could afford to buy a ride on mower."

They continued their survey in silence. A large bathroom was fitted with a shower cabinet and a bidet as well as the usual furniture and there was another separate lavatory with a washbasin.

"Is this the last room? Caroline, for crying out loud, we could run a blooming boarding house here."

"What, with all this expensive stuff. I wouldn't dream of it. It's just all so beautiful, I feel I've died and gone to heaven. Right, have you got the camera? You did remember to bring it didn't you. Take several photos of every room and then we'll go into the garden. Wait a minute, we didn't go into the conservatory."

Dennis turned his eyes to heaven and then dutifully followed her through the drawing room into a small study, which opened out into a very large conservatory. Dennis sat down on one of the cane chairs, "This cushion is lovely and soft, you can leave me here."

"Oh no you don't. Come on take a photo of this and then we'll go back over each room."

Over half an hour later Caroline and Dennis stepped out of the kitchen door into the garden, "Oh Dennis, isn't it lovely. Look at all the roses and the lovely pond. Hey Dennis, look, it's got big goldfish in it."

"Yeah, more bloody work."

"Don't swear. You know I don't like it."

He followed her in silence as she slowly walked around the large garden, "D'you know, I remember some of this quite clearly."

"Have you seen enough now because the M6 will be solid if we don't get a move on."

"Alright, alright. I'm coming. You have got the camera haven't you. I can't wait to get the photos developed and show them to Julie and Madge."

Dennis, a careful driver, drove home faster than usual and was reprimanded by Caroline, "For heaven's sake Dennis, you only just missed that car. What's the matter with you? You've hardly said a word."

"You've been saying enough for both of us. You've hardly stopped since you got into the car."

"That's not fair. I've only been talking about the house and all the lovely things in it."

"Yeah, that's what I mean."

They let the dogs out into the garden as soon as they got home and Caroline made some tea while Dennis went out for some fish and chips for their dinner. Caroline laid the table thinking how small everything seemed.

"I needed that, I was really hungry Dennis."

"Um, the old chippie always does us proud. Couldn't do this if we were up there."

"For goodness' sake, you make it sound like Siberia."

"It is as far as I'm concerned. No chippie, no pub."

Tired and exasperated, Caroline launched into all the reasons why they should accept her inheritance and live in the house her Aunt had left, her ticking each one off on her fingers. Dennis steadfastly refuted all her arguments and then stated why he thought that they should stay put. Caroline got really angry and Dennis got up and got his jacket from the hall.

"Where are you going?"

"I've had enough of this, I'm off to The White Horse. See you."

The next day Caroline tried to bring the subject up again but Dennis refused to discuss it further so when, on Monday morning the solicitor, Mr Carruthers phoned, Caroline was at first lost for words.

"Good morning Mrs Amery, I am phoning to see if you enjoyed going round the property?"

"Oh, hello Mr Carruthers, I wasn't expecting to hear from you so soon."

"I hope I haven't rung at an inconvenient moment."

"No, I was just surprised that's all. Yes, we did look at the house."

"Beautiful, isn't it."

"Yes, it is absolutely beautiful."

"Oh good, I knew that you and your husband would like it. Now if you would like us to act for you in the sale of your property, or in any other capacity, we would be more than happy to do so."

"But, we haven't..."

"That's alright Mrs Amery, just give the estate agents our address. Must go now, so glad that you are coming to live here. Goodbye."

"Mr Carruthers wait I....." the line had been disconnected.

All that day - she only worked at the florists on a Thursday, Friday and Saturday - she busied herself with the housework. She changed the sheets and pillowcases on the bed, made up a load for the washing machine, dusted, put the vacuum around the carpets but all the time her mind was on the other house. It was obvious that Dennis did not want to move and deep down, she understood his reservations but, they had no family ties here now except Dennis's brother and they never saw him or any of his family. Yes, they had friends, good friends but they could always come up and visit. Heavens, they could even come and stay, there were enough bedrooms! With her mind so occupied, she soon finished her household chores, made a cup of coffee and took it out to the grooming shed that Dennis had built for her in the garden years ago.

She smiled as she opened the door, the smell of dogs, leads, brushes, shampoo, ear cleaner, coat spray and all the other necessities for grooming dogs for the show ring, assailed her nostrils and she breathed in deeply. Grooming always calmed her and enabled her to think clearly, she often thought that she would have made a good hairdresser. She could spend several hours out there, talking to the dogs as she groomed and tidied them, clipping their nails, cleaning their teeth or whatever other part of the dog needed attention at any one time. She loved her dogs, she loved them even more than Dennis if she was honest. They hadn't had any children so, after they had been married for five years, she had bought a Cumbrian terrier from a local breeder who had advertised in their local paper. She realised now that Bertie hadn't been show material but, at that time she hadn't known any better and she had adored him. Having joined the local dog society and gone to Open shows with him she began to see his flaws; undaunted, she then bought a bitch puppy from another exhibitor. Dennis hadn't objected at all until the bitch came in season and Bertie started to whine and bark and howl! They had ended up putting him in kennels for two weeks until the season was over. Caroline smiled as she patted the bitch that she was grooming, what a couple of ninnies we were. They had found a good home for him and she had bought another bitch with the money.

Had they lived in Aunt Ellen's house then, they could have erected a corridor kennel somewhere up the garden, put the bitches down there and all would have been well. Caroline's eyes widened, what potential that house had, she was only just beginning to realise, and they would have more money to spend. She stopped grooming the dog and put the brush down on the table. Thoughts tumbled through her head as she thought of all the avenues living up there might open. She had known all along that it was the lack of money that had held her back in showing but now.... she hurried indoors and grabbed the Yellow Pages, what was the name of that Estate Agent in the High Street, Mortimer's that's right. She'd ask them to come round just to give her a rough estimate as to what it was worth. She wouldn't tell Dennis, after all, it was only a valuation. It wouldn't do any harm.

"Hello, Mortimer's? Oh, good morning, I wondered if you would come and give me a valuation on my house."

CHAPTER FOUR

"Simon, for heaven's sake, it's nearly ten-o-clock! I've just about finished here; how are you getting on?"

"OK, on the last kennel, we've only got to shower and change. We've plenty of time."

"What! I've got to tidy my hair, put my make-up on, do my nails, it takes us twenty minutes to get there and the wedding is at eleven fifteen!"

"Well, I've just about finished now. Look, you go on down and have your shower and I'll just tidy up here. Ruth will be able to do anything else. By the way, have I got a clean shirt?"

Fiona rolled her eyes to heaven and pulled a face at him then hurried down to the cottage and upstairs to their bedroom. Having shed her working gear, she put on a shower cap and went into the bathroom. As the hot water ran over her body she thought about Natalie and Paul, she had really wanted to tell Natalie what Paul was really like but, seeing how lovely she had looked in her wedding dress and how happy, she had stayed silent. She hadn't told her about her love affair with Paul, she hadn't told her how he had dropped her when he thought that he could have Natalie and her lovely, old manor house, her friends in high places at the Kennel Club and her money. She hadn't even told Simon. She had tried to several times but he had silenced her with a kiss every time; she wondered if he already knew. Now, today, she and Simon were going to Natalie's wedding to Paul. Her thoughts were interrupted by the shower door being opened and a kiss being planted on the back of her neck, "Simon, you startled me."

"Come here me proud beauty and I'll startle you a bit more."

"Simon, stop it, we'll be late," she turned off the shower and grabbed a towel.

"Come here Fee, I'll dry your back for you."

"Oh, no you won't. I know what that can lead to," Fiona laughed, wrapped the towel around her and ran into the bedroom.

Just over half an hour later, when Fiona was just putting the finishing touches to her make-up, Ruth called up the stairs, "Hello, Simon, Fiona, I'm here."

"We're just coming down Ruth."

Ruth had been helping them out with the kennels for several years now so she only needed to know if any dogs were going out or coming in. All the dogs were well and no medication was required and there were no special diets.

"Well, I've got an easy day then, I must say, you are both looking very smart. I love the hat. That peachy colour really suits you Fiona. Is that a new suit Simon?"

"Yes, Fee made me buy it, under protest I might add, because I refused to hire a morning suit."

Fiona and Simon got in the car and drove off towards the town. They couldn't find a parking space anywhere near the Registry Office and had to drive a couple of streets away before they found a gap between cars. Locking up they walked quickly back, Fiona found it hard to keep up with Simon in the high heels she was wearing, she looked at her watch, it was ten past eleven. As they neared the Registry Office, Fiona could see Natalie smiling and waving to them, she had obviously lost more weight and was looking very smart in the turquoise blue dress and matching coat. She had shoes to match and a really lovely hat that blended perfectly with her outfit. She was holding a small posy of pale pink flowers.

"Natalie you look absolutely lovely. Hello Paul," Fiona kissed Natalie on the cheek but Simon did not shake hands with Paul.

"Oh, Fiona, I was so worried that you wouldn't get here in time. Candida, this is my good friend Fiona. This is my daughter Candida and her husband Jason. She is going to give me away."

The tall, dark girl at Natalie's side held her hand out, "Hello Fiona, I have heard so much about you and how you have helped my mother. You must be Simon. I am so pleased to meet you both at last."

Paul interrupted their conversation, "I think that it is time that we went in don't you."

Neither Simon nor Fiona actually heard much of the ceremony, Fiona was remembering her marriage to Simon in this very room as well as looking at the dresses of the other women and Simon was noting how many members of the Kennel Club were there as well as one or two well known all-round judges. Altogether there were about twenty or so people there. My, our Paul is hoping to really go places he thought. The short ceremony was coming to an end, everyone seemed to be smiling and moving forward to congratulate the couple.

Simon and Fiona hung back and were some of the last to leave the room so that, when they walked out into the street, it was to see the happy couple getting into a car with ribbons on it.

"Hello again Fiona, where is your car?" Candida was standing beside her.

"It's a couple of streets away. We couldn't find a parking space."

"Jason and I will see you back at Mummy's then. I should very much like to have a chat with you some time. Mummy has told me so much about you."

As they walked back to the car, Simon was asking her if she had noted the various members and the all-rounders, "Quite the rising star isn't he," he said bitterly. Fiona decided that, today, discretion was the better part of valour and remained silent..

The reception was to be in a marquee erected in the large grounds at the back of Natalie's house, the drive was already full of cars but they were able to park in the road quite near to the house. As they walked up the drive they could see Natalie and Paul greeting their guests at the open door to the house. Fiona felt Simon's hand tighten on hers but he said nothing.

"Hello Fiona, do please go through, you know the way," Natalie's happy, smiling face beamed at her, "Isn't it a lovely day."

"Yes it is Natalie," she looked across at Paul and managed a strained smile as she walked past him. Simon gave Natalie a kiss on the cheek and, without looking at him, briefly touched Paul's hand. I'd like to murder the conniving bastard he thought.

"This is gorgeous," exclaimed Fiona as she and Simon walked into the marquee. Hanging from the roof were swathes of silky, pale blue material caught up with small bouquets of pale pink and white flowers. There were matching flowers on the tables too. The entire colour scheme matched the blue of Natalie's dress and the pink of her bouquet and the white of the marquee and tablecloths. The lights shining on the silver cutlery and polished glasses, showed everything off to perfection. There was a two-tiered cake standing on a side table, it too was decorated with the palest of pink flowers.

They were each handed a flute of champagne and, as they sipped the cold liquid, they mingled with the other guests.

As they walked round smiling politely at everyone, they saw Harriet and Larry, Natalie's neighbours from the Christmas party, who, when they recognised them, smiled, said "Hello" and then quickly excused themselves. Fiona felt herself blushing at the memory of the party but Simon turned to her and grinned, "Well Fee, at least they recognised us. Come on, let's find someone interesting and corner them. The someone was Stanley Benson who was on the judges committee of the KC. Simon walked up to him hand outstretched, "Hello again Stanley, haven't seen you since Windsor, or was it Bath?"

"Hello um....."

"Simon Philips and this is my wife Fiona. Remember now, the Simfell Cumbrians?"

"Oh yes, yes of course. How are you both? This is a splendid 'do' isn't it."

"Yes it is. I was pleased to see that Audrey and Ian were able to come. Weren't they judging in America recently?"

"Yes that's right, only just made it though. Got back last Wednesday I believe."

"I must speak to them later. I'd like to know what they thought of the Cumbrians out there now. As a matter of fact, Fiona and I have only just got back from Germany. Fiona was judging the Cumbrians, they could compare notes. I was judging..."

"How interesting I...." someone was tapping a glass and then they heard Jason ask everyone to find their place names and to take their places at the table.

There were three long tables set out with a top table and two long tables forming three sides of a rectangle. Natalie, Paul, Candida and Jason were already seated at the top table and Simon could see that Audrey and Ian were there as well; at that very moment Paul was smilingly calling Stanley Benson, Harold Manningtree from the KC and the two all-rounders Peter Everton and Charlie Waters to their places at the top table.

"Look at the bloody creep," Simon murmured under his breath.

"Shut up Simon. Someone will hear you. Anyway, what were you doing just now?"

"That's different, it's not my wedding day."

Fiona finally found their place names, they were almost at the far end of one of the long tables. She was a little surprised that Natalie had put them so far down the table but then, it was her prerogative. The food would be the same anyway. The caterers were extremely efficient and the four courses were served with the minimum of delay between each course. The food was excellent and the portions generous.

Natalie sighed with contentment, the caterers were living up to their promise and everything was going without a hitch.

"Did I hear you sigh my dear? Is everything alright?"

"Yes Paul, of course it is. I was just sighing with pleasure."

"Then my dear, I am happy. I think that you chose the caterers very wisely. The food is excellent."

Natalie looked around at the guests now onto the fourth course, a selection of biscuits and cheeses with fresh green grapes. Where was Fiona, she scanned the faces near her, she had asked for them to be placed next to her good friends Harriet and Larry at the top of one of the long tables. Harriet and Larry were there but where... she slowly looked down the table until she saw them seated at the far end. That was odd, she had checked the placings herself last night when the caterers had set it all up. Paul had helped her.

"Paul. Paul, do you know someone has made a mistake...." she was interrupted by Jason standing up and asking everyone to be silent.

Simon and Fiona listened to Jason's speech in silence but when Paul indicated that he wished to say a few words Simon murmured, "This ought to be good."

"Firstly, may I on behalf of my wife and myself," he smiled at Natalie and lifted her hand to his lips, "may I thank you all for coming today and helping us celebrate our wedding day. Thanks to Candida and Jason for all their help. Thank you all for your good wishes and for your wonderful gifts. There are several people here today prominent in the world of show dogs. This to me would seem most fitting, since it was through this media that I had the good fortune to meet Natalie. I shall be eternally grateful. Thank you all once again."

Natalie leaned across and whispered something to him, "Oh yes, if you would all remain seated, we are about to cut the cake. Thank you."

"Puke, pure bloody puke."

The people across from Simon looked at him with puzzlement on their faces at his words. Simon grinned broadly, "Don't worry, must have been something I ate."

"Sh. Simon, it will all be over soon."

"Aren't we having a knees up afterwards?"

"No, they are leaving almost straight away. They have a flight to catch, remember?"

"Where are they going?"

"Ceylon."

Jason got up to speak.

Shortly after this, Natalie and Paul left the marquee, it was a signal for everyone else to get up and wander around, to talk and to look at the wedding presents laid out on a trestle table, to drink coffee and eat their piece of wedding cake.

"Nice cake Fee, pity there wasn't more of it. Do you think we can disappear now?"

"No, we've got to wait until they leave for the airport. It would look so bad if we left first."

"For heavens' sake," Simon frowned and looked around him. When he spotted Stanley Benson talking to Harold Manningtree his face lit up and he moved towards them. At the same time Natalie's daughter, Candida approached Fiona, "Ah, there you are Fiona, I was worried that I would have missed you. It was a lovely meal wasn't it?"

"Yes, excellent caterers and I think the marquee looks beautiful."

"Mummy used to have these caterers when we gave dinner parties, that's when Daddy was alive."

"Didn't you think that your mother looked very pretty today?"

"Yes, I haven't seen her so happy since Daddy.... Fiona, you and your husband have known Paul for quite a while haven't you."

"Yes, for a number of years now."

"I know that he is your friend but... oh dear.... he is all right isn't he? He will look after Mummy won't he... Daddy did leave her comfortably off and... well you do know what I am trying to say don't you? I'm sorry Fiona, but I don't know who else to ask."

Fiona looked into the girl's face, she'd have to be careful what she said, Candida was quite astute. "That's alright Candida. I do understand. Well, all I can say is that I think that Paul will look after your mother, from what she has told me they seem to get on very well together and share several interests. As you noticed, he seems to make her very happy. As far as I know, because he works hard and is a successful accountant, I think that he is financially sound."

Candida was silent for a moment as she watched Paul coming back into the marquee. He had changed out of his morning suit into something more comfortable for travelling. Seeing Simon in conversation with Stanley and Harold he purposefully made his way over to them. Natalie then appeared in her dark blue going away suit and started to make her way over towards Fiona and Candida. Candida watched Paul walk across the marquee and, turning to Fiona said, "You didn't say that you and Simon liked him Fiona."

CHAPTER FIVE

The day after the wedding as Fiona prepared lunch, Simon was doing a few minor repairs on one of the kennels; she frowned as she cut some bread to make a cheese sandwich. At the reception Paul had only said a few words to her, "I presume that you will be going to Midland Counties?" She realised immediately that that must be Paul's way of telling her which shows would be advantageous for her to attend. She had replied that she would be entering and they had parted company without speaking again.

After lunch she would have to look it up in the dog paper and send for a schedule as she hadn't gone to that particular show last year. She had other schedules for Richmond and Birmingham, it must be nearly the deadline for sending in the completed schedule for the Richmond show. She must do that today, since Simon had come back to the cottage everything else had seemed less important to their happiness and the shows had faded into the background. They had both had lessons to learn about their relationship and were both determined that nothing like that would happen again. The niggling worry in Fiona's mind was that she hadn't told Simon about her affair with Paul.

"Any more tea in the pot Fee?"

"Yes, I'll get it for you."

"No, you sit there, I'll get it. Mind out of the way Sapphire, I nearly fell over you."

Simon placed the newly filled mugs on the table, "You OK Fee? You seem a bit quiet."

"Yes, I'm fine. I was just thinking that I ought to fill in some schedules this afternoon."

"Damn the schedules, I have a better idea for this afternoon," he grinned at her and raised his eyes upwards.

"Simon, don't you think of anything else."

"Yes, but not when I'm with you and it is Sunday and it's pouring with rain outside."

Fiona smiled, "Oh Simon you are incorrigible. Look, let me just fill in those schedules and prepare something for dinner and then I'm all yours."

"Better still, let me do the schedules and I can get you up those stairs quicker."

About twenty minutes later, when Fiona had prepared the vegetables for their dinner that evening, she picked up the dog paper for that week. Smiling, she turned to the pages displaying the forthcoming shows, Midland Counties, there it is, now who's judging the Cumbrians. The smile left her face as she saw the name of the judge, Mr Alan Burgess! No, not Alan! Had Paul done this deliberately just to be nasty, to get his own back? Surely not, because he didn't know about her and Alan and that awful afternoon at the hotel. Simon would never have told him; but had Alan? Oh please God, no. She thought that that day was behind her. She frowned, she couldn't tell Simon that she wanted to show under Alan! He would go mad. She just couldn't go and that was that; but, if she didn't go would Paul take that as a breaking of their agreement? She'd have to phone Paul and tell him to change it. Oh lord, when did the entries close because Natalie and Paul were away for a month on their honeymoon.

"Ever heard that saying about spare parts at a party."

She turned to see Simon standing on the bottom step of the stairs and it was very obvious to what he was alluding.

"If you don't come soon I'll just have to frighten the life out of the dogs and have you on the kitchen table."

Fiona burst out laughing, "It wouldn't be the first time would it."

"Right my girl, you're for it now."

She laughed as she ran around the table and up the stairs closely followed by Simon.

During the following weeks, Fiona or Simon attended several Open shows with the young dog, Stream and a bitch that they thought was promising material for the forthcoming championship shows. The dog performed well in the ring and each time they got BOB and, in fact, did well in the terrier group as well. Simon though began to notice that dog showing was subtly changing with more and more emphasis being put on going to Champ shows and less and less on open shows, especially by the newer exhibitors. Everything was costing more, with the Champ shows costing far too much considering the way exhibitors were treated. Petrol was dearer and, perhaps because of the cost, people seemed to not enjoy the shows as they once did. There seemed to be a lot more complaining about 'face judging', 'the same people always winning', 'too many all-rounders doing the circuit and certain breed judges judging every year' and so on. The little people were beginning to revolt at last. The backbone on which the whole industry hung was beginning to realise that they were being 'seen off'. So why the hell didn't they go back to the Open shows? Thank God that they were no longer part of it, he and Fee could just enjoy their dogs and their showing, for him, it didn't matter. Funny that, he thought as he drove home from one of the shows, I used to be so ambitious, so wanted to win at any cost, to be there at the top. To be looked up to and now... I must tell Fiona how I feel sometime, she'll be pleased.

Fiona too had noticed that, in general, the Open shows were losing entries badly because everyone wanted to make up a champion. It made her feel a little guilty about her arrangement with Paul but then, if it wasn't her it would be somebody else. The system was in place and had been for a long time, the people at the top, the cliques holding power, weren't going to change it for a few moaners. She would soon have to have a word with Simon about Midland Counties, that was if she couldn't get hold of Paul before the entries closed.

"Simon, did you take this stud booking for a Mr Harding?"

"Oh yes, he's going to bring the bitch round for us to see. I didn't recognise the dam's side of the pedigree when he read it out over the phone, it's definitely not show stock. The sire is OK, it's one of Phil Leonard's dogs. Anyway, I thought it best we saw it first as he wants to use Samson."

"OK, he's coming tomorrow evening then?"

"Yes, I told him to make it after six so that I'll be here."

They both liked Rob Harding as soon as they saw him but the bitch, although extremely well looked after, was not show quality at all.

"Did you buy her as a puppy?"

"Yes, saw an ad in our local paper. When our last child got married and left home, we thought that a dog would be company."

"So, may I ask why you want to mate her?" Simon asked.

"Well, my wife and I have been taking her to obedience classes and we heard people talking about going to a show near us, so we went to watch. It was a very pleasant day out and we thought that perhaps we could try it. The people who run the classes said that they didn't think that Annie was good enough for showing but why didn't we find a good dog and have a litter; they recommended your kennels, so here I am."

Fiona asked to look at the pedigree and, when they looked at it they both quickly realised that the breeder's name was linked to puppy farming.

"Look Mr Harding..."

"Please call me Rob."

"Well Rob. To be honest we are not happy with this pedigree and do not wish to use our champion on your bitch, but, as she is partly of good stock, we will let you use one of our less successful dogs of similar breeding. Is that OK with you?"

"Well, yes, if you think that's OK but, what's wrong with her pedigree?"

"Nothing's wrong with it, but the breeder, the owner of the bitch, breeds an awful lot of litters in a year. The poor bitches are often over-used and the puppies are not reared as well as they should be. People like us would never let her use any of our dogs. We wouldn't want our name associated with her at all. She is basically a puppy farmer."

"Puppy farmer! It was a private house, I thought that I had been careful. I saw the mother That's what they tell you to do isn't it? She said that they were bred from show stock."

"Well yes, they were on the sire's side, but not everybody who breeds dogs is totally honest. I'm afraid that you haven't got a very good specimen of the breed here, although it's obvious that you, have taken very good care of her."

"But how would I know?"

"That's just it. That's how they get away with it. Unless you are in the know you wouldn't. It's always best to go through the Kennel Club. Actually you've been lucky. She seems to have a nice temperament and she is sound."

Seeing how disappointed Rob Harding was looking, Fiona interrupted the conversation, "As we said before,, we would be happy for you to use another of our young dogs."

"Well yes, thank you."

"May I suggest that you and your wife, go to watch more shows and read some books on the Cumbrian Terrier. There are several in the library."

"Yes, I will, that's a good idea."

Phil Leonard was most concerned when Simon phoned him later that evening. "Good God, not one of those dogs. That person lives in this area and is turning out dogs like bloody sausages, seems to have loads of bitches out on terms. Advertises all over the place and no questions asked. God knows how the puppies are reared and where the poor devils end up. I remember now, Nancy did that mating because I was up North at the time, I bet she never thought to look at the pedigree. Blast, I don't want my prefix linked with that one. I think I'd better tell the club so that they can warn others to be on their guard. Thanks for letting me know Simon, I owe you one. See you around, we'll have a drink. Bye."

"God Fee, what the hell is happening to dog showing?"

"Nothing much, puppy farming is nothing new."

"I know it's not illegal but surely the KC could somehow legislate properly to see that these bastards can't keep having litter after litter. You can shoot holes in every new rule they make. I wonder if they know anything about the people they are dealing with."

"Oh, come on Simon, you know and I know that some breeders do it too just to make money. It's even been known for some 'big' breeders to buy in litters from their stud dogs and sell them at a handsome profit. Dozens and dozens of pups can pass through their kennels in a year."

"Hey, you're changing your tune aren't you Fee. Don't tell me you are beginning to live in the real world of showing after all these years?"

Fiona did not reply, she was definitely living in the real world now, but how could she tell him, "Simon, about Dar......" the phone rang and Simon went out into the hall, "Hi Peter, how was the holiday?" Fiona could hear Simon laughing at something his brother was saying," Yes, next Sunday, fine as far as I know, have a word with Fee," he passed the receiver over to Fiona.

"Hello Peter, yes, we'd love to see you both next Sunday. Yes, come for dinner. Don't forget the photos. Give my love to Beryl. Bye."

Fiona shoved a pile of clothes into the washing machine and switched it on. Another Monday morning! Where did the time go? Entry for Midland Counties closed next Monday and Paul and Natalie were due back from their honeymoon this Saturday evening, Fiona had spoken to Jessie who had told her that, as far as she knew, they would be home on time. She was certainly dusting and vacuuming right through ready for their arrival. Fiona put the phone down, she couldn't phone on Saturday, Sunday they were having Peter and Beryl over for dinner so that only left Monday; too late no doubt to ask Paul to change their arrangement.

As soon as Beryl walked into the cottage on Sunday morning she knew that something was not right. Something in Fiona's face reminded her of the time when she and Simon had been parted. She had thought that that was now all behind them, they had seemed so happy to be together again, "Hello my dear, lovely to see you."

"Hello, did you have a lovely holiday? You're both so brown."

They all chatted away while they drank coffee and then Simon suggested that he and Peter went for a pint at the local pub while the girls had a natter and got the dinner ready. As soon as the door had closed Beryl looked at Fiona, "What has happened?"

"Nothing. Why?"

"Why? because your face is like an open book to me. You are unhappy or worried about something aren't you? Is it Simon?"

"No, well yes and no. Oh Beryl, I don't know what to do." She proceeded to tell her about the arrangement with Paul. Beryl raised her eyebrows once or twice but said nothing.

"..so you do see the problem Beryl, if I can't get Paul to change it, I shall have to go and I don't know what Simon will say or do."

"I've got a pretty good idea Fiona and so have you. You must get this man to change it."

"And suppose I can't?"

"Oh Fiona, surely no amount of CCs is worth your happiness."

"Beryl, you know and I know that Simon has always been mad about dog shows and winning CCs. If I don't go to this one I think that we can kiss goodbye to ever winning again."

"I do realise that showing is not what most ordinary people think it is but, is it really this cut-throat?"

CHAPTER SIX

Caroline was just loading the washing into the machine when she heard the phone ringing, hurrying into the hall she picked up the receiver, "Hello Caroline Amery speaking."

"Good morning Mrs Amery, this is Justin from Mortimer's the estate agents. We have a Mr and Mrs Jenkins here and they are very interested in your property. Would it be convenient to bring them round shortly?"

"What! I didn't know that you had put it out. I mean, I didn't tell you to put it out yet. I don't know if..."

"I'm sorry Mrs Amery if I've surprised you, we haven't actually circulated the particulars as yet. It was just that Mr and Mrs Jenkins are very keen to buy a property in your area and they are cash customers having already sold their own property. It seemed far to good an opportunity to miss but, if you would rather I didn't bring them ......"

"No, wait a minute, you say that they are cash customers?"

"Yes and very keen to find a suitable house as soon as possible. Yours seems to fit the bill perfectly."

"Oh, well I suppose it wouldn't do any harm just to let them see over it. I mean it's not as if I'm...."

"Well, as I said Mrs Amery, it seems much too good an opportunity to miss, it might be some time before we get another customer like Mr & Mrs Jenkins."

"Alright then, but could you give me about an hour. I wasn't expecting to..."

"Would half an hour be all right, only they do have other properties to see. Not in your area of course but..."

"Yes, all right then half an hour, but as I said, we haven't decided..."

"We'll see you soon then Mrs Amery."

Putting the phone down Caroline stood looking around at the hall for several minutes incapable of movement but then, she was suddenly galvanised into action. She raced upstairs and into their bedroom, it was a shambles. She hadn't put the clean sheets on yet! Too late to do it now, she thought, as she grabbed the duvet and

41

started cramming it into the clean cover. Smoothing the pillows and the cover she looked around the room, she grabbed two pairs of her shoes and a pair of Dennis's slippers and threw them into the wardrobe, banging the door shut. Picking her dressing gown up from a chair, she hung it on the peg behind the door. Some used tissues from the top of her dressing table went into her pocket and a couple of fresh tissues were brought into service as a duster. The tops of the furniture were then quickly dusted with the tissues. Her lipsticks and sprays, on the dressing table were stood up in orderly rows like toy soldiers. She scooped up last night's newspaper from the floor, put her library book inside her bedside cabinet drawer, tweaked the curtains, smoothed the duvet again, plumped the pillows again and sprayed the room with some of her perfume. Satisfied with the effect she then hurried to the bathroom, where she proceeded to spray cleaner in the washbasin and bath, wash it off, put some disinfectant down the toilet, put Dennis's shaving stuff into the cabinet together with a few other sundry items, opened the window, straightened the curtains, put out fresh towels, breathed on the mirror and used the tissues from her pocket to polish it. After a quick look at her watch, she just glanced into the other two bedrooms and then hurried downstairs to the lounge cum dining-room.

She plumped the cushions and straightened the armrest covers on the three piece suite, grabbed a pile of magazines and slipped some of them underneath the cushions of the settee and the others under the armchairs, opened a window, straightened the curtains and stood back. Seeing the discarded flights from some of Dennis' darts poking out from under one of the armchairs, she hastily picked them up and ran into the kitchen where she proceeded to put all bits and pieces of cutlery and crockery into drawers and cupboards, including the old dart flights. The dogs meanwhile were getting quite excited at this new and interesting game and decided to add to the fun by bringing in their hard rubber balls, rings and various other, rather grubby, precious items. Caroline did not appreciate the help and shouted at them to get out whilst throwing their toys after them. This set off another chain of thought, she looked at her watch, only five minutes left! She ran out into the garden to get the pooper scooper and hurry around the garden collecting dog faeces as fast as she could. She usually put it down the manhole cover but there wasn't time, she just dumped everything into the dustbin and hid the pooper scooper in the shrubs. She'd sort that out later. Hurrying back into the hall, she caught sight off her red face and dishevelled hair so she ran upstairs again and had just put a comb through her hair when the doorbell rang. The dogs immediately sent up a chorus of barking and Caroline, by now thoroughly hot and dishevelled, ran down the stairs and opened the door with a smile, "Hello Justin, do come in."

"This is Mr and Mrs Jenkins, Mrs Amery."

"What have I done," Caroline, utterly exhausted, was sitting on the settee with a mug of coffee, "Dennis is going to be furious." The dogs, now reinstated, were listening to this one-sided conversation. "What is he going to say when I tell him?" Worried, Bonnie lay down and put her face on her paws and Patsy came and licked Caroline's hand.

"I mean, they thought the place was wonderful, perfect, just what they'd been looking for. They didn't even quibble over the price! They even want to buy some of the curtains and carpets. I mean, what was I to do?"

Bonnie closed her eyes, whatever it was it was too awful to contemplate.

"I told them that we could move as soon as we could make the necessary arrangements! Oh lord, why did I say that? I just got carried away. What about Dennis's job! He hasn't even asked for a relocation! He doesn't even want to move! It's no good is it, I'll just have to phone Mortimers and tell them it's all off, I shall feel such a fool. They'll think I'm crazy."

Bonnie opened one eye and seeing Caroline's face, closed it again sighing.

Dennis let himself in, "Hi, it's only me."

Caroline came out of the kitchen, "Oh hello Dennis, had a good day?"

"Not as you'd notice, all much the same as usual."

"Dinner's almost ready so sit down and I'll bring it in. Do you want a drink first. A beer or something?"

Dennis raised an eyebrow and pulled a face as he walked into the lounge. He sat down and easing off his shoes wriggled his toes, what's she been and bought now he thought as he switched on the television. Bonnie came up and put her head on his knee, "Hello Bon, old girl. Had a nice day?"

"Here we are then, shepherd's pie. I cooked it especially for you."

Blimey, thought Dennis, it must have been dear whatever it was. I hope we can afford it. Caroline's inheritance was too new to have changed his mental processes over spending money.

"Been out today?"

"No, of course not. I had to change the bed and do some washing."

Dennis finished his shepherd's pie, she must have ordered something from a catalogue, she would no doubt tell him soon.

Later that evening as they were watching their favourite 'soap' Caroline said, "Dennis, have you asked Mr Smithers about the possibility of a relocation?"

"What, er no, course I haven't. Why?"

"I just wondered, only we're going to have to do something soon about my inheritance."

"I've told you, sell it."

"But I can't, you know I can't. Anyway, I don't want to, oh Dennis, it's such a lovely place, we could have an outside kennel and loads of other things and...."

"Caroline, I don't want an outside kennel or anything else for that matter. I'm perfectly happy here, we can let it to someone or something, now can we drop it. We're missing all this and we'll lose the plot."

Caroline sat there and looked at Dennis watching the TV. What a boring man he'd turned into, all he wants are his creature comforts. No imagination, no sense of adventure. She had been thinking all afternoon about the possibilities open to them when they moved up to Aunt Ellen's house, all that extra space, all that lovely furniture, the garden, more money, everything, just everything would be better, she might even have her own car. She was bored with living here. Always seeing the same people. She could go to lots of different dog shows, meet lots of other people, it would be great. As for Dennis, well he would soon find another pub with a darts team, if he relocated even his job would be the same. It was perfect, he could be the same if he wanted and she could - well who knew what she could do. Her mind made up she picked up the remote control and turned the television off.

"Dennis. Dennis!"

"What.! What did you turn it off for, he was just about to..."

"Dennis, I sold the house today to a Mr and Mrs Jenkins."

"Well good, glad you've seen sense. That was quick though, did the solicitors do it? How much did it fetch?"

"The solicitors? No, Mortimers in the High Street."

"What sold the house up there? Why did you get them to sell it?"

"No silly. I wish you'd listen. This one, the one we are in now; you know I can't sell the other one. Look! I sold the house today, this house."

She now had Dennis's undivided attention, "What! You what! You did what!"

"At last. Don't keep repeating yourself. As I just said. I've sold the house, this house to a Mr & Mrs Jenkins. They came this morning to look at the house and liked it. The best bit is that they are cash buyers and want to move in as soon as possible. Isn't that great."

"Now, hold on. You say that they came this morning. How the hell did they know that it was for sale? It isn't for sale."

"Ah well. I got in touch with Mortimers the other day just to see what it was worth. You know, just to get a valuation."

"And."

"Well that's it. Justin told them about this because they wanted to live in this area."

"Oh did they. Who the hell is Justin?"

Caroline sighed, "Dennis, I do wish you'd listen." She proceeded to explain the day's events in more detail, ending with the news that the Jenkins wanted to move in as soon as possible.

Dennis turned back to look at the empty television screen and said nothing for at least five minutes, "And supposing I don't want to go up there?"

"We've been through all this Dennis. A chance like this won't happen again will it. We'd be throwing away a fortune. On your salary we'd never be able to afford a house and garden like that one up there. Never. Surely you're not going to stop me having the chance to live in a house like that. We'd have no mortgage to pay, we'd have the money that Aunt Ellen left and we'd have the money from this once we've paid off the mortgage. Dennis, we'd be daft not to, we'd be better off than we have ever dreamed of being short of winning the football pools or the lottery... ......you could even have a new car. Look, I was thinking, I can't remember anything in the will to say that we couldn't sell it later, that's after we've lived in it. Look, if we really hate it up there we could sell it and come back here."

"Supposing I can't get a relocation?"

"Have you asked?"

"No, not yet, but supposing..."

"Well then, we cross that bridge when we come to it. Now, I don't know about you but I'm shattered. It's been a busy day. Are you going to walk the dogs later?"

"Yes, I suppose so."

"Right, well I think I'll be off. Don't be too long, I'm tired."

As soon as she had left the room, Dennis turned on the television set and continued to sit in front of it but saw nothing of the drama being played out on the screen. He had enough drama of his own to worry about. After about half an hour, he sighed heavily and turned off the TV with the remote control. Getting up, the three dogs who had been laying near his feet, immediately got up and raced out to the kitchen where their leads hung on a hook behind the door, it was in the shape of a Cumbrian terrier.

As he tramped the dark streets he knew that he was, in all probability, looking at the inevitable. She was right, he could never give her money like that, he couldn't buy her a house like that. His only hope was that he couldn't get a relocation but he knew, although he hadn't told Caroline, that his insurance company had only recently opened a big branch up that way and needed experienced office staff, a memo had come round only the other week about it. He sighed as he turned the corner into his road, perhaps he'd be lucky, perhaps they wouldn't want him. He would have liked the new car though but then, would the pubs up there want a good darts player. Scenting the familiar smells, the dogs towed him through the front gate.

That night saw little sleep in the Amery household. She lay there in the dark imagining her new life in that lovely house, they could have parties with all that lovely china and cutlery. They could invite some of their friends and even some dog people and judges. She could have a big kennels and more dogs if she wanted. She and Dennis could have some new clothes, he could have his new car, she could have a nice little car for herself, an estate perhaps, easier to load the dogs, good holidays - anything - the possibilities seemed endless.

Dennis was thinking too, this house was fine. Didn't need much doing to it, it was convenient for getting to work. He got on with everybody at his present office, even his boss and his days were mostly trouble free. The neighbours were good friends, it was convenient for the pub and there was a nice little parade of shops a couple of streets away. She'd miss the florists, had she thought of that? He'd been a member of the pub's darts team now for years. They all knew him at the pub and the newsagents, Fred always asked after the dogs and that was how he liked it, no hassle. God knows what he could be facing up there, there wasn't a pub for sure and he hadn't seen any shops nearby either. They were both townies born and bred, if he was absolutely honest, he'd rather stay here and miss Caroline than go up there and miss his comfortable life and his mates. She wouldn't like it either and then what; they'd be stuck up there and couldn't come back. Had she thought of that? He turned over and settled down to sleep, he'd be tired in the morning.

Why did people have to complicate life so much?

CHAPTER SEVEN

Paul replaced the receiver and smiled, he looked in the mirror in the hall, smoothed his hair and smiled again at his reflection.

"Natalie, Natalie where are you my dear?"

"I'm in the utility room drying the dog's feet."

He walked through the kitchen into the utility room, "Natalie, we have just been invited to a dinner at Clarges Street. Apparently several overseas judges and members of other kennel clubs will be there and it should be quite a pleasant evening."

"Oh, how lovely. When?"

"On the third of next month."

"I must check in my diary. There you are Jamie, off you go," Natalie stood up and smiled at Paul, "Dogs are so much easier to live with when the weather is dry aren't they."

Paul stood there seemingly deep in thought, "Yes, yes, especially now that you don't show them. Um."

"Yes, I do feel so guilty about not showing them, they so love the outing and seeing all the other dogs. I think Jamie really misses it but, now that we have our little trips abroad and our busy social life, there never seems to be enough time."

"You don't regret anything do you my dear?" Paul took her hand in his and looked at her face, "You are happy aren't you?"

Natalie reached up and kissed his mouth, "What a silly thing to ask, just being with you is enough. The trips, the outings, the dinner parties, accompanying you to the championship shows, they are just the icing on the cake. You have transformed my life and yes, I'm very happy." Paul enfolded her in his arms and they stood there content to be close to each other.

Later that week, as he was quietly sipping a post-prandial dry sherry, Jamie ran in closely followed by Natalie. Jamie jumped up knocking Paul's hand and spilling a few drops of the contents of the glass, "Get down you wretch. Get down!"

"Oh Paul, I'm so sorry I just couldn't stop him, he does love to see you."

"Send him out. He shouldn't be in this part of the house anyway. You know Natalie, you are far too soft on those dogs, they should be outside in kennels."

"Paul they are my friends, they were such a comfort to me when I was on my own."

"Yes, but you're not now are you."

Natalie grabbed Jamie's collar and took him back to the utility room. After washing her hands she continued preparing dinner. She frowned as she sliced the tomatoes, it was true what Paul said about them. The dogs did keep running into the house as they had done when she was on her own. They did sometimes keep barking when they were having a small dinner party. They did scratch at the utility door in the evenings wanting to join them. It had surprised her very much when Paul had decided not to bring any of his dogs with him when he sold his house, he had, of course, found a couple of the older ones very good homes, the others had gone to a handler to be shown. Had he perhaps been right all along when he had said that, with their new life together, too many dogs would be an encumbrance? He himself had cut his work load so that he could be with her more, have more time to help her entertain, go abroad, play golf. He had given up a lot for her. But on the other hand, Fiona and Simon always boarded her dogs when they went away, so they really weren't that much of a problem. She must be more firm with them in the house; they would soon learn to be quiet and behave. As she finished her preparations she called, "Paul dear, dinner is ready. Would you like to pour the wine?"

As Paul sipped his coffee, he turned to Natalie with a smile, "By the way my dear, you will arrange for the dogs to board with Fiona when we go to this dinner won't you?"

"Of course if you want, but do you think it really necessary just for the evening?"

"Well, Clarges Street is renowned for its sumptuous dinners, we don't want to hurry away do we."

"No, I suppose not. Have you been to many before?"

"Er, no, but their reputation is well known in the dog world."

"Do you know if Audrey and Ian will be there?"

"Yes, it is they who invited us and best not mention this little dinner party to Fiona and Simon when you take the dogs."

Natalie looked up and frowned, "Oh why?" She shrugged, " well, all right, if you think it's best.".

When, a few weeks later Natalie drove into the drive of the cottage with her three dogs in the back, Fiona, in dungarees and wellington boots greeted her with a wave of the hand, "Hi there Natalie, lovely to see you. How are you?"

"I'm fine. You seem to be busy."

"Yes, the two puppies, I've had them out on a lead for the first time. They thought it was a good game. It was a bit muddy too but then, who cares."

"What's all this about new puppies. I didn't even know that you had mated one of your bitches. How is Simon?"

"He's fine, really fit and well again. I have mated a couple of my bitches since I last saw you but these puppies I bought in. They're Glencastle terriers."

"What! I don't believe it. When did you decide on this?"

"Oh, I had thought about it when I was on my own for that time but, when Simon and I got back together, he was all for the idea as well so we booked one from two litters that Simon was rather keen on. We were very lucky and managed to get a dog and a bitch."

"Where are they? You must let me see them. Gosh, that's so exciting."

As they came out of the puppy kennel, Natalie was smiling broadly, "Oh Fiona, they are gorgeous and what a lovely colour. Those little black eyes looking at you. How clever of you to buy them unrelated, I suppose the idea is to breed from them?"

"Yes, ultimately, the gene pool in this breed is quite small so I tried to get as much difference in the pedigree as possible. They both seem sound but whether they'll both make the show ring is a different matter but, the whole prospect is interesting and exciting for the future."

"It is, I'm already excited for you. Paul will be so interested.. I can tell him all about them on the way up to London."

"Having a night out at the theatre?"

"No it's a dinner at...... well it's a dinner with friends of ours."

As they sat by the Aga that night having their hot chocolate, Fiona told Simon of Natalie's pleasure at seeing the two puppies.

"Yeah, pity that Paul has stopped her from showing, I think that she really enjoyed those dogs."

"Well, he hasn't actually stopped her from showing. It's just that, now he doesn't have to work so hard with Natalie's money to back him up and the sale of his house, they seem to go out more and go away more, you know how often the dogs come here for a couple of days. Don't knock it Simon, it represents quite a steady income for us."

" Yeah, do you wish that you could go away more, Fee?"

"No, I'm fine, as we are," she yawned.

"Good, come on then wench, time for you to warm your master's bed. I'll settle the dogs and lock up."

Natalie, full of apologies, arrived to pick up the three dogs the next afternoon, "Hello Simon, Hello Fiona, I'm so sorry I'm later than I said. I know that Saturday is a busy day for you."

"That's OK Natalie. We're not full up. Fee tells me that you like our new pups."

"Oh yes, I adored them both. I told Paul about them on the way to Clarges Street last...."

"Ah, so, dining with the famous and influential now are we. Well, I suppose that, with Paul's ambitions it had to come."

"What do you m....."

Fiona quickly linked her arm with Natalie's, "Natalie, I have a favour to ask now you're here, I've bought some new curtains, ready-made, for the kitchen and I don't know if they are right or not. I'd value your opinion," she shepherded Natalie towards the cottage. Once inside she filled the kettle and placed it on the Aga, "Now Natalie, what do you honestly think of these?"

They chatted about this and that and the old warmth of their friendship, missing a bit since Natalie's marriage, was re-established.

"Do you know, we haven't had a natter like this over tea and biscuits for ages Natalie. I've missed our chats."

"Yes, so have I, since my marriage to Paul there seems to have been so much to do. Every time I've been going to come round for the afternoon, Paul has always wanted to do something or other and, of course, with more cooking etc., time just seems to fly. That's no excuse though, I must try to make time, I've missed our heart to hearts. I must go now though, I've so much to do, we were rather late up this morning."

Fiona noticed Natalie blush and smiled inwardly. It looked as if Paul was still pleasing her in the bedroom anyway. Simon walked into the kitchen, "Great, where's mine then. I hope you two haven't eaten all the jammy dodgers."

As Fiona came back into the kitchen having seen Natalie off, Simon helped himself to another biscuit and said, "So, dining at Clarges Street were we. I wonder how many committees and or judging appointments, he managed to wangle himself onto? Soon be seeing his mug in the dog papers every week. The smarmy bugger."

"I know you're right but please Simon, don't say anything in front of Natalie. She's so happy."

As far as Fiona was concerned, she didn't want to talk about Paul. She still hadn't got round to telling Simon that she had entered Darlington under Alan Burgess. She was worried that Simon would put two and two together and guess that Paul had something to do with their present popularity in showing. After worrying about going to the show for days, she had decided that the only safe course of action was to start out for the show and then for the car to break down. Paul couldn't say that she had broken the agreement and Simon would be a little happier at the thought that she hadn't been near Alan Burgess. All that remained was to tell him that she had entered!

"Don't let's spoil our evening talking about him. We'll have to think about taking those babes to training classes sometime. I hope that we can show at least one of them."

"Yeah, me too. Being such a numerically small breed, even though we know the top honours are totally sown up, with the usual few constantly winning all the CCs on offer, at least, with such small classes, we get placed more often that not. Pity Paul knows about us having them, I'm dying to see the expression on old Mick Piper's face when I walk into the ring with a Glencastle," Simon laughed at the thought, "Paul will no doubt spoil it all now by telling him."

"Why should he?"

"What, he'll be busting a gut to tell Mick and the other prominent ones in Glencastles what a rotten, unreliable, trouble-making bastard I am and to watch me like a hawk and not let me win. The bugger will try to finish us before we start."

"So why are we doing it then?"

"Come on Fee, it's a bloody challenge isn't it. It's a lovely old breed that's being ruined with bad breeding from dogs with defective genes. That's the trouble with such a small gene pool, especially when some of the CC winners are the ones with the defects. If we can breed some decent stuff, all the big wigs will soon be sniffing round to use one of our stud dogs or have a pup. I'll then have something to bargain with." Simon rubbed his hands, "it's a challenge Fee, a bloody good challenge."

"But what about the Cumbrians?"

"What about them. We're beginning to do well again and we'll see that we continue to do well. It's always a good thing though to have two strings to your bow. When we give CCs in two breeds it opens up a lot more horizons doesn't it?" He gave her a hug, " the future looks rosy for the Simfell kennels."

Suddenly it seemed the right time to say something, "Simon, I was thinking about Darl...."

"We're on the up Fee. Now we're back together we'll show 'em. Glencastles, Cumbrians, the lot," he hugged her again. "Shall we have a sandwich, I'm starving."

Fiona smiled and went towards the fridge, perhaps it wasn't the right time after all.

CHAPTER EIGHT

Dennis sat staring at the back wall of the substantial red brick double garage; he wasn't actually staring at the wall but rather trying to fathom out how he could have let himself get to this stage where he was actually staring at the wall of Caroline's Aunt Ellen's garage.

They had handed over the keys of their house to the estate agent that morning and then driven over to Fiona and Simon Philip's boarding kennels to see how the dogs had settled in. The car was full of suitcases and dog gear but apart from that they had brought hardly anything else. It had upset him very much to think that that had been their first home, they had lived there nearly all of their married life together and she had either sold stuff to the people who had bought their house or she had sold it through adverts. What she couldn't sell she had packed into boxes ready for the local charity shop! Every time that he had mentioned items that he would like to keep she had countered it with, "Aunt Ellen's is better quality". He had got so sick of hearing her say that! He had finally had to resort to subterfuge; taking things round to Arthur and Madge's house so that he could come back and pick them up at a later date. He had even had to hide things like his darts trophies and odd little mementoes that he had kept from school in one of the suitcases containing his clothes.

Even the tools from his garage, some of which his Dad had given to him, he'd even had to take them round to Arthur's.

"Dennis, for goodness sake what are you doing just sitting there, bring the suitcases in. I've put the kettle on, Mr Carruthers has seen to it that the water and electricity are on, everything is working and we can have a nice cup of tea."

Dennis looked at her face, she still looked pretty; he'd noticed that small women often looked pretty until they were quite elderly as long as they didn't put on too much weight.

"Dennis!"

He slowly opened the car door, stood up and, taking a deep breath, picked up two of the suitcases lying on the back seat.

"It feels a bit chilly now but I've put the heating on and it will soon be warm."

Caroline had been coming up for the odd day over the course of the last couple of weeks, familiarising herself with all the equipment involved in the running of the house, sorting through the various drawers and cupboards. She had come home every time absolutely bursting to tell him how marvellous, how expensive, how useful everything was, he'd just switched off after the first few minutes. Blast Aunt Ellen!

"It was a good thing Dennis that I came up here for those days, we can move in so easily now. Oh, just take those cases upstairs to our bedroom will you. We can put them away later. I'll pour the tea."

"Where is our bedroom?"

"Where... Dennis, you know which one it is. I told you only last week that I'd aired the bed and made it up ready. I knew that you weren't listening."

"I've forgotten."

Caroline stopped what she was doing and turned to face Dennis emitting a deep sigh as she did so, "It's the ivory and apricot one overlooking the back garden. I told you that we would be able to look out onto the patio and the pond."

Dennis could hear her singing as he trudged up the stairs to find the ivory and apricot bedroom. The pile was so thick that you couldn't hear your steps! Dumping the two suitcases on the bed, he had just started back for some more when he stopped, turned and removed the suitcases from the bed and placed them on the floor.

Over the course of the next few days, Dennis had a week's leave before starting in the new office, he reluctantly familiarised himself with the house. It all seemed so much bigger than he remembered it from his one and only visit. There were more rooms and they were so much bigger, even the damned windows were bigger. He'd often had to clean them at their old house but he wasn't going to tackle these. She could moan all she liked. After a few days he did manage to turn in the right direction from one room to the other, but he hated all the furniture. Caroline had impressed on him just how 'good' it was and he was worried in case he knocked, scratched or, heaven forbid, broke any of it. The contents of all the damned drawers were a complete mystery to him and he didn't know how Caroline already knew where everything was kept, he still spent half his day looking for things. Even the blessed china was Royal Derby or some other posh name and all the cutlery was silver, he was terrified of touching the stuff. Thank goodness he'd given his favourite mug into Arthur's keeping, he couldn't enjoy a cuppa until he had it back.

He had been very relieved to find that there was a good burglar alarm in place, with all this expensive gear it was important. He would be glad when they got the dogs back, they'd help to guard the place. He suddenly found himself in the large conservatory, he had to admit that he quite liked this room with its' cane furniture, pots of flowers and bright chintzy cushions, it was the only place that he felt that he could relax. Opening the door to the garden, he stepped onto the patio, Caroline had asked him that morning to look out the best place for the new corridor kennels that were arriving any day now. He took a deep breath and the scent of the roses filled his nostrils, the garden wasn't bad either. He hadn't really had the chance to explore it yet. He walked past the roses in search of a flat piece of ground. Poor devils having to go in kennels because of damned chinese vases and things. Why couldn't they stay in the conservatory, it was big enough, worse they could do would be to chew the cane chairs or pee on the tiles.

Wrapped in his thoughts he realised that he was in part of the garden he hadn't noticed before because it was hidden from the house by a large beech hedge. Although rather covered in weeds, it had obviously been a large vegetable and fruit garden at one time. It instantly brought back old memories of school summer holidays and his grandad's garden in Worcester. For two weeks, right up to the age of sixteen, Dennis had gone to stay with his grandparents as soon as he had broken up for the summer. They had always made a great fuss of him and he had loved going there and helping in the garden. Dennis walked over to a large fruit cage and opened the door, yes, there were raspberry canes and yes, loganberries too. He hadn't had a loganberry since lord knows when. He found a couple of deep red fruits and popped them into his mouth. The flavour was so evocative he could almost hear his grandma's voice as she poured cream over a large bowl of loganberries for tea. He smiled and ate another one as he looked around the cage, he'd look in the library and see if he could find a book on fruit growing. They certainly looked as if they needed pruning. Didn't you have to prune them in the Autumn or something?

Stepping outside the cage, he found a clump of rhubarb, gooseberry bushes and some blackcurrant bushes still with the odd plump berry or two clinging to them. When he found the mound for the Asparagus bed he knew that, whoever had gardened here must have liked to grow the same things as his grandfather. He next looked into a large moss covered greenhouse with dead desiccated plants trailing on the floor, while nearby was a slightly dilapidated potting shed. There he found a lot of gardening tools and cloches, seed trays, pots, canes, an old bag of compost and some faded packets of weedkiller and fertilizer. Dennis sniffed, yes, it even smelled like his grandad's shed. What a find, it was.......

"Dennis. Where are you?"

Not wanting to share this little bit of happiness with Caroline yet, he hurried back past the hedge and then angled over to the left so that she wouldn't know where he had come from, "Hi, I'm coming."

"Have you found a place for the kennel?"

"Not yet. I wanted to ask you how close you wanted it to the house because you'll need a path up to it won't you."

"Yes, I will. When they lay the base perhaps they could do that as well if we pay them. Isn't it lovely to be able to afford to do these things."

"Um, if you say so. What about here?" Dennis indicated a stretch of lawn to one side of the pond."

"Good heavens no. It's got to be out of sight of the conservatory. We don't want them barking all the time do we, especially if we have guests. Use your common sense Dennis. By the way, could you take me to the shops now please."

"OK. I'll just change my shoes."

"I was thinking, as the roads are quieter here, I might get a little car for myself, a hatchback or something. I could go to more dog shows then and you wouldn't have to come if you didn't want to."

Dennis, who hated even the thought of dog shows, was quite pleased to hear this, "Good idea."

Parking at the local supermarket and watching Caroline disappear into the jaws of the building, he settled down for a snooze. Finding that plot today had, for some reason made him feel more relaxed than he had done since she had dropped the bombshell of selling the house. He must try to remember exactly what sort of things his grandad had grown, potatoes, yes, definitely potatoes, he remembered the excitement of digging them up, buried treasure his grandad had called them, and then............

"Dennis wake up, I'm sorry I've been so long but you'll never guess who I've just met."

"What... who?"

"Ophelia Hammond-James!"

"WHO!"

"Ophelia Hammond-James. Oh Dennis. She's ever so big in the dog world. Everyone knows her."

"Ah. Do they."

"And what's more, when I introduced myself and told her where we were living, she said that she would call on us sometime!"

"I see."

"I knew it was the right thing to come here. I just knew it. If I can get to know her it will help me a lot."

"Have you finished shopping, can we go now?"

"Yes."

Two and a half weeks later, with the kennel block erected, they drove down to see Fiona and collect the dogs. Fiona came out of the cottage followed by a couple of Cumbrians wagging their tails furiously, "Hello again, did you have a good trip down?"

"Hello Fiona, yes, the roads were fairly quiet weren't they Dennis. It's so much nicer where we are now, very peaceful."

"Good, and you're settling in alright?"

"Oh yes, we are already settled in aren't we Dennis, you see everything was there. My aunt wanted for nothing you know. The whole house is so beautifully furnished isn't it Dennis."

Dennis nodded, "How are the dogs er... Fiona?"

"They're absolutely fine, haven't been any trouble at all. Annie is a dear isn't she."

"That's good," Caroline said, "because we've bought one of those corridor kennels for them and had it erected. It's a good make so they should be very comfortable."

"Are you going to breed then Caroline?"

"What? No! I just don't want the dogs to ruin the carpets and furniture."

58

" Ah I see. Now, before we collect them, would you like a cup of tea, I've got the kettle on."

"Yes please, and we must settle up with you," Dennis replied.

Over tea in the warm kitchen, Caroline continued to extol the joys of Aunt Ellen's house, its' contents and its' surroundings while Dennis sat quietly looking at Fiona's dogs now lying by the Aga and just drank his tea.

"And Fiona, you will never guess who I bumped into in the supermarket up there."

"No, who?"

"Ophelia Hammond-James."

Fiona broke into spontaneous laughter, "Did you, what was she wearing?"

"Wearing?"

"Yes, didn't you know that she buys all her clothes from Paris, Harrods or from those dreadfully expensive London boutiques. It's always a talking point when she's judging."

Caroline was slightly taken aback that Fiona should be so well informed about Ophelia, after all she and Simon weren't really up in the world with that sort of person.

"Of course I knew that. I can't remember what she wore exactly when I last bumped into her. It was something blue and silky I believe, anyway, she has promised to call on us in the near future."

Dennis sighed, the stupid girl had done nothing for the past fortnight but rush round with a duster every morning in case this damned woman turned up - and she hadn't.

"She has Cumbrians and....."

"She has several breeds of terrier and a few toys as well I believe. Simon says that her kennels are marvellous. Best that money can buy."

"Has he been there then?"

"Yes, once or twice in the past."

"Yes, well, I shall no doubt see them for myself soon. We are quite close neighbours you know, anyway, Fiona, we must be on our way now. Thank you very much for the tea and for looking after the dogs, now how much do we owe you?"

Dennis went with Fiona to collect the dogs, they were delighted to see him, jumping up and barking excitedly, "Hello you lot, come on let me put your leads on, we're going ho...... to the house."

CHAPTER NINE

"You take Stream and I'll take Star Quality, OK."

Simon and Fiona both hurried down the path to the car each carrying a dog, "OK Star, in you go, right Fee give Stream to me. Good that's all three in, Saxon's already settled down. God why does it always seem to pour with rain for these 'early morning start' shows Fee?"

"I don't know but I think I'm getting too old for them."

"Don't talk daft."

They ran back to the cottage and took off their old raincoats, "Now, have we got everything, schedule, passes, food, money. You did put the box of trimming tools in the car didn't you Simon?"

"Yeah, and some extra towels, we're sure to need them."

"Right, well, I'll just pop into the loo and then I think we're ready."

Simon went and sat in the car, it was a reasonable drive to Ascot and he hoped that the rain eased a bit soon, the motorway spray would be bad otherwise. Fee plumped down in the passenger seat, "OK Simon, I've locked the door, let's away."

They were fairly quiet for the best part of the journey, they had had a bitch in for mating the previous evening and she had proved to be a right prima donna, refusing to stand, trying to bite the dog. It had taken a lot of patience to calm her and get her mated. They had got to bed later than they had intended and were pretty tired into the bargain. As they neared the show their spirits rose and they started to talk about their chances of a win.

"I do hope the youngsters get pulled out today at least."

"What! I hope they get at least a third. Wish we hadn't entered Saxon though, he's too good to be put down."

"He won't be put down. He'll be a champion."

"Come on Fee it's Gwen Fairfield. It's anybody's guess what she'll put up. Could be us, could be anybody. At least it keeps him in the public eye, good for studs."

"That's a bit unfair Simon, you make it sound as if she doesn't know what she's doing. She has some good dogs, which she herself has bred. She does have quite a good eye for a dog."

"Did I say she hasn't? I meant that she's not beholden to anybody, not in anybody's pocket, independent."

"Yes she is and I like her, she has principles and that's getting to be a rare commodity in showing nowadays. She hardly ever gets asked to judge simply because of that."

"No, course not, they're uneasy bedfellows. They don't want people to judge who have principles."

"Simon, you make it sound so hopeless."

"It bloody is if you've got principles! You of all people should know that."

"Well, she has managed to get this appointment and I am really looking forward to watching her judging, whatever she puts up will be her honest opinion."

"Agreed," they drove on in silence, the subject of honest judging was still a tender one where Fiona was concerned.

Simon joined the queue for the car park as Fiona sat still contemplating what Simon had said. It was so true, she knew from Paul how it was all arranged. It was obvious that people like Paul wouldn't want the Gwens of this world judging too often. It upset the orderly system. She still hadn't told Simon about her arrangement with Paul. She couldn't as yet gauge his reaction. Would he be angry or would he be pleased? He certainly wouldn't be happy that it was Alan Burgess judging! Blast Paul! How could she have ever liked him?

"Cheer up Fee, we're here and, thank God, it's stopped raining."

As they joined the throng of exhibitors pulling loaded trolleys or walking their dogs over the grass to the benches, several people greeted them including Caroline Amery who smiled and waved enthusiastically. There was a very good turn out of Cumbrian exhibitors, due, no doubt, to the unknown factor in the judging. Ring seats were quickly claimed with a jumper or plastic bag and there was quite a buzz round the ring when judging started. The young dog Stream was the first of their dogs in the ring and Fiona set about brushing him out. Simon studied the catalogue to see what they were up against.

"Um, the competition's not bad Fee. he should get placed."

Simon's prediction was right as the young dog came third in his class of seven. As their next class wasn't until the Post Graduate class, Fiona hurried off to the toilets. As she passed the Glencastle

61

benches, she was haled by Monica Worth, "Hello Fiona, how's that bitch I sold you?"

"Hello Monica, she's fine. Can't wait to bring her out."

"Good, she should do you proud you know."

The grapevine had it that Monica all but ruled the roost in the Glencastle breed. That was why Simon had wisely insisted that they bought the bitch pup from Monica. Her prefix was behind half the stock in the country and, as Simon said, rumour had it that she held sway over the choice of quite a few of the Champ show judges. As Fiona joined the inevitable queue for the ladies toilets, she listened to various conversations going on around her.

"I tell you, she does damn well dye that dog's coat. How I'd like to take the poor little bugger home and bath it. The water would be brown I'd like to bet." Both women nodded in complete agreement. Two older women further along the queue were in deep conversation, "It's always the same isn't it, we run welfare, giving it a lot of our time, money and effort. All the little people support and give money or buy things and the big breeders, and let's be honest, we get far more of their dogs than anyone else's, they don't give us a damned thing except at the club show where they make a big thing of giving to rescue! Honestly, I get so fed up with it."

Some women joined the queue behind Fiona, "There's no doubt in my mind that that dog who won that class today was not the same dog that I saw the other week! Did you go to SKC? No, well I did, that dog absolutely crawled round the ring there. Today, the damned thing went round like a greyhound, you saw it!"

Two women came out of the van and the queue moved up. As they passed Fiona one said, "How is it then that you can say that he's a puppy farmer because he breeds for money, when all the big breeders, some of whom breed and sell in large numbers, often buying in their stud dogs' litters as well and selling them on, how come no-one says that they are puppy farmers?"

At last Fiona had got into the van, ".....and the exhibitors are the last people to be considered as always. Give us your money and shut up that's the motto. Just look at the state of this place. When are they going to consider the exhibitor, we damned well pay enough."

Fiona would have loved to hear more but she was now at the head of the queue.

"Good you're back, she's getting along quite smartly. I've brushed him out. I'll go now and watch the judging if I can get a seat. I'll say something for Gwen, people are actually watching the judging for once and applauding! Got to go back quite a few years for things like that." Simon hurried away and Fiona sat on the bench and drank some coffee. There was another round of applause; it was getting more and more rare these days. She was just tidying up a couple of stray hairs when Simon hurried back, "OK? she's just pulling them out in Grad. I'll brush Saxon out while you're in the ring."

Post Grad was a big class with fourteen dogs entered, Fiona looked round and counted thirteen in the ring. Good class to win, she could see several nice looking dogs. She was ultimately pulled out fourth.

"Not bad Fee, it was a good class. Here's Saxon, I've brushed him out."

Fiona smiled at Simon and touched his hand, "Thanks."

They had agreed that it would be better if she continued to show Saxon until he was made up so she walked into the brightly lit ring looking full of confidence and smiling. There were eight other dogs already in the ring with one more to come. When that one entered the ring, she moved and settled Saxon at the end of the line-up. She knew that he really stepped out well when watching the other dogs move ahead of him and it kept his attention. He was looking in really good condition and she felt proud of him.

It was decision time and, as Gwen walked up and down the line of dogs Fiona tried to keep Saxon alert and keen. Gwen stopped in front of her and examined his mouth again then moved on to do the same with two others. After a final look she called Fiona out first. A big smile broke over Fiona's face as she accepted the red card; she looked round the ring and caught a glimpse of Simon grinning broadly.

In the challenge Fiona was praying that she would get the CC this time. She desperately needed an honest win to make her feel better about the others that she knew that she would get through her agreement with Paul. After no more than a moment's hesitation Gwen firmly walked across to Fiona with her hand outstretched, "Congratulations, a worthy winner." Fiona shook Gwen's hand vigorously, she was so thrilled. He was a true champion!

With tears in her eyes she ran round the ring followed by the Res.CC the applause was spontaneous and rippled all round the ring. Simon grabbed her in a bear hug, "Bloody marvellous. Fee. You'll see it's Stream's turn next." Fiona quickly looked at his face but saw only happiness. He obviously didn't know about the arrangement with Paul.

"Come on Fee. I need a stiff drink after that. I could see that she liked him, she kept looking at him but...."

"Yes, that's a wonderful idea. Let's settle him down and get someone to keep an eye on him first. My legs are still shaking, I could do with a stiff drink."

Several friends were invited on the way and a small party of Cumbrian exhibitors assembled in the bar and grabbed a table and several chairs.

"Here's to Simfell Saxon. Long may he win."

Everyone raised their glasses and sporadic talk broke out. Fiona listened quietly but heard no bitchy remarks about her win. Caroline, whom they'd met on the way, seemed busy trying to impress everyone with her new house and her new kennels, one or two immediately offered to sell her a decent dog. She did just manage to join in the ensuing laughter. A couple had to leave to prepare their puppy bitches so the little party broke up amicably. When they were driving home at the end of the day, Fiona remarked on the general atmosphere that had prevailed, it had seemed so much better than some of the Champ shows they'd been to recently.

"Yeah, well, it didn't leave a rotten taste in your mouth, no-one really knew who was going to win beforehand did they. Dog show people appreciate a bit of fairness, especially now that it's all so damned expensive."

For the rest of the journey home, Fiona sat huddled into her warm cardigan, deep in thought. She had seen Alan Burgess at the show and he had raised his hand and winked. She had felt acutely embarrassed, she hadn't appreciated before that several judges were going to know that she had an arrangement with Paul. Now they were all going to know that she had either slept with him or that she and or Simon had some sort of arrangement. It got worse the more she thought about it and how long would it be before someone said something to, or winked at, Simon. She looked across at his familiar profile, she couldn't bear it if their relationship were to break up again. She really must find the right moment to tell Simon about Darlington and quickly.

"Nearly home Fee. What a day, another champion for the Simfell kennels, Stream did well considering and Star Quality got a second at her first Champ show. Couldn't be better." He looked across at her, "You're quiet Fee. Something the matter?

"Er, no nothing. Tired that's all."

CHAPTER TEN

"Do you know you've been sitting here for an hour?" Dennis had entered the conservatory from the garden. There had been a slight frost the night before and he had wanted to see if that big old greenhouse was frostproof or not so, finishing his coffee and wandering off casually into the garden, he had managed not to arouse Caroline's interest. He felt a bit guilty not telling her about the garden behind the hedge but, for some reason that he couldn't explain, he wanted to keep it as his own secret for as long as possible.

Caroline engrossed in formulating her own plans for the future was startled at Dennis's sudden entrance, "Good lord Dennis, don't creep up on me like that, you nearly gave me a heart attack!"

"What have you been thinking about then?"

"Nothing much," she said with an exaggerated shrug of her shoulders.

"Come on Caroline, it must have been something important."

"No, not really, just thinking about the dogs and things. You know shows and things."

"Oh," Dennis smiled and went into the house, she didn't suspect anything then. She had the dogs and he didn't question her about them, in fact, now that she had bought that Renault estate, he wouldn't ever have to go to the damned shows again. He had been rather surprised that she had gone off and bought the car, he had taught her to drive not long after they were married but she had never been a very keen or, for that matter, a very competent driver, far too nervous. This money seemed to have given her a lot more confidence, she had asked him to come out with her a couple of times when she had first got the car but, after that she had trotted off to the supermarket and the next village on her own.

Caroline had actually been thinking about Fiona and Simon, she had heard from her old doggy friend Joan that Simfell Saxon had won his third CC at the Richmond show the other week. This news had started a train of thought, up till now she hadn't gone to that many championship shows not only because they hadn't been able to afford it but also because she knew that her little dogs weren't that

66

good. It was the big breeders' dogs that won at champ shows, they had so many puppies to choose from, they always had the best but now, now she could buy from the big breeders! She might not get the best ones but they would be better than the ones she had; she had been debating whether to phone Fiona or Ophelia when Dennis had startled her. She felt that Fiona, as she knew her, might let her have a nice one. She also knew that her old friend Betty had paid a fortune to Alan Burgess for a puppy and it hadn't been that good, in fact it hadn't won much at all and she had gone to no end of Champ shows with it. As for Ophelia! Now she was a very big breeder, she had looked up her address in the Cumbrian Year Book when they had first met; it was way out in the country and she wasn't sure if she could find it. Could she find her way to Ophelia's? Would Ophelia be angry if she turned up? Would she sell her a good puppy?

"Come on Caroline, your money's as good as anybody's," she said as she went upstairs, "Get your jacket and go now."

As she slowly turned into the long, gravelled drive leading to a big, old, white-painted farmhouse Caroline's nerve went, she slowed the car, perhaps this wasn't a good idea after all. Ophelia may be too busy to see her, of course, she should have thought and phoned first! She could just introduce herself again this time, say she was passing and popped in. Yes, that's what she'd do. Slowly pulling up outside the front door, she opened the car door and immediately a large wolfhound appeared round the side of the house and came enquiringly up to the car. Oh God, she should have phoned! Quietly shutting the car door, she sat there for a moment not knowing what to do, she daren't start the car, supposing she ran over the dog! She was almost in tears when a plump girl dressed in a big sweater, jeans and wellington boots came round the corner, "Here Hector, come here boy," the dog dutifully went to the girl, his tail wagging furiously from side to side.

"Can I help you?"

"Yes, oh yes, I wanted to see Ophelia Hammond-James please if that's alright?"

"Oh, I'm sorry, but she's in America at the moment. Can I help? Was it about dogs, only I'm one of her kennel maids. Did you want to book a stud?"

Caroline's courage failed at this point, "No, no, it's quite alright. I'll come back another time when it's more convenient."

"It's best to ring first, she's a very busy person and not always here. It might save you a journey."

"Yes, I'll do that. Thank you. Goodbye," Caroline started the car and drove down the other side of the horseshoe drive. The size of the place had surprised her, she had glimpsed a long row of kennels as she had driven in and stables when she had driven out, she had had no idea that Ophelia Hammond-James was so well off. Perhaps it would be best to stick with Fiona for now she thought as she slowly drove home. Ah well. She knew where she lived now anyway.

Dennis had worked in the garden for most of the afternoon and after dinner he felt like having a pint or two. In the last couple of months since they had moved he had sampled the brew in several pubs but had either not felt comfortable in them or hadn't liked the beer. Things were looking pretty bleak as he put an anorak on and he fervently wished he was back home. The job was pretty much the same as his old job had been but he didn't feel he fitted as well as he had in his old office. The rest of the staff were younger than him and keen on partying, football and foreign holidays, everything was 'cool', it made him feel old at forty- three. He definitely didn't like the house either or the furniture, too bloody grand altogether and it didn't have a decent pub for miles. He had seen a little pub one day when he had been out with Caroline and tonight he was going to see if that was any better. Unfortunately 'The Bricklayers Arms' turned out to be very little different from the other pubs in the area. He finished his pint and putting his hands in his pockets, he nodded to the landlord as he left. He felt so fed up that, if it wasn't so far, he'd drive back to The White Horse just to see a few friendly faces and have a game of darts; this reminded him that he hadn't even been down there to pick up his stuff from Arthur yet. In this miserable frame of mind he passed 'The Fox and Hounds' which was the pub he had first gone to when they had moved, it being the nearest. There had been no atmosphere there, it had been quiet and nearly empty and, they didn't have a darts team so he hadn't stayed long. He looked in the car park, there were only a couple of cars in there, no, not worth the bother. He drove home.

"Hello, you're back early."

"Um, didn't like the pub I went to. Caroline, how long have we got to stay in this mausoleum before we can move back home?"

"Move back home, this is our home now and it's not a mausoleum. Really Dennis you are so fuddy duddy. It's a lovely house and much better than our old pokey place. You know your trouble don't you Dennis. You've got no ambition."

Dennis looked at her for a minute then, taking his coat off went into the sitting-room and turned on the TV. Getting a can of bitter from the kitchen he went back and sat down to watch a gardening programme.

Caroline meanwhile was pouring over her Cumbrian year books for the past five years. She wanted to have some of the Simfell pedigrees firmly in her mind before she spoke to Fiona. She had loved their bitch called Sapphire, perhaps she might be having puppies. Should she have a dog or a bitch? Now that she had the corridor kennel, wait a minute, having seen Ophelia's, she could have another kennel. She could have two corridor kennels, one for bitches and one for dogs. Yes, she could then have some stud dogs and..... no, perhaps not stud dogs, she wasn't too keen on that side of things; but, puppies, yes, bitches would be better for her. She could build up her own line. Yes, she'd apply for a prefix and breed beautiful puppies that everyone would want. She'd make a name for herself in Cumbrians. Getting up she went to the phone and dialled.

"Hello Caroline, how's life in the frozen North?"

"It's not the frozen North Simon and life is very good thank you."

"How is Dennis?"

"Fine, he loves it up here, all the peace and quiet. Could I speak to Fiona please?"

"Certainly, I'll get her for you."

Caroline had rehearsed exactly what she was going to say but it was useless when she heard that, not only was Sapphire not in whelp, but neither was anybody else at that moment.

"No, you see Caroline, with the boarders and so much to do, we try to not have a litter at this time of the year."

"I see, that's a pity. I so wanted a nice one to show next year. I want a good one to take to Championship shows you see."

"I see."

Fiona thought for a moment, Caroline had made a point of telling them, and everyone else it seemed, that her aunt had left her money. Perhaps she could now afford a slightly older one, "Look, let me think about this Caroline only I might have a youngster I could let you have if you're interested. It would, of course, be dearer than a puppy."

"I hadn't thought about an older one but yes, if she's good enough, yes, I'd be interested."

"What about a dog?"

"No, not really, I'd rather stick with bitches."

"Well look, leave it with me and I'll have a word with Simon. I'll phone you tomorrow."

Caroline put the phone down. Well, that would be marvellous, a Simfell bitch! She could start showing her almost straight away. She had already joined the local dog society, she could start at their matches before the New Year, she hugged herself with excitement. Skipping into the sitting-room she said," Dennis, I'm so excited Fi......" Dennis was sprawled on Aunt Ellen's beautiful sofa, sound asleep with two empty beer cans laying on the carpet.

When the phone rang the following evening, Caroline almost ran into the hall, "Hello, oh, hello Fiona."

Fiona and Simon had spent a while the previous evening considering their various young stock. Since Simon's return they had run on several pups to evaluate their potential. Knowing the arrangement with Paul, Fiona had been very keen to run them on. They had one or two who were showing great promise.

"Well, if her money's good, we might as well have it as anybody else. At least we'll give her a decent one and not totally rook her as some of them would."

"That's true."

"If she is going to show it at Champ level, well that does us good too, we might even help her a little bit."

"Yes, so, which one do you think, she definitely wants a bitch."

"Yes, that's a bugger. Both of those young bitches look too good and we don't want to bring a dog out until we've made Stream up and that might take all bloody year. I'll have another look at the next year's judges list."

"How much should we charge her Simon?"

"A couple of thousand?"

"What!"

"That's what every other sod's doing."

"Well I'm not every other sod then. I'd be embarrassed asking her for that much."

"Fee, we're not putting terms and conditions on as well. She's bloody lucky that she's come to us. A hell of a lot would. She's so bloody naive they could easily see her off."

"That's true enough. It still seems a lot of money though."

"Now, come on Fee, don't get all sentimental about this."

"I'm not being sentimental."

"Yes you are. She's got the money, we want it. She's getting a bargain after all, in fact, now I think more about it. I'll make it two and a half."

"What!"

The conversation rapidly deteriorated from then on and they began to argue, suddenly Simon got up and walked out of the room returning shortly with two glasses of whisky, placing one beside Fiona he sat in the opposite chair, "Here's to us Fee."

Fiona raised her glass and sipped the smooth liquid but said nothing.

"Now my lovely girl, let's start again shall we. While I was away from you I had a lot of time to observe, read and think and I came to the conclusion that dog showing is changing out of all recognition from the showing I knew when I first started. It was changing when you came into it but, since then, the process has accelerated. With the KC and the championship shows turning the screw even more by increasing prices all the time, ambitious people want more out of it, more power more glory. It's not enough now to win and be seen to be a successful kennel and make a living, now it's money and more money with the success that counts and...."

"Don't you think that you are overstating the situation a bit."

"No, understating if anything. Look, even a lot of moderately successful people think of success in money terms now. Gone are the days when a rosette was enough. Now it's money that counts, the more you can win, the more puppy sales you get, more studs too, people abroad are more interested so you put the prices up and the money starts coming in. Sell stock on breeding terms getting even pet people to have litters to your stud dogs and you get even more money, you get the stud fee and get to sell the litter as well. Sell promising youngsters at expensive prices and people are happy, you go up in their estimation not down Fee. Success breeds success. Fee we're seen now by 'little' exhibitors as these sort of people. Like it or not, we are in the business of dogs and must in part obey the rules....."

"But I hate the rules," Fiona interjected thinking of her arrangement with Paul.

"Well, you know the alternative, we get out."

"No, we could just..."

"No we couldn't Fee. Not now."

They talked on for a while longer and it was decided that they would offer Caroline the dog for two and a half thousand no terms or two thousand and they would have the sole rights to sell the first litter save one puppy, the stud for the litter to be chosen by them.

The next morning, Fiona felt quite worried about telling Caroline of the terms that she and Simon had decided upon but Caroline, much to her surprise, didn't hesitate when she told her and readily agreed to the arrangements. Fiona showed her the young bitch in question and Caroline was over the moon. She immediately wrote out a cheque for two thousand, collected the necessary papers and left. Fiona breathed a sigh of relief as she put the cheque in her handbag.

CHAPTER ELEVEN

"Heavens Simon I nearly missed that," Fiona was trawling through last week's dog paper before consigning it to an already huge pile of previous dog papers in the kennel office.

"What's that?"

"There's an Open show on at the Sports Centre. It's perfect for putting our Glencastles in for their first show. Not far to travel and a nice venue, not too noisy."

"Who's the judge?"

" Brian Johnson?"

"Can't say that I know him, but then, most of them are going to be new to us aren't they?"

"True, it's a bit more exciting in a way. I'll put the bitch in the puppy class and the boy in Junior. It'll be interesting to see how we are received by the hound fraternity."

"With deep suspicion. They'll all be frightened we are going to try to take over. Pinch some of their precious bloody CCs. The old drums will be beating out there almost as soon as we enter the ring, they'll need to get organised in order to keep us out!" Simon grinned, "bloody funny really. I'll take great pleasure in worrying some of them anyway."

Fiona smiled at him, "Simon, you are utterly incorrigible."

"Well, the whole bloody thing is a set up. The CCs are, without any shade of a doubt, organised for the next couple of years at least. It's only if we can go under an overseas judge or a neutral one, that we'll stand any sort of a chance. By the way, have you heard from Caroline Amery how that bitch is getting on?"

"OK. She settled in quite well apparently. I was wondering if we could help her a bit?"

"Yeah, I should think we could. At least tell her which shows to enter anyway and, if we know the judge, we could drop a word in his ear. I hope she bloody well shows it properly. That's our prefix she's got."

The subject of their conversation was in her new corridor kennel proudly showing off her latest acquisition, "Just look at her Dennis, isn't she marvellous. Just look at her head!"

73

"What's wrong with it?"

"Nothing's wrong with it. It's a lovely head. Just look at the others heads and then look at hers."

Dennis dutifully looked at the heads of their three dogs and then at the head of the new one. Shrugging his shoulders and turning to walk out of the kennel he said, "All look the same to me."

"What! I paid..... a good price to get that head."

"How much did you pay then?"

"As I said a good price, after all you only get what you pay for, especially in the dog world."

Dennis again shrugged his shoulders and walked away. He hated having the dogs in the kennel. They had been alright in their old house, no bother, and they hadn't had a quarter of the room that they had now. He missed them. He missed saying hello and letting them out in the garden first thing in the morning. He missed them laying at his feet and missed them looking at him in the evening when it was time to take them for a last walk round the streets. What was the point of having them if they were stuck out there. He turned right and made towards his greenhouse.

Caroline was busy brushing the bitch, she talked to her as she brushed her, "Now Sesame, I don't like calling you by that name. What shall we call you, Beauty? No, Sarah? No. Now I've applied to the KC for an affix and if I get it, your show name will be Simfell Sesame at Carellen. Carellen! Doesn't that sound good; but what shall we call you. I know.... Mimsy! Aunt Ellen told me that she used to call my mother Mimsy when they were little girls. There you are Mimsy, that's you all brushed." She took the dog out into the pen with the others and stood looking at her. She was beautiful; she knew it had been right to go to Fiona. It was such a pity that Dennis wasn't interested in dog showing. She was dying to take her to ring-training classes this coming Thursday. Wouldn't everyone be surprised. She wished that Ophelia Hammond-James went to ring training, she would love to show Mimsy to her. Of course, she could call on her again. If she took the bitch it would look more professional, perhaps ask her advice on something. Yes, she would do that. She hugged the bitch, "Oh Mimsy, I'm so glad I've got you."

Consequently, on the following Tuesday morning, Caroline once again drove into the long drive leading to the farmhouse and, once again was confronted by Hector the wolfhound. She wound her window down to speak to the dog but Mimsy immediately started to bark and she hurriedly wound it up again. Oh heavens, she sat there for a while and was just wondering whether to sound the horn or not, would Ophelia think it rude? Nobody appeared from around the corner when finally Caroline plucked up the courage to give a tiny peep on the horn. She sat there for several minutes before she peeped again. There was no result so, after another couple of minutes of Hector walking around the car and Mimsy barking her head off, Caroline started the engine to quietly drive away. Out of the corner of her eye she saw the front door to the farmhouse open and Ophelia Hammond-James came out, "Did you want the boarding section? Just drive up there and the office is on the right," she turned to go back inside the house.

"Oh no, wait, wait please," Caroline was hastily undoing her seat belt and trying to get out of the car, "It's me Ophelia, Caroline Amery. Do you remember that we met in the supermarket a little while ago. We had just moved up here."

Ophelia turned and looked at her, she was quite certain that she had never met this small pleb before.

"I've got Cumbrian terriers like you have and I show them. Do you remember now?"

Ophelia didn't, but she was rather out of sorts having had a row with her friend Deborah with whom she was supposed to be lunching. This little person might amusingly pass a few hours, "Of course, I remember now. Why don't you come in."

"Well, I've brought my dog."

"Oh, he'll be alright there for a while won't he?"

"It's a bitch. I've only recently bought her."

Ophelia's interest was slightly aroused, "In that case do come in, I'll make some coffee and you can tell me all about her."

As soon as Ophelia left the room, Caroline, full of curiosity, looked around her. The large room had a huge, walk-in brick fireplace which could have looked most attractive had it not been full of ashes, covered in dust and with a miscellany of chocolate wrappings and old crumpled letters littering the floor. Most of the furniture was large and old. Caroline wrinkled her nose, the chintz covers on the settee and the two big, armchairs were decidedly in need of cleaning; as were the curtains at the windows. Caroline turned at looked at the rest of the room. Every available space seemed to be covered with books, magazines, papers and letters. She was just about to get up to go and peer into a small china cabinet when Ophelia crashed the door open. She was carrying a wooden tray with cups on it, "Sorry about that. Couldn't find the coffee. Just shift all that stuff that's in front of you and I'll put the tray there. Haven't got a cleaner at the moment, the last one only lasted two weeks."

Caroline quickly grabbed a pile of letters and papers and placed them on the floor beside the settee.

During the next hour, Caroline told Ophelia all about her inheritance, how lovely Aunt Ellen's house was and how much she was looking forward to showing Mimsy.

"Mimsy! What a quaint name," Ophelia said as she poured Caroline another cup of coffee, "and what about you. You are obviously married. Have you any children?"

"No, Dennis and I weren't lucky enough to have a family. The dogs are our family."

"I see, and how long have you been in dogs, I don't recall your face."

"Only six years or thereabouts."

"And how many champions have you made up?"

"Oh, er.. well none as yet. That's why I bought Mimsy. She's a Simfell bitch and they do very well."

Now that Ophelia had the full picture, this silly woman had a bit of money, was totally naive and was a no-hoper as well; she lost interest, "Well... er.... Caroline, it has been so nice meeting you. Good luck with your dog." She stood up and started walking towards the door, Caroline hastily placed her cup on the tray and followed her out of the room. As she started up the car, she realised that Ophelia had not looked at Mimsy, she switched off the engine but Ophelia had already gone in and shut the door. Never mind, she had made friends with her. Perhaps she could ask her over for coffee now. Contented, she switched on the ignition again and drove round the long horseshoe drive towards the road.

Ophelia took the tray back into the big stone-flagged kitchen and snorted as she put the tray down. How Deborah would have loved to listen to the stupid girl's silly ramblings. She frowned at the thought

76

of Deborah, she was being very cagey of late, this was the fourth or fifth time she had cried off coming to stay, had she found someone else? No, she and Debs had been together since boarding school days when they had been 'new girls' together. They'd then gone to the same University where they had fallen in love. Even when they had left University and got jobs in different parts of the country they had always remained faithful to each other, meeting as often as they could, snatching weekends together and always spending their holidays together. It was a wonderful romance that had lasted over the years, surely she couldn't have found someone else? She had a judging appointment this coming Saturday, but until then she was free. She'd go up and surprise Debs. Debs always loved surprises. The girls, two of whom lived in, could cope well enough with the kennels and the horses. She phoned through to the kennels, "Ophelia here, have we any studs in the next few days? In other words can you cope if I go away for a couple of days?"

Hearing that the girls could cope, she ran upstairs and started rummaging through her wardrobe. Deborah taught French at Leeds University; it was often a bit colder up there so she might need a jumper or two. She threw underwear, a negligee (she never wore pyjamas when she slept with Debs) a couple of pairs of trousers, blouses and tights into a suitcase, packed her make-up and her toilet bag, checked her handbag for money, credit cards etc. and hurried downstairs and out to where the girls were mucking out the stables.

"Annie something urgent has come up and I'm going away for a couple of days. You can manage can't you. There's not a lot in the diary, just one dog mating I believe and Diana says that she can manage that. There is that chap coming over to look at Minuet. You know the one who lives near Peterborough and who is considering him to cover his mare. If you want me urgently you can phone me at Deborah's. You know the number. OK?"

A couple of hours later, Ophelia let herself into Deborah's flat. She breathed deeply as she closed the door, she would know that smell anywhere. It was Deborah! She ran her fingers through her long blonde hair, it was good to be here, she had done the right thing. She picked up a decanter and sniffed the contents, different from her usual, she must have been splashing out, she smiled and poured herself a drink, just being here, near to Deborah, she felt relaxed. As

77

Ophelia walked around the rooms touching a coat of Deborah's which was hanging on the wall, picking up and smelling the dressing-gown laying across the bed. She looked at her watch; she should be home in about an hour unless some student held her up. There was just time to pop out and get some of that smoked salmon that Debs liked so much, some salad and a bottle of French wine.

When Deborah saw the lights on in the flat she stopped for a moment, only one person had the keys to her flat. She opened the door and called, "Ophelia is that you?"

"Yes my darling, I'm in here."

Ophelia resplendent in an oyster coloured silk dressing gown, her shining hair let loose from it's usual pleat, was pouring some wine into two glasses, "Here you are dear, something to take the tiredness away and then....." She untied the sash of the dressing gown and let it fall from her shoulders onto the ground revealing her nakedness, "and then we can shower together and spend the night making love."

Diana was amazed to hear a car racing up the drive on Thursday morning, "Who the hell is that madman," she said to the other kennel maid, "must be bloody daft. You alright to carry on here?"

As she came round the corner of the house, she first saw Ophelia's car screech to a halt sending stones flying in all directions and then Ophelia. She got out of the car slamming the door and then dragged her suitcase out of the boot, shouting at Hector, "Get out of my way you bloody cretin."

Diana had been working for Ophelia for three years and knew her moods, quietly turning round she disappeared back to the kennels. It was definitely best to keep one's distance at times like these. Seeing Annie she said, "Keep your head down Annie, she's back and in a foul mood."

CHAPTER TWELVE

"Thank heavens she's going," Diana the head kennel maid said to Annie who looked after the two hunters together with the Falabella mares. Ophelia had successfully bred these tiny horses for a few years now and made a good profit from their offspring. "God knows what's got into her this past few weeks but it's got to be something diabolical."

"If you ask me it's got something to do with Deborah. Have you noticed that we haven't seen her here for quite some time."

"Yes, you could be right there. Perhaps they've had a lovers tiff."

Both girls grinned as Ophelia, the subject of the conversation, screeched down the drive, stones flying from the tyres. She just missed an oncoming car as she turned onto the road and slammed her hand on the horn in return when the driver admonished her bad driving.

"Bloody cretin," she observed as she put her foot further down on the accelerator, "thinks he owns the bloody road."

It had actually been three weeks since her 'spur of the moment' visit to see Deborah since when she had written several letters to her, sent innumerable e-mails and had tried to phone but Deborah had not replied to anything. Surely to God she had seen sense now! She and Debs had been together for so long. They had been the best of friends at school, almost inseparable, and had realised their love for each other when they went to University. Their love had grown and they had vowed to be together for the rest of their lives. How could she say those awful things. How could she say that she had fallen in love with one of her mature students! She had never even looked at anyone else since she had first found out that she loved Deborah. How could Deborah be unfaithful!

Her foot pressed down on the accelerator and the speedometer steadily rose. She was thundering along a straight road when her eye was caught by some Cumbrian terriers being walked by a woman. One of them particularly caught her eye. Jamming her foot on the brake she came to a screeching, tyre wearing, halt quite a bit further up the road. Looking in her rear vision mirror she could just see the woman, she appeared to have stopped walking and was turning around to walk the other way. Slamming the car into reverse gear, she drove back to the woman and leaning across, wound the nearside window down, "Hello there, saw your dogs. You've got a lovely bitch there, do you mind if I ask where you got it from?"

"Oh, hello Ophelia, you startled me a bit."

Ophelia frowned, "I'm sorry, do I know you."

"Yes, don't you remember, we met in the supermarket. I'm Caroline Amery and I live near here now."

Ophelia, who could not remember meeting the woman at all replied, "Of course, I remember now. How are you settling in.... Caroline?"

"Very well thank you. The house is so lovely, my Aunt Ellen left it to me when she died."

"Oh, do you live on your own then?"

"No, Dennis my husband is here too."

"You're married then." Blast she thought, a germ of an idea was slowly taking shape in Ophelia's mind, "And how many children have you got?"

"None, I'm afraid, Dennis and I weren't lucky in that respect."

That was a relief anyway thought Ophelia eyeing Caroline up and down. Not too bad in an insipid way. Obviously from the lower to middle classes but then.... better not be too curious at the moment, "That's a nice looking bitch you've got there. Caught my eye. Did you breed her?"

"No, I've only recently bought her from Fiona and Simon Philips. Her kennel name is Simfell Sesame."

"Oh yes, I know them, how's she bred then?"

Caroline saw her chance, "I can't remember exactly just for the moment, look the house isn't very far away, why don't you come in for a cup of tea and I can show you the pedigree."

Ophelia looked at her smiling face. Why not, poor devil was obviously smitten with her, you never know, could be a bit of fun, the thrill of the chase and all that. Deborah had apparently found it thrilling, as she had told her that day, "It was a wonderfully fulfilling adventure," she'd show her that two can play at that game.

"How kind of you, I'd love to have tea with you and see your new house. Why not pop the dogs in the back and I'll drive you there." Caroline eagerly agreed and put the dogs in the back of the estate car.

"Good, now, you give me directions."

That evening Caroline was over the moon, she couldn't stop singing Ophelia's praises to Dennis. Ophelia had been so complimentary about Aunt Ellen's house, she obviously knew quite a bit about antiques and advised her on several pieces telling her to make sure that her insurance covered them adequately. She had admired the new kennel and had been most interested in Mimsy's pedigree. She had advised her on the shows in the local area and had suggested that she get to as many Champ shows as she could with the bitch. She had squeezed her hand as she left and thanked her for a very pleasant afternoon. It would be wonderful when she saw her at Champ shows and spoke to her. She thought of the people she knew in Cumbrian terriers; wouldn't they be surprised when they saw that she was a friend of Ophelia Hammond-James!

Dennis, however, had been singularly unimpressed. He had hardly spoken to Ophelia and had quickly disappeared in the direction of the garden and he hadn't reappeared till long after Ophelia had left. That reminded her, what did he do up there for hours? She really ought to go up there some time. His only remark when she had asked him what he thought of Ophelia was, "Is she married? No. I thought not." Caroline smiled as she prepared their dinner. What a silly remark to make.

"Do you know Dennis, I think that we ought to go ski-ing next year, Ophelia says..."

"For goodness sake Caroline, change the record will you, and anyway, we can't ski can we!"

"That's the point, they show you how, Ophelia says....."

Dennis threw his newspaper on the floor and went out to the kitchen. Caroline watched him go and shrugged her shoulders, men were so boring, they never liked anything new!

Simon Philips was reading through the Breed Record Supplement to keep abreast of all the information of who bred what to whose dog, who bought in a puppy and who was selling abroad, it often helped to explain wins in the ring. The phone rang and he went into the hall, "Hello, is that Simon? This is Ophelia Hammond-James. How are you and Fiona?"

"Ophelia! This is a pleasant surprise. Er, we're both well thank you and you?"

"Fine, thank you. Now Simon, to the point of my call. I've just seen a bitch of yours, a Simfell Sesame."

"Oh yes, we've just sold her to Caroline Amery."

"That's right. I've been to her house today. She tells me that you have a dog and another bitch from the same litter."

"Ye-es, I have."

"How much do you want for either of them?"

"Now, they're not really for sale. I've decided to run them both on."

"So they're both promising are they?"

"Well, I wouldn't be wasting the space if they weren't would I."

"Right, how much do you want for them?"

"Hey, hold your horses Ophelia, you'll have to let me think about this. I would have to consult Fee as well and anyway it would only be one of them if we did agree."

"Righto, I'll leave it with you. Come back to me when you've decided which one."

Simon put the phone down and stood looking at it for a moment deep in thought before going back into the kitchen, "You will never guess who that was and what she wanted."

"No idea apart from it being a woman."

"Ophelia Hammond-James no less and she wants to buy either Sinbad or Salome! We have really got to get our thinking caps on Fee. I wonder what's behind it. Her stock hasn't been so good of late, perhaps she wants some new blood, or is there an alternative reason we know not of. This could do us a power of good though Fee."

"How? I thought she was a...."

"Yeah, so what, it doesn't stop her doing us some good as well if we see her all right does it."

"Like what?"

"Come on Fee. She exports a lot to America and is well in there for starters. Possible puppy orders or even a judging appointment? She has contacts all over the world. With the help of her lady friends she'll make the dog up in no time, that will be another Simfell Champion in the records. She'll then either breed from it or export it which will also spread our name far and wide and, don't forget, if we don't let her have one she'll bloody well see that WE don't make either of them up. You've seen all the tricks that can be pulled to stop someone winning."

"But what are her kennels like. If you believe the stories of how the dogs are kept in some of the big breeders kennels; locked in cages for most of the day without human contact, never taken out for a run - except perhaps to ring training classes. Got rid of quietly to God knows who or where if they don't make the grade and so on."

"Yeah I know, I've heard it all, poor buggers, you'd never know it to see them in the ring would you. From what I've heard though, she has a reasonable reputation for a breeder. Breeds horses too, you know those little ones, can't think of the name, rumour has it that everything is well looked after, she employs good staff.

"We-ell, can't we make a few enquiries before we decide?"

"Fee, I've told you before, you can't be so soft. If you are going to do well in dogs you've got to think of them as a business commodity not a pet. If we don't let her have one of them she'll do us harm eventually and you know it."

"I do know but, well, let's just find out if she has a bad name for her kennels. It wouldn't do us much good to let one go there if she has would it."

"OK Fee, I'll phone Bob, he'll know."

Simon again came back into the kitchen shortly after with the information that her kennels weren't that big, only about ten to twelve bitches and a couple of stud dogs. Her kennel maid had been with her for a few years so she must be treated fairly well too, not treated as a skivvy or given a filthy old caravan to live in. They talked on for a bit more about it, Fiona knew that she was facing the inevitable, "Damn the women, why did she want one of ours. I suppose we shall have to let her have one, but which one, the dog or the bitch?"

"Let's go out there now and decide shall we."

"Yes all right, I'll not sleep anyway until we've decided. Blasted woman."

The 'blasted woman' was drinking a gin and tonic at that moment and priding herself on a good day. Her stock hadn't been really up to the mark for a year or so now and, although she had continued to win top awards, she felt that new blood was needed. The solution to this was only a phone call away and the solution to her present problems with Deb was only a few miles away! Yes, a real departure from the humdrum, the day was ending far better than it had started. She smiled and took another sip of gin. The more she thought about

Caroline Amery, the better it looked. It would be exciting to pursue her, it would be most exciting to make her fall in love with her. The silly fool was half way there already, even if she didn't realise it. Best of all, she'd be on equal terms with Debs.

CHAPTER THIRTEEN

"That sounds wonderful Duncan. When did you say that you were going, April was it? Well I'm certain that Donald will adore every moment. Switzerland is pretty at any time. Now, I'm afraid I really must go, we are expecting a customer and I think that I heard a car draw up. Goodbye Duncan and thank you so much for phoning. Do give my regards to Barbara and a big hug for Donald. Bye."

Putting the phone down, Fiona sighed. She still felt a little guilt about the divorce and everything that had happened before it, he really was such a kind man. He had phoned her regularly ever since that terrible time when she had lost her baby. She sighed again at the memory of that day but then, hearing Simon talking outside the door, she shrugged her shoulders and putting a smile on her face, opened the kitchen door, "Hello Ophelia, how are you? Do come in, it's a bit damp out there today."

Ophelia came in and looked around the large, stone flagged kitchen with interest. Seeing the Aga she went towards it with outstretched hands, "Yes it is, I shall have to look out some gloves for driving soon." She sniffed the air and continued to look around mentally noting that the kitchen actually looked and smelled clean! She had been in some breeders' houses where she couldn't bare to sit down let alone eat or drink something. This one didn't even stink of dogs although there were a couple wandering round and inspecting her, "Are these related to the dog I'm having?"

"Yes, similar lines but all mostly Simfell. Not too close though. Would you like a cup of tea or coffee?"

"No thanks. I'd like to get on with the job in hand if that's all right with you."

Good old Ophelia thought Simon, who had been standing in the doorway listening, blunt and to the point. He and Fee had been up until late last night debating the pros and cons of this sale. She had wanted to keep the bitch, they already had Saxon and Stream, both doing well, they didn't need another dog. He had had a hell of a job to persuade her that they had to look ahead. There was a golden opportunity here to get a foot in the door so to speak. Not only was Ophelia a member of the Kennel Club but her mother had been before her. She had clout and could do the Simfell kennel a lot of good. She would, without doubt make the bitch up and then, when she had had a litter from her, might ultimately, sell her abroad for a damn good figure. Whatever, it had to be good for their name. He had explained to Fee that their job today was to say the right thing as to what they hoped to get out of the deal! She had been very funny last night, insisting that they didn't need to do deals and things, their dogs were good and should win on their merit. She bloody well knew how the cookie crumbled with regard to dog showing, he couldn't understand her reasoning, she must have been tired

"Right then Ophelia, shall we go and see the bitch? This way. Are you coming Fee?"

"Yes, I'll just get my coat."

Although she made no comment, Ophelia was also impressed with the kennel arrangements. Almost as good as hers. These people knew what they were doing when it came to dogs, "So this is the bitch." Simon had put the bitch on a lead and brought her from the kennel, together they all went over to the stripping shed so that Ophelia could go over her. She was very thorough in her examination of the bitch, and then asked to see her move, "Um, not bad. I'll take her if the price is reasonable."

Fee looked across the stripping shed at Simon, she did not look happy, he looked at her and raised an enquiring eyebrow, after a moment, she nodded her head slightly.

"Well now Ophelia............"

The bargaining went on for some while, mostly in half sentences but the meaning was clear. Fiona felt acutely uncomfortable during the whole procedure, how would this affect her arrangement with Paul? Simon still knew nothing about that! She couldn't but admire though the delicate and diplomatic way he was going about it. Finally it was agreed, a small amount of money would be required for the bitch to keep the books straight, Simon would get an overseas judging appointment, Fiona would get a Champ show in this country and the bitch's litter brother, the one that they were keeping would be made up into a champion and Ophelia would then get three free studs from him or any of the other Simfell dogs. They shook hands on it, Simon gave her the necessary paper work and Ophelia loaded the bitch into her car. She hurried back into the warm kitchen where the kettle was now boiling merrily.

"Will you have tea or coffee now Ophelia?"

"Yes, coffee thank you, black."

They started talking about the show scene in general and their breed in particular as they drank the coffee. Suddenly, Ophelia put her cup down and stood up, "Must away, things to do and people to see."

After Ophelia's car had disappeared down the drive Fiona turned to Simon, "God, Simon however did you do it. How did you think up those things?"

"Fee, for God's sake, I've kept my eyes and ears open and I've watched, looked, listened and recorded for years. I only needed the right opportunity. It's bloody marvellous isn't it, a guaranteed champion and at least one overseas appointment. She drove a hard bargain, I was hoping for more. Now, at least, we won't have to sit there for ages with only two CCs".

"But Simon, how do you know that she will honour it now that she's got the bitch?"

"I know," he smiled and sipped his coffee. "I know she will because of this." Out of his pocket he took a tape recorder and rewound it, "This will go to our solicitor if there is any funny business, I managed to call her by her full name, I mentioned today's date and what the transaction was about. I called you by your name and brought you into the conversation as well. She'd have a hard time denying it."

Fiona looked at Simon's smiling face, it surprised her how much he had enjoyed the wheeler dealing, "Promise me one thing."

"What's that my sweet girl?"

"Don't get like the others will you."

"What me! You know me better than that Fee. Come on let's have another cuppa."

Fiona sat holding her cooling mug of tea and staring at Simon's grinning face, he was still elated with his success. "Simon, I can't believe what you're saying. You make it sound so sinister, so machiavellian, it's like MI5 not dog showing. I mean I know the fiddles, the wheeler-dealing the lies, the underhandedness and the cheating but this, this cloak and dagger stuff, I mean, tape recordings!"

"My darling girl; still the sweet innocent really aren't you. Believe you me, this is nothing compared with what goes on, nothing!"

Fee thought of her own guilty secret and said no more. Simon was elated all that day and, in the evening broke out an expensive bottle of wine they had been given by Rob Harding, his bitch had had a lovely, healthy litter and he was keeping a bitch. "Here you are Fee, taste that, it should be good." He poured himself a generous glass, "Here's to us Fee and the Simfell kennel."

They sat by the log fire, his arm around her shoulders and enjoying the rich taste of the wine. Soon his fingers began to caress one of her nipples and she arched her back slightly, "I know that I talk a lot of rubbish Fee but, I'll tell you something, none of it, not the winning, the judging, the wheeler-dealing, none of it is worth losing you again. If you are ever unhappy, if you ever want to pull out. Just say so. OK?"

She turned to look into his warm brown eyes; she remembered it was his eyes and his hands that had first attracted her. She leaned forward and kissed his mouth, "I love you Simon."

He kissed her back with growing passion, pulling her jumper up he started to caress both her nipples with his fingers as his tongue explored her mouth. Pulling her bra down, he licked and kissed her erect nipples, "Well then my girl, I think it's time you showed me just how much."

Fiona laughed, her face was flushed from the wine and Simon's caresses had made her body glow, "Right my great entrepreneur, you've asked for it." She jumped up and quickly kicked off her shoes, removed her jumper and bra and then the rest of her clothes. He sat back admiringly until she bent forward and started to strip off his jumper and shirt. They caressed each other's body with practiced ease knowing just where to tease or kiss for the desired effect until finally they laid on the rug by the fire and soon after he had entered her they climaxed together. They stayed locked together in the warmth from the fire secure in their own world.

The next day being Sunday, after they had seen to the dogs, it was their custom to have a leisurely breakfast and read the daily papers and the dog papers. Fiona who was reading one of the dog papers suddenly stopped and hurriedly turned back a couple of pages. Her face flushed, good heavens she thought, it's true, I hadn't realised, here could be a neat way out of the Alan Burgess problem.

"Simon, we have a small problem."

"What?"

"Well, you know that I entered the Glencastles for that Open show next weekend."

"Yeah."

"Well, it clashes with Midland Counties, same day in fact."

"Midland Counties, didn't know that we were going. Who's the judge?"

Fiona flushed deeply, "It's Alan Burgess."

"What! You've bloody entered under him! What the hell were you thinking of!"

"Well, you said that we had to get back again and be seen so I thought..."

"You mean that you didn't bloody think. For God's sake Fee, how can you enter that bloody ring with him there. How can you stand there with him looking at you, being near you. Have you gone stark raving bloody mad woman. Did you honestly think that I meant any bloody show. I'd throttle the bugger given half a chance," Simon stood up knocking over his mug and raged around the kitchen, finally going outside and slamming the door so hard that the walls seemed to shake.

Fiona sat very still but her mind and heart were racing, she had been dreading this moment ever since she had filled in the entry form.

As suddenly as he'd stormed out he stormed in shouting at her, "I can't bloody believe you would do such a thing. What in heaven's name possessed you? Do you want the rumours to start up all over again? You know what a reputation he's got damn it. I thought all this was behind us. I believed you when you said that it meant nothing to you. I bloody well believed you and now you go and do this! Well, I'll tell you something, you're not bloody going."

"But Simon, I've entered, there won't be any rumours, and truly Alan doesn't mean anything to me, you know that. I just thought that it would be good for Stream to be seen."

"There are always rumours surrounding him, the randy sod. Fee, you are NOT going to that bloody show, do you hear me Fee. You - are - not - going."

"Well, I must admit that's a load off my mind. I really didn't want to go, I just thought...."

"Well you thought wrong."

"I know but, what about if I take the Glencastles to the Open show and you take Stream to Midland Counties."

Simon looked at her for a moment, "Why do I get the feeling that I'm being organised here? Have you been planning this all along?"

"No, honestly Simon no, I thought that it would be good to keep him in the public eye because we're only going to LKA after that and I doubt we'll do much there. Then there's nothing until Crufts. You always said that we must be seen..."

"I know, I know but... Hell, Fee, I don't know, why did you have to load me with this? As for going under the bastard... I don't think I can do it. Almost anybody else but not him. Honestly Fee, I still can't believe it. I've never known you to do something as stupid as this."

He continued to pace around the kitchen; the dogs had long retreated into their beds and kept looking at him and showing the whites of their eyes. They were very worried. Meanwhile, Fiona sat quietly sipping her tea, cursing Paul for eternity. She'd forget their silly bargain, what did it matter anyway now that Simon had made the deal with Ophelia. She opened her mouth to tell Simon not to bother, it had been a stupid thing to do when he stopped in front of her, "All right Fee, I'll go, but I'll only take Stream in one class and then I'm on my way home. People will then think that I wanted to go, there'll be no rumours and that's an end to it. Don't you ever, ever do anything like this to me again Fee. Do you hear me. Never ever again. I'm warning you, I still want to kill that bloody man."

Fiona realised that she had been holding her breath through this conversation. She inhaled deeply, "Thank you Simon, I think that your reasoning is very logical. It would be best if you go and I'm sorry. Would you like another cup of coffee?" Her legs were shaking as she got up and went across to the Aga. She was rather worried at what Simon might do when he got the CC. She assumed that he would, surely Paul wouldn't have stipulated that it had to be her! On second thoughts, she wouldn't put it past him.

At the same time as this argument was taking place, Natalie was looking across her lounge at Paul. How lucky I was to find him she thought, how very lucky. He is so kind and considerate, so loving and gentle, well read, interesting to talk to, knowledgeable about so many things. He got on so well with all of her friends and they all seemed to like him. How her lonely life had changed. It was a bit of a pity that her friendship with Fiona wasn't encouraged by him. She couldn't understand it, she knew that he and the Philips were old friends, he didn't mind her taking the dogs to board there when they went away but, she just felt that he didn't want her to be as friendly as she had been with Fiona in the past. Could he be jealous of her friendship with them, it was so pleasant to think that he could be jealous. She looked at him and smiled and he smiled back at her, "Penny for your thoughts my dear?"

"Oh nothing really darling. Just silly woman's things."

He smiled and went back to his paper, just at that moment the phone rang and Natalie hastened to answer it, she hoped that it was Candida phoning from New Zealand, "Hello, Mrs Paul Aston speaking," she still loved to say that name. "Oh yes, I'll get him for you," she called out to Paul, "Paul there is an Ophelia Hammond-James wants to speak to you."

She could hear him speaking and he seemed quite annoyed about something, she could hear snatches of the conversation, "......you should have had a word with me or one of the others first...... this totally mucks up the CC schedule for the next two years...... just forget it, he can't prove anything.... you didn't sign anything."

When Paul came back into the lounge he was frowning, his face was flushed and he seemed very annoyed.

"Anything the matter darling?"

He stared at her for a moment and then smiled, "No, nothing to trouble yourself about my dear. Nothing that I can't solve with a bit of time."

CHAPTER FOURTEEN

Dennis was enjoying himself, he had started to repair, clean and disinfect the big greenhouse down at the end of the garden in what had been the vegetable and fruit growing area. He had bought a couple of books on vegetable and fruit growing and was making plans for the Spring. He had already thoroughly cleaned out the big garden shed and cleaned the window. He now not only had room for all the tools but also a small table and a chair, a single Gaz burner, and a teapot. In a plastic box he had a supply of tea bags, some sugar, dried milk and some ginger nut biscuits. He finished his dunked biscuit and the last drops of tea, closed the book and prepared to start work again.

Caroline was at a show today and, apart from looking after the other dogs and a few delegated chores, he could relax and enjoy the peace and quiet of the garden. Suddenly Annie and Patsy came wandering round the big beech hedge, he bent down and patted their heads, he still hated the fact that their three older dogs were kept in the kennel. Today, he had let them all out to wander around the garden at their leisure and it had been obvious from their faces that they had enjoyed the freedom and the company.

He looked around at the new panes of glass he had put in the greenhouse to replace the broken ones and the new pieces of wood which he had bought to replace the rotten parts. He was now taking out one pane of glass so that he could insert a ventilator for the summer months. All the dirt and lichen had been cleaned away from the inside and the outside, he had replaced some of the broken slabs, which formed a path down the middle of the greenhouse and repaired a long table on which plants could stand. He nodded his head as he stepped back to look at the ventilator in place.

Going back to the shed he returned with several, new, propagating trays which he placed on the table, yes, he was really looking forward to the Spring. Over the last few weeks he had bought several geranium plants, which he had seen reduced in a Garden Centre. He should be able to overwinter them in here if he lit the old paraffin heater that he had found in the greenhouse and cleaned up. They'd give him a bit of colour through the winter. Finishing the job in hand and again testing that the ventilator opened and closed easily, he decided to wander back to the house for a cup of tea. Calling the dogs, he put them back in the kennel.

As he neared the house he was surprised to see a woman standing by the conservatory, as he neared her she called out, "Ah, there you are, do you know if Mr or Mrs Amery are in?"
He found himself looking at that damned women Ophelia whatsername, "Well, I'm here."
"Yes but..... oh, are you Mr Amery then?"
"Yes."
"Ah well, I've just bought a bitch from the Philips and I wanted to compare the two together, your wife has one from the same litter."
"Oh yes."
"So, will you tell her to give me a ring so that we can arrange for her to pop round with the bitch. Right. Bye."
He heard the car start up and the gravel fly as she charged out of the drive, "Snobby bitch," he said as he walked through the conservatory, " who does she think she is."

He had just finished his second mug of tea when he heard the key turn in the front door, "Hello Dennis, Dennis, are there you are. Dennis, I've had a marvellous day. I got Best of Breed with Mitsy AND came third in the Group. What do you think of that! I mean I know it was only an Open show but there were several Cumbrians there and I've never come anywhere in the group before. It was wonderful and I'm so excited. I must phone the Philips, they'll be so pleased. I just can't wait to go to the other shows I've entered. Oh Dennis, isn't it marvellous. I must enter the Championship shows now too. Oh Dennis."
Her cheeks were flushed, her eyes were shining and she was laughing and talking at the same time. He didn't think he had seen her so happy since their wedding day fourteen years ago. Dennis shook his head, for the life of him he couldn't see what was so exciting about dog showing, all that rushing around, all that fussing the dog about and for what, a couple of minutes running around a dirty bit of grass to win a bit of paper.
"Do you want a cup of tea love, there's one in the pot. By the way, that posh dame from up the road with the fancy name came to see you. Wants you to take your dog up there so that she can look at it."

"Does she? Which dog? Why?"

"Don't ask me, I'm only the messenger boy or the gardener!"

"Right, I'll phone her after I've phoned Fiona."

Fiona put the phone down, "That was a very excited Caroline Amery, apparently she got BOB and 3rd in the Group at an Open show today. Now, Peter, more tea?"

They had invited Peter and Beryl down for tea today; it had been an awful rush because tomorrow was Midland Counties and the Open show. It had been Peter's birthday in the week and this was a celebratory tea. They had been so busy of late that Simon hadn't seen his brother for a couple of months and Fiona was always pleased to see Beryl. At the moment that Fiona walked back into the room, they were having a heated discussion about the merits of a certain footballer, who had recently been transferred for a massive sum of money and the chances of that team winning the cup. Beryl smiled up at Fiona, "Don't bother Fiona, they can't hear you. Come and talk to me. Will you be busy for Christmas and the New Year?"

"Yes, I think we will, we have quite a few advanced bookings already."

"So we might not see you then?"

"No, look, why don't you and Peter join us for Christmas. Peter can help Simon with the dogs and we can share the cooking. We'll have a wonderful time."

"That sounds lovely. I'm sure that Peter would like that too. I'll ask him when I can get a word in edgeways."

"Good. I'll look forward to that."

Later that evening, when Peter and Beryl had gone, she told Simon of the arrangements that she and Beryl had made.

"Great, yes, I'd like that. By the way, are we having our usual New Year Party this year now that we're back together?"

"Yes, if you like."

"Well, I know we've got this arrangement with Ophelia but, we could still do with a bit more help don't you think?"

Fiona looked down at the floor, she just hated this subterfuge, she hated the whole business with Paul, "Yes, perhaps we could."

"Right, that's on then. You see to the grub and I'll do the booze. Now, who shall we invite?"

Ophelia sat by the fire with a vodka and tonic, Caroline had phoned her to arrange a time to come and to tell her of her win, so that bitch might be as good as she had thought. She wanted to go over it again in order to compare it with hers. That stupid woman might be persuaded to swap if she flattered her a bit. She thought of Debs, she still had not phoned her, she thought that she would have come to her senses by now. This mature student must be a wow in bed for it to have lasted so long it couldn't be anything else other than a fling. Debs loved her, had always loved her and had told her so many times. She still couldn't really believe that Debs could have been unfaithful to her, she felt so angry every time she imagined them in bed together, she wanted to hurt Debs as she had hurt her.

She poured herself another generous V and T and sat down again. She missed her lover; she missed the thrill, the anticipation, the warm feeling of satisfaction afterwards. She groaned, why the hell should I be the loser? Why should I sit here waiting for the phone to ring? Why should I remain faithful to her? She wouldn't hesitate any more, she would put her plan into action.

The next day, Caroline drove up to the farmhouse at exactly eleven'o'clock. Diana appeared in her usual gear accompanied by the dog. This time Caroline was not so frightened, she opened the door of the car, "Hello, I've come to see Ophelia."

"Yes, I know, if you like to wait in the car, I'll call her and then you can bring your bitch into the courtyard, OK."

Diana soon appeared again and beckoned to Caroline. She got Mimsy out of the back of the estate and put her lead on. When the bitches met up it was obvious from the wagging tails that they recognised each other and Caroline was happy to let them play but Ophelia told Diana to move her bitch away so that she could go over Caroline's bitch. She then told Caroline and Diana to move them side by side.

As they walked back Caroline looked at Ophelia's face, her nose was all creased up and she was frowning.

"I like your bitch, I'm willing to buy her from you. How much?"

"I couldn't sell Mimsy. She got third in the Group the other day. I'm going to show her at Championship shows."

Ophelia drew a breath in through her teeth, "Champ shows, dicey. She'd be all right for breeding though. That's what I'd want her for."

"Don't you think she's good enough for Champ shows then?"

"Well, if you want to win firsts... no."

"Oh, the judge was so complimentary on Saturday I thought.."

"Well, you don't have to take my word for it but...."

Caroline was crestfallen, her Mimsy, not good enough to win, she looked down at the bitch and suddenly she didn't look as good after all. Perhaps Ophelia was right.

"Look, I can see how disappointed you are, how about we swap the bitches. I can guarantee that you will win firsts with the one I've got at Championship shows."

"Do you think so?"

"I'm certain of it. Look, you're welcome to look round my kennels at any time, you'll see that she'll be well looked after."

Caroline looked down again at Mimsy and then at the other bitch, yes, Ophelia was right. Perhaps that's why the Philips gave her this one, they kept the best one for themselves. Ophelia must have paid a fortune for her bitch for them to let her have it. Firsts at Champ shows! She'd never won anything at all at the few Champ shows she had gone to and she desperately wanted to win and show off like others did. She imagined herself going up to her friends, "Hello, I got a first at Crufts with my bitch and she has had no end of firsts and BOBs, I'm hoping to make her up next year," she looked down again at Mimsy "Well, if you're sure that your bitch is good enough to win firsts at the shows..." Ophelia, sensing victory butted in, "You won't regret it Caroline. I promise you she will get some firsts. Why don't you come in for a drink to seal the deal. We can get to know each other better."

At these treasured words, Caroline nodded and followed Ophelia into the house.

CHAPTER FIFTEEN

She only had to load the Glencastle babes into the estate and she was ready but Ruth hadn't arrived yet. What a week it had been, rain and yet more rain, the row with Simon, having Beryl and Peter to tea, it was a blessing really that there were no boarders at the moment. Fiona looked at her watch, Ruth should be here by now, perhaps she had better phone her. Simon had left about six-thirty with Stream to Midland Counties. He had looked angry and upset and she had felt so guilty, she had kissed him goodbye and wished him luck but he had hardly said a word. She wouldn't have been at all surprised if he had refused to go, blasted Alan Burgess seemed to hang over them like a cloud. She was now absolutely sure that Paul had done this deliberately, was there no end to the viciousness of some people, "Hi Ruth, you haven't forgotten that you are coming over today have you?"

"Hello Fiona, I was about to ring you, no I am coming, we all overslept this morning and it's like a mad house here. I should be with you in about a quarter of an hour; I'm awfully sorry."

"That's OK just as long as you are coming. See you."

Thank heaven she could come, this extra quarter of an hour would give her time to throw a few more of the washed dog beds in the dryer. Mud and wet, she was sick of the sight of it she thought throwing the beds in and starting the machine. If this week is anything to go by I shall come last today.

The hall was quite crowded when she finally arrived pulling the heavy trolley with the two pups in their cages. There seemed to be very little space left to put up her grooming table but, after wandering around the perimeter for a while, she eventually found a small space to squeeze into. The people on either side glared at her and shuffled their belongings a bit closer to them. This is a good start, Fiona thought as she discarded her wet jacket and shook the rain from her hair. Her classes would be in ring four which was further up the hall so she would have to keep an eye on it, a few Bedlingtons were in there at the moment. These would be followed by Welsh terriers and then the Glencastles, she poured a much needed cup of coffee from her thermos and talked to the pups to keep them happy, not that they seemed too perturbed by the proceedings. She wondered how Simon was coping? Judging at Midland Counties had started at nine-thirty so they must be well into the dogs by now. Would Simon going instead of her alter the arrangement? Had Alan Burgess been told to give her the CC or her dog? If he did give Simon the CC what would he do? Throw it at him? Choke him as he said he would? Punch him in the face? Or would his commonsense and good manners prevail? She was glad she wasn't there.

Deep in thought she looked towards ring four and realised that the Open class for Welsh terriers was being called in and there were only two entries. She grabbed her grooming box and took the dog puppy out of its' cage and started grooming it. Thank heavens she had got them well prepared first thing this morning. She then hurriedly groomed the bitch puppy. Putting a lead on the bitch she walked her up to the ring just as the puppy class was being called; altogether there were five entries. A couple of the other exhibitors looked at her unsmiling, looked at the bitch and looked away, the other one ignored her. The little bitch behaved well enough when it was her turn and, although it was obvious that the judge knew the other exhibitors, Fiona thought that she might get somewhere. She did, fifth and last! Hurrying back to her space, she took the dog out of his cage, slipped the lead on him and walked him up to the ring. There were only three other entries this time and the dog walked very well. Having pulled out the first two quite quickly, the judge then seemed to go into a reverie as to which of these last two should come third and fourth, she asked them to move again, she looked at their teeth again, she deliberated again, she smoothed their coats down their backs, she considered again and finally, making up her mind, she gave Fiona the third place and the other poor specimen the fourth. Looking at the fourth placed dog, Fiona couldn't but wonder how the woman could have spent so much time deciding.

Pouring another cup of coffee from her flask Fiona smiled wryly. It was what she had expected but she had to smile. She had gone up to the other exhibitors after the judging was over and introduced herself, but had met with a very tepid reception. They did not want someone else horning in on their preserves. Well, thought Fiona, my pups must be good then, if they were lousy the reception would have been warmer! Finishing her coffee and her sandwich she started to load her trolley. As she left the building, the rain was still lashing down as she pulled the trolley towards the car. Who in their right mind would show dogs she thought as, soaking wet, she started the car and went home.

It was getting dark and she was putting her wet clothes to dry near the Aga, having got soaked again seeing to the kennel dogs, when she heard Simon's car come up the drive. He drove straight up to the kennel area and it was a while before he came into the kitchen.

"Hello Simon, how did you get on?"

"Don't you know?"

"No, no-one has phoned."

"I got the dog CC, but didn't get BOB. Alright?"

Fiona looked up at his face, he looked older and strained. It must have been an awful ordeal for him. She shouldn't have done it. Now, that Simon had an arrangement with Ophelia, she should have dropped her arrangement with Paul. It just wasn't worth this.

"I'm so terribly sorry Simon, it wasn't meant to be like this."

"What wasn't?"

Once again, she couldn't bring herself to tell him about her affair with Paul, she was so frightened of losing him again, "When I was silly enough to enter the show, I should have thought more. Oh my darling, I'm so sorry, it must have been awful for you."

"It was, I wanted to ram the bloody CC down his throat and he knew it. If I didn't know better I'd have said that you were.... with him. God, Fiona, for God's sake, tell me you haven't.... I didn't get that bloody CC because you...."

There were tears in his eyes and he looked haggard, "No Simon, no, no, no. I haven't, I didn't. I wouldn't. No. Believe me, please believe me, no." She flung her arms around him and tried to pull his stiff unyielding body towards her, "Simon I love you," she kissed his wet face," I don't ever want anyone or anything else. I only want you. I'd give all this up tomorrow just to have you with me."

She stared at his set face, this was terrible, she should have thought more about the implications of the reputation that Alan had. What a fool she was, of course, this was Paul's revenge wasn't it, not making her go under Alan but the fact that everyone would be saying that she had won because she had slept with Alan. That was his revenge on Simon as well and she had walked into it blindly.

She continued to stand there holding him, tears quietly running down her face and gradually, the tension went out of his body and he put his arms around her and put his cheek on the top of her head. They stood without moving or speaking for some time until Simon moved slightly, put his hands on her arms and moved her back from him. He looked into her eyes for a moment or two before he kissed her wet cheeks and then her lips, "Come on, enough tears wench, let's have a cuppa and then we'll break open·a bottle to celebrate Stream's first CC."

" Oh Simon, you are a lovely man and I love you so much."

"Yeah, funny business dog showing isn't it."

"Why do you say that?"

He kissed her mouth, "Because of today. There's something bloody funny going on, it was obvious that Alan didn't want to give me the CC. He made me bloody work for it the sod."

"How?"

"Well, after he'd gone over him and I'd done a triangle, he asked me to go straight up and down."

"Yes."

"And then the bugger said, 'Again,' so I walked him up and down again and then he said, 'Do it again please.' I watched very carefully Fee and Stream was walking perfectly well. There was no need for it. The old bugger was just having a bit of fun at my expense! Can you imagine my surprise when he pulled me out first! He did the same bloody thing in the challenge too, made me walk again and again. Honestly Fee I wanted to throttle him as he stood there grinning all over his slimy face! I still don't understand why he did that and then gave me the CC? I'll find out though!"

Fiona's heart sank, she hoped that Simon would never know how Stream got his CC. She knew one thing though, she would be phoning Paul first thing tomorrow and cancelling their agreement.

As it happened, Natalie called round early the next morning, "Hello Fiona, may I come in."

"Natalie, what a lovely surprise, come in and get dry. Will it ever stop raining do you think and it's so dark isn't it. Gosh, you look well, marriage certainly agrees with you."

"Fiona, I'm so lucky to have found such a dear man. He is so kind and thoughtful."

Fiona thought otherwise but refrained from speaking.

"I don't think that I knew just how lonely I was before. We get on so well together it's amazing how much we have in common and he is so considerate."

"I'm so pleased that you're happy Natalie. My only regret is that I don't see you so often nowadays."

Natalie's smile left her face, "No, I don't get over as often as I would like, Paul always seems to find something for me to do. Not that I'm complaining, it's lovely to be needed."

"How are the dogs?"

"Fine, they're fine. It's partially about them that I have come to see you."

"Oh?"

"Well, Paul has a couple of overseas judging appointments next year and wants to make them into a holiday for us. He also thinks that he may have more meetings and things here next year so...."

"So you want to book the dogs in advance. That's fine Natalie, pleased to have them."

"Well no, not quite. Paul thinks that, with our social life expanding, we shall not have the time to show dogs so he thinks that it would be kinder to find mine good homes and that's where you come in."

"Natalie! You can't, not Jamie."

Natalie looked down at the table and swallowed hard, "Well, yes, Paul thinks that they should all go. He says, quite rightly, that it would be better to find them a permanent home. He has already parted with some of his dogs you know."

Fiona looked at her unhappy face for a moment and then reached out and took her hand, "OK Natalie, don't worry, I'm sure that I can find the right homes for them; but you should keep Jamie you know, he really is a nice specimen of the breed."

Natalie looked up, " Thank you for saying that Fiona, perhaps I'll have another word with Paul about Jamie. As for the other two, I know that, if you say the homes are good, they will be. I think that I've been in dogs long enough to realise that not all so called dog

101

lovers really care for their dogs. I think that Paul might agree about Jamie. If he can go to the same kennels as his, it will help matters."

"The same kennels?"

"Well yes, as I said, Paul reckons that we will have so many engagements next year that the dogs would be a tremendous liability. He doubts that we shall be able to show them ourselves so he has made an arrangement with the kennels that they will handle them for us. That way our name will still feature in the catalogues and the write-ups, he did explain it all to me and it does make sense Fiona."

"Oh yes, that bit makes sense."

There was a short silence and Natalie fiddled with the buttons of her jacket. Fiona felt so sorry for her; it was true she wasn't lonely any more but, was she losing her independence? She had always admired the enthusiasm with which Natalie, not a doggy person really, had embraced dog showing. Changing the subject and, in order to break the silence, Fiona said, "Well, you do sound as if you'll have an exciting year ahead, I feel quite envious."

"Yes, not only have we these two appointments but Paul has promised that, if all goes well, we can go to New Zealand to see Candida. She is expecting her first baby in May. I did tell you didn't I? They phoned me last week, they were both over the moon and so excited."

"What wonderful news Natalie. I'm so pleased for you."

"Yes, it's turned out to be a marvellous year for me."

"Thank you Fiona. I have so enjoyed this visit, I don't see enough of you. I miss our chats. Now, I must be away, I promised Paul that I would pick up some of his suits from the cleaners."

Just as she was about to get into the car she turned and took hold of one of Fiona's hands, "Thank you for being such a good friend Fiona and not minding about the dogs. I just don't understand why Paul was so adamant that his dogs should go to the other kennel to be shown. I did say that I thought that you and Simon were the best people to show them for us."

Fiona waved as Natalie's car drove away, she nodded her head and said, "Oh Natalie, I understand why. I also know that the kennel concerned is run by two of the biggest crawlers in Cumbrians. They'll show your dogs and win and not show their own for a while just to curry favour with Paul. A fat lot of good it will do them too. At least, you might be able to see Jamie though."

CHAPTER SIXTEEN

Fiona was sitting on a bench at the LKA show, the last championship show of the year. Simon was off somewhere, chatting to someone no doubt, she couldn't leave the bench because, not only did she have the two Glencastles on their bench but also Stream and the young Cumbrian dog, Skiddaw, the brother to Ophelia's dog. Simon was going to show them. She was smiling to herself as she listened intently to a conversation which was taking place on the benching adjacent to her. The two ladies were having a heated argument, one had accused the other of spreading malicious gossip about her dog. The other was just as vociferously denying it. Apparently, according to the first lady, rumours were being circulated that her dog was firing blanks and yet, knowing this, she was still using him at stud and taking the money under false pretences. In consequence, her stud work had dropped off in the last couple of months. She had been told, by a reliable source, that the second lady was to blame for starting the rumours.

"Now why on earth would I do that?"

"You know perfectly well why; you and your husband are well known for it. You just want all the studs in the area for your dogs. Not to mention the fact that my dog is siring lovely puppies, far better than your rubbish."

Fiona sighed, a different breed of dog but exactly the same problems.

"I've a good mind to report you to the club for that."

"Of course you do. It's common knowledge that you've got them in your pocket as well. The whole of the committee are at your beck and call, including your husband. They even pick the judges to please you."

Fiona nodded, she herself had heard this said several times about this breed, and many others. Being a numerically small breed, when only a few people and their friends seemed to win all, or nearly all, the CCs, these things were certain to be remarked on.

"What utter rubbish."

"It isn't. You and your husband between you organise the judges, shows, everything, no judge would dare put you or your few cronies down, if they did you'd see that they never judged the breed at CC level again!"

"That's it! I've heard enough! I'm reporting you under the code of ethics."

"Do what you like, this is my last show anyway. I'm sick of just being ring fodder for you and your cronies to smugly walk in and get the top prizes. I'm sick of spending money to see my dogs put down to inferior stock. You're so damned greedy that you even have to turn up at Open shows, you can't bear for anyone to make a bit of a name for themselves. You are a greedy, conniving, vicious and downright evil bitch. Glencastles are a lovely breed, they don't deserve sods like you. I'm going."

Totally enthralled, Fiona popped her head over the top of the benching in time to see a lady, very red in the face and almost in tears, pick up her dog and walk away. Fiona was just getting down when she realised that the other lady was looking straight at her. Monica Worth's angry face glared at her for a second, "Who the hell do you think you're staring at," she shouted.

It was on the tip of Fiona's tongue to say, "A downright evil bitch I believe," but commonsense prevailed, there would be no future in Glencastles if she said anything. She was saved by the appearance of Simon, "Simon, I was looking for you."

"Hi, sorry darling, got cornered by Bob. I'll take Skiddaw and Stream to their bench. OK?" turning he nearly bumped into a stoutish, middle-aged woman, " Sorry. Oh, hello Monica, we're pleased with that pup you sold us." Monica only managed a tight smile. He turned again to Fiona, "Good Luck sweetheart."

"Yes, OK. I'll see you later. And may the best man win." She knew that she'd be very lucky to get anything to speak of at this show being an interloper, so to speak, but it would be interesting, nevertheless, to see how the dog fared in his class. Simon with the Cumbrians was another matter. Stream should do well today and Skiddaw, he should do well next year with Ophelia's help. Simon winked at her and hurried off with the two dogs.

As the Minor Puppy Dog class was called, Fiona had to admit to a little bit of nervousness. How silly I am she thought, after all this time and knowing what I know now about dog showing, to be nervous. She entered the ring with her youngster trotting happily beside her. Good, he's not overawed by the occasion. There were only three other competitors. It seemed as if the lady in the argument was not the only one to be fed-up today. One dog would not walk round the ring and had to be almost dragged around by the owner who was constantly squeaking a plastic duck at the puppy. The other two walked fairly well, one, however was very big for a Minor puppy and the other had an obviously poor tail set. Fantasy stepped out well for Fiona and looked the part, she wanted to pick him up and hug him. These two puppies had given her so much pleasure. They were a delightful breed, full of fun and willingness to please. The judge asked the girl with the uncooperative puppy to walk again, and once again it was very reluctant to walk, pulling away from its' owner and looking slightly distressed. Fiona was, therefore, a little surprised when the judge gave it the first prize, the big puppy was pulled out second with Fantasy third. She got over her surprise when, putting Fantasy back on the bench, the same girl gave the puppy who got the first prize, to Monica and said, "I'm so sorry Mrs. Worth, he didn't want to walk for me."

"Never mind dear, no harm done. I'll take him in for the challenge."
Let's hope that she hasn't got a bitch puppy in those cages thought Fiona, we won't stand a chance in that either.

"Would you mind keeping an eye on my dog for me please? I must dash off to the loo."
A youngish woman was looking at her, she looked quite pale and drawn.

"Yes, of course I will," Fiona didn't want to leave her bench and was having a cup of coffee. With such a numerically small breed it wouldn't be long before the bitch classes were in and she didn't want to miss her class. It wasn't long before the woman returned, "Thank you so much, that's very kind of you."

"Not at all. Pleased to help."

"Is this your first show?"

"Yes, with this breed, my husband and I show Cumbrians as well."
They got chatting and Fiona was amazed how similar her early experiences in dog showing had been to this girl's.

"My husband hates it all, says that it's silly and a waste of money and now that the entry fees to these shows are getting dearer and dearer, it is hard to justify." The woman blushed slightly, "You see I'm expecting our first baby."

"Congratulations."

106

So taken up was Fiona in listening to the girl's experiences that she suddenly realised that a few people were clapping around the ring, "Good heavens, that must be the dog CC. Please excuse me, I just want to see who got it. I wonder if they'll go straight on?"

"They usually do. There's so few of us."

As she entered the ring she saw Monica having a chat at the judge's table, the steward said something to her and she left. There were three other bitch puppies in the class. All looked quite nice, all walked quite well. All Fiona could do was to present the bitch as best she could. When she was pulled out second, she was thrilled. As she walked out of the ring a now smiling Monica Worth congratulated her profusely, "Well done Mrs Philips, Fiona isn't it. I didn't meet you when your husband collected the pup. I've only just made the connection. That's a nice bitch, I shouldn't have parted with it should I! I'm sure that you will do well with her."

Over a cup of coffee, Fiona looked at her catalogue, yes, it was as she thought, hers was the only Monica bred dog in the ring. Good old Simon, he knows what he's doing. Thank heavens I didn't say that she was a downright evil bitch!

Just at that moment Simon came round the end of the benches, "Good, a cup of coffee, just what I need. How'd you get on?"

"Third with Fantasy and second with Fleur."

"Not bad, not bad at all for a first Champ show. More to the point, how did they behave?"

"Fine, absolutely fine, just like they do at training classes, absolute poppets, most promising. Have you been in with Skiddaw?"

" Yes, he got a third so he'll be in the write-ups. There were eleven in the class so it's far better than we could have expected. It'll be good for next year though," he winked an eye at her.

"What's the current gossip?"

"Not much, some of those stupid women are trying to outdo each other in attending these blasted seminars they're all on about now. Silly buggers, it won't alter the status quo one iota."

"I don't know, we might get some judges who know what they're doing AND who are honest."

"And how long do you think they'll last. Won't be asked to judge will they. Anyway, who cares about them. We're doing all right Fee and that's what counts. Now, where are those rolls, I'm starving." He ate one roll and then, taking another one with him, he returned to the Cumbrian benches to get Stream ready.

Later, as they were packing up, Fiona remembered that she hadn't given out the Christmas cards that she had written the night before, "Oh Simon, wait. I must give out these cards. Look, you go on and I'll come to the car when I've finished."

As she raced round to the Cumbrian benches, she kept getting stopped by other Cumbrian exhibitors giving her cards and wanting to chat about their latest wonder dog. It was well over half an hour before she got down to the last few cards. She stopped Irene Allsop, "Hello Irene, nice to see you. How are you?"

"Fine, it's always a good day when I'm away from my husband. That's why most of us show isn't it?" she laughed. Fiona smiled, "Have you seen Mrs Emsworth today Irene?"

"No, but I did hear that she's not too well. By the way, Alan Burgess was looking for you."

Fiona stared at her for a moment her mind shying away from the information, "Thanks Irene."

"Look there he is now, Alan, Alan, Fiona's here."

With a sinking heart Fiona turned round, "Hello Alan."

"Hello Fiona my dear, I've been looking for you."

"Well, now you've found her Alan, I'll be off. Happy Christmas."

With a pounding heart Fiona watched Irene walk away to the benches.

"Now my dear, do you mind telling me what happened at Midland Counties."

"What do you mean?"

The smile left his face, "Come on now, don't play the innocent with me. You know bloody well what I mean. I was told to put you up and you didn't appear, Simon did. It left me in a hell of a mess, I didn't know what to do. If I had done the wrong thing it could have done me irreparable harm and you know that. So once again, what game are you playing now?"

"I'm not playing any game. I couldn't come so Simon came instead."

"Ah yes, so he knows about your sordid little affair with Paul does he. He knows that you are blackmailing the poor man does he?"

"How do you know about that?"

"My dear, Paul is not the gentleman I am. Although don't tell him I said so."

Upset and frightened now, Fiona wanted to escape, she told Alan that Simon was waiting and hurried to one of the exits, now full of people all with trolleys, boxes, bags and dogs, all looking weary and eager to be on their way home. As she threaded her way through the masses she was full of admiration for the fortitude, the dedication and the seemingly unquenchable optimism of these people. Their dedication knew no bounds and it was a great pity that they were not given more consideration by many of the organisers.

She felt sick after her encounter with Alan, how many other people had Paul told? Supposing Simon found out, supposing Alan or someone had already spoken to him. She had hurried away too soon, she should have asked Alan if he had said anything to Simon. Did anyone else know? She had so wanted to tell Simon about her relationship with Paul but Simon always stopped her. Now, now that they were so happy again, it was much more important that this was cleared up between them. She would have to make him listen to her and soon. She hurried out into the cold, dark, car park.

Once home, having paid Ruth and listened to the answerphone messages while Simon nipped out for some fish and chips; Fiona let out a long sigh of relief, thank heavens, they could have a bit of a rest from showing now. It would give her time to sort something out. She knew now that she must end this arrangement with Paul and quickly. She could not trust him at all. She wanted to look forward to this Christmas and to the New Year's party. Heavens, the party, surely no one would say anything then, not with Paul and Natalie there. Her unhappy thoughts were interrupted by Simon returning with their supper. As they sat in the warm kitchen, Fiona was still thinking about how to terminate her arrangement with Paul when she heard Simon say,

"Hey, aren't you hungry, don't you want those chips?"

"No Simon, I'm not terribly hungry and I had an awful lot of chips. You have them if you can eat them." She grinned as he poured some brown sauce over the chips and ate them, she loved him so much nothing must be allowed to destroy it.

"You're quiet tonight."

"Um, just a bit tired. I'm glad it's the last show of the year."

"Yeah, so am I in a way, gives us time to think of other things. By the way Fee, I heard that Mrs Emsworth isn't too great. Perhaps you'd better give her a ring."

"Yes, I heard that. She has always been so kind to me. I hope that it's nothing serious."

Later that evening she dialled her number, "Hello Mrs Emsworth, it's Fiona Philips. I missed you at the show today, how are you?"

Her face grew serious as the elderly lady spoke, "But, surely they..." She continued to listen with a grave face, "Of course I would. I'll speak to Simon and come back to you. Now do take good care of yourself."

"You look serious Fee."

"Yes, I'm afraid the news is not good. In fact it's very bad. She's very worried about her dogs. She has found homes for some of them but she has a young one of only a year old and a favourite of nine years. She was wondering if we would have them. She was going to write to us. She wants to pay us to keep them until the old one dies and to show the other."

"She doesn't have to pay us."

"No I said that but she says that it will take up a boarder's space and she doesn't want us to be out of pocket."

"Rubbish."

"I know Simon but I owe her such a lot, I wouldn't have met you if she hadn't let me have Sally; and you know what Sally means, meant to me."

"OK, we'll have them, I know it means a lot to you. Try and persuade her though that we don't want paying. Tell her to donate it to Cumbrian rescue."

"She is already giving them a tidy sum apparently, I think that she would rest happier if we took some money. She is a proud, old lady."

"OK, OK, I give in."

Fiona gave him a hug, "Oh Simon, I do love you so much."

CHAPTER SEVENTEEN

Having put the new bedding, bowls and toys in the kennel block and said hello to the dogs, Caroline opened the kitchen door where Dennis was cooking the evening meal, "Hello Dennis."

"Hi, did you have a nice day? How did you get on?"

"Yes I did thank you and yes I went straight there," Caroline had been to the LKA. She had not actually been to any Champ show before, other than Crufts, not that she told people that, and she had been pleasantly surprised. At this show the noise and bustle had been less, there were less pushing people, and it had been easy to park and get a bus.

She had dreamed last night that Mimsy had won the CC and everyone had applauded, it had been wonderful. Actually, in real life, she had hoped that Fiona and Simon might win the CC with Skiddaw so that she could tell everybody that she owned his litter sister. She had told all her acquaintances that were at the show anyway. She had also told them of her plans for the shows for next year and how much she was looking forward to them now that she could drive herself round. Although she was, in actual fact, still a little worried that she had done the right thing by letting Ophelia swap bitches with her and hoped that it would not spoil her chances.

The trip today had been a trial run for Crufts because she had never driven to the NEC before on her own. Dennis had given her detailed instructions and she had been rather pleased that she had got there and back without a hitch.

"Sausage and mash OK?"

"Yes, I'm starving. I'll lay the table."

"Can't we have it in here Caroline, just for today. It's nearly ready." Caroline was rather tired after her exertions and agreed. They had often had their meals in the kitchen in their old house but it seemed wrong somehow here. As they ate the meal she told Dennis about Simon's third place with Skiddaw and his first with Stream. How everyone seemed to be giving Christmas cards to each other and what she had bought at the various stalls.

"Did you get any cards?"

"No, of course not, I didn't know about it but I will next year. I'll go out tomorrow and send one to every one of the Cumbrian exhibitors that was there. Which reminds me, on the journey home I was thinking about Christmas, it'll be our first one here. Shall we have a little party?"

"Good idea, this place could do with livening up, but who could you ask?"

"All our friends that used to come to our other parties of course."

"They won't come all this way for a party, they've all got children or other relatives to consider."

"Some would if we offered to put them up. After all we've got the bedrooms. I'll get on with the list after dinner. It would be nice to see them all again, I'm dying to show them the house."

Dennis continued to eat his dinner quietly and didn't look up from his plate. He knew that their friends wouldn't come up here for Christmas, they wouldn't want all the fuss and bother. If the truth was known, he didn't want them to come up here. He wanted them to invite him and Caroline down there! He could go to his pub for a pint or two, have a game of darts and thoroughly relax. He sniffed and put his knife and fork down on the plate, "Want a cup of tea and a piece of cake?"

"Just the tea please Dennis, you know that I have to watch my weight. Not too much milk mind."

As Dennis poured the tea into the cups he mimed, "Not too much milk mind". Had she asked him what he'd been doing all day? Had she asked him if he'd enjoyed himself? He could have told her that he had now completely lined the greenhouse with bubble plastic ready for the winter. He could have told her that he had ordered a lorry load of manure from a nearby farm and had also ordered some seed catalogues from his gardening magazine. He had even cleared and dug a bit more of the vegetable patch and had a bonfire. He and the dogs had felt tired but happy by the time it was going dark; well that was before Caroline came home with her big ideas for Christmas.

Later that evening, when Caroline was on the phone, he looked into the sitting room and told her that he was popping out for a jar. She didn't even break off in her conversation merely waving a hand in his direction; so he got his anorak and went out. It didn't seem too cold tonight and as he didn't feel like driving after his day's exertions, he thought that he'd walk to the nearest pub, namely, The Fox and Hounds. He hadn't been back to it since the first week that they'd moved up there. Then the landlord had been such a surly bastard, coughing all the time he pulled the pint that Dennis hadn't even bothered to finish the beer, he had left and never gone back. Dennis thought that he might treat himself to a whisky tonight, a double. Better still a pint with a chaser. He'd worked hard today and he'd been pleased with the results. He noticed that there seemed to be more cars in the car park than at his first visit and, as he opened the door, warmth and noise greeted his ears.

"And what can I get for you sir?"

Dennis stared at the tall, well-built man behind the bar, this wasn't the man he'd seen before, "I'll have a pint of bitter please and a whisky chaser."

"Single or blend?"

"Blend please."

The landlord then named four well known brands. He watched as the pint was expertly pulled into a clean glass, and the whisky taken from the optic, "Here you are sir, I hope that you enjoy it."

Dennis took his pint to a corner table, sat down and quietly studied the bar. The whole atmosphere of the pub seemed to have changed! He then noticed a sign over the bar stating that the pub was under new management. Another sign on the nearby wall then caught his eye,' Anyone wishing to form a darts team, a quiz team or a cricket team please inform the landlord'. Dennis rose and went up to the bar, "Excuse me but are you still looking for people to form a darts team?"

"We most certainly are. Are you interested?"

"Yes, used to be in a team where I lived before."

"Good, we've had two other enquiries so, with you, I reckon that we can make a team up quite quickly. Do you live near here?"

"Yes, in walking distance."

"Even better. Could I have your name and phone number please."

Dennis was smiling as he returned to his table and finished his pint and then his whisky chaser. He put on his jacket and made to leave but then stopped, what the hell he thought, it was about the best day he'd had since he came to this god-forsaken spot, turning to the bar he said, "Same again please."

As soon as Fiona and Simon had decided how to accommodate the Emsworth dogs so that they needn't be moved when they got busy with boarders, Fiona asked Ruth to come in one morning and drove up to Mrs Emsworth's cottage. It was a grey, cold, wet day and the motorway was a sea of spray, Fiona was not looking forward to this visit at all, she was fond of Mrs Emsworth. She smiled to herself, how silly, as far as I can remember everyone has called her Mrs Emsworth, I don't know her Christian name, it must be on Sally's pedigree but I can't recall it. Fiona felt a pang as she thought of Sally. She still missed her very much and often visited her little grave in the woods to have a chat and sort out her problems. As she neared the lane leading to the cottage, Fiona thought of how very excited she was the day that she and Duncan came up to collect Sally, she had been just eight weeks old. How things had changed since then, she had been a different person then, or had she? Just then her thoughts were interrupted by the sight of a familiar sign blowing in the wind and rain, ARAMINTA. The cottage looked just the same and, as she walked down the wet path, the front door opened and Mrs Emsworth her face wreathed in smiles, beckoned her to come in quickly.

"Thank you so much for coming Fiona, I'm so sorry that you've had this foul weather to contend with."

The house was quieter than she remembered, there were always several dogs barking or crying to come and greet the visitors.

"I'm sure that you would like a hot cup of tea wouldn't you?"

Fiona gratefully drank the hot tea, Mrs Emsworth didn't look at all well, she seemed a pale shadow of her former bustling self, "We have sorted out a kennel for the dogs and I think that they'll be comfortable and happy together."

"Thank you my dear so very much, I know that you will look after them, it has taken a weight from my mind. I have packed all their belongings in this cardboard box. Just as a small reminder of home so to speak. I hope you don't mind."

"Mrs. Ems.... please forgive me but I really can't remember your Christian name."

The elderly lady smiled, "Ah, well I was christened Anastasia Araminta, but my family called me Stassy and my husband called me Minta. I didn't want the dog world calling me by either name so I was quite happy with Mrs Emsworth!"

Fiona smiled, "Yes. I see, but they are such beautiful names and your prefix is Araminta."

"Yes. but people thought that it was a name from a book, which it was. Now, let's talk about the dogs."

After they had sorted out all the little idiosyncrasies of the two dogs and the old lady had discussed the terms of their staying with Fiona, she smiled, "I'm glad that we have been able to sort all this out satisfactorily. I know my dear that you would have them without payment but I should be happier if you let me arrange something, so please humour me in this. You have given me such peace of mind. It is possible that I shall not see you again my dear so a word of caution; be careful in the show world, it can be an evil place. Take care of Simon, I know that you have had your ups and downs," she smiled, "ah yes, the jungle drums, but don't let the show world destroy what you have, it so easily can do and has many times in the past."

"I know it can, both Simon and I are aware of the pressures."

"Good, well then that's all there is to say. Thank you once again my dear. I'll call the dogs now. Will you please go quickly; I shall not wave goodbye," Mrs Anastasia Araminta Emsworth put her frail arms around Fiona and kissed her on the cheek. It was all that Fiona could do not to cry as she quickly took the dog leads handed to her and hurried back down the path.

The two dogs were very quiet as she drove home through the pouring rain. Ruth had the kennel all ready and warm and she put the dogs in straight away, speaking to them by name and stroking their heads. They seemed rather worried and she quietly tried to reassure them; at least they had each other for company. She'd pop up later with Simon to see that they were all right.

"Dennis, Dennis, close your eyes."

"Why."

"Because I want to show you a surprise."

He dutifully closed his eyes and Caroline got hold of his arm and led him from the hall into the sitting-room, "Right, you can open them."

"Good God," he found himself looking at a large Christmas tree ablaze with golden light. Large! it had to be at least eight feet and it was completely decorated with golden things. "Where the hell did you get all this."

"Isn't it just lovely. Everything matches, look at these dear little angels and these stars and, and..... just everything. I had such a wonderful time picking everything to match."

"But it must have cost a bomb."

"Well, it's a one off and everybody will be amazed when they see it."

"Everybody? Who?"

"Well, no-one has actually replied but several of our friends have said that they'd let me know when they had sorted out their arrangements."

Dennis looked at her narrow face all alight with pleasure. God, he felt sorry for her, she was in for a big let down. He had always thought her more sensible but this damned house and the money had gone to her head. He shook his head; it was going to be a bloody awful Christmas!

"Look Caroline, don't go buying masses of food until they do reply will you."

"No, of course not. I'm not silly you know."

Later that evening, as he was making them a bedtime drink, he saw that the jar was nearly empty, he opened one of the many cupboards in the kitchen to see if there was a replacement jar. There before him were Christmas puddings, several jars of mincemeat, cranberry sauce, two large tins of savoury and two of sweet, biscuits and.... he shook his head. It was going to be a truly bloody awful Christmas!

CHAPTER EIGHTEEN

Simon was sitting on the settee with Fee beside him in front of a warm fire. Taking another sip of whisky he said with a smile, "Well, I think that that just about wraps it up now. We'll phone most of them shall we and send an invite to the others."

"Um." Fiona was blissfully relaxed sitting beside Simon, they had been deciding on the guest list for the party. Simon, as always, had his list of judges etc., whom he thought it would be wise to include in the invites even if they weren't able to come.

"You start the ball rolling by asking Natalie and Paul, that devil is certainly using Nat's friends in high places, he's getting himself on various little committees, dinners and so on. Our Paul is set to do well for himself in other ways too. Have you noticed that he is quietly going to these blasted seminars and getting himself on even more 'A' and 'B' lists. I only noticed when we got our club book from the Glencastle Club the other week. He's already on the 'A' list of that! God knows how many more he's on. We'll have to take a leaf out of his book and do the same because our Paul never does anything without a reason."

"What, get ourselves on the 'B' lists too?"

"Precisely! the 'A list', if we can. If he's doing it so quickly, after all these new-fangled ideas from the KC are new and only just getting going, he's trying to steal a march on everyone else. I bet quite a few of the charmed circle are doing the same thing don't you?"

"Yes, possibly. We'll try and suss it out at the party."

"Good idea Fee. In fact, I might make a phone call or two now."

"Well, wait until I've phoned some of them about the party. I'll start with Natalie."

"Paul that was Fiona on the phone. She has kindly invited us to their New Year's Eve party. Isn't that lovely, it should be a pleasant evening."

"Did you accept?"

"Why yes, you don't mind do you?"

"Well, actually, I had thought of asking Ian and Audrey and a few of our neighbours in for a drink or two," Paul thanked heaven that he could think on his feet.

"Oh Paul, what a kind thought. That would be lovely but what about the Philips?"

"I think that they will have plenty of other people there. I shouldn't worry too much; I doubt they'll miss us. Would you like me to phone and make our apologies?"

"No, let's see first if Audrey and Ian can come shall we?"

"Hey, you're shivering, come here and I'll give you a cuddle."
Fiona gave a feeble smile and sat close to Simon. Paul had just phoned and had said that they would not be coming to the party. He had then proceeded to tear her to ribbons for not going to Midland Counties in person, ending with, "don't think that you can get around our agreement like that."

"Tell me Paul, why did you pick that show in particular."

"Surely you don't have to ask why Fiona. Surely your memory isn't that bad or perhaps there have been too many men for you to remember them all."

"How dare you! That remark was totally uncalled for and incorrect and you know it. As far as I'm concerned Paul the deal between us is definitely off! I want nothing to do with you."

"It's off when I say....."
She slammed the phone down. Did he really know everything about that incident with Alan or was he just guessing because of Alan's reputation? Suddenly shivering with the cold, she returned to the settee and the warm fire.

"Who was that?"

"Only Paul to say that they can't make the party, apparently Natalie forgot that they're having a party themselves."

"That doesn't sound like Natalie," Simon frowned but said nothing more, just wondered what that devil Paul was up to, "I'll do some phoning now if you like."

"Would you? I must start thinking about Christmas day and make a list of all the things I need to buy. I'm so glad that Peter and Beryl are coming I'm looking forward to it."

"Yeah, better than last year Fee eh?"

Dennis put the phone down, shrugged his shoulders and sighed. He'd known it all along; he'd known that nobody would come. Poor girl. He shrugged his shoulders again and returned to the sitting-room still bathed in its' golden aura, sitting down heavily on the sofa he said, "That was Jim Parsons, they can't come either because they have been invited to the Williams for Christmas together with the James's."

"What you mean is that Julie and Ray are having Christmas there and didn't ask us as usual."

"For heaven's sake Caroline, we invited them here!"

"Yes and they said that they couldn't come but they didn't say that they were having Christmas there and inviting our other friends AND NOT US," she shouted.

It was obvious that Caroline was working herself up into a state, the next thing she'd have was a migraine.

"Now Caroline, don't get so upset, you'll only make yourself ill. We'll have a nice meal on our own. I tell you what, we'll have the dogs in like we always have before."

"THE DOGS! For heaven's sake talk sense Dennis, I have a kennel now, proper dog people don't have their dogs in for dinner!"

"Bonnie misses being indoors and so does Annie, I don't like them in the kennel. Keep the new one in there if you like but let our three old ones in. You used to like the dogs."

"Do you know your trouble Dennis, you are a small person. We have been given this chance to make something of ourselves. I want to impress people and so should you, it's the only way to get ahead. I want to get ahead in the dog world. I was only having Julie, Ray and the others up here to impress them with all our lovely furniture and things. To show them how well we are doing. You ought to do the same at work. Invite the boss over. Honestly Dennis, you are just too easy going. You'll never make management!"

At a loss for words, Dennis stayed silent. He knew that Caroline had changed since they moved up there, she was still fussy and bossy, still concerned with everything being tidy and 'looking nice' but these ideas that she had now!

"Whatever am I going to do with all the food? We can't eat it, we'll put on weight. I was so sure that they'd come."

Dennis got up, he'd heard nothing but the party for weeks, he just couldn't take any more of her moaning, "I'll just pop down to the pub, will you be all right or do you want to come?"
Caroline shook her head and Dennis sighed thankfully.

Ophelia quickly scanned the writing on the envelopes. There were at least twenty of them waiting on the hall table when she got in; Christmas cards mainly. She never knew who half of them were from, bloody crawlers mostly trying to curry favour for when she judged next year. As she got to the last one she realised that, once again, there wasn't one from Deborah. She had sent her two cards so far with a note inside saying that she was expecting her to come, as usual, for Christmas but had not, as yet, had a reply. Her phone was always on the answerphone these days. The University term was over now so she must have had time to write a card or phone. She could be very busy though and would be intending to just turn up perhaps full of smiles and funny stories as she always did. She must have got over that silly fling with that student by now and although Ophelia was still terribly hurt, she desperately needed Deborah in her life and was prepared to ignore it this once. After she had had a meal, she picked up the phone and dialled Deborah's number, a youngish female voice answered the phone, "Hello Dr Illingstone's residence."
"Who's that speaking?"
"It's Sandra Edwards. Can I help you?"
"Could I speak to Deborah please."
"Who's calling?"
"Would you tell her it's Ophelia Hammond-James."
"Ah, um, I'll see if she's in."
After only a few seconds the voice returned, "Hello, are you there? I'm afraid that Dr Illingstone is not back yet from shopping."
"When do you think that she will be back? It's a bit late for the shops."
"Not for a long time I'm afraid. Perhaps you could try tomorrow."

When Ophelia phoned the next day, the monotonous ringing tone went on and on. Furiously she slammed the phone down and poured herself a stiff drink. How dare Debs treat her like this! After all these years, after all they had meant to each other. Why! Why!. She slammed out of the house and shouted that she wanted her mare

Reza to be saddled up. Twenty minutes later she rode away from the farmhouse with the horse on a tight rein.

Diana looked concerned, "God, whatever's made her so angry I hope she doesn't take it out on the horse."

"No, I'll give her her due, I've never known her to harm any animal," Annie replied.

Ophelia returned two hours later. The mare was muddied up to her belly and blowing slightly but otherwise unharmed. Without a word Ophelia slipped from the saddle, handed the reins to Annie and went into the farmhouse. Not bothering to change out of her mud-spattered jodhpurs and jacket, she picked up the phone directory, ran her finger down a page and then picked up the phone and dialled a number, "Hello is that Caroline Amery? Caroline, it's Ophelia Hammond-James here. I'm having a few friends round for drinks on Christmas Eve, I would love it if you could come too."

"Oh, oh I'd love to Ophelia and I'm sure that Dennis would love to come as well."

"Ah yes Dennis. Actually it's a party for some of my women friends, I think perhaps that he might feel a bit uncomfortable, don't you?"

"Oh I see, yes perhaps he would. I'm sure, in fact, that he would rather go to the pub."

"Good, that's settled then, shall we say eight-o-clock?"

CHAPTER NINETEEN

It was the evening of the 24th of December and Caroline was in a fever of excitement, she had started her preparations in the morning with an early hair appointment. Dennis had been left to clear up the breakfast things, make the bed, put the vacuum cleaner around downstairs and have a plate of mince pies ready to warm up 'just in case someone popped in'. When she returned from the hairdressers' she then spent ages agonising over what to wear, finally deciding on the outfit she had bought especially for her own party. It was a very expensive 'little black number'. It fitted her closely and showed off her neat, petite figure, she had also purchased a pair of high heeled, strappy sandals and a pair of sheer, black tights these, together with one of Aunt Ellen's necklaces and matching earrings completed the ensemble. She surveyed her image in the full-length mirror turning this way and that. Yes, it looked smart and it suited her, she felt confident that she would be as well dressed as Ophelia's other friends.

While all this had been going on upstairs, Dennis had started to defrost the smaller of the two turkeys that Caroline had bought. It was obvious that, if they were going to have anything like a decent dinner tomorrow, it was up to him to get it ready. All she could think about was this blasted party up the road. He had fed the dogs earlier and now went to let them have a run in the garden. They would have a good time this Christmas at least, if he had anything to do with it.

During the course of the afternoon while Caroline tried various types of make -up on to see which went best with black, Dennis wandered down the garden to check on the temperature in his greenhouse, made sure that his rhubarb was well protected from the frost, let the dogs have another run, checked the cupboards for vegetables, stuffing and bread, he was looking forward to a cold turkey sandwich on Boxing Day, and wrapped Caroline's present. She, on the other hand had spent the entire time wrapping a bottle of perfume that she had bought for Ophelia, having a shower and asking Dennis's advice on whether she looked 'right'. She was ready to go by seven-o-clock and wandered around the house like a caged lion in a state of nervousness. She knew that she mustn't arrive too early, that was not good manners at all, her mother had always impressed this on her when she was young. When, finally, it was seven-fifty by her watch she called to Dennis, "I'm off now Dennis, don't wait up for me, I don't know how long the party will go on for."

"OK but don't drink too much, you know you can't hold your booze."

"Dennis, I'm not a child!"

"Well, I'm off as well, I promised old Harry a game of darts tonight and I said that I'd be there about now. You go and I'll lock up and put the alarm on."

"Wait a minute Dennis." She hurried upstairs again, she had to go and spend a penny again, she was so excited. Looking in the bathroom mirror, she fluffed up her hair a bit and cast a critical eye over her make-up. She had spent ages getting her eye make-up just right. It was important to make the right impression. Some of Ophelia's friends must also be high up in dogs. Satisfied with her appearance, she hurried back downstairs as fast as her high heels would let her, blew Dennis a kiss and went out to the car.

Dennis watched from the front door as her car slowly drove away, "Have a nice evening Dennis and a Happy Christmas Eve, Dennis." With a shrug of the shoulders he put on his jacket, turned on the alarm system and shut the front door.

"Hello, do come in, you're a little early no-one else is here yet but you can help me with the nibbles and things if you like."

Caroline looked at Ophelia and thought that she had arrived much too early, Ophelia was still in a plaid shirt and jeans, "You do look smart, - er - Caroline."

She hadn't turned a hair though thought Caroline, that's what money does for you, gives you confidence. She'll shortly pop up and change into something quite glamorous and look marvellous. As she placed a few dishes of nuts, pretzels, crisps and other assorted things on various occasional tables, Caroline took the opportunity to look around the room. There appeared to be no sign of Christmas, no tree, no decorations, nothing other than some cards on the top of a large writing bureau.

There was a hammering on the front door and other guests arrived. Caroline was introduced to several women but couldn't remember any of their names, she was only concerned with the fact that none of them were dressed up for the party. A couple of women had a skirt and jumper on but others were in trousers or jeans with loose shirts or jumpers on. Hardly any of them had much make-up on. She began to feel very uncomfortable and very over-dressed.

"What will you have to drink, er, oh yes, Caroline?"

"A small sherry please Ophelia. I'm not much of a drinker."

She sat there quietly as the conversations flowed around her. Somebody was speaking about dogs but they were only running down certain lines, some of them were big, successful kennels with a good name and they were saying all sorts of awful things about them. She took another sip of sherry. A variety of breeds were then discussed and well-known names were bandied around. Caroline was concentrating very hard but she just couldn't seem to remember it all. Ophelia came up to her, "Your glass is empty Caroline, another sherry?"

"Oh no, I've had three already. I mustn't have any more, I've got to drive home. Could I have an orange juice do you think?"

"Of course, I'll get it for you."

She sat back in the deep comfortable chair, what a lovely party this is, such friendly, nice people, even if they dress casually. I shall have quite a lot of friends here soon and I shall give my own party, blow all her old friends, they weren't worth bothering about. She had secretly been annoyed that Dennis had joined a darts team and had been able to make several friends. One had even come over and helped him move an enormous pile of horse manure! She had been horrified when it had been delivered and so worried that Ophelia might see it. The orange juice was ever so nice, by now she'd had three of them. Oh, one or two ladies seemed to be going. She supposed that she should go soon too. What was the time, she had a bit of a job focusing on her watch, whoops it was nearly midnight; she struggled forward on the chair and her skirt rode up on her thighs. She was trying to pull it down when Ophelia gave her another orange juice.

"Thank you, I'll drink this and then I must go home if that's alright. I've had a lovely time."

She sat back in the comfortable chair again, Ophelia and another lady were talking about horses and hunting, Caroline tried to look interested but found it difficult. It was so warm and cosy here she could fall asleep.

Dennis put the phone down, it was well past midnight and he had been worrying about Caroline driving home so late but the Ophelia woman had just assured him that she would give her a bed for the night and send her on her way in the morning. I told her not to drink, the silly girl, he thought, he checked on the turkey now almost completely defrosted and was about to go to bed when he stopped. Why not, when the cat's away.... He grabbed his anorak and went out to the kennels and brought the three older dogs in, Bonnie was ecstatic and ran around his legs, "Now, you lot had better behave yourselves or there will be hell to pay. Come on." They followed him upstairs and lay down on a blanket which Dennis had put on the floor.

"Happy Christmas Caroline."
Caroline slowly opened her eyes, she had an awful headache. Surely she wasn't going to get a migraine. As she took in her surroundings, she sat up quickly and then put her hand to her head, "Why are you here Ophelia?"

"Because I live here you ninny."

"What.... where..." she looked around the unfamiliar room.

"You are in my house. You tied one on last night and weren't fit to drive. Don't worry I phoned your husband and told him. Incidentally, you have very pretty breasts, lovely little nipples too."
Caroline's eyes and mouth opened wide. She looked down and saw that she was naked, blushing furiously she said, "Did you.... did you undress me?"

"Yes, of course I did and you are very pretty. I cuddled your breasts all night. Your belly is very flat too, nice to stroke. I would have made love to you if you had been awake enough to enjoy it too."

Caroline stared at her for a moment with her mouth open, then, when she realised the implications of what Ophelia had just said, she shot out of the bed trying to hide her nakedness with the sheet and looked for her clothes. The 'little black number' was lying on the floor together with her underwear. With fumbling fingers she tried to put everything on while still clutching the sheet. Once or twice the sheet fell and with a whimper she snatched it up again. When finally dressed she turned around to see Ophelia looking at her and smiling. Trying not to meet Ophelia's eyes, she made a rapid apology and said that she must get home now to her husband, he would be expecting his dinner. She grabbed her handbag and ran down the unfamiliar stairs and out to her car.

"Hello Caroline, Happy Christmas, I've put the turkey in the oven." Dennis's smiling face greeted her at the door. She couldn't look at him, she just couldn't face him yet. Saying that she wanted to spend a penny, she rushed up the stairs to their bedroom. Their bedroom, hers and her husband's, she was a married woman. She wasn't like that, it was dirty what Ophelia had said. Her mother had always told her that anything like THAT was unnatural, shameful, disgusting. She had to have a shower, a long, hot shower before she could even face Dennis. Dennis! he must never know. He would be horrified if she told him. Not that he was very keen on sex anyway, neither of them were. Even when they were first married it had been boring and not what she had thought it would be like. It had got less and less and, after a few years they just hadn't bothered.

She turned the shower onto hot first and soaped herself all over thoroughly. What had Ophelia done? Her mind shied away from the thought. Turning the shower to cold, she gasped as the droplets of water hit her body; then she turned it to hot water, that was better, she felt clean at last. Shivering slightly, she dried herself off, she couldn't resist though having just a little look at her breasts in the bathroom mirror. No, she shouldn't, she mustn't, her mother had always said that it was wrong to admire oneself.

Dressed in trousers and a warm jumper, she took a wrapped present out of the drawer and went downstairs, "Happy Christmas Dennis. Now how is the turkey? Have you done any potatoes yet? I'll take over shall I, you check on your greenhouse or something. Now where are the brussel sprouts? Oh, you picked them this morning, oh good. Now I must put the water on to boil for the Christmas pudding, get the crackers and serviettes out and lay the table. We'll have the dogs in shall we? They must have a slice of turkey. Shall we have our presents after dinner, while we watch the Queen's speech? Yes. Right, now you toddle off and I'll get the dinner." Hastily donning her pinafore, she bustled around the kitchen. Dennis stood there for a moment before donning his jacket and going outside, shaking his head, he sighed, he would never be able to fathom women out.

CHAPTER TWENTY

Dennis put the clear plastic cover over the seed tray and then placed the tray beside several other similar ones. It was the beginning of February and he had been busy this past week sowing some of the seeds, which he had ordered from the catalogues. It was still a little early perhaps but he couldn't wait to start on the programme of planting he had worked out since Christmas. The heater would protect them from frost and this part of the garden was fairly well sheltered from the worst of the winds. He was so looking forward to the Spring and Summer when he could plant them all out into the garden. He had plans for a big display of various annuals in the beds in the front garden and some geraniums in tubs. He had also ordered quite a few plugs from a well known seedsman; plugs of mixed geraniums, dahlias, cabbages and brussel sprouts. He looked around the greenhouse, he would soon be able to set his seed potatoes out, his tomato seedlings would soon be up and he could put all his new canes up for the runner beans. He planned to bring Caroline down here soon and surprise her with it all. Thinking of Caroline reduced some of his euphoria, she had been so quiet since Christmas, he had asked her several times if she was alright, did she feel ill, should she see the doctor but she just shook her head and said she was fine.

She wasn't fine though, he knew that something was bothering her. She even seemed to have lost interest in this new dog of hers, hadn't been to any shows although he knew that she had entered one or two. Aunt Ellen's marvellous house didn't even seem to cheer her up. She dusted and put the vacuum around, washed the odd vase or ornament but not with her usual bustle. She didn't sing any more, didn't even keep on about that damned woman up the road thank God. No, he supposed that he'd have to say something and insist that she see the doctor. Why was life so hard? He hadn't wanted to come here, he'd tried to make the best of it but it hadn't been easy and now, now that he had found a decent pub, got on the darts team, got going with all this gardening, Caroline had to throw a wobbly! Shaking his head, he closed the greenhouse door behind him and made his way down the garden to the kitchen door, "Any chance of a cuppa?"

127

Caroline screamed, "Dennis! What did you do that for. You made me jump!"

Her pale, startled face stared at him wide-eyed and it bothered him greatly, "Hold on, I only came down for a cup of tea. Why are you so nervy lately? I honestly think that you should see a doctor Caroline, you know, get yourself sorted out."

"Sorted out! Don't be silly Dennis, I'm perfectly all right. I just haven't been sleeping too well, that's all. I'll put the kettle on if you want a cup of tea."

It was true she hadn't been sleeping well, she was off her food, she kept dreaming such weird dreams, it was awful because she couldn't tell anybody about them. She just couldn't. Since Christmas Eve her whole world had been turned upside down. Ophelia had phoned her a couple of times and had even called round but she had put the phone down each time and had not answered the door when she had called. She was terrified to go out for fear of Ophelia calling round when she wasn't there and talking to Dennis! She couldn't get the whole ghastly episode out of her mind and it was driving her crazy. She had been thinking about it then when Dennis had suddenly appeared. She put a hand to her aching forehead, "Perhaps you're right Dennis. Perhaps I need a tonic or something. I'll make an appointment."

"Good, you do that," he drank his tea and then went to the back door to put his boots on again, "You OK now?"

She nodded and he went off up the garden pleased that that was sorted.

Caroline went upstairs and sat down in front of the big dressing-table mirror. She put one hand up to her face, apart from the dark rings under her eyes and looking a bit pale, the same face stared back at her as had always stared back at her. She didn't look any different but she was different. She was terribly, horribly different. The dreams that she had been having were disgusting, she dreamed that Ophelia was making love to her and that she was enjoying it! She had hoped that, with time, the dreams would go away. She closed her eyes, it was awful, what would her mother have said! What would Dennis say if he knew? It was just all too terrible, she started to cry, she would have to do something about it, but what? Seeing a doctor wasn't going to help. What about a Marriage Guidance Clinic? No, what could she say, she and Dennis got on fine. There wasn't any sex but neither of them minded, they were quite happy really. She would have liked a family but, well that wasn't anything to do with this. She was going to go mad if she didn't do something though. She knew that she should go and see Ophelia and find out just what did happen, she thought that she knew from her dreams but she just couldn't face her. She sat still wiping the tears that ran down her face and looked at her reflection, she couldn't face her but she could write her a letter or she could phone her. She would have to wait until Dennis went out but then she really must phone Ophelia. Her mind finally made up she went to the bathroom to splash cold water on her eyes and then went downstairs.

The next afternoon Dennis said that he was popping out to the nearest garden centre because he wanted a few more things like compost and stuff. Caroline managed a weak smile, "Yes, you go Dennis, I've a lot to do in the house."

"Leave it, everything looks fine. You have phoned the doctor haven't you?"

"No, but I will do it while your out. OK?" It took several false starts before she finally managed to dial the complete number and wait for an answer. The answerphone clicked in and she heard Ophelia's voice. She immediately put the phone down. Tears started up in her eyes and she fiercely wiped them away, swallowing hard she picked up the phone again and re-dialled. This time when asked to leave a message she said in a choked voice, "Ophelia it's Caroline."

She had hardly got back to the kitchen before the phone rang again, "Hello it's Ophelia. You rang."

With her heart pounding in her throat Caroline said, "I want to know exactly what happened on Christmas Eve. I need to know, it's driving me mad."

"And you've waited all this time? Well, nothing actually happened as you put it, you were spark out. I just caressed you."

Caroline swallowed hard, "Yes, but I don't know what you mean by that."

"Well it's perfectly obvious my sweet girl, I undressed you and you looked so lovely that I stroked your lovely soft skin. I didn't arouse you if that's what's troubling you. We could do that next time."

"Next time!"

"Of course, don't say that you didn't enjoy it. I know how you responded."

"Responded!"

"Yes, responded, before you fell asleep! Don't play the innocent with me Caroline; you know perfectly well what I mean. Now, why don't you come over here and we can sort it out. I was going to ask you if you wanted to come with me to Crufts?"

Caroline was silent for a moment, it would be such a relief to get everything sorted out, she couldn't go on like this, "Well, I'll come but only if we just talk about things."

"Fine by me, we won't do anything you don't want to do. OK?"

Caroline quickly changed and, wishing that she had washed her hair, hurried out to her car and shakily drove towards the farmhouse. Halfway there she put her foot on the brakes, she couldn't do this, she was too scared. After a few minutes, she started the car again, like it or not, she had to do it or go mad. As she drove up the now familiar drive she felt sick with apprehension, as her sweaty hands turned off the ignition switch, Ophelia opened the front door and asked her in. Caroline blushed deeply when she first saw her but gave a faint smile and surreptitiously wiped her hands on her skirt as she walked into the sitting room. She sat there looking round and clutching her handbag until Ophelia came back with a tray of tea, "Brought some biscuits, thought you might like some."

Caroline drank the tea quickly but refused a biscuit, it would have stuck in her throat.

"A good friend of mine is judging Crufts this year and I particularly wanted to go so, are you going to come with me?"

Caroline hesitated for several seconds before replying, did she really mean just that, they would drive to the show together and no more? She had so wanted to go to Crufts to be seen with Ophelia but perhaps if she didn't drink anything, she would be in control of herself and could stop anything happening couldn't she. Caroline thought of the logistics of actually going with Ophelia and decided that it might be all right, "Yes, I would like to go to Crufts very much. Thank you. We would be coming straight home that evening wouldn't we?"

"Of course."

"Right then, I'll come."

"Now that's out of the way, what is your problem with what happened on Christmas Eve?"

Faced with the question, Caroline didn't know where to begin but, gradually, with half sentences she managed to say the things that were troubling her. About how she felt about that sort of thing.... she didn't want to offend her but... her mother had always said that.... and how she wasn't like that, she was happily married. She was just interested in the dogs and ...and just being friends.

"I see, don't go on I've got the picture. Well it's a great pity but, I'm not forcing myself on you. Let me tell you this though, I know that you enjoyed it. I know what you feel, even if you won't admit to it. Just think about it."

Caroline stood up quickly, "I must go now and get dinner ready for my husband. I don't.... I'm not... you've made a mistake... I don't want to think about it any more but I would like us to be friends."

"OK. Friends it is. We'll do it your way."

"I can still come with you to Crufts though."

"Of course, I invited you didn't I?"

Caroline walked swiftly to the door and got into her car and breathed a sigh of relief.. Thank goodness it was all sorted out now, she felt better already.

As Caroline's car disappeared down the drive Ophelia shut the door and leaned on it. How exciting, she hadn't felt so excited for ages. Here was a real challenge. This would be much better than trying to get Debs back. Debs wasn't exciting any more, this pretty girl was.

CHAPTER TWENTY- ONE

Fiona yawned, she felt rather tired as she drove home from visiting Mrs Emsworth in the nursing home. This was the second visit she had made and, she thought, it might very well be the last. The old lady was fading fast, without her dogs and the necessity each day of caring for them, she seemed to have lost the will to live. They had had a wonderfully long and interesting conversation on her first visit but this time she had been much quieter and reluctant to talk about the old days. On the first visit she had asked after her dogs and then told Fiona about the wonderful times that she had experienced when she was much younger and had started showing her dogs, of the characters she had encountered, of people she had met, those who had helped her a lot and those who hadn't. Her face had lit up as the memories flowed and she had become quite animated.

"Oh no my dear, it was so very different in those days. It was far more relaxed for one thing. There were less people showing then and a lot of those people seldom went to a Championship show you know. We all went to the Open shows, they were such fun, everybody was so enthusiastic and helpful, we used to chat about dogs for ages, it was a really lovely day out. I didn't even think of going to a Champ show until I had been showing for at least six years, the Open shows were quite enough for me. Exhibitors today almost start off going to Champ shows, no wonder so many give up in a couple of years, it all becomes far too serious. The judges always came round the benches afterwards then too, I'm talking about the Open shows as well you know, and you could actually talk to them about your dog and ask advice, they were often a lot of help. Everybody seemed to talk to each other then and I for one picked up so many tips and good advice that way. It was always such a pleasant day out."

Mrs Emsworth paused to drink her tea, her face was flushed and her eyes shone, " I do hope I'm not boring you my dear."

"Not at all, in fact I'm fascinated."

"Now where was I... Oh yes, nowadays people don't seem to want to go to the Open shows, such a pity. Of course, in those days even a lot of the Open shows were benched you know Fiona. We were so proud to receive a card, any card, that we always pinned them up over the bench, yes, even VHC. Now, you see people throw a second or third away in disgust. Such a pity you know. Why do they bother to go if they feel like that? Do you know my dear that we had to serve an apprenticeship in those days. Yes. We had to show at Open shows for five years before we could even hope to judge a show ourselves. Fancy that now! Most have given up dog showing by then. You Fiona would have liked the shows so much in the old days, such nice people, such characters, especially some of the all-rounders! Some of them were dyed in the wool, doggy people. If you know what I mean. You had to learn to be an all-rounder in those days by constantly watching and looking, asking and remembering for years. You can't do it now because you just don't see the number of dogs at the Open shows and the Champ shows are divided up into several days and Groups. This modern idea of seminars doesn't in any way give you the experience needed to judge you know my dear. It takes time, a keen eye and honesty to be a good judge, not a one-day seminar and a few years showing. We were in absolute awe of some of those all-rounders. Fiona I could tell you such stories, you'd never believe them!" Mrs Emsworth laughed and put a hankie to her eyes to wipe them.

"I'm afraid that I'm getting a little tired now dear but perhaps we can talk some more when you come. Give my old fellow a hug, I do miss him."

"Of course I will, they both get hugs I can assure you."

Mrs Emsworth smiled and held out her hand, "I know they do dear."

When Fiona went a month later, a nurse took her on one side and advised her not to stay too long today as Mrs Emsworth was very tired. When Fiona saw her sitting in a chair she immediately saw the difference in her old friend.

"Hello Fiona, I'm so pleased to see you. How are the dogs?"

"Very well. Simon sends his regards."

"Thank you and how are you?"

"Very well, I've been busy taking some of the dogs to training classes, just to keep them up to scratch. I love going, everyone is always so relaxed."

"Yes dear."

"You were telling me last time about the old days of dog showing."

"Was I? Oh yes I remember now, such good days, such good days."

It was obvious that she was very tired and didn't want to speak very much so Fiona chatted a little about this and that, had a cup of tea with her and then said goodbye. What a pity Fiona thought, I'd have loved to hear some more of those stories and they seemed to cheer her up so much to remember them, perhaps next time. Driving home in the car, she thought of Mrs Emsworth's cottage and the sign swinging outside. How she must miss it. The street lights were on and it was quite dark as Fiona neared home. As she stopped the car, Simon opened the kitchen door and the light streamed out from the kitchen, "Hi, had a good day?" He said as he flung his warm arms around her, "How was the old lady?"

"Not so good this time. It was so sad Simon. I think that, apart from a lady who had a couple of her dogs and who lives nearby, I'm the only other doggy person to visit her and she is just going downhill fast. I think that she misses the dogs and being busy and useful."

"Yeah, I expect she does. Pity. I'm not surprised that people don't bother to visit her though, she can't help them any more can she?"

"Simon! That's an awful thing to say. You are such a cynic."

"Or am I a realist? You know the dog world. By the way, Natalie phoned but said that she'd phone again later. Anyway lass, take your coat off. Dinner's nearly ready and here's a cup of tea to be getting on with."

"Wonderful."

Later that evening, Natalie did phone again and Fiona answered it, "Hello Natalie, nice to hear your cheerful voice. How are you?"

After a few minutes of inconsequential chatter Natalie said, "Fiona, what I want to discuss with you is Jamie?"

"Jamie? I hope that there is nothing wrong."

"Well no, he's well enough. You know that I sent him to the kennels where Paul's few dogs are?"

"Yes."

"Well, I decided on the spur of the moment to go over there to see him today and he seemed terribly unhappy. He was so pleased to see me and I hated walking away and leaving him there. What I wanted to ask you is do you think that I'm being silly?"

"Silly, no of course not, nobody likes to see their dog unhappy."

"Well, Paul says that I shouldn't have gone. He thinks that I'm being silly about it. His dogs are fine there, the people are showing them for him and winning with them but Jamie, he is just left in his kennel most of the time. I mean, why can't he be shown too?"

"What did Paul say?"

"He said that we can't expect them to show all the dogs. They have their own to show as well."

"Um. Perhaps you ought to take Paul there to see just how unhappy he is."

They talked for a little longer and then Natalie rang off.

Fiona told Simon about her conversation with Natalie. They both agreed that it was a mistake for Jamie to go there. The kennel owners were the ambitious sort to say the least, Jamie wasn't much of an asset to them but showing Paul's dogs could lead to favours being done for them if they did well with them. At least, it seemed, Jamie had a kennel and a run, some so- called breeders kept their own dogs in cages for most of each day or in small pens!

"Enough of dog talk Fee, you'll only get depressed. How's about we take the rest of this wine into the lounge, drink it and let the rest of the evening take care of itself?"

Fiona smiled as she looked at his handsome face and dark brown eyes, "Yes, why don't we. But I have a pretty good idea how the evening will progress if we do."

"Good, I don't like having to force my women," he pulled her out of her chair, put his arms round her and kissed her, "Do you know that I fancy you rotten. Come here wench it's been far too long." Laughing, he led her into the sitting-room. They sat there with just the glow of the fire reflecting on their glasses of wine. He put his arm around her shoulders and gently cupped his hand around her breast, " Fee. I love you."

She turned to kiss him and later, when the logs dropped down in the fire causing a myriad of sparks to fly up the chimney and fresh flames, licking around the logs to illuminate the room, the reflections danced across their naked bodies. Fiona stirred as the logs burst into renewed flames and watched the reflections on Simon's body, which was so closely locked with hers that she couldn't tell where her body ended and his began. She lifted an arm and stroking his hair kissed his forehead, he grunted, pulled her even closer and rolled back on

135

top of her, 'Good God woman, you're insatiable." He started to slowly move inside her as he kissed her and she wrapped her legs around his firm body and pulled him even closer as the rhythm got faster and faster until, once again, they climaxed together. As they gradually came back to earth and their surroundings, Fiona realised that the fire was dying down and the floor was getting a little cold, "Simon, I must move sweetheart, I'm getting cold."

"Yeah, I suppose we'd better," suddenly she felt his ribs expand as he laughed, "I tell you what Fee. It's a bloody good thing we didn't meet when we were in our twenties."

"Why?"

"I'd be bloody worn out by now!" He pulled her up and they clung together laughing.

The following day was memorable in that two unexpected things happened, about midday, the nursing home phoned to say that Mrs Emsworth had died peacefully in her sleep and they thought that Fiona would want to know. Fiona had been rather upset at the news and Simon had made her a cup of coffee, consequently they had been late starting to clean the kennels and exercise the dogs so that they were still busy when Natalie's car appeared in the drive, she got out closely, followed by Jamie, and walked towards them, "Hello Fiona I've brought...." she got no further but burst into tears in front of them both. Fiona immediately went over to her, "Whatever's the matter Natalie?"

"Could you.... would you have Jamie for a short while Fiona please?"

"Of course, you know I will; but why, what's happened?"

"I went back to the kennels again today and this time I just couldn't leave him there. When I brought him home Paul was really cross and insisted that I take him back! I just couldn't believe it. I've never seen him like that. He was so angry and I just don't know why."

Fiona just put an arm around her and said nothing but signalled to Simon to go down to the kitchen and put the kettle on. Simon hung the leads on the peg and shut the door of the shed, he felt a little tired today and could have done without all this trauma. He smiled at the recollection of why he felt so tired, their love making had been marvellous and was well worth being tired for something like that.

"Fiona, it's my house, it's my dog, how can he say things like that! It won't affect him or alter anything so why, why was he behaving in such an irrational manner?"

"Bad hair day perhaps. I'm sure I don't know Natalie."

"But you do agree that his behaviour was over the top."

Fiona shrugged and refrained from comment, she felt that discretion was definitely the better part of valour here.

"Well anyway, I'm not taking him back to that place so would you have him for a couple of days while I organise something for him at home."

"So you're going to keep him?"

"Yes, I am. To tell the truth Fiona I'm not used to being spoken to like that. Paul has hurt and surprised me. He is usually so kind, understanding and considerate."

Fiona raised her eyebrows but kept her mouth firmly shut. She walked with Natalie down to the kitchen. After a cup of tea, Natalie had regained her composure. Simon came back into the kitchen having been asked to kennel Jamie, "Well, that's done Natalie. He's all settled in."

"Thank you both so much. I'd better go now."

As soon as her car disappeared down the drive Simon said, "Now, what was that all about?"

When Natalie got home, Paul was very contrite, he realised the mistake he'd made. He'd thought that Fiona had, in some way, been behind Natalie, egging her on to do this but had realised too late in the argument that he was wrong. It was Natalie's natural kindness and tenderness, which had caused her to bring the dog home, not some Philips' plotting. Good God, he'd have to be more careful with Natalie, he hadn't fully understood what a gentle nature she had, he just could not afford to do anything to upset their happiness. He could have ruined everything! Bloody Philips though, they were getting too big for their boots. What with making deals with that Hammond woman and winning with that young dog, judging abroad; it was time that he did something about them.

"Natalie my dearest, I do apologise for my stupidity. I have been onto the kennels and they said that Jamie has definitely been pining for you. I've had no idea that there was such a bond between you or I would never have suggested that he go. I've been thinking, how about we order a good kennel for Jamie. You could place it in the garden near the house where you could see him. Then, if we wanted to go away at any time, the gardener perhaps could feed and walk him. How do you feel about that? My darling, please forgive me. I've been on my own too long and have become insensitive to other peoples' feelings. Am I forgiven my dearest?"

A week later, Fiona and Simon attended the funeral of Mrs Emsworth. It was a very small gathering at the local church, just a couple of elderly neighbours, the lady who had some of her dogs, a nephew and Fiona and Simon. The sky was grey, the wind cold and, when it started to drizzle, everyone was quite relieved when it was over. The nephew and the neighbours had arranged a small tea at the cottage but Fiona and Simon thanked them but declined, it held too many memories for Fiona. She thought of all the photographs of the dogs on the walls together with the award cards and rosettes, that Mrs Emsworth had been so proud to show her and Duncan the first time that they had met, she didn't want to see them, she would cry. When they got home, Ruth told them that Mrs Aston had collected Jamie and taken him home, "She said to say thank you very much and that she would ring you tomorrow. A Mrs Amery phoned too, she said to tell you that her bitch had come first in the group at an Open show last weekend."

"That's nice. OK Ruth and thanks for looking after everything." She turned to Simon, "That's a bit of good news anyway. Sesame was a nice bitch, I'm glad that she's showing her and doing well with her."

Simon picked up the phone when it rang later that evening, "Hello, oh yes, Ruth said that you had rung earlier. Congratulations on your win with Sesame. Oh, so it wasn't Sesame it was Saffron! How did that come about? I see. So she's showing Sesame now then. I see. Right, well thanks for letting us know. I'll tell Fiona. Bye," Simon walked back into the kitchen saying," Fee you're never going to believe this."

CHAPTER TWENTY-TWO

In only a few days now it would be Crufts, Caroline was deciding what she should wear on the day. This year the terriers were on a Saturday and Ophelia had said that it would be a very busy day with crowds of visitors. Next year she herself would be an exhibitor because Ophelia had assured her that she would definitely qualify Saffron in the year ahead. She had only been to Crufts once and that was several years ago and without a dog as she had never qualified a dog. She hated, therefore, seeing some of her friends there with the dogs that they had qualified, she had felt in some way inadequate. This year, however, being seen arriving with somebody as important and well known as Ophelia would be enough. What was more, since they had had that discussion, Ophelia hadn't tried to do anything horrible, in fact she had just been very sweet and friendly. She actually enjoyed her company very much. She got out yet another ensemble from her wardrobe and, holding it up against herself, she regarded her image in the mirror.

"Caroline where are you? I'm home."

Dennis already! She hadn't finished getting the dinner prepared, "I'm up here. Put the kettle on and I'll be down in a minute." She quickly put all the clothes back into the large wardrobe, looked in the dressing table mirror as she passed it and tidied her hair with her fingers.

"Been busy?"

"Yes and no, apart from cleaning the silver, I was deciding what to wear on Saturday, you know for Crufts."

Dennis nodded and sipped his cup of tea. Terrified of breaking the Crown Derby, he always held his cup in two hands and sipped the tea. When Caroline was out he used a mug.

"Looking forward to it?"

"Oh yes, very much."

Dennis nodded and continued to sip the hot tea. She certainly seemed to be a lot better lately, more her old self. Whatever the doctor had said or given her it must have done her good. She was always grooming the dogs and filling in the forms for the shows, beetling around with a duster or vacuuming. She had even talked about getting some new settee covers and things. He must pop out soon to the greenhouse.

Natalie came back from her walk with Jamie, it was a cold, windy day with the clouds positively racing across the sky but it had been exhilarating. She had so missed these walks during the day. Opening the box of shaped dog biscuits she gave him two of them. He crunched them up with obvious delight, wagging his tail and looking for more. Since she had brought Jamie home, Paul had never complained of his presence, in fact, he was his usual, charming, attentive self and she felt very happy again. She still had no idea why he had been so angry but had put it down to a bout of dyspepsia or some problem at work. They were off to Crufts tomorrow for four days and staying at a nearby hotel, the KC had kindly made all the arrangements. Paul was officiating in some capacity every day so she would be able to have a chat with her friends in the dog scene. They were going to have lunch every day with Ian and Audrey and several of the Crufts committee. Paul was very pleased that there would also be members of overseas kennel clubs and overseas judges there too.

As he had said, it would be four very pleasant days. She was particularly looking forward to Saturday because it was terrier day and she would see a lot of Cumbrian exhibitors that she knew. She looked at Jamie and with a little regret in her voice said, "You know you should have been there as well Jamie, you are looking lovely." Taking the pleasant tone of voice to be complimentary, Jamie looked even more hopefully at the box of biscuits.

Fiona was nearly blown off her feet as she struggled back from the field where she had been exercising the dogs. There were no boarders at the moment, well there were the two of Mrs. Emsworth's but she no longer considered them as boarders. The youngster was shaping up nicely and they had added their affix to his name at the Kennel Club. She would feel proud to show him, it was nice to think that the Araminta affix would still appear in the show catalogues. She had a busy day ahead, with a bit more time to spare she could do all the little jobs about the place that tended to get left when they had a lot of boarders in. She also needed to get to the Vet with two of the dogs who were due for boosters. Fiona was just collecting some blankets to take down to be washed when she saw a van stop near the house, a man got out and walked up to the kitchen door.

She walked down the path smiling, "Good morning, isn't it windy today, how can I help you?"

"Mrs Philips?"

"Yes."

"Is Mr Philips here?"

Suddenly Fiona felt concerned, "No. Why? Is there something wrong?"

"Mrs Philips, you are the owner of these kennels?"

"Yes."

"I'm here on behalf of.... He named a well known animal welfare organisation. We have had a complaint about the conditions in your kennels. I'm sorry but I must ask if you will let me look round the kennels."

"A complaint, who from?"

"I'm sorry but we are not allowed to disclose that information."

"But wait a minute; I can't believe," she paused for a moment, "Well of course, look round the kennels if you want, you won't find anything wrong."

"Thank you Mrs Philips. I shan't be long I hope."

Fiona utterly dumbfounded stood and watched him as he walked in and out of the kennels making notes, he inspected everything, the whelping shed, the grooming shed, he even looked at the exercise field before he came back to her, "I see that you only have two boarders here at the moment?"

"Actually they aren't really boarders," she proceeded to explain about Mrs Emsworth.

"I see." He made some more notes on a sheet of paper he had attached to a clip board, "May I ask where you keep the food for the dogs and where is it prepared?"

"Of course, it is all separate from ours," she led him to the small utility room off the main kitchen. "All the food is stored in these cupboards and, as you can see, the bowls are all washed in hot water and detergent and left to drain. This washing machine is for the dog blankets, I was just going to wash some when you arrived."

"Yes, I see. These arrangements apply to the boarders as well. Um. Well thank you for being so co-operative Mrs Philips. By the way, do you have any other dogs in the house, I see there are two in the kitchen."

"No, only these two, they are the older ones."

"I see. Right, you will receive a letter from us with our comments and any alterations that we feel could be made but may I say that I'm very pleased with what I've seen."

"But.... that's not good enough, surely you can tell me what you are going to say?"

"All I can say at the present time Mrs Philips is that it is our duty to check every complaint. Would you have it any other way?"

"No, of course not. I do understand. It was just such a shock."

"Yes, I'm sorry but, well it's my job. Well good morning Mrs Philips and I'm sorry to have bothered you." He got back in his van and drove off.

Letting her breath out in one long gasp, she hadn't realised that she had been holding it, she hurried into the hall to phone Simon. He was, at first, just as surprised as she had been but then he paused in mid sentence.

"Simon what's the matter?"

"Nothing, I was just thinking. Now look love, don't fret over it any more. We'll talk about it when I get home OK?"

"Yes, OK only it was such a shock."

"More a shot across the bows I think but, don't worry Fee. I'll see you soon. Bye love."

The rest of the day passed slowly, she phoned Beryl and told her about it, she was equally horrified and very sympathetic. She phoned Ruth but she wasn't in so she made some cakes and an apple pie to pass the time. Cooking in the warm kitchen always soothed her. The cakes would do to have with their sandwiches at Crufts, they were going for two days and Simon was always hungry. At last, she heard Simon's car in the drive and opened the kitchen door, "Am I glad you're home Simon. I just can't get it out of my mind."

"Yeah, I bet. Bit of a shock."

"I phoned Beryl and told her about it and she was horrified."

"Damn. I meant to say, you haven't told anyone else have you?"

"No, I phoned Ruth but she was out."

"Good, with any luck, it won't break 'til after Crufts."

"Break?"

"You don't think it's going to stop there do you Fee? Whoever did this is going to spread it around the dog fraternity. You know the 'there's no smoke without fire routine', somebody's out to blacken our name, there's no point in doing it otherwise is there. The buggers, it'll be somebody who's jealous of our success, or we've rattled someone's cage somehow."

"But who? I've thought about it all afternoon and I can't think who would do this."

"We might never ever know but I'm sure as hell going to try to find out. This is just how it all started with Viv. I wonder what's next?"

"Next?"

"Yeah, next. Good old Viv. She put me wise to a lot of things. I can't recall upsetting anyone for ages. Can you Fee?"

Fiona shook her head, "No, I can't think of anything. No-one has complained to me about the boarding or any of our puppies or studs."

"No, perhaps it's nothing. Now, what's for dinner I'm starving, is this apple pie for pudding?"

"Yes, but how you can think of eating!"

"Come on Fee. Remember the golden rule, don't let the buggers...."

"Grind you down, OK," she smiled and started to lay the table for dinner.

CHAPTER TWENTY- THREE

Fiona stared at her somewhat pale and dishevelled appearance in the mirror. My God she thought, these blasted overhead strip lights they put in these places make you look ghastly. As usual, she had had to queue for ages. When were The Kennel Club going to allocate more ladies' loos than mens' at this event? Trouble was that The Kennel Club was predominantly men, and exhibitors were predominantly women. She quickly applied a bit of make-up and combed her damp hair. It had been still fairly dark and pouring with rain as she and Simon had pulled the trolley through the busy car park, through the tunnel and then into one of the massive NEC buildings. She had been working hard on the grooming of the dogs all week to have them in the peak of condition for Crufts. She knew that everybody else throughout the country would have been doing the same thing. She looked around at her fellow exhibitors, a motley collection of young, old, fat, thin, eager and resigned, some were dressed for the occasion while others were in their usual rather nondescript 'doggy' outfits.

"Oo, Oo Fiona."

Fiona saw Monica Samuels' smiling, fat face; she was standing at the row of washbasins. She loathed Monica Samuels, if anyone beat her in a class or in the challenge, it always seemed to be Monica Samuels and boy, didn't she always lord it over her when she did; in the nicest way, of course!

"Hello Monica," Fiona was saved from saying anything further by a toilet becoming vacant, "See you later."

Washing her hands, she again looked in the mirror, heavens, she thought, I'll have to change my make-up or something, I look as if I'm on death's door!. Giving a last look at her reflection in the mirror she pinched her cheeks, shrugged her shoulders and proceeded to make her way through the crowds and back to the Cumbrian benches. Because of the visit from the animal welfare in the week and concerned about Fiona, Simon had suggested that they only take the Cumbrians, even though they had qualified and entered one of the Glencastles. He had made the excuse that it was such a nuisance trying to keep a look out for classes in two rings, especially at Crufts with all the visitors and Fiona had agreed although she had been a bit disappointed. This way Simon felt that they could stay together. The person who had organised that visit was not going to stop there, of that he was certain. He was also concerned that their dogs were never left alone on the benches; either he or Fiona must be there for every minute of the day.

As she approached their benches she could see Caroline Amery talking to Simon. What a transformation! Her hair had been beautifully styled and she was wearing a very smart suit. Her Aunt or whoever it was must have left her a lot of money as well as the house.

"Hello Caroline, how are you and how's the bitch?"

"Hello Fiona, I was just telling Simon all about her. She is doing ever so well at the Open shows and I shall be at several of the Champion shows this year with her too. Ophelia Hammond-James, who lives near me you know, has offered to take me in her car to some of them, in fact I came with her today. Have I told you that I have a car of my own now so I shall be driving myself to a lot of the other shows. Can't afford to miss the Championship shows can I," she giggled coyly.

Fiona looked at her little ferrety face, I'm obviously supposed to be terribly impressed with all this she thought, "Are you!" she said, "Well, we shall look forward to seeing you more often Caroline and hope that you do a lot more winning, she's a nice bitch."

"Yes and Ophelia is very pleased with Sesame as well, I'm sure that she will do well with her. She is very hopeful of doing well today with her champion dog."

Surprise, surprise thought Simon, "Is she! and I'll tell you what, that bitch of ours that she's got is bloody good compared with some of her own stock."

Caroline's eyes and mouth opened wide, "Oh, well yes, well, I must be off, I've some shopping to do. Good Luck."

They both watched her retreating figure weaving her way between the throngs of people.

"Well, the story's not out yet then, if anybody would have heard about it, it would be her. I thought that she was going to bring it up when she stopped at the bench."

"I think you're worrying unnecessarily Simon, it was just a mistake that's all, but all the same, you shouldn't have said that about

145

Ophelia's dogs. You know what a tell-tale Caroline is. Ophelia will be none too pleased."

"What the hell! I know, but, well sometimes you just get sick of these hallowed breeders always having the best dogs - always. That's how these buggers get away with it. What's more, that rule goes right to the top echelons, the well-known breeders at the top always have the best dogs. They can get away with murder. Never mind that now, what's more important is that, at the moment she doesn't know and it's a girlie friend of hers that's judging!"
Fiona smiled at Simon and agreed with him but she knew that he was tense and worried, had he rubbed somebody up the wrong way. He did tend to speak his mind.

Fiona went into her class with Stream and came third to Ophelia with one of her own stock and Monica! Simon said that the judge was, 'one of them' and not to worry because it was only to be expected. When Simon took Saxon into the Open class however, he ended up coming first with him. Fiona couldn't resist saying as he came back to the bench, "My, my Simon, how do you account for that!" He laughed a bit shamefacedly, "Well, just because she's... well she still knows a good dog when she sees one." He did not, however, go on to higher things in the challenge as Ophelia got the dog ticket. During the period when the judge went to lunch, he went over to Ophelia's bench and grabbed her arm, "Hi, you did well today getting the dog CC."

"Hello Simon, yes, but I don't know about doing well. He richly deserved it."

"Come off it Ophelia. It's me you're talking to. Now Stream on the other hand.... You haven't forgotten?"

"I haven't forgotten but this is neither the time nor the place.... Mind you, I didn't know that you had upset some people when I agreed to do it!"

"Oh, who?"
She looked at him for a moment or to, "I think you must know who don't you. Just be very careful from now on what you say and do."

"Right thanks. How's the bitch by the way. I hear you've got Sesame now."

"Yes, I suppose Caroline told you. Nice little thing isn't she."

146

Simon raised his eyebrows, so, that was the way of things; he was rather surprised. He made his way back to their bench, "Hey Fee, have I got news for you!"

They had just finished their sandwiches and Simon had gone to watch the bitches being judged when Natalie appeared at the bench. She was wearing a lovely, dark blue suit with a prettily patterned matching blouse. Fiona looking up and smiling felt decidedly drab, "Hello Natalie, it's lovely to see you and don't you look smart! That colour really suits you. Are you here with Paul?"

Natalie bent and kissed her on the cheek and a waft of exquisite perfume assailed her nose, "Hello Fiona, yes I am, he's busy talking at the moment, do you mind if I sit down? I'm so pleased to see you. Paul has introduced me to so many new people both yesterday and today that my head is buzzing. He is so keen and interested; it's lovely to watch him chattering away. They think quite highly of him at The Kennel Club you know."

Fiona fixed a smile on her face, "I'm sure they do and I'm so glad that you are enjoying it too Natalie. By the way, how is Jamie?"

"Fine. He has a lovely kennel in the garden now and the gardener looks after him when we are away. It was Paul's idea."

"Yes, I see. Are you going home today?"

"Oh no. We're here for the next two days as well. We are staying at a very nice hotel. A lot of the officials and some of the judges are there too. Paul has a great time chatting to people. I go to our room usually, I find all this quite tiring. Anyway, have you been in yet? How did you get on? I do so miss the excitement of showing you know."

Fiona told her of Stream and Saxon's placings and urged her to start showing Jamie again but Natalie only smiled and said that they were so busy nowadays.

Natalie had not long departed when Simon came back to the bench, "Well Fee. I don't know why, but nothing seems to have been said as yet. There are no funny looks, nobody is trying to avoid me, nothing. Mind you, I can't say the same for poor old Caroline, she's getting the treatment. Lots of knowing looks, winks and nudges."

Just at that moment Caroline bore down on them her hands full of bags, "Hello again, I've been shopping. There are so many gorgeous stalls here aren't there. There are things here that I've never seen before. I think that Crufts is marvellous. It's just like a big Sunday market. Dennis is going to be quite shocked when I get home."

Simon dug Fiona in the ribs, "Dennis didn't come with you then?"

Quite unperturbed Caroline relied, "Dennis, no, I told you I came with Ophelia, he hates dog shows. Anyway, he's busy in his greenhouse. Since we moved to my Aunt's house, he has become a gardening fanatic. He's joined the local gardener's club and sends for loads of seed catalogues and things. I hardly see him until it gets dark. He thinks that I don't know about it but I've sneaked down the garden to his greenhouse and seen it all. He is very happy in his greenhouse."

Bet the poor bugger doesn't even know about her and Ophelia thought Simon.

"Well, I must be on my way, we're staying with a friend of Ophelia tonight and travelling back tomorrow. She apparently has a house nearby."

As Caroline retraced her steps to Ophelia's bench, she noticed several admiring glances from other Cumbrian exhibitors, she smoothed the skirt of her new suit over her hips. They must be so surprised and envious to see her so well dressed and friendly with one or two of the 'top' breeders.

All the fun of the fair was gradually slowing down as various judging rings emptied of exhibitors and they sat on their benches patiently waiting for the time when they would be allowed to leave. Tired with the early start, the driving to get there, the tension of the judging ring and, for most, the disappointment and dashed hopes for their wonderful dog. They sat having the last cup of tea, chatting idly and watching the vast crowds constantly surging past them, sometimes answering their inane questions but also, hearing stories of loved pets, having overseas visitors asking if they might take a photo of their dog and even, sometimes, getting a puppy order. Thinking about the poor standard of judging, thinking about the deals and fiddles, the tired dogs, thinking about the crowded loos, the poor food facilities, the lack of seats, the cramped conditions of the benches and aisles and the long journey home. And these stalwarts of the ring, these gladiators had paid a large sum of money to be treated with such lack of consideration by the organisers.

Simon shook his head and looked at his watch, "Good, only another fifteen minutes and we can get out of this monumental farce. This isn't a dog show any more."

As Fiona and Simon were joining the throngs of exhibitors making their way to the exits, Fiona spotted a couple of familiar faces, "Hello there, Bob and Annie, hello, haven't seen you for ages. How are you both."

Their faces lit up in a smile, "Hello Fiona and hello Simon. We've been trying to see all our friends but it's so crowded that we just gave up. How have you done today?"

"Third in Junior and First in Open."

"Well done. I never ever got a card at Crufts when I was showing," Bob shrugged his shoulders and grinned, "That's why I gave up in the end."

"Do you mean that you're not going to show any more? We thought that we hadn't seen you much of ...."

Annie interrupted, "That's what he says but he's driving me mad. Doesn't know what to do with himself any more. This showing lark is a drug you know, you can't give it up. We've shown dogs for the past thirty years, so all our friends are in dogs. We never took up any other hobbies because of all the time and money it took to show the dogs. He's miserable and bad-temp...."

"I'm sure that Fiona and Simon don't want to hear about us although I do agree, I am suffering withdrawal symptoms. Got any plans for the coming year Simon? Got anything nice coming out? That looks like a new one, he's got a lovely head," he pointed to the young dog's cage.

"That's Stream but we've got a couple of even better ones at home, watch out for Skiddaw and Solitude. We expect great things of them." Simon smiled.

"Now look Bob. Why don't you just come to the Open shows. At least it's a nice day out with people to talk to, not so expensive and usually not so far to travel," Fiona said.

Annie nodded her head, "You tell him Fiona because he won't listen to me. At least if we don't win we haven't travelled miles and spent a fortune we can ill afford, have we?"

"Yes, but the excitement's not there. I just can't understand why the KC don't introduce a points system for Open shows, leading

149

perhaps to a different sort of champion award. An Open champion! That would make all the difference. Mind you, if the Champ shows get any dearer, people won't be able to afford Open shows at all."

Fiona told them about the death of Mrs Emsworth and, after a few more enquiries concerning other old doggy acquaintances, they both said their goodbyes and continued on their way to the exit and home.

CHAPTER TWENTY-FOUR

It was quite late as Ophelia and Caroline drove towards the house where they would be staying overnight. It had been arranged that they should stay at the house of a friend of Ophelia's in case she had to return to Crufts for the Best in Show award. Unfortunately her dog had not won the Terrier Group so they would only be staying for the one night before returning home. Ophelia had been fairly quiet during the short drive and Caroline put it down to tiredness and possibly disappointment. She had suggested that morning that she had felt quite confident of winning the group. Caroline was rather curious to see this friend and also to see what sort of house she lived in. As the car stopped in front of a small, detached house in a tree-lined road on the edge of a small town she was rather surprised, she had expected something much grander. This was nowhere near as good as Aunt Ellen's house. As they got out of the car the front door of the house was opened and light spilled onto the path. Caroline could just make out a fairly short woman in a jumper and trousers, "Hello Ophelia lovely to see you again, it's been ages and this is your friend Caroline. Hello Caroline, I'm Jessica." She shook Caroline's hand and kissed Ophelia on the cheek.

"Hello Jess. You're looking well. My God I'm shattered."

"You must be, what time did you set out this morning? Do come in and I'll put the kettle on or would you like something stronger?"

"A cup of tea to start with Jess. What about you Caroline?"

"Oh yes, tea for me please."

"Do sit down Caroline, I'll pop the kettle on."

Ophelia lay back in the chair and closed her eyes. Caroline took the opportunity to look around the room. It seemed fairly small compared with the lovely, big rooms in Aunt Ellen's house but it was very pretty. Everything was in soft pastel colours, there were some very nice pictures on the wall of cats and, she noticed that there was a china cabinet full of ceramic figures of cats of all shapes, sizes and colours. There was a large, wooden cat curled up on the floor near the fireplace too. Turning the other way she observed that the dividing wall between the two downstairs rooms had been partly demolished and she could see the dining table and chairs in the unlit part of the room. It gave a feeling of space and Caroline nodded approvingly. This was just what she and Dennis had done at their old house. In fact she'd go so far as to say that she liked the decor and the furniture too. This Jessica must have similar tastes to her. Caroline's thoughts were interrupted by the arrival of Jessica carrying a large tray and followed by two beautiful cats.

"Here we are. Now girls, don't get under my feet. I hope you're not allergic to cats Caroline."

"Not as far as I know. We used to have a cat when I was small, not like these though. What are they?"

"These two are long-haired Persians."

"But they are different colours."

"Yes, this one with the brown points and the more creamy coloured coat is a seal-point and the slightly lighter one with the bluey-grey points is a blue-point. There are about twenty different colours, there's......"

"Don't get Jessica talking about her cats. We'll be here all night."

"Well you will be, Ophelia, anyway," Jessica smiled at Caroline. "Have you noticed she's awfully bossy?"

A well aimed cushion caught Jessica on her side and the two cats fled from the room. Caroline quickly looked at Jessica but she was laughingly throwing the cushion back at Ophelia.

Jessica had prepared a meal of ham and salad followed by a delicious fruit cheesecake which she had made. Caroline suddenly realised that she was hungry. Over coffee Jessica and Ophelia were reminiscing over mutual old friends, Caroline gradually deduced that they were cousins of a sort and had played together and had summer holidays together when they were small. When Jessica enquired about someone called Deborah, Caroline noticed that the convivial atmosphere changed and Ophelia instantly got up from the table saying that she had a headache and was rather tired.

"Of course, how thoughtless of me, you must both be so tired after such an early start," she looked across at Caroline and smiled.

" Yes, I am a bit tired now, we left Ophelia's house at six-o-clock this morning."

"I'm going to the car Caroline, I'll get your overnight bag for you as well," Ophelia left the room.

"I'm so sorry Caroline, did I put my foot in it. Has Ophelia completely finished with Deborah then? They were together for such a long time."

Caroline stared at Jessica for a moment, "I'm sorry, I don't know what you're talking about."

"Oh, I thought that you and Ophelia were an item, I mean that.... I'm so sorry Caroline. I didn't mean to offend you; look, excuse me." She got up and carried the tray out to the kitchen.

Ophelia came back into the hall and shut the front door with a bang, "Where are we Jess?"

"Oh dear, you're in the front bedroom, you see I thought that.... I didn't know that..." Rather flustered Jessica walked upstairs and opened a door. Ophelia walked in and dumped the bags on the bed. Just behind her Caroline noticed that the walls of the room were decorated in a beautiful primrose colour. The drapes were of the same colour as were the lampshades, what a wonderfully relaxing room she thought. There was an exquisite white, cotton and lace duvet cover on the bed and the pillowslips had, she paused in her appraisal of the room, the bed was a double bed! She hurriedly looked around the room for another bed knowing somehow that she wouldn't find one. She swallowed hard, she would have to say something, this was a mistake but as she turned to Jessica, she saw her disappearing quickly downstairs and saying as she went, " I hope that you will be comfortable. Sleep well. Goodnight."

"God, I'm tired," Ophelia grabbed her bag and unzipped it, hauling out a pair of silk pyjamas she started to undress. Caroline hurriedly turned away and tried to get hold of her bag by putting her hand behind her and feeling for the handle. All she succeeded in doing was to make the bag slide onto the floor. She turned and bent down to retrieve it and, as she stood up, saw that Ophelia was standing on the other side of the bed completely naked rubbing her hands up her belly and round her breasts, "God, that feels good to get those clothes off."

Covered with confusion and feeling totally out of her depth now, Caroline hugged her bag to her chest and hurried out of the room saying, "I must go to the bathroom." There, she looked at her red face in the mirror. What could she do? Was there another bedroom?

Could she ask Jessica to make up another bed for her? Quietly she tip-toed out of the bathroom and along the landing to the first of the doors. With her heart thumping she slowly turned the handle, opened the door and looked inside, she could make out another double bed with two or three cats asleep on it. This was obviously Jessica's room. She quickly tip-toed to the other door and opened it. She jumped and nearly ran back to the bathroom as the door squeaked, swallowing hard she quickly looked inside. She could see a desk, a computer and lots of books and..... no bed. Hearing Jessica coming up the stairs, she quickly tip-toed back to the bathroom and shutting the door, locked it. She let out a breath which she had been holding in her vain search for a bed. Sitting on the toilet she reviewed her options, she could go out and sleep in the car.... but she didn't have a key. She could walk out of the house now and call a taxi to take her home... but she didn't like the idea of walking along unknown streets at this time of night. She could...... A bang on the door caused her to jump up from the toilet seat.

"Come on Caroline, I'm bursting."

Oh God, that was Ophelia! What could she do? She didn't want to upset her, she had promised her so much help with Saffron this year. She so wanted a CC. The banging on the door started up again. She had spoken to Ophelia hadn't she and she had said that she understood. I mean, it surely wasn't like going to bed with a man, they couldn't control their feelings but Ophelia.... Making up her mind she shouted, "Sorry, I shan't be a minute."

Caroline was in bed and as near to the edge as she could get when Ophelia came back into the bedroom, she squeezed her eyes shut and tried to make her breathing sound as if she was sound asleep. Ophelia got into bed beside her, "Sorry my little pigeon, I really am bushed tonight. See you in the morning."

Caroline lay there in the darkened room for hours but finally dropped off with sheer exhaustion as the first birds started to twitter outside. An hour or so later, Ophelia partially woke up stretched and turned over, Debs, I love you, but no it wasn't Debs. She pulled the bedclothes back and in the dim light looked at the sleeping form of Caroline. Being used to the size of Debs, Caroline looked so small and neat. She was a pretty little thing, she put her hand around the sleeping form to fondle her breasts. Good God. She had her bra on!

154

Gently lifting the hem of the white cotton nightie she almost laughed when she saw that Caroline also had her tights and knickers on! She liked a challenge and this was going to be a good game to win. She lifted the nightie slightly higher and undid the hooks of Caroline's bra and, slipping her hand inside the bra proceeded to fondle her right nipple, Caroline groaned slightly but did not wake. Ophelia continued to fondle Caroline's breast and slowly Caroline turned over onto her back. Ophelia caressed both nipples and when they were erect and proud she slid one hand down inside Caroline's knickers and tights. As she caressed her, Caroline started to respond and arched her back. As she woke up and opened her eyes, she was assailed with tremendous, wonderful emotions and feelings such as she had never experienced before. What was happening, she was panting hard as she involuntarily arched her back. Waking fully, she found that Ophelia was touching her breast and her... Oh God. It was wonderful, the feeling was.... was... she involuntarily arched her back again and started to writhe and moan. Part of her mind told her to stop this, stop it at once but... Ophelia had pulled her knickers down now and was.... Oh my God. No. She mustn't.

"Stop it Ophelia. Please stop it."

"Oh my little one you know that's the last thing you want at this moment. Wait a minute while I...."

Caroline's body seemed to have a mind of it's own, she wanted to stop but couldn't. She seemed to be soaring on huge waves that were lifting her up and crashing her down until... until, she grabbed at Ophelia's arms and cried out.

"Shush. Shush now. You'll wake Jess and it's still early. Now, wasn't that lovely? Didn't I tell you that you'd enjoy it."

Caroline lay sprawled on the bed, her nightdress up around her neck. Her eyes were closed and she was red-faced and breathing heavily. After a while, she opened her eyes, "What happened, what did you do to me?"

"Nothing, I just loved you and you had an orgasm. That's all."

"An orgasm?"

"Don't tell me that you've never had one before."

"No, not if that was what it was."

"Poor you. You don't know what you have been missing."

All the emotion was suddenly too much for Caroline and she burst into tears. She was trying to say something but it was unintelligible.

"What are you saying? I can't understand you. Look come here and let me cuddle you and tell you how pretty you are."

Caroline hurriedly shuffled away from her frantically pulling her nightie down as she did.

"I said that you made me do a terrible thing. It's wicked and bad, I know it is and I feel awful."

"You weren't saying that a minute ago. It's no different than you do with your husband. Why is it wicked?"

"Because it's not normal and anyway, Dennis has never done that to me!"

"What! Well I repeat. Poor you and poor Dennis too."

"I have a very good marriage. Dennis and I are very happy. We don't need that sort of thing. And now I'm going to the bathroom."

It was a very pale, quiet and subdued Caroline who appeared for breakfast. She wouldn't look at Jessica and just picked at her breakfast. Jessica asked if she would like to see the garden and the house where her stud cat lived before she went but, after one horrified look at Jessica, Caroline shook her head. After Ophelia had seen to the dog and put him in the car, they packed up, said their goodbyes and left for the journey home. Caroline, confused and frightened sat slumped in her seat as far from Ophelia as she could get and did not speak all the way home. When they arrived at the farmhouse, Caroline declined Ophelia's offer to come in for a drink and, putting her bag into her car, drove home. About a mile from her house she stopped the car, she had to calm down, she had to think about what had happened before she went indoors and faced Dennis. She was having such mixed feelings and thoughts, on the one hand, if she allowed herself to think about what had happened, she remembered how marvellous she had felt, how powerful and strong, how beautiful! How could she when she didn't particularly like Ophelia as a person? On the other hand, she could hear her mother telling her how wrong it was and she couldn't imagine what Dennis's face would look like if she told him what she'd actually done! It just didn't bear thinking about. The whole thing was a nightmare! She started the car and drove the last mile to Aunt Ellen's house. Aunt Ellen, now what would she have said?

CHAPTER TWENTY- FIVE

Fiona bent down and laid a few of the daffodils on the little grave in the woods, "It's me again Sally. Thought that you might like a few daffs. Remember how you used to love to run in the woods and how, sometimes you used to bite off the head of a daffodil as you raced past? I've got to go to training classes soon with Solitude, your grandson, or is it great-grandson now! Let's hope that he proves to be as good as you. It will soon be summer again Sally and I can come and see you more and bring Sapphire. We haven't had any more problems lately so perhaps it was just a mistake after all. Let's hope so. Simon is fine and sends his love. Bye for now Sally." She stood up and walked back through the field to the cottage musing on the fact that, although she had Sally's daughter, Sapphire and her granddaughter in the house, she just didn't feel the same affection for them as she had for Sally. It was strange how one particular dog could wind its' way into your heart so effectively. She had often heard other exhibitors remark that now and again a 'special' dog comes along. They are different, closer to you, have more understanding of your feelings, they don't have to be fantastic in the ring or anything; they are just 'special' and you love them for just being who they are. As she neared the cottage Simon drove in, "Hi Fee. Had a good day?"

"Yes all right. Just picked a few daffodils from the woods and said hello to Sally. It's lovely in there at the moment, the leaves are beginning to burst on the trees and it all smells damp and 'leaf mouldy' you know, just like Spring."

Simon put an arm around her waist, "Glad you enjoyed yourself. Did you said hello to Sal for me?"

They were just having a cup of tea after dinner that evening when they heard the phone ring; Simon got up to answer it. When he came back into the kitchen he was frowning, "That was a bloody funny phone call."

"Why? Who was it?"

"Woman called Stephenson. She said that she had a mating booked with Saxon for Friday. That right?"

157

"Yes, he's got two bookings, one for this week and he's got another one for next week with one of Mrs Mortimer's bitches. Why?"

"Well, this Stephenson woman has cancelled. Gave me some cock and bull story about the bitch not being suitable, said that she had been advised that her line wouldn't be compatible with ours."

"What rubbish. I went into all that with her when she first booked. It should have been quite a nice mating. You know the bitch in fact Wilcora Watersprite, she has had a couple of firsts at the Champ shows recently. She's owned by a tall women, quite thin with black hair in a pony tail, hasn't been showing for very long but seems a nice person."

"Yeah, think I know. When I asked her who had advised her she wouldn't tell me. Anyway, she's not coming."

"Damn. I cancelled going shopping with Beryl because of that mating. I think I'll ring her and see if she still wants to go."

"Um. OK."

When she came back into the kitchen Simon was still sitting at the table, "Right that's settled. Beryl was pleased. Peter sends his regards."

"What? Oh yes. Um. Look Fee if we get any more cancellations, let me know straight away."

"More! That's not likely."

"No, but let me know all the same."

On the following Tuesday Fiona smiled as Mrs. Mortimer came up to the kitchen door, "Hello Mrs. Philips, lovely day isn't it. She's absolutely ready I can assure you."

Fiona smiled at her, Mrs Mortimer had been using their dogs for several years now. She didn't show her two bitches but did look after them very well and, as they were from good lines, Fiona was happy for her to use her dogs. "Good morning Mrs Mortimer and how are you and your husband?"

"Fine, Len is keeping well too."

Fiona knew that Len Mortimer had contracted Parkinson's disease and could no longer work. The two litters each year helped financially.

With the mating successfully completed, Mrs Mortimer had hardly left when the phone rang, "Hello Simfell Kennels."

"Hello Fiona it's Di Sharpe."

"Hello Di. What a coincidence, I was just thinking of you. All ready for Saturday?"

"Ah, well, that's why I'm ringing. I think that I've decided not to mate Penny this time."

"Oh why? Nothing wrong I hope."

"No. Just that I don't think that I want the bother of it all. You know, all the worry when they're born and all the feeding etc. Don't think I'll bother that's all. OK."

"Yes, if that's how you feel. See you at one of the shows then. Bye."

Fiona put the phone down. How strange, Di had been so keen to use Stream, said that she'd loved him the moment she'd seen him. What a pity, she'd been looking forward to seeing what that particular mating produced. Funny though that Di should say that, she was always such a bundle of energy.

That evening over dinner she told Simon about the phone call from Di.

He sat looking at his plate for a moment and then looking up at Fiona said, "This is what I was afraid of. So this is the next move. Who the hell is doing this Fee?"

"The next move? You think that this is deliberate then."

"Yes, don't you?"

"But why? Couldn't it be a coincidence?"

"It could but I don't think so. Someone out there thinks that we're doing too well. Someone out there is trying to put a spoke in our wheel. First the call from that welfare inspector and now this."

"But they might not be related."

"They're related; and don't think that this is the end of it. Someone is obviously spreading the news that our dogs are throwing deformities."

"WHAT!"

"Come on Fee you know it happens. Now who hates us that much or who's jealous enough or ambitious enough to do it."

"Well that remit just about covers over half of the Cumbrian exhibitors."

"No it doesn't because they've got to have clout as well."

They sat in silence for a while. A name immediately sprang to Fiona's mind but she dismissed it. No, he wouldn't be so petty would he. She

159

was startled out of her reverie by Simon jumping up from his chair, "Well, we can't just sit here. I'm getting on the phone and calling in a couple of favours." About twenty minutes later he came back into the kitchen, "Well, I had a job to get it out of anybody but I did in the end. I was right; it was going round the benches at Crufts after we left. Apparently, our kennels are so badly run that there have been complaints. The story has since done the rounds at other shows. Damn, blast and bugger. I knew I was right Fee. I had a gut feeling about this."

"But, why do people believe it? Surely the people who've been here won't, will they?"

"God Fee, you know how these damned things spread. It's a knee jerk reaction, somebody tells one and they tell another. Doesn't matter if it's true. They don't stop to think about that, it's just good gossip and it might stop you winning. As for the genetic defects in puppies, for one thing they're frightened that it might be true. Secondly, they're afraid that if they use our dogs, knowing that we are in trouble with someone with authority, then they may also be in trouble. You know the damn silly phrase, 'it might harm you in the ring'. What I now need to know is what are they planning next?"

About two weeks later, as Simon was looking through the diary he said, "Fee, did I ever get the paper work for that show I was asked to do later this year?"

"I don't know. I'll have a look."

When she couldn't find anything relating to the show Simon looked grim, "So this is the next thing is it?"

"Now you don't know that yet. They may just be late in sending it."

"Well, we can soon find out."

Simon put the phone down and came back into the sitting room, "I was bloody well right. They aren't asking me."

"But they already have. They can't go back on their word."

"They already bloody have. Lots of apologies and they'll ask me another time but this time, they hadn't realised that they had already asked someone before. So terribly sorry and all that."

The following Sunday they took the two Glencastles to an Open show. Fiona got them ready for the ring while Simon restlessly walked around the show speaking to various people. As Fiona walked in with the dog she couldn't recall having ever seen this judge so was interested to see if she knew anything about Glencastles and how she judged them. She was awarded third out of five with the young dog so wasn't too disappointed. She could tell the judge at least knew what she was doing by the way in which she went over the dogs. When she brought the bitch into the ring there were only two other exhibits. She was awarded the first prize and subsequently went on to get Best of Breed with her. This was met with complete silence until Simon loudly clapped his hands. She suddenly thought of Viv, when that had happened to Viv Fiona had always thought it was because Viv was such an unpopular person.. How she had misjudged her. She herself had been one of those who refused to congratulate or even speak to her at this very show. She had believed everything she had heard about Viv. How had she coped with it for so many years?

"Oh Simon, I don't like this. The unpleasantness spoils the enjoyment."

"I know Fee, but until we can find a way to find out who's doing it and stop it, we've got to put up with it. My biggest worry is that bloody Ophelia Hammond-James will chicken out of our agreement. She's got the bitch now so there's nothing I can bloody well do about it is there if she does."

"But who is doing all this?"

Having confronted her fears that it might be Paul, and desperate for answers, Fiona, not being able to get Natalie on the phone for several days, had made a few discreet enquiries at Natalie's house. The gardener had told her that Natalie and Paul had apparently left for Sweden a few weeks after Crufts, they were then going on to Germany and France. Paul had some business out there. I bet he does thought Fiona but, it was good news in a way, if Paul was out of the country and busy, he was hardly likely to be the person arranging all this trouble for them, he appeared to have bigger fish to fry.

When Simon received a phone call from Ophelia telling him that, in her opinion, he should enter a certain Champ show because she felt sure that the judge would like his young dog, he felt better. The mood lifted at the Simfell kennels, at least, something was coming right. The following week, however, Fiona got a call from a council

161

official, he had had a complaint about the noise that the dogs made at night. He informed her that he would be making recordings of the noise one night and, if it exceeded the permitted noise level, she would be required to do something about it or risk being closed down as a boarding kennel. Before this could be resolved, two weeks later another official arrived saying that they had had a complaint about how she disposed of the dogs' waste matter, Fiona felt near to tears, it was all getting too much. She was able to reassure him that everything was done according to the requirements that they had made when issuing her licence. She phoned Simon at work to tell him about the latest episode, "Simon I can't stand much more of this, I really can't. Where is it going to end?"

"Don't worry Fee, calm down. I'll get off early today and we'll sort something out, somehow."

"Simon, what can we do! I'm dreading what's next! I even had Monica Samuels on the phone this afternoon, commiserating with me about all my problems! The bitch! I really think it's time that we informed the Kennel Club of what's going on."

"And say what? Where's our proof. You know as well as I do that everything that goes on in the dog world, any fiddles, anything underhand, is done by word of mouth. What could the KC do? That is supposing that they even wanted to."

"Well what about Di Sharpe, she could tell the KC that she was told not to use our dogs. Especially as she then subsequently mated that bitch to another dog. We could phone round people who have had our puppies in the past, going back over the last two or three years in fact, and get statements to prove that they haven't got defects."

"Sorry Fee but that's just bloody ridiculous. Di Sharpe knows that she daren't open her bloody mouth. One word and she'd be finished in showing for good. As far as your other idea is concerned; it wouldn't make any difference. People would just say that you haven't shown them the bad-uns, only the good-uns."

"But Simon, we've got to do something! We'll be finished in showing if this goes on, and the kennel too, the boarders, everything, all our future in ruins.People are already avoiding us if they can. Even our so-called friends seem frightened to speak to us. I hate it Simon. I hate it, it's driving me mad!"

"Yeah, I know, I know Fee. It's a bloody awful situation; but let me think about this for a bit. There's got to be a clue somewhere and I'll try and get to the bottom of this. It's just a question of thinking like these bastards that's all."

CHAPTER TWENTY- SIX

"Do you know Fee, I've been thinking and I'm beginning to think that all this trouble is down to Paul bloody Aston."

Fiona and Simon were sitting up in bed drinking tea; it was four-o-clock in the morning and neither of them had been able to sleep. There had been several mornings in the last couple of weeks when, tossing and turning unable to sleep because of all the problems with the kennels, one or the other of them had got up and made a pot of tea.

Fiona dunked her ginger nut biscuit into her tea and ate it while, at the same time, mentally telling herself that she really must stop eating biscuits or she'd not get into her clothes soon.

"I don't know that you're right there Simon. When this all started he was so busy with Crufts and then, after Crufts, he and Natalie were getting ready to go abroad. Surely he wouldn't have had the time to organise all these things and, anyway, what's his motive in trying to close the kennels."

"Well, going abroad wouldn't have stopped him making a phone call or two to arrange things before he went, would it. Don't forget, with those in a position of power, there are always plenty of climbers and crawlers willing to do their dirty work. There'll be nothing in writing, that's for sure, so what harm can come to any of them. Hey, what about that unsavoury pair looking after his dogs? Now there are two likely candidates!"

"But Paul? He's happy with Natalie, they are both so happy together, it's obvious he adores her. He's also getting on well in the KC, with the help of her money and friends. He's surely got everything he wants, why should he even think about us, let alone want to destroy us?"

Simon looked at Fiona for a second or two, her hair was dishevelled, she had no make-up on and was looking a bit pale but, to him, she looked gorgeous. They had never discussed her affair with Paul. He had refused to listen to her in the early stages of their getting back together for fear of rocking the boat but now, in view of what was happening to them, perhaps it was time to speak about it, "I think perhaps you know why Fee, don't you? We've never spoken

164

about it and I don't want to even now but, did something happen between you and Paul that might make him want to do this?"

Fiona looked worriedly at Simon and took his hand, "Oh Simon, I've thought and thought about that and.... I can't think of anything that would cause him to do this to us. I could, perhaps, understand him wanting to hurt me by stopping me showing the dogs but Simon, the business as well! I can't believe that I honestly can't. He was always such a kind man."

"My dear girl, you'd believe well of the devil! I can think of one thing anyway, he's never forgiven me for bashing him at Natalie's party." Simon suddenly smiled, "God, I can still see the surprise on his face." He then burst out laughing, "and I can still see the look on Caroline and Dennis's faces! Their eyes nearly popped out of their heads! They looked like two little squirrels about to fall out of a tree!"

Fiona laughed, "Yes, I suppose it must have been quite something for them. But surely, do you think that that could be the cause of all this. It's got to be something much bigger. That's why I'm not sure that it is Paul."

"Come on Fee, I hurt his pride! You must know that his standing with people is his main concern in life, he likes adulation and the feeling of power. Good heavens Fee you of all people must have seen that and you as good as turned him down didn't you?"

"Well yes, I agree that he is a very proud man but he's not stupid. Everything has turned out for the best for him ever since he married Natalie. He lives in that lovely old house, he's got plenty of money to spend on whatever he wants. Natalie is an enormous asset for a proud man, she's intelligent, attractive, she is marvellous at entertaining. He's got on in leaps and bounds at the KC since meeting Natalie's friends, if he'd stayed with me he wouldn't be much better off at all would he. I'm not the asset that she is so, no, I am still inclined to think that it's not him but someone else with a grudge."

"Who then?"

"Oh Simon I'm so tired of all this, who ever it is I wish they'd leave us alone. Cuddle me and let's try to get some sleep."

Simon turned off the bedside lamp, bashed his pillow and lay down. He put his arm around Fiona and she pushed her bottom against his warm body as he circled one of her breasts with his hand. Soon her regular breathing proclaimed that she, at least, was asleep.

165

Simon was still worried, he had found out that day that another possible judging appointment, this time for Fiona, was not going to materialise. It was obvious that someone was ringing around the secretaries and a mark was being placed against their names on the judging lists. That would mean no more judging for either of them. Tomorrow he'd phone Joan Skipton, she was the secretary who had phoned to say that there had been a slip up, although she had asked Fiona to judge the next show, she had discovered that someone on the committee had already asked someone else. It was fortuitous that he had taken the call not Fiona. Simon turned over in the bed and adjusted the pillow again; that was one of the standard excuses for putting a judge off. He'd heard of it happening so many times over the years and you never got asked for the next show. He'd ask her point blank if they had been 'marked' but Joan had just laughed nervously and assured him that that was not the reason. Simon sighed, how long would it be before Ophelia reneged on her promise?

Many miles away Caroline was lying in bed looking at the ceiling and unable to sleep, her mind was in overdrive. She and Dennis had been watching TV yesterday evening; a fairly unusual occurrence now for Dennis was either at the pub playing darts or in his greenhouse most evenings, when they heard the phone ring. Fearful that it was Ophelia, she had asked Dennis to answer it. He came back into the sitting room, "It's a Jessica Mason. She wants to speak to you."

Caroline stared at him for a second or two and she blushed, "Tell her I'm not here."

"I can't, I've already told her that you're here."

"Oh Dennis! Can't you ever get anything right."

Surprised at her anger, she was usually so eager to talk to people, Dennis said, "How was I supposed to know you didn't want to talk to her?"

Caroline got up and went out into the hall, closing the door firmly as she went.

"Hello."

"Hello Caroline it's Jessica, sorry to bother you if you're busy, but you left a silk scarf here and, as it's such a pretty one, I wondered if you would like me to send it back to you?"

"Yes please, I'll pay for the postage."

"Nonsense, it doesn't weigh anything. I enjoyed meeting you the other evening. I was sorry that you had to leave so quickly without seeing the cats and the garden."

"We had to get back."

"Yes, I was wondering, as you didn't see the kittens either when you came, whether you would like to come over for the day, see the kittens and have a spot of lunch. They will be going to their new homes shortly. You could collect your scarf then."

Caroline's first instinct was to refuse, she didn't know what sort of friend Jessica was to Ophelia! She had so liked Jessica, she felt that they could be good friends and she really did want to see the kittens and the garden.

"I couldn't stay long. I'm rather busy at the moment. It would have to be just a quick lunch because I have to get my husband's dinner. That was Dennis, my husband you spoke to, we have been married for years and are very happy."

"Good. I'm so pleased. Now how about this Friday, I don't have an appointment until two-thirty."

"An appointment!"

"Of course, we really didn't have much chance to talk did we? I'm an Aromatherapist."

"Are you? I didn't know that. I've always thought about doing that myself. Those lovely flowery smells but I didn't like the idea of....... I preferred working in a florist's shop."

" Oh yes, that sounds very nice too. When you come, you can smell all the oils, see which ones you prefer and I can explain what they are all for; and you can see the garden. I expect that you could give me a tip or two about flowers. Shall we say eleven-o-clock for coffee?"

"Yes, I'd like that. Thank you very much Jessica."

Caroline's heart was pounding as she, once again, walked up to the front door of Jessica's house and knocked. The adrenaline was flowing and she was ready to run away the moment anything seemed untoward. A smiling Jessica opened the door and immediately welcomed her in. Once again, Caroline was impressed with the decor and furnishings of the house. The sun was shining through the windows and the extra brightness showed up the colours. Yes, she had been right before, they had similar tastes in colours and furnishings and flowers. Surely Jessica couldn't be like Ophelia. After all she was only a sort of cousin. Did it run in families?

"Coffee's nearly ready, how do you like it?"

"Milk please and one sugar."

"I've got these gorgeous crunchy biscuits too. I hope that you like them."

When Jessica left the room Caroline let out her breath which she had been holding. So far so good, she looked around the room noting again the cat statues and the large wooden cat asleep on the floor. Perhaps she could start a collection of Cumbrian statues? She was just about to get up and look at some photographs on a side table when Jessica bustled in with a tray, "Coffee and biscuits. Oh do take your coat off Caroline."

Still with a few misgivings, Caroline stood up and removed her coat.

"I'll hang it up for you."

"No. No. It's quite alright," Caroline quickly folded her coat into a neat pile and put it beside her against one of the arms. Jessica looked at her sharply as she did this but said nothing and got on with pouring the coffee. They chatted while they drank and found, as Caroline had suspected, that they really did seem to have a lot in common. She began to relax and enjoy the visit.

"Shall we go and see the kittens now?"

"I'd love to. How many have you got? What sort are they?"

"This litter are Abyssinians, ticked tabby in fact."

"Ticked tabby, what does that mean. I've never heard of them."

Jessica smiled, "I'll explain the markings when you see them. I don't know an awful lot about dog breeds so we're equal. Would you mind if I asked you to wash your hands first before you see them?"

"Of course I don't mind. It's the same with some dog breeders. It's very sensible."

Jessica took her through the neat and tidy kitchen and Caroline noticed how clean it was. Once out in the garden, Jessica opened the door to a well-built substantial shed. When they were both inside, she then opened a wire door into the main part of the shed, "Would you take your shoes off here please."

After they had both removed their shoes, they entered the large, warm room where they were immediately greeted by a beautiful long-haired cat who brushed against Jessica's legs making little mewing noises.

"This is Elizabeth. Isn't she lovely and these are her kittens." Five bright pairs of eyes surveyed them critically and, as one began to stretch and rouse itself from sleep, Elizabeth ran back and started to make little noises in her throat.

"Is she talking to them?"

"Oh yes. She is a fantastic Mum."

Gradually all the kittens stretched and yawned, blinked once or twice, stood up and one by one came towards them.

Caroline knelt down, "May I stroke them?"

"Yes do. I like them to be socialised."

The next half an hour passed rapidly with Caroline stroking and talking 'kitten talk' to all the kittens and Elizabeth, who was more than proud to show off her children. She constantly purred and rubbed her sleek coat against Caroline's leg. Jessica just sat and watched, a smile on her face.

"How old are they Jessica?"

"Ten weeks now."

"Aren't any of them sold then?"

"They're all sold. Unlike puppies, most breeders don't let the kittens go until they are about three months old. Elizabeth isn't feeding them anymore but she just pops in now and again to see them."

"I think they're all absolutely beautiful. I'd love to see a litter of those long-haired ones you've got."

"My long-haired Persians. Yes, I'm sure that you would love them too they are utterly adorable as kittens, just a ball of fluff. I have just mated one of my girls, I'll show her to you when we go indoors. She is a brown seal point with a wonderfully loving nature and she has done well at the shows."

"You show them as well?"

"Yes, the cat show scene is quite like the dog show scene. Instead of the Kennel Club we have The Governing Council of the Cat Fancy, they are very keen to promote the well-being of cats generally. Our pedigree cats are registered with them and we have shows and Championship shows just like you do with the dogs. Have you ever been to a cat show?"

169

"No never. It's one of those things that, when I've read something or seen something about it on the TV, I've thought how interesting it would be to go and see them. I never had a cat as a child. My mother didn't like pets in the house."

"Oh, what a shame. Well, in that case, if I see a show on in your area I'll give you a ring and let you know details. You'd see all sorts of breeds of pedigree cats then."

"That would be marvellous, I'll look forward to that. Thank you so much Jessica."

"Look, I don't want to rush you Caroline but it's already gone one-o-clock and we haven't even had lunch."

"Good heavens. How time flies when you are enjoying yourself."

After a pleasant light lunch, Caroline drove home; she was feeling relaxed and happy. All her fears had been unfounded, Jessica was a sweet person, not a bit like Ophelia and she liked her very much. They hadn't even got around to talking about the Aromatherapy. Jessica had invited her up again to see the other kittens when they were born. She could see them when they were very tiny then and she could smell all the Aromatherapy oils too, something to look forward to. She frowned, that would be weeks away though.

CHAPTER TWENTY- SEVEN

Natalie picked up a card from the many on the shelves, it depicted a man swinging a golf club on a beautiful green under a blue sky. Paul would like it she thought, he had recently joined the local golf club; both she and Richard, her first husband, had played golf there when he had been fit and well. Now, she and Paul would soon be able to play a round or two. She was looking forward to the pleasure very much; she smiled as she gave the money to the man behind the counter. It would soon be Autumn again, how the summer was flying by she thought as she made her way back to the car. It had been a blissful summer, one she would never forget. Paul had been so attentive and loving, introducing her to all the various doggy acquaintances in the countries they had visited, taking her for meals, visiting interesting museums and churches, explaining their histories and the various architectural features, he was so knowledgeable and she enjoyed every minute. Their nights together had been romantic and often quite passionate, he was a very considerate lover. A smile lit her face as she got into the car, marrying Paul had been the best thing that she had done for years, even better than buying Jamie from Fiona. Some of the happiness faded from her face at the thought of Fiona, she just had a feeling that all was not well at the kennels, although Fiona always shrugged the question aside if she asked if all was OK, she nevertheless, looked quite stressed sometimes and preoccupied. Surely it couldn't be that their marriage was going wrong again! Something else that she had noticed was that Paul seemed unwilling to talk about Fiona and Simon if she brought them up in conversation. He would shrug his shoulders and say that it was really nothing to do with them and that she would do well to leave things alone. That wasn't like Paul, he was usually such a kind and caring man.

The recipient of all this concern was, at that moment, up in the woods tending to Sally's grave. Fiona often walked up to the woods and 'had a word or two' with Sally; in the quiet dampness of the wood, with only the sound of the wind rustling the leaves, she was able to assemble her thoughts and sometimes find solutions to small problems.

"As I've told you before Sally, Simon thinks that all these things are down to Paul. I've always said that I didn't think that they were but now, well, I'm not so sure. This persecution has been going on for months now. Last week it was the dog food order, when it didn't arrive, I phoned up the firm to be told that we had cancelled our order as we were selling the business! We certainly haven't been doing well at the shows right through this summer. Neither of us have received any invitations to judge, the studs have dropped off, even for Saxon. One or two of our regular boarders have not come this year; poor Simon is very worried, he tries to hide it from me but I know." She finished cutting the dead heads from the flowers on Sally's grave and stood up, "Time to go now Sally, sorry if I've been a misery," she gently touched the earth on the little grave.

The following afternoon, Natalie arrived at the kennels, to find Fiona in tears.

"Now Fiona enough is enough, you must tell me what is the matter and don't fob me off this time. I know that there is something not quite right. Is it Simon?"

Fiona wiped her tears away with a tissue and smiled weakly, "Oh Natalie, thank you for being concerned but, no it's not Simon. The business is going through a rough patch at the moment that's all."

"Well, that's good. I mean, that's good that it isn't Simon. All businesses go through rough patches though Fiona. Perhaps Paul could help. I'll ask him shall I?"

"Er, no, I don't think it's the kind of thing that Paul could help with."

"Ah, I wouldn't be too sure Fiona. Do you know, he constantly amazes me with the depth of his knowledge about all sorts of things and, don't forget, in his line of work, business is a big factor."

"Yes, I'm sure, in fact I know that he is very good at his job. Tell me Natalie, does he ever talk about me or Simon?"

"What an odd question, we often talk about you, you are our friends. He always asks me what you've been doing when I tell him that I've come round here to see you."

Fiona, on hearing this, regretted having said anything to Natalie. If Paul was behind all this, she didn't want him to know that it was upsetting her.

"Don't take any notice of me Natalie, I haven't been sleeping too well lately, it must be my age."

"Nonsense. Look, I've just had an idea Fiona, it's Paul's birthday in two days and I was going to take him out for a meal but, if you aren't doing anything, why don't you both come to dinner. It's ages and ages since we had a meal together." .

It was time to think on her feet. Fiona knew that, knowing how Simon was feeling at the moment, he would not be the best person to sit at a table with Paul, "Natalie, what a lovely idea, just let me look at the calendar......... What a pity! We have a stud booked for Saxon that evening because the people couldn't come during the day. I'm so, so sorry. Perhaps we could arrange it for a bit later on.... When the boarders die down a bit. We're quite busy at the moment."

"I'm so disappointed I would really have enjoyed that, but I do understand," she got up to go, "You would tell me Fiona if there was anything really wrong. I feel that I owe all my present happiness to you and Simon and I'm so grateful."

Fiona watched her retreating figure and sighed, she could destroy all that happiness with just a few words. She turned and went back into the kitchen. Damn Paul Aston.

Telling Simon of Natalie's invitation as they ate dinner that evening she again questioned whether Paul could be responsible for all the trouble.

"Fee, with this last couple of things, that anonymous letter to my boss and now, two suppliers being told that we are packing up the business, yes, I'm bloody well certain it's that lying bugger."

"But why Simon. Why?"

"It's got to be someone who has been in the business long enough to know most of the wrinkles and, God knows he does, and the reason? Jealousy perhaps?"

"No, not jealousy, he's got everything, lovely wife, enormous old house, money, he's just going up and up in the KC world, why should he be jealous of us?"

"God knows what it is then. I'm certain of one thing and that is that it is him. Who else knows so much about our affairs, where we buy our food etc. Who else but him has so much influence in the dog world to stop our winning and stop our judging appointments. Who else! Answer me that!"

Fiona remembered what Natalie had said about Paul always questioning her when she had been over to see them. It was something she would keep to herself for a while because, she decided, it was something that she herself would have to investigate. Simon was getting so angry about it.

"So I take it that you don't want to go to Paul's birthday dinner?"

"What! I hope it bloody well chokes him."

Fiona smiled, "It's as well that I refused then isn't it."

Simon looked up at her and grinned.

Dennis was selecting blooms for the local Annual Flower Show. The greenhouse was warm and colourful, he shook his head, "And to think that I didn't want to come here." He found that talking to the plants did seem to improve them. Once, when Caroline had walked into the greenhouse and heard him talking to the plants, she had poured scorn on his theory, "Dennis, for goodness' sake, they can't hear you or understand what you are saying."

"Don't you be too sure. Prince Charles says that flowers respond to talking and I for one, absolutely agree with him."

He continued along the row of dahlias, "Caroline seems to be a wee bit happier now that she has made a friend of this Jessica women, she's up there again today. It looks as if we shall be having a kitten before long though Lord knows how it's going to get on with the dogs. I shall have to make sure that it doesn't come up here scratching around too, can't have you beauties damaged." Finishing labelling the blooms that he would be picking for the show, he moved further along the greenhouse to the tomatoes, he had grown several varieties and they were ripening well; he selected one or two for lunch. He had suggested to Caroline that he sold them at the front of the house but she had vetoed the idea saying that it was common. He didn't know where she got these ideas from, her mother had been a bit like that come to think of it, perhaps she'd thought that he was common! On the other hand, it could be that Ophelia dame. Not that she went to as many shows with her now, in fact she didn't seem to be quite as keen on showing as she had been. She was going to a show with Ophelia this coming weekend, he remembered because it was the day of the flower show and he had wanted her to come and meet his friends. All his pals from the gardening club would be there and several of the pub regulars had said that they would come, pity she wouldn't be there. Going out of the greenhouse into the garden, he called the dogs who ran up to him tails wagging, "You lot had better go back into your kennel just in case your Mum appears. She'd have my guts for garters letting you get dirty. I'd better clean your feet up."

The phone was ringing as he entered the house and he hurried to pick it up, "Is that Dennis. It's Ophelia Hammond-James, will you tell Caroline that I shall pick her up at 6 am. As we shall be second in the ring and, therefore, later finishing, I propose that we spend the night in a hotel. It's too far to drive back in the dark so tell her to bring an overnight bag will you."

"Er. Yes, I'll tell her when she comes in."

"Right, that's 6 am on Saturday. Bye."

The phone went dead before Dennis could reply and his goodbye just floated away in the air as he replaced the receiver. He just couldn't see what Caroline saw in that woman, she was so rude and bossy. Later that evening, as they were having a cup of coffee and Caroline was telling him all about the latest kittens and how she couldn't make up her mind which one to have because they were all gorgeous, Dennis remembered the phone call and informed Caroline of the arrangements for Saturday. He was very surprised to see how she reacted, she suddenly went quite pale and looked almost frightened.

"Blimey, what's wrong?"

"Nothing, why?"

"Why? you should see your face."

"Well, you surprised me, I was thinking about something else and, for a moment, I'd forgotten about the show. That's all."

Dennis could have had no concept of what he had just said. Staying the night! An overnight bag! She knew what that meant, she had had a couple of firsts at Champ shows with Saffron this summer, Ophelia had behaved herself up till now but she felt sure that it was now pay back time. Her stomach turned over at the thought. She'd have to refuse, say she felt ill or something. I know she thought, I shall say that I have got to go to the flower show, Dennis insists that I go. Yes, that was a good excuse. She'd do it now and get it over with.

"I must spend a penny Dennis," she hastily got up and left the room. If she used the phone upstairs Dennis wouldn't be able to hear what she said. Hurrying upstairs and shutting the bedroom door, she composed herself and then picked up the phone and dialled Ophelia's number.

Dennis, who was going into the kitchen with the coffee cups heard the phone in the hall 'ting' and picked it up but before he could say anything he heard Caroline's voice, "Hello Ophelia, it's Caroline, thank you for your message but, unfortunately, I shan't be able to come on Saturday Dennis insists that I go to his flower show."

Not an eavesdropper by nature, Dennis had been putting the phone down when he had heard his name mentioned. Now intrigued he listened on.

"It's his first flower show you see and it's very important that I go. I'm so sorry."

"Not as sorry as you'll be if you don't come. I've set this show up for you, you stupid woman. I'm telling you now that, if you don't come on Saturday, you can forget dog showing for the rest of your life because I'll see that you never do anything again ever. Got it. I'll see you at 6 am."

Dennis put the phone down gently and hurried into the kitchen, what the devil was that all about. Several minutes elapsed before Caroline came downstairs again. She found Dennis in the sitting-room reading the paper. Noticing how pale and strained she still looked, he smiled at her as she sat down in her armchair, "Just looking to see if there is something good on the television."

CHAPTER TWENTY- EIGHT

"Here's your sandwiches," Dennis came into the hallway carrying a plastic box. Looking up he saw that Caroline was just coming down the stairs with a small suitcase. She looked pale and tired, he knew that she hadn't slept very well because she had woken him a couple of times with her twisting and turning.

"Have you got everything?"

"Yes, I think so, just got to get the dog and....."

"That's the car now," he looked at her face, "are you sure that you ought to go? You look as if you're coming down with something."
Ophelia sounded the horn outside.

"Yes, it's my big chance today, what I've been waiting for; I must go. Put this in the car for me and I'll get the dog."
Dennis watched as she put the dog into the back of Ophelia's car and got into the passenger seat. Ophelia didn't get out to help her.

"Have a good day. Bye."

By the time that Caroline remembered to wish Dennis good luck and had wound the window down, her, "You have a good day too," disappeared into the early morning breeze.
Dennis looked up at the sky, smiled and turned towards the house. Now, all he had to do this morning was to tidy up the kitchen, feed and walk the dogs and then he could get on with his preparations for the show. He had to carefully select, cut and wrap each bloom and stand them in a big bucket of cold water. An hour later with all his chores done and with excitement building in him, he looked up at the blue sky; the weather forecasters had said that it would be a fine Autumn day and it looked as if they were right for once. Pity Caroline had decided to go to the dog show instead, he'd have liked her to come to his first show. He'd have liked to introduce her to the other members of his gardening club. Some of the pub regulars had also promised to turn up; they could have had a nice day. He carefully loaded his blooms into the car making sure that the buckets were firmly held, then he laid some of his choice vegetables on the floor, all well wrapped, he stood back to admire the picture they made, all his own work. Nodding and smiling, he went to lock up the house.

Caroline sat hunched into the jacket of her new, blue trouser suit. She was thinking about Jessica and how, when she had last gone up there, they had picked out a kitten together for Caroline. Jessica was such a sweet person, so easy to get on with and so like herself. She was just wondering when she could next go up there and if she might be able to show the kitten when her thoughts were interrupted, "Well, what do you think?"

"Pardon."

"I knew you weren't listening. What the devil were you thinking about?"

"Er... I was thinking of Dennis. It's his flower show today and he wanted me to go with him."

"A flower show! Today! This show is more important to you than that. I've had to do a lot of talking and organising to get this show for you."

"Why have you?"

"Why, for God's sake. Why? Because it's all set up for you to get the Res CC today with that bitch. That's why!"

Caroline sat in silence for a moment while she digested this bit of information, "Set up?"

"Yes, set up. How else do you think that you'd get one?"

"I don't understand, I thought that my bitch was good. I thought that you'd just point that out to the judge."

"Good God, give me strength. You know how the system works, you know about all the various cliques, heavens there's enough of them. If the boys can have their clique and help each other, so can the girls. The straights do it all the time so why can't we."

"Straights? I don't know what you mean, what's any of that to do with dog showing?"

"Heaven preserve us, you really don't know do you. How long have you been in dogs?"

"A long time, about eight years now."

"And how many Champ shows have you attended?"

"Only one some years ago, it was my first dog. Everyone told me he wasn't very good and to stick to Open shows, so I did. Couldn't really afford them anyway."

"I suppose that's some excuse. What an innocent you are, I can see I've got a lot of work to do on you. It's rather quaint in a way. Well, to win CCs you need something, power in high places is the best, then money, gifts, the bigger the better too, a holiday home, furniture, cars, crates of expensive booze, the list is endless. Free puppies and studs is another one of course. There are other ways too like doing down the opposition in any number of underhand ways. It's quite a sport in itself."

"But surely a good dog, a really good dog will win eventually."

"God, haven't you seen some of the lousy specimens that win at Champ shows? No, of course you haven't so you've never wondered why."

"But, I..."

"But you have only one thing to do and that is to love me. That isn't hard is it?"

"But why me? I'm not a......."

"Oh yes you are my girl. You know the old saying, takes one to know one; well, I spotted you a mile off. It's a small price to pay and you'll enjoy yourself into the bargain. With a bit of time I could make your bitch up into a Champion, guaranteed. Now, do you understand?"

"Yes, I see it all now."

"Good, I've booked us into a very comfortable small hotel that I know of, they've got a good chef as well. We'll have a lovely time."

Caroline settled further into her seat trying to make herself as small as possible. She realised that this must all be true although she didn't want to believe it. Little things that she had overheard and seen in the past, little things that had happened at Open shows when obviously the best dog had not won, all began to float into her mind. She thought of the couple of Champ shows she had recently attended, had all this been going on and she just hadn't noticed! Everyone seemed nice and normal, did they too not know about all this! She had seen dogs win who she thought weren't very good but had put it all down to bad judging, perhaps she had been wrong. But now, now today, she had to concentrate on getting through today and tonight! It truly was pay back time but not in money! Looking paler than ever, she sank even further into her seat.

The AA signs for the show began to appear and they passed several cars with stickers of their particular breed displayed on the side window and with dogs in the back, all making their way to the show. They soon joined a queue of hopeful exhibitors all waiting to get into the showground, gradually the enormous marquees came into view, standing out so white against the green grass and the buzz of excitement that always seemed to accompany Champ shows began to build. Caroline looked at the various occupants of the other cars as they drove along to a car space. Did they know all this? If so, why did they come? Why did they look so happy? Could Ophelia be lying to her just to get her into bed again? The thought was so worrying that she sat up and undid her seat belt ready to get out. Together and in silence they unloaded the car, put the dogs in their cages and Caroline pulled the trolley along the car park towards the entrance to the show. Ophelia waved and smiled at one or two show officials and then told Caroline to take the dogs to their respective benches and settle them in as she had one or two people she needed to speak to first. Caroline watched her retreating figure as she made her way towards the judges' tent. How could she have thought that she was such a nice, important person?

"Hello Caroline. Are you all right?"
Fiona was walking towards her, a look of concern on her face.
"Yes thank you."
"Well, you don't look it. You are as pale as a ghost."
"I've got a bit of a headache that's all."
"I think I've got some Aspirin in my bag. Would you like a couple?"
"Thanks all the same but I've got some in my bag."
"Well, good luck today."
Caroline snapped at her, "Why!"
Fiona, quite taken aback, looked at Caroline again, her face was quite pasty and she looked so strained, "No reason, just good luck."
"Right then, thank you and good luck to you."
Fiona walked away quite puzzled by Caroline's aggressive attitude. Caroline watched her retreating back. Did she and Simon do these things with other people in order to win? They had made up a couple of champions hadn't they, what did they do for them. She shook her head, she had thought that they were nice people, Fiona had been a librarian! What about Paul Aston and Natalie? Now they were really nice people. They wouldn't be party to any of the things that Ophelia had mentioned. No, they wouldn't. Ophelia must be exaggerating everything just to get her into bed. Oh God. Tonight. She scrambled

about in her handbag for the Aspirins. Damn there weren't any. She had to buy some things from the various stalls, did any of them sell Aspirin? She'd go now and see.

As she wandered amongst the colourful stalls her heart didn't seem to be in it. Normally, she couldn't wait to get to them. They had some lovely things to buy for the dogs, "Hello Caroline, my you look smart today. Are you OK you look a bit pale?"
She smiled at a fellow Cumbrian exhibitor, "Yes, I'm fine, just got a bit of a headache that's all. Looking for some Aspirin."
   "They'll have some at the First Aid tent I expect."
   "Oh yes. I'll go there, thanks."
As she walked along, she felt quite sick with the pain in her head. Perhaps she ought to eat something, she'd only had a bit of toast early this morning. She passed the refreshment tent. She felt quite shivery too, perhaps a small brandy would warm her up. Then she could get the Aspirin. As she drank the brandy, she could feel it warming her stomach. Why had she never thought of doing this before, it was well known as a stimulant, perhaps if she had another one, it might even take the headache away; then if she had the Aspirins and something to eat she'd be OK to show Saffron. She bought another small brandy, after all, brandy was medicinal wasn't it and it certainly seemed to be doing her good. Feeling much better and more confident, she obtained two Aspirin from the First Aid tent and took them. She didn't feel like eating yet so just sat on her bench and cuddled Saffron contemplating the evening. It was well into the afternoon before Saffron's class was due in the ring and, in the meantime, Caroline was feeling a bit cold and shivery again. Ophelia had popped over and spoken to her for a couple of minutes but only to tell her that she had got the Reserve CC with her dog and to ask why she hadn't been watching. Caroline said that she had felt too cold to come outside. She got out the sandwiches that Dennis had made for her, tinned salmon, one of her favourites. She took one bite and then put them back in the box, she just didn't feel hungry. Did she have time now to pop over to the tent for a small brandy to warm her up and settle her stomach before she went into the ring? Perhaps she should have a large one because the other two had certainly helped to settle her stomach before.

As Caroline walked into the ring to meet her fate her head was held high, her cheeks were very rosy and she was smiling. Completely relaxed, she stood Saffron beautifully and, when the judge smiled at her and asked her to walk her dog, she walked around the ring and the dog, not feeling any tension from her, walked beside her at a good pace. When the judge asked her to do it again please, she smiled so sweetly at her and sailed around the ring again. The judge then called her out into first place, she nodded at the crowd and walked out, still smiling, to the centre of the ring and stood Saffron beautifully. When the steward handed her the card, she curtsied to her and then to the ringsiders, who cheered her to a man. After the judge had written her critique Caroline curtsied to her, thanked her and walked out of the ring head still high, cheeks still rosy red and still smiling. She was met by Fiona, "Caroline, are you all right. I mean would you like me to take her in for you for the challenge?"

"No, I'm abso-blooming-lutely fantastic. I shall sow... I sall... show my own dog thank you."

Fiona could smell the fumes on her breath, she didn't know that Caroline drank, "Did you have your Aspirin?"

"Yes thank you I did, got them from the... the... tent place over there. My headache has com.... completely gone thank you and thank you for asking Fiona. Thank you, I app... appreshiate that. Thank you."

Fiona now knew that Caroline Amery was completely drunk, "Please let me take Saffron in for the challenge. I think it would be best Caroline."

Caroline put a finger up to her nose and tapped it and, at the same time, she winked at Fiona, "Aaah, you're wrong. I must take her in you see. I must. It must be me, only me d'you see."

"Well, if you're sure."

Giggling, Caroline replied, "I'm sure all right I'm abso..lute...ly sure. It must be me," she giggled again and wandered off with the dog.

Simon won the Open class with their bitch, as Ophelia had arranged, so Simon and Caroline walked into the ring together. There were six unbeaten bitches in all. Having been warned by Fiona about the state that Caroline was in,, he gave her as wide a berth as possible. It didn't stop her calling out to him across the ring, "Good luck Simon. Good luck," she then wished the other exhibitors in the ring, good luck.

Simon did not reply but concentrated on showing his bitch. Caroline then turned to the ringside crowd which had swollen in numbers with the promise of a bit of fun, "I got this lovely bitch from this man over there. I paid him for it with money you know. My Aunt Ellen..." The judge very quickly made her decision and awarded Simon the CC and Caroline the Res CC. Caroline beamed at the judge and winked as she handed her the card, Caroline then did a deep curtsy before shaking the judge's hand vigorously, then she insisted on shaking the stewards' hand and t turning to Simon, shook his hand, "I'm so pleased for you Simon. Where are sleeping you tonight?" Simon, after a couple of seconds silence, burst out laughing but, urged by the steward, who had been told in no uncertain terms to get that bloody woman out of the ring, asked Simon to please do his lap of honour. Simon got a round of clapping as he ran around the ring but Caroline, still, rosy, still smiling and blowing kisses at the crowd, took her turn around the ring to tumultuous applause from the delighted ringsiders.

This time as she left the ring a woman whom she did not know grabbed her by the arm, "Don't do that you are hurting me."

"I've been told to bring you back safely to the bench. Come on," as she stumbled along behind the unknown woman, people were patting her on the back and saying, "Well done."

"Stop pulling me. People want to talk to me. Who told you to pull me?"

"Ophelia. And am I glad not to be in your shoes. She's furious with you."

"Why. I won didn't I?"

"Come on," she continued to drag the unwilling Caroline towards the Cumbrian benches.

As they neared them, Caroline saw Ophelia and her face creased into a big smile, "Hello Ophelia, look. I got it. Just as you said I......"

"Shut up. You're drunk," shouted Ophelia drowning out Caroline's voice, "Now give me the dog and go with Sue to the refreshment tent for some black coffee."

"I don't like my coffee black."

"Too bad. Now go," she yanked the lead and the card from Caroline's hand and pushed her towards the other woman.

Once inside the refreshment tent, Caroline refused to drink the coffee so Sue left her there. Caroline's headache was coming back with a vengeance as she made her rather slow way back to her bench; there she found all her stuff packed up and a note pinned to the bench.
YOU CAN MAKE YOUR OWN WAY HOME. GOODBYE. O.

For a moment Caroline stood there looking intently at the note. She had to read it several times before the full implication of it hit her; she then burst into tears. Going in search of Caroline, Fiona found her sitting on her bench crying, her face bright red, her nose running and tears rolling down her cheeks, "Whatever is the matter Caroline?"

"Ophelia has gone and left me here."

"What! I'm so sorry. Look, we can perhaps take you home, or at least well on the way and you could get a taxi. Don't upset yourself."

"Upset, I'm not upset, I'm pleased, so pleased," and she started giggling as she tried to stand up.

CHAPTER TWENTY- NINE

Caroline opened her eyes and shut them again quickly. She'd been having such an odd dream, she had dreamed that she had been making very passionate love to...... She opened her eyes again and, in panic, looked around the room and sighed with relief as she saw her own dressing table and the pretty curtains at the window. Thank goodness, it was her own bedroom not an hotel room. She looked across the bed to the other pillow and saw an indentation, dear old Dennis, he always slept with his pillow slightly sideways. She closed her eyes and sighed, thank heavens it had all been a dream after all, she hadn't slept with Ophelia again and she hadn't done all those awful things. Gradually the events of the previous day returned to her. Ophelia had been cross with her in the car, yes, that was right, she'd had a headache, she remembered that and she had felt cold, yes, she'd been shivering before she had gone into the ring and had had a brandy to warm her up. How had she done? Did she get the Reserve CC? She was trying to remember when the bedroom door opened quietly and Dennis came into the room.

"Oh you're awake then." She thought that he was looking at her rather oddly, "Yes, I'm awake. Why?"
Dennis' face blushed a deep red as he looked across the room at the window, "Nothing, I thought perhaps you weren't yourself or something."
Did he know! Had Ophelia spoken to him? "Dennis! Oh, my head hurts, don't make me shout, please. What do you mean 'or something'?"
Even redder if that was possible Dennis mumbled, "Well, you weren't yourself last night were you. I mean I was so surprised when you... I mean, you were so different weren't you."

"Dennis, I don't know what you are talking about. Would you be a dear and get me a cup of tea please. I'm so thirsty."

"Oh, yes," Dennis hastily disappeared and she heard him going downstairs. She sat up. Her head hurt so much, she put her hands to her head and... she was naked! She looked down at her breasts and blushed. In the dream she had been...oh no, she put her hands to her face. Dennis appeared with a cup of tea in his hand, she hastily grabbed the sheet and covered her breasts. He stood by the bed and, without looking at her said, "You didn't do that last night did you."

There was silence in the room as Caroline sipped her tea and desperately tried to remember what had happened last night, if only her head didn't hurt so much. She couldn't even remember coming home except, without looking at Dennis she said, "Did Fiona and Simon bring me home?"

"Yes."

"I think I can vaguely remember them saying that they would take me home because..." Suddenly she remembered Ophelia shouting at her, she remembered getting the Res. CC and everyone laughing and smiling and being so pleased for her and then.... She couldn't clearly remember anything else!

"Why did they bring me home?"

Dennis said nothing for a minute or two but then, thrusting his hands into his trouser pockets and looking out of the window, he said, "Because you were dead drunk."

"Drunk! Dennis, you know I don't drink. I've never been drunk."

"Well, you were drunk last night, plastered in fact. I suppose that's why you.... Did all those things."

"For goodness sake Dennis. What are you mumbling about? What things! Dennis will you look at me please."

He looked at her briefly then looked back at the garden, "You honestly don't remember what you did?"

"At this moment, no, so tell me please so that we can stop all this talking," she put a hand to her head and closed her eyes.

Dennis, still looking out at the garden said, "Well, I put you to bed and..."

"What, like this?" Caroline opened her eyes and dropped the sheets to reveal her breasts and then quickly pulled them up again.

"No, not like.... that. I put your blue nightie on you and tucked you in. It took me a while because you kept on wanting to kiss me. Anyway, when I came to bed, you were sound asleep and snoring."

"Snoring! I never snore."

"Well, you were snoring last night! As I was saying, I came to bed and I was just going to sleep when you suddenly woke up, put your arms around me, started kissing my neck and undoing the buttons on my pyjamas. You th..."

"I did no such thing."

Suddenly Dennis turned around to face her, " Yes you did. I tried to stop you but you took off your nightie and started to pull my pyjama trousers off. You danced round the room naked waving yourself at me and turning all the lights on...."

"Waving myself at you?"

"Yes, and then you flung yourself on top of me and started to...." Dennis looked embarrassed, " you grabbed my.... and then you started to... Oh my God. You just did things that... you were all over me. I tried to stop you but, you kept kissing my.... You just kept on until..... Well you know what happened then. I mean, I didn't mind but, well, we don't, we haven't, it's been ages since we did anything, we've never done that sort of... well, then, you started all over again waving and twisting yourself on top of me... you wanted me to do things to you that.... well I mean.... Caroline! For God's sake, I can't even say the words!"

Dennis sat down on the bed and put his head in his hands, "I didn't know that you knew such things. How could you know such things. I mean, are you having an affair with someone? Is that how you know?"

Caroline had been listening to Dennis with ever mounting horror. Her dream, it was all true then! Oh my God, had she really done all those things in her dream to Dennis! She hid her face in her hands and in a muffled voice said, "Dennis, would you mind leaving the room so that I might shower and dress please."

"Leave the room, you don't have to keep up this modesty thing any more. There's not much I don't know about you after last night and to think that all these years you've made me turn my back when you've undressed! We always made love in the dark too!"

Caroline shrivelled inside, visions of the dream kept appearing in her mind, her head hurt and she couldn't cope with them.

"Please Dennis, please go and let me have a shower."

Dennis snorted and left the room, Caroline got out of the bed, she felt tired and stiff as if she had been doing a lot of exercise and.... it was true, Dennis had made love to her... she hurried into the shower. As the hot water cascaded over her, more pictures of last night's lovemaking came unasked into her mind and she groaned.

When she came down later, Dennis was nowhere to be seen. She knew where he would be, in his greenhouse. She had forgotten to ask

187

him how he got on at the flower show, she must ask him now even though she didn't want to face him at the moment. She was crossing the hall when the phone rang, "Hello Caroline. It's Fiona. How are you?"

"I'm very well now thank you. Thank you for bringing me home yesterday. I was not at all well."

Fiona laughed, "You can say that again. Anyway, congrats once again on getting your first Res CC. It was a Simfell double wasn't it. CC and Res CC in bitches!"

As she listened to Fiona's voice, the rest of the events of yesterday slotted into place in her mind. Caroline started to cry.

"Are you crying Caroline. What's the matter. Can I help?"

"No, I'm all right really I am. Just a bit tired that's all. Congratulations to you too."

"Thank you. We just wanted to know that you were OK. See you at a show soon I expect. Must go now, masses of work to do. Bye."

"Bye." Caroline put the phone down and sighed. What a fool she had made of herself. No wonder people had been laughing. She could never show her face in the ring again! She was just going out of the kitchen door when the phone rang again. As she picked up the phone she could hear Ophelia's voice shouting at her, "How dare you humiliate me like that, you stupid little nobody. I should have known better. You petty, common, hopeless little cretin. Don't you ever show your face here again or at any other show for that matter. I'll see that you never win anything again with that bitch. You're finished in dogs. Do you hear me finished. I'll arrange it so that you never ever win and never ever judge and nobody will speak to you. I'll see that no-one ever buys anything that you might breed from that bitch. Do you hear me you apology for a woman. You're finished." The phone was slammed down and Caroline stood in the hall holding the receiver, too stunned to return it to its' cradle. She couldn't believe such nastiness, such venom. This was dog showing, a hobby, not world politics. Yes, she'd got drunk but, she hadn't hurt Ophelia, she hadn't even seen her in the afternoon. Of course, in a way, I suppose that she had got the Res CC and hadn't slept with her but... Caroline sighed, her head hurt again, she couldn't think about that any more. She went towards the kitchen door just as Dennis was coming down the garden, "Dennis, I'm so sorry, I didn't ask you how you got on yesterday."

Dennis looked at her for a brief moment, "Since you have remembered to ask, I got a third with my dahlias and a second with my leeks."

"That's good isn't it. That was nice wasn't it?"

"I've fed the dogs and they've had a run round the garden."

"Thank you Dennis," they stood there neither knowing what else to say.

"Would you like a cup of coffee?"

"Had one."

"Oh."

An awkward silence followed and after a few seconds, Caroline went back indoors. What had she done! Dennis couldn't bear to look at her. What should she do tonight? Should she make up another bed? She opened the kitchen door again; Dennis was still standing there, "Dennis, I don't know what to do. I mean, do you want me to sleep with you tonight? Or would you rather I made up a bed in one of the other rooms."

He stood silently contemplating this question for several minutes before he said, "Yes, I think that's best for now don't you, unless you want to go to the bloke who taught you all those tricks? You might learn some more!" He turned on his heel and went back up the garden towards the greenhouse.

Shocked, Caroline went upstairs, "What have I done!" she said to herself. "I wished I'd never started dog showing. I wish we'd never come up here. I wish I'd not met Ophelia. I wish....," she burst into tears again, she couldn't stay here tonight. She'd go to a B&B or something she'd...

The phone rang and she stared in panic, it must be Ophelia again and she just couldn't bear it. She had just finished her packing when, once again, the phone rang, she grabbed it, "Hello, who's that?" Caroline was overjoyed to hear Jessica's voice.

"Oh Jessica!" Caroline burst into tears afresh at the sound of her friendly voice.

"Whatever is the matter?"

"Everything, just everything."

"Now calm down and tell me all about it."

After a somewhat garbled and edited report on the happenings of yesterday, leaving out how drunk she was and completely leaving out her torrid night with her husband, Caroline finished with how terribly upset she felt. Jessica promptly invited her to come up ending with, "You could stay the night and take your kitten home the next day if you like."

"Oh, you're so kind Jessica, that would be lovely."

That evening, when she told Dennis of her plan he remarked, "Oh yes. I get the picture now, I'm beginning to think that this Jessica wears trousers and shaves."

"Dennis, you're wrong. Honestly, she is just a friend, a nice person. Look, come with me if you like, you can talk to her, see the cats. I'm sure that she wouldn't mind."

"No, you go, it gives both of us a breathing space. I just can't get my head round this yet Caroline. No, you go and I'll see you Tuesday."

Packing the small suitcase once again Caroline looked at the rumpled bed and colour rushed into her face. Stripping the bed and hurrying to the airing cupboard she pulled out clean sheets and clean pillowslips. She opened all the windows in the bedroom and then made up the bed again.

CHAPTER THIRTY

"Paul my dear, I'm terribly concerned for Fiona and Simon. I was over there yesterday and things don't seem to be improving for them at all, not at home or at the shows."

Paul put down the piece of toast and marmalade, which he was eating and looked across the breakfast table at Natalie, "I didn't know that you had been to see them."

"Well, I had to take one or two things to the cleaners and I thought that, as I was passing, I'd just pop in for a few minutes. I'm glad I did because Fiona seemed to be awfully low."

"Did she now, and why was that?"

"Oh, you know, things in general. I've told you about various problems all this year, don't you remember, the welfare people coming and the cancellations etc."

"Now you mention it, I remember you saying something about not having so many boarders."

"Well yes and it still hasn't picked up. People still think that they have moved away. Remember I told you all about it at the time, the estate agents came to view the cottage. Announcements were made in the local papers and in the dog papers that they were closing down. The feed people insisted that they pay cash each time because a rumour had gone round that they were nearly bankrupt. What ever is going on Paul? Do you think that you could look into it and perhaps help them?"

"I'll certainly look into it if you would like me to but I'm not sure that I would be able to help. These sorts of things have, regrettably, happened before in the world of dogs. I, and possibly the KC are completely unable to do anything to bring the perpetrators to book. There are some very competitive people out there my dear who will stop at nothing to win."

"How terrible. I had no idea; but who would want to do this to Fiona and Simon? They are such nice people and always willing to help."

"Natalie, there are things that people do that you could have no conception of. Believe me, it's best to stay out of it. It's not all bad is it. They did get a CC this year with that young bitch."

"Yes that's true but, ever since then, so Fiona was telling me the other day, she has been unplaced. How can that be?"

191

"Have you thought my dear that one judge didn't know what they were doing and the other judges did? Even some championship show judges really don't know how to judge."

"Well, what about their stud dogs not being used, what about the phone calls that they get and no-one speaks, what about someone actually writing to Simon's boss at work and saying that he was responsible for Viv's suicide! Paul, this is serious. Please see if you can find anything out. You know so many people on the KC and on the various committees. Surely someone would be able to help. Fiona is convinced that it is a doggy person behind it."

Simon put the phone down firmly, "Bloody madman."

"Not another one."

"Yeah, my fault, I forgot to put the answerphone on this morning."

"I feel besieged, under threat. I'm so glad that we're going out to that Open show today with the Glencastles. Thank goodness all this nastiness doesn't seem to have filtered through there."

"Give it time; Paul, or whoever this bastard is, is bloody thorough."

"Please don't say that, I think that I'm just about at the end of my tether."

Simon looked at her white, strained face, "Come on love," he put his arms around her and kissed her cheek and then her neck, "you know the saying."

"Yes I know, I know, but I'm afraid it's getting awfully hard to stay positive. Every way I turn something is going wrong."

Simon hugged her close to him and kissed her hair, "Um, you smell nice. Are you ready?"

As they entered the building where the show was being held, the usual noise and bustle assailed them and Fiona's spirits lifted a little.

"That's it Fee head up and smile."

It always gave her such a buzz seeing all the different breeds. She had always wanted to buy a puppy from each breed and watch them grow and develop. It was all so interesting. Her thoughts were interrupted by a familiar voice, "Hello you two, long time no see. How are you?"

"Joan! Lovely to see you. Have you brought your Cumbrians today?"

"No, actually, I'm stewarding for someone."

"Who?"

"Well, actually it's the best in show judge, you know Anthony Jackson."

She had named a very up and coming all round judge who was very well in with the KC, and who was in frequent demand to judge shows. Simon looked at her smiling face and nodded. She had got onto several committees in the past couple of years and now this! Could he scent a little affaire in the offing? Our Joan was certainly out to improve her standing, it's a wonder that she wants to be seen with us; perhaps it hasn't filtered through to her yet. He'd test his theory.

"Joan, you won't be needed yet then will you. Come and have a cup of coffee with us and we can catch up on all the gossip."

The smile briefly left her face, "What a lovely idea. I'd love to and we could have a good chat about old times, but I promised to see the Secretary about something. Must go now but perhaps later? It was so nice to see you both."

Simon watched her as she hurried away smiling and waving to other exhibitors, so it had filtered through.

"Nice to see a friendly face isn't it Simon."

"Um."

Looking through the catalogue, there were only a few Glencastles listed for the classes, "Simon, we should do well today. I don't know most of the exhibitors, they can only be hobby people."

"Yeah, well we'll see, I think I'll wander round and see who's here OK?"

The Glencastle classes weren't called into the ring for a couple of hours, Fiona and Simon had eaten their sandwiches, drunk all their coffee and were getting pretty fed up by the time the steward called for the Glencastles. Fiona was the first to go in. There were only two others in the ring. One was obviously a pet person. The dog would not stand or walk properly and was poorly presented, the other wasn't much better. Looking down at her dog she couldn't see how she wouldn't get the first prize. When she was pulled out third of three she couldn't believe it. She looked over to Simon standing beside the ring with their other dog. He was looking very serious and just shrugged his shoulders.

When Simon got similar treatment, she was furious, "Simon, we can't let her get away with judging so badly. It was ridiculous. I'm going to say something."

"Don't bother sweetheart, she'll only say something like, 'I preferred the other two' or ' he wasn't walking too well today'. You won't be able to pin her down. We've been blacked and that's all there is to it. Come on let's pack up and go."

They sat by the fire that evening discussing their future. It was becoming apparent that, whoever was doing this was not going to give up until they had finished them off. Simon carefully listed all the things that had happened and when but it still gave them no ideas as to who was doing it.

"You still think it's Paul don't you Simon, but why?"

"Yeah, I do. He is the only person I can think of who knows us well enough and who has the clout to make all these people do these things for him. You've got to remember that, when this has happened in the past to other people, they have never been able to prove anything because all the toadies are on small promises 'in the ring' or suchlike. People will do anything, say anything, to get on in the ring or get a promising youngster, or a judging appointment or whatever." They sat on for a while discussing the financial aspect for the forthcoming year and the social ramifications.

"So you don't think that we can hold our usual New Year party, Simon?"

"Oh yes, we will hold it I doubt it will be the usual success but we will hold it," he made a gesture with his hand, "and that to whoever's doing this."

"Do you think that we should give up showing then?"

"I hate to admit it but, unless we can smoke out who's doing it, yes; it's a waste of time and money to go on showing. The longer these things go on, the worse your name becomes."

"And the business?"

Simon shrugged his shoulders.

Fiona cuddled up to him, "Simon, you're really frightening me now, it's our whole future we are talking about, what can we do?"

They sat on talking as the fire died down and the shadows faded from the walls. Suddenly Fiona shivered, "I'm getting quite cold, come on Simon, I'll make us a drink and we can go to bed."

They lay cuddled up together in the dark so intertwined that she was not sure where she ended and Simon began. As long as she had

Simon, Paul or whoever it was couldn't totally win. He'd find a way through it somehow.

Some miles away, Natalie lay awake looking at the moonlight shining through a small chink in the curtains. Paul's regular breathing told her that he was sound asleep. He had made love to her this evening. It still gave her a thrill to be wanted by a man again, it made her feel womanly and gentle and warm. A tiny thought insisted on strolling into her mind; she tried to stop it, to block it out, but it persisted. It was that Paul always said the same things and did the same things in the same order when they made love. She frowned, how can I be so ungrateful, he has made me so happy. I'm never lonely now. He buys me flowers... another little unbidden thought strolled past.... they are always the same flowers, red roses. But roses are the flowers of love she argued with herself. Yes, said the little voice, but does he think of you when he buys them or is it just a regular order? Natalie turned over in the bed and screwed up her eyes, you ungrateful woman, think of something else, something different and you'll fall asleep. She placed an arm on Paul's broad shoulder; he was so nice and warm to cuddle up to. Fiona, yes, think about her plight, poor girl. What could she do to help her? Perhaps, if Paul couldn't help, she ought to phone Audrey and tell her about it. Yes, Audrey had had dealings with the KC for a lot longer than Paul, she might be able to find out who was doing this and why or, at the very least, tell the Philips what they could do to minimise the damage. After all, the KC are a monopoly, they are in sole charge of everything to do with dogs in this country. Show people pay them a lot of money one way or another for them to look after their interests. They would be horrified when they knew about this terrible situation.. Perhaps Audrey could have a word with the Chief Executive or the Chairman of the KC. Richard, her first husband had always said that, if you want to know something, go to the top. She turned the other way and plumped up her pillow, first thing tomorrow morning, I'll phone Audrey. Having made this decision, her mind relaxed and she fell asleep.

Paul had to go out early the next morning, he had a meeting with an important client so she was able to phone Audrey about nine-thirty, "Hello Audrey, how are you? Good, and Ian. Good. Oh yes, I'm fine thank you, yes, Paul is well, he's out seeing a client this morning. Now Audrey, have you a minute or two to spare, I want to tell you about something that is disturbing me."

She proceeded to tell Audrey all that had been happening to Fiona and Simon ending with, "so you see Audrey, I'm terribly worried for them and don't know how to help, they have both been so kind to me. I suddenly thought that, if anyone could help them it would be you. Could you make enquiries at the KC? Simon says that this sort of thing has happened before to people so the KC must have heard about it in the past. They may be able to help."

"My dear, I can tell that you are very concerned about this. Have you told Paul? What does he think?"

"Yes I have told him but ....well, he doesn't seem to be very interested."

"Ah. Well, perhaps they are exaggerating the situation a bit. Paul is very knowledgeable about show issues you know. I think that you should be guided by him."

"But, as I told you, it's not just show issues, it's their business as well... their livelihood. They may have to shut down or sell up!"

"In that case, the KC couldn't interfere. They only deal with matters appertaining to shows etc."

"But Audrey, I told you that they're not winning any more and....."

"Natalie, you're so kind hearted and trusting, perhaps they don't deserve to win, a lot of people do think that their dogs are better than they are you know."

"But Audrey, it seems that people are told not to let them win."

"That old chestnut! Natalie, please be guided by Paul or myself, if all that you say was true, don't you think that the KC would know about it and act accordingly."

"So you're saying that you can't do anything."

"My dear, if there was proof, positive proof, that shows were being rigged don't you think that the KC would be down on them like a ton of bricks. Do these people have any proof?"

"Well no, they say that it's all done by word of mouth and...."

"Well there you are. In any competitive sport I'm afraid these things can happen. Don't upset yourself any more my dear."

Natalie put the phone down; she had been so sure that Audrey would be able to help. Perhaps Audrey and Paul were right and that

Fiona was too wrapped up in things to see them clearly. All the same, it did still seem a bit odd.

She had cooked Paul's favourite meal, an Italian dish, that evening, they had just finished it and were having a glass of wine when the phone rang. Paul got up, excused himself and went out into the hall. Natalie smiled, he was so polite and well mannered, so appreciative of her cooking.

"What the devil do you mean by phoning Audrey this morning. All that garbled rubbish about the Philips. What did you think that you were doing woman?" Paul was standing in the doorway shouting at her.

Natalie turned a startled face to stare at him, her wine glass still halfway to her mouth. She quietly put the glass down onto the table, "I beg your pardon."

"I said what the hell did you think you were doing phoning Aud...."

"I heard you the first time Paul, and if I may paraphrase what you have just said, what the hell do you think you are doing talking to me like that in my house."

"Your house?"

"Yes, my house. I own it outright still. MY house!"

Paul, who had never seen Natalie so angry and realising that, in his anger, he had overstepped the mark tried to calm the situation by apologising and excusing himself by saying he had experienced a very trying day.

"I'm sorry Paul, but your apology is not, under the circumstances acceptable."

"But why, my dear I..."

"As I have said, I am not in the habit of being spoken to in my own house like that. I do not expect anyone to question my right to make a phone call to one of my friends, I repeat MY friends. I am more than surprised that you should be the one to do it. I, therefore, realise that I have stumbled upon something that bothers you greatly and indeed Audrey, if she felt it necessary to tell you so quickly. So will you please acquaint me with the details."

Struggling for words and thinking rapidly on his feet Paul said, "Natalie, Natalie, you are reading far more into this than there is. I didn't.... I wasn't going to tell you but, well, as I've already said, I've

had a pretty awful day. The client I was supposed to meet didn't turn
up and.... there have been one or two other little occurrences lately ...
I didn't want to alarm you my dear but, I think, in fact I'm pretty sure
that I might be the next victim of this unknown person. I am being got
at now!"

CHAPTER THIRTY- ONE

Fiona was singing as she groomed one of the show dogs. The last show had been interesting for several reasons and it had helped to take her mind off her and Simon's worries. All the gossip had not been about them as she had feared but about a mysterious phone caller. Apparently one or two Cumbrian exhibitors had been receiving threatening calls and being told not to enter certain shows or their dogs would be at risk. They had also had a couple of 'heavy breather' calls. Fiona had been asked if she had received any such calls and had been so relieved to be able to say no. That, at least, was one thing that had not happened to them so far. On a lighter side, she had heard of one exhibitor turning up to a show with the wrong dog; they had all been able to laugh and sympathise at that. She had wandered round the various stalls and noticed just how many grooming products there were now; far more than when she had started, dog showing was being taken over by hairdressers! She would have to look to see what other exhibitors were using, one had to keep up with all these new products in order to stay in the game. So many new judges and exhibitors seemed to be more keen on the grooming of the dog than anything else.

When she heard the beep of a car horn, she put down the brush and looked out of the grooming shed door. It was Natalie's car parked in the drive, "Hello, Natalie. I'm up here in the grooming shed."

Natalie waved and started walking up to the shed, "Hello Fiona, I can see you're busy, sorry if I'm bothering you. Would you rather I went?"

"Good heavens no, I'm just trying out something I bought at the last show. So many of the dogs seem to have such shiny coats now that I made a few enquiries. Everyone appears to be using this."

She showed Natalie a spray can, "Actually you've come at a good time. If we walk this dog outside with another one that I haven't put it on, we can see if there is any difference."

After a few minutes they both agreed that it had improved the look of the coat slightly, "You know Fiona, Viv once told me, when Jamie was quite young, that I could put on something to make the coat grow. I bought it but never used it, I'm sure that I've still got it. Would you like to try that on one of your dogs?"

"I don't know. Supposing they ended up looking like shiny Old English Sheepdogs."

They both burst out laughing, "Or perhaps the steward would come up to you and ask if you'd got the wrong ring."

"Seriously though Natalie, I've always been a bit wary of using these products in case the KC objected to them, you know like chalk, but they must know that everyone uses stuff. The various stalls are absolutely full of cans and bottles that purport to do almost everything and they don't seem to object to them."

"It's a bit like us then and all the anti-wrinkle and ageing creams, I think it's time I stocked up on those."

"You! Natalie, being married has made you look years younger."

Laughing, they made their way back to the cottage, "This is like old times Fiona. I do really miss showing you know, all the excitement and anticipation."

"Well, why not come back. Jamie has still got several useful years ahead of him."

"It's a bit difficult. Paul just doesn't have the time to show now and he likes me to be at home at weekends."

"But surely you..." Fiona stopped, she didn't want any more antagonism from Paul and she wasn't going to persuade Natalie to go against his wishes, "Perhaps, when he's not so busy, you could show again."

"I don't know when that will be. What with all the committee work and his judging engagements, not forgetting his own work, the phone never seems to stop ringing some days. He's far too kind I think. People are always phoning him up about various judging matters and things. He's terribly loyal too, he never discusses anything with me."

Fiona, while inwardly digesting this information, poured two cups of tea and got out some cake that she had made, "You're lucky, I've made your favourite chocolate cake and Simon hasn't eaten it all yet."

"Oh, chocolate cake! I hate to say no but I must. Paul does like me slim," she blushed, "he says that I look so much more attractive now that I am slimmer. I do so miss my little outings to that lovely tea shop, you know Fiona that one with the gorgeous pastries, we went there several times."

"Yes, I remember," she looked at Natalie, " you are happy aren't you Natalie?"

"Yes, very happy. Fiona! I count my blessings, it's so wonderful to not be on my own and to be wanted and needed. Oh, I almost forgot to tell you, it's partly the reason why I came, do you know you're not the only one to be getting these nasty things happening to you. Paul is certain that he is too."

"Paul! What do you mean exactly?"

"Well, last week, a client whom he was supposed to meet didn't turn up and later said that he had not arranged to meet Paul. He says that he has had several calls at his office and the caller has put the phone down. He was a little late the other night because, when he went to get into his car, one of his tyres was flat. The garage told him yesterday that they couldn't find anything wrong with it. He is beginning to think that he is the next victim. How have you and Simon been getting on?"

"You haven't had any funny calls then Natalie?"

"No, have you?"

"No I haven't but some people at the last show were talking about just that. It's strange because all the other problems have eased off for us in the last week or so."

"Well there you are. It very much looks as if Paul is right doesn't it. Who can it be though and why? It's a complete mystery, but, whoever it is, they must be pretty sick in the head and in need of treatment. Well, I must be away. Thank you for a lovely chat and the tea. Bye Fiona."

Fiona was deep in thought as she cooked the evening meal, sausage toad-in-the-hole with potatoes and peas. Who could be doing this to them? Were they now targeting Paul? If so, why? She frowned and shook her head; it just didn't make sense. Some part of the jigsaw was missing.

Over dinner that evening, she and Simon went through everything that had happened to them recently and then what had happened so far to Paul.

"Well, I don't believe it Fee," Simon said whilst tucking into his toad-in-the hole, "unless we have an anti-dog madman in this area."

"Well, we could have I suppose but then, Paul and Natalie only have the one dog now, and that's Natalie's."

Simon continued eating, "True, but why wait 'til now? Has anyone new moved into the area? This dinner is great Fee. Thanks."

The subject was then dropped and not mentioned again that evening. Having told Simon that she had tried out the coat-shine spray, she took him up to the kennels and showed him the results, "What d'you think Simon?"

"Well, it's looks OK. You know my feelings on all this stuff. It ain't real dog showing! You should get the healthy shine from good food and exercise. Ask the old-timers in hunting or the gamekeepers, they'll tell you."

"Yes I know but, if everyone else enhances their dogs with this stuff and judges put them up and the KC doesn't complain; why shouldn't we? I'll just pop into the grooming shed, I want to read up how often I can use it."

"OK. OK. I know when I'm beaten," he took her in his arms and kissed her, "Um. that was nice. Let's do that again."

This time the kiss lasted longer, "Um, I can still taste your toad-in-the-hole. Kiss me some more, I didn't have enough."

His tongue licked her lips as his hands cupped her breasts, "Um. What about some afters."

He pulled her blouse up and, pulling down her bra he licked her nipples until they were hard and proud, "Um. they're sweet."

"Simon stop, stop there."

A muffled "Why" came from Simon as he started pulling her trousers and panties down and licking round her navel. She tried to pull his head up, "Simon, not here."

"Why not" was the even more muffled reply.

He looked up for a second, "Come on Fee. It'll be fun, I don't think we've ever made love in here have we? Get out of those bloody trousers will you."

Laughing now, she obligingly stepped out of the trousers and took off her shoes, "Simon, the floor's too hard."

"Who said anything about the floor?" She looked at Simon who was by now completely naked and very much aroused. He came towards her and pulled her to him as he kissed her, he then turned her away from him and, putting his hands around her, he started caressing her nipples as he kissed and licked the back of her neck and ears.

She bent her head back so that her breasts stood out even more proudly, "Simon, stop. You know I can't bear that. It just sends hot waves all the way down my body."

"I know, that's the general idea. How's about this as well then," he bent her body forwards until her breasts were hanging full and heavy in his hands and entered her; with a deep sigh, she braced her legs and pushed backwards.

"My God Fee, that's bloody marvellous."

It was the next morning when Fiona received a phone call from Caroline, "Hello is that Fiona Philips?"

"Yes, is that you Caroline?"

"Yes."

Fiona, totally relaxed and at peace with the world after making love to Simon the night before was somewhat taken aback by Caroline's next sentence.

"I want to give Saffron back to you."

"Saffron, why what's wrong with her?"

"Nothing, no nothing's wrong with Saffron, I'm just getting out of dog showing."

"Getting.... Is this because of what happened at the last show?"

"No of course not.... well partly.... well yes in a way. Look Fiona, I shall be the laughing stock of everybody and I just couldn't bear it. I couldn't honestly."

"Caroline, surely you've been in dogs long enough to know that anything like that is only a five day wonder. Something else will have happened by now and....."

"Fiona, it's not just that, it's other things as well, I can't tell you about them, I just don't want to show any more that's all. I don't enjoy it any more. Look, I've made up my mind and I thought that you might like to have Saffron back as she is so nice. If you don't then..."

"Of course we'll have her back Caroline, no question,"

"Right then, when would it be convenient to bring her down?"

"Well, any time, there is always someone here but are you sure that..."

"If you're not going to a show then I'll bring her tomorrow; in the morning. Goodbye Fiona."

Fiona worked a little faster the next day so that she would be finished when Caroline came. She prepared a kennel for the dog putting extra bedding in because she wasn't sure if the dog usually slept in the house or not. She had told Simon about the call and they had speculated on the real reason for her giving up the dogs, "I tell you Fee, there'll be a man involved somewhere," he paused and grinned knowingly, "or a woman."

"No surely not. Caroline! No. It wouldn't be Dennis either, I always got the impression that he was definitely under her thumb."

"What like me! It's always the quiet ones you know Fee. I betcha it's Dennis having a fling."

She was smiling at the memory of the conversation when she heard a car stopping. Walking down the path she saw Caroline getting out of the car. She was on her own so Dennis hadn't come then. Perhaps Simon was right after all.

"Hello Caroline, nice to see you again."

Caroline gave her a weak smile, "Shall I get Saffron out?"

"Yes, I've got a kennel ready. She is still used to being kennelled?"

"Oh yes. You know I bought a brand new corridor kennel when we moved."

"Yes, I remember now."

"Would you be willing to give me something for her? I wouldn't charge you much. I just want to know that she has a good home."

They chatted about it while they settled Saffron into her new home, "Right, that's agreed then if you are happy with the price, so am I Caroline. Now that we've sorted that out, come and have a cup of tea."

Caroline drank her tea so quickly that Fiona was sure that it must have burned her throat.

"I'll be off now Fiona, thank you once again."

"You've got a bit of a drive ahead of you. Wouldn't you like another cup of tea; or perhaps you'd like to see Saffron again and see that she has settled."

"No, no I'd rather go," as she was opening the kitchen door she suddenly turned, "Fiona, would you please tell me something."

"If I can."

"Have you ever slept with someone for a CC?"

Fiona felt her face flush as she replied, "No, I have not slept with someone for a CC. Why do you ask?"

"It was something that O...someone said to me recently."

"About me?"

"Well not actually about you, more in general, but you were mentioned. This person said that, generally speaking, people had to earn their CCs one way or another. Money or s... something else."

"I see. Can I presume that this person was Ophelia?""

"I'd rather not say. That's really why I'm giving up though. I always used to say to Dennis that I didn't win at Open shows because I didn't have a good dog. I bought Saffron from you because you are successful breeders and have good dogs so..."

"But you have won. You got a Res CC."

"Yes, but I wasn't prepared to pay the price for it afterwards."

"I see. You've been blacked then."

"Oh, you know about it then already."

"No, but I have heard of this happening before to someone else." Caroline looked near to tears and Fiona took a step towards her, "Look Caroline if you want to talk about it."

"No thank you, it's kind of you Fiona but I just don't want to, I couldn't... not to anyone. Well, that's that. Thanks Fiona for being kind and honest with me. I shall let my other dogs go as well so, if you hear of anyone wanting a pet."

"Yes, I'll put a few feelers out and let you know if I get anyone suitable. Well it's goodbye then Caroline. Good luck. By the way, what does Dennis think about all this?"

"Dennis, oh, I haven't told him yet, he's too busy with his garden nowadays."

"But what will you do now?"

"I don't know yet. I might buy a pedigree cat, or help Dennis in the garden. I just don't know."

She watched the car disappear up the road and then turned to go in, another victim of the damned show system, what a shame. When she told Simon of her conversation with Caroline he laughed and said, "So, Caroline didn't fancy a romp in the hay with our Ophelia. Never mind, it's an ill wind. When I looked at that bitch Saffron just now, I thought that she'd improved tremendously since we sold her. We'll have to show her."

"Simon, how can you be so heartless, I felt really sorry for Caroline. She's obviously had a terrible shock."

"I bet she has," he burst out laughing.

"Simon! It's not funny. Anyway, you don't know that that was the reason."

"No, but I've a pretty good idea," he burst out laughing again and even Fiona had to suppress a giggle at the thought.

CHAPTER THIRTY -TWO

Dennis was picking the last of the tomatoes from the trusses in the greenhouse, the TV forecaster had said that there would be a frost tonight and he wanted to pick the last of the crop and take them into the conservatory to finish ripening off. As he picked the last semi-green tomato from the last plant in the row and placed it in the trug he sighed, it was nearly Autumn now, soon be winter, what the hell was he going to do with his time apart from potting up some spring bulbs for the conservatory and getting the Asparagus bed prepared. He did have a full calendar of darts matches though, what with that and the digging etc., perhaps it wouldn't be so bad.

There was definitely still something very wrong with Caroline, he couldn't put his finger on it quite; she was certainly keeping it to herself whatever it was. He closed the greenhouse door and started to walk down the garden. Thank heavens that there hadn't been a repeat of that ghastly night, he'd since often wondered if she'd been on drugs or something. The subject had never been mentioned again and she was sleeping in one of the smaller bedrooms. Then there was the business with the dogs. After all these years she'd suddenly sold the lot not to mention the brand new kennel! He'd had the biggest row with her over the dogs that they'd ever had but she had been adamant. He'd only managed to save his two favourites, Patsy and Bonnie from disappearing altogether by asking round at the Gardening Club. His pal George had a sister who was willing to have them. All he had been able to get out of Caroline was that she was fed up with showing dogs and didn't want them any more as she was going to have cats instead. He looked at the spot where the kennel had stood; only the concrete base remained. Pity, he'd always enjoyed the company of the dogs especially when Caroline had been out and he could have them with him in the garden. They so enjoyed their walks with him too.

That was another thing, she was always up at that Jessica's place now. She was up there today, had been there for the past three days in fact, buying a kitten she said. The trouble was he still hadn't seen this damned kitten! All she talked about now was how Jessica did this with the cats, how Jessica did that. He opened the conservatory door and placed the trug on a table. He looked up at his marrows hanging in their slings. He hoped to keep them for Christmas dinner; he'd have his home-grown potatoes as well. Point was would Caroline be there to eat it? This had all seemed to start after that night! What a night! He ran a tomato stained finger around his shirt collar, thank goodness there hadn't been a repeat performance! He walked into the kitchen. The fact remained though, how did she know about all those poses and positions and all those other things she did, who told her what to do and why had she changed so much? It was no good, he must face facts, there was someone else and he bet his bottom dollar that it was this so-called Jessica. She often called her Jess and that could be a man's name as well. He knew that he ought to go up there and catch her out but the very thought of seeing her doing all those things with someone else! He just couldn't bring himself to do it. Or could he? More to the point, should he?

On an impulse, he went into the lounge and started to rummage through her correspondence. He kept furtively looking at the door as if he expected her to walk in and find him. Suspicion was a terrible feeling, it made you do things that you would never do normally. He found nothing incriminating so went upstairs and looked in her bedside cabinet. Yes, there was a photograph of cats in there. Turning over the photo he saw a phone number. With his heart pounding in his throat he picked up the bedside phone and dialled the number, "Hello is that Jessica Mason?"

"Yes, Jessica Mason speaking. Did you want to make an appointment?"

My God, she was a prostitute. Dennis almost dropped the phone in his haste to put it down. My wife is friendly with a prostitute! Now that explained everything. Caroline, his wife was up there now doing God knows what, helping her out! Is Jessica her pimp, or whatever is the female equivalent, a Madame? Oh God, it gets worse. Dennis walked into the kitchen, his mind in orbit, so that's where she learned to do all those things. That's why she's always up there; she must be good at it and in demand. He sat down heavily, no, he must have it all wrong, not Caroline, she wasn't really keen on all that sort of thing. She was small and pretty though, perhaps she dressed up as a schoolgirl or a nurse or something. He put his head in his hands unable to cope with the kaleidoscope of pictures now entering his mind. Perhaps she was into torture or leather or chains or - Oh my

God. He staggered up, went into the lounge and poured himself a stiff brandy.

Jessica came back into the kitchen, "Sorry about that Caroline, it was some man too shy to make an appointment. I get it sometimes."

"I've been meaning to ask you about that Jessica. Do you get many men, I mean do they get the wrong idea?"

"I did get a bit of that sort of thing when I first started up but, when I kept refusing the male appointments, they got the message. Now I have my regular clientele, all women and they all come on recommendation so I don't have any problems in that direction."

"I'm so glad to hear that. I really ought to be going home soon Jessica. Poor old Dennis will be out of food soon."

"What a pity. I'm ashamed almost to say it but; we get on so well that I wish you could stay all the time."

"Do you? So do I Jessica. So much, you are the very best friend that I have ever had. You're right, we do get on well together don't we, in fact, I get on better with you than I do with Dennis. You have been so kind to me and understanding."

"Nonsense."

"But it's true, I think of you all the time when I'm at home. I love everything about this house and all the cats and especially you."

"What. Love me?"

Caroline sat there for several minutes staring into her empty cup and it was as if time stood still for several minutes. Then, with a sigh, Caroline looked up and met Jessica's eyes, "Yes, I think I do love you."

Tears sprang into Jessica's eyes and she leaned across the table and took Caroline's hand in hers, " Oh Caroline, how I've longed to hear you say that. I return that love completely my dearest Caroline."

Minutes ticked by as they sat holding hands across the table, there seemed no need for words. Suddenly Caroline looked at Jessica and then looked down again at her cup, "Jessica, are you? I mean have you? I mean have you, I'm sorry I have to ask, have you loved anyone else before?"

"No. I have never found anybody I liked enough; that is until I found you. The moment you walked into my house with Ophelia I knew that I was going to like you very much." She got up and walked round to Caroline and bending, kissed her gently on the lips, "I knew that that would be sweet. I love you Caroline."

Standing up Caroline put her arms around Jessica and kissed her mouth, "I've dreamed of doing that Jess. I think you're lovely."

With their arms locked around each other they kissed again and again.

"Caroline, you have no idea how much I have wanted to do that."

With tears running down her cheeks Caroline hugged Jessica close to her and murmured in her ear, "Oh Jessica. I have. I have."

Jessica took Caroline's face in her hands, "Caroline. I must ask you. Do you want to take this any further?"

"Do you mean?"

"Yes. I have to tell you that this would be my first time. I have never done this before."

Caroline was silent for a few moments and then putting a hand up to stroke Jessica's face said, "Yes, I do then. I'm frightened, but yes, I do want to."

"Then shall we?" Jessica looked upwards.

"Yes please, I want to show you just how much I love you. I want to love you more than I have ever wanted to love anybody Jess."

"Then lets go upstairs shall we? I do hope that I am not a disappointment to you."

Holding hands, Jessica locked the doors and, still holding hands they went up to Jessica's pretty, flowery bedroom. They both found, in the discovery of the other, profound happiness and the two lovers talked well into the night as they cuddled up close and kissed and touched and stroked each other.

Next morning though, hard and difficult decisions had to be made and, with tears in her eyes, Caroline said goodbye to Jessica, promising to phone her every day and to be back as soon as she could sort something out.

During the drive home she was rehearsing little speeches. How did you tell your husband of fifteen years that you had fallen in love with a woman? It was so hard, Dennis would never believe her, never understand. It was almost impossible for her to understand! She would leave it for a few days because there were so many other things to be sorted out before she told him. The house for instance, he could go on living in it, she couldn't, wouldn't turn him out but then, there were all the bills to be settled. Who would pay what? Suppose he didn't want to stay there? She'd have to look at the terms of the will again. Suppose he found someone else? A little worm of jealousy squirmed in her mind at that thought. Thank goodness all the dogs had gone, she didn't have to think about that. He had his gardening club mates and his darts mates so he wouldn't be lonely. They had hardly been out together since they moved up to Aunt Ellen's house; they hadn't even shared a bedroom since that awful night.

She shuddered and felt slightly sick when she remembered what she had done to Dennis that night; it was awful! Especially when she compared it with loving Jessica last night! It didn't bear comparison. She suddenly heard her mother's voice talking about such things so she immediately drowned it out by switching on the car radio. She felt several pangs of conscience about Dennis, he didn't really deserve this but, she just couldn't help it. She remembered the outings they used to enjoy when they were first married, the pictures, the bowling alley, swimming, walking; going out with friends. Had she always been a les.... different then? She couldn't answer that. She thought of how pleased her mother had been on the day she had married Dennis. How happy she herself had felt standing there in her lovely dress with all her friends throwing confetti. All the smiling faces at the reception, leaving for the honeymoon in her new outfit, she sighed, the honeymoon had been all right but, the big mystery, the secret of romance, the becoming a woman, it hadn't been very thrilling after all. Buying their new house and planning the furnishings had been wonderful, she was the envy of so many of her old friends, it had been so exciting planning little dinner parties and, she was startled by the sound of a car horn blasting near her. She saw an angry, male face peering at her and making a gesture with his fingers as he passed her. Heavens, what had she been doing. Concentrate on the road Caroline. As she later drove into the gravelled drive of Aunt Ellen's house, she still thought of it as that, she felt rather worried at the thought of the ordeal ahead.

Dennis was sitting in an armchair in the lounge fast asleep, the cut-glass brandy decanter and a glass were on the floor beside his chair. Her heart missed a beat, something dreadful must have happened for

Dennis to drink during the day! She shook him vigorously, "Dennis, Dennis wake up. What's wrong?"

Dennis slowly opened his eyes and then rubbed them with his knuckles, "Oh hello Caroline, didn't expect you back yet."

"Have you been drinking?"

"Yes," now fully awake he sat up in the chair, "Yes, I have. What was it this time, black leather and whips?"

"Black leather and whips! Dennis, how much of that did you drink?"

"Enough, enough to know just what you've been doing, you, you.... slut!"

Caroline's eyes opened wide with shock, how could he know about last night, who had told him? He couldn't know unless Jessica had phoned him. No, she wouldn't do that so how, of course, Ophelia. But how would she know unless... Jessica was a friend of hers. A terrifying thought came into her head, Jessica had told Ophelia! No, please no.

"Has Ophelia rung?"

"No."

Caroline breathed a huge sigh of relief, "Then what, what are you talking about. What has happened, tell me."

Dennis pushed himself up from the chair and angrily pushed past her causing her to step back a few paces, "I'm going for a pee."

Caroline's eyes opened wide, she didn't expect Dennis to speak so coarsely to her. Ever since they were married she had discouraged words like that, "Don't speak to me like that Dennis."

Undoing his flies in front of her he replied, "Why not, I bet you've heard and seen a lot worse than that in the last few days you whore," he stomped out of the room.

Caroline's jaw dropped and putting her hand to her aching forehead, Caroline sat down; he couldn't know about her and Jessica, it was impossible. If he hasn't spoken to Ophelia, how could he know anything? It was only last night after all and... Her thoughts were interrupted by Dennis storming back into the room. He stood in front of her and shouted angrily, "I phoned your precious Jessica yesterday. I know what you two have been up to....

"What! How! When?"

"Yesterday."

"When yesterday"

"Does it matter? Somewhere around lunchtime I suppose."

Caroline shut her eyes with relief, he didn't know then. Heaven knows what he does know, but he doesn't know about me and Jessica loving each other thank goodness.

"Now I know why you were all over me like a rash that night. Now I know where you learned all those positions and ....and things you wanted to do. You dirty slut! You didn't even need the money. What have you been doing it for, excitement, pleasure, fun? I wasn't good enough for you I suppose. Have you done this before? What's worse, have you given me anything?" Dennis sat down in the armchair and put his head in his hands, "Why? That's what I want to know why? Didn't I give you enough money? Was it boredom? Wasn't I good enough for you?" He looked up and shouted at her, " Well come on say something or has the cat got your tongue? Ha, ha, that's a joke, get it. Perhaps I should say kitten, sex kitten."

He suddenly got up and grabbed her by the shoulders and shook her saying, "Come on then sex kitten, tell me you dirty slut. Have I got to see a doctor?"

As he continued to shake her, the tears ran down her cheeks and she gasped for breath, "Dennis let me go you're hurting me."

"Hurting you am I well it's not as much as I want to hurt you. Not as much as you've hurt me you whore. I came up here just to please you, I didn't want to come but I came. It was hard and lonely for me, in a new office, stuck in this great mausoleum of a house with no mates but I've gradually made a life for myself, made a few friends and..."

"And I'm pleased for you Dennis I knew..."

"Shut up and listen for a change. You knew bloody nothing. You have been so busy prancing round like Lady Muck that you haven't noticed or cared what I did."

"That's not true Dennis. I know you like the greenhouse. I'm so sorry that I didn't get to the flower show. I..."

"Shut up, just shut up you liar."

He suddenly released her and she sat down heavily in a chair.

"I'm going in the morning."

"What do you mean Dennis?"

213

He turned and made towards the door shouting over his shoulder, "What I said, I'll be gone in the morning."

She ran after him calling up the stairs, "No Dennis, please don't go. I want to talk to you, I'm sure we can sort something out. You've got it all wrong. Please wait for a day or two so that I can explain, please." She heard their bedroom door slam and then silence. This was turning out all wrong. She didn't want him to go. She must make him see sense.

Having taken some Aspirin for her pounding head, she got a chair, placed it at the bottom of the stairs and sat down for her vigil. Dennis would not be able to leave the house until she had spoken to him and tried to clear her name. Through the night her head would fall down on her chest and she would wake up shivering with the cold, she put one of Dennis's anoraks around her legs and one round her shoulders. When Dennis came down in the morning, he was astounded to see her sitting there pale faced but determined, "Dennis, I have done something, not what you think, but something. I don't want you to leave; I want you to stay here. I'll go, I'll leave but, until I can see the solicitors, I don't know quite what the situation will be if I go. So please stay, at least until I can sort something out. I shan't bother you. I shan't even speak to you if you don't want me to but, please, please stay Dennis. Please."

Dennis looked at her for a moment and then walked straight past her and into the kitchen. Caroline stayed where she was as she heard him put the kettle on and then make a cup of tea. Later when she heard the back door open and close she crept into the kitchen and poured herself a cup of tea. Seeing that Dennis had left some toast on the table she ate that too. She must stop him from leaving; it would ruin all her plans. She hurried up to the greenhouse.

CHAPTER THIRTY -THREE

Replacing the mobile phone in her pocket, Fiona looked at her watch, that time already! It was lovely having the mobile phone, Simon had bought her one when they had had so many nuisance calls on the house phone, but it did stop you working. They had only given the number to a very few personal friends and it had been so nice to get up in the morning and not worry about nuisance calls. Perhaps though, it was time to go back to the answerphone. Duncan had kept her talking for such a long time, now that Donald had started school, there was even more for the proud father to tell her. Not that she minded, it was wonderful to hear how well he could read, how good his writing was, how quick he was going to be at Maths. His drawings were exceptional for a child of his tender years, he had a beautiful pitch when he sang; the list of achievements was endless. Fiona smiled wistfully as she recalled the conversation, how she would have enjoyed bringing up a child, introducing him or her to all the wonderful things there were in the world, music, books, flowers, animals, sport, in fact, just life in general. She would choose some books to give him for this year's Christmas present, being a librarian had some advantages. She put the three dogs back in their kennel and leashed up three more. Duncan had been so good with his monthly reports that she felt that she knew little Donald quite well. She looked down at the dogs, "Come on you lot, let's have a run," she started off for the field.

She had hardly put the dogs back in their run before the mobile rang again, it was Beryl this time to say that they would be able to come for dinner on Sunday as the builders had finished the conservatory at long last and she and Peter would have everything tidied up and put back again. As always, she had asked if everything was all right, was there anything she could bring, Beryl truly was the sister that she had never had, a good friend and confidante, she had supported her through all the difficult times, losing the baby, separating from Simon, Peter too was always there for Simon, she would look forward to seeing them on Sunday. She was putting three more dogs on their leads when the phone rang again. She couldn't believe it, so few people had this number, "Hi Fiona, sorry I haven't phoned for ages have I."

"Laura! How are you all?"

"Fine, we're all fine. Now that Amanda has started school I have more time to myself. I just can't tell you what bliss it is to have the house to myself for a few hours. I know you must think I'm mad."

"No, of course not. How is Michael?"

"Fine, that's partly why I'm ringing you. There's a chance that we might be moving to Scotland."

"Scotland! How, why?"

"He has been head-hunted. What about that! The money is much better and there are other hidden perks he says. Of course, it would mean moving the boys and Amanda to new schools, we have done nothing but talk about it for ages going round and round the pros and cons and we were wondering Fiona, if we could come over to see you both on Sunday and talk it over and get your input. A fresh approach would help iron things out. He has to give his answer this coming week."

"On Sunday, well yes I think so. You see we already have Peter and Beryl, you know Simon's brother and sister-in-law coming to dinner."

"Well, in that case we couldn't intrude."

"No, wait a minute. I could manage it. Tom could help Simon with the kennel work couldn't he and that would leave me free."

"Michael would help as well and I'd willingly help with dinner but, our six is an awful lot more, are you sure?"

"Well, what I was thinking was, I can easily pop a roast in the Aga, could you bring a dessert of some kind?"

"Yes, no bother. Thank you Fiona. It will be such a relief to talk it through with someone who has known us for a long time and Peter and Beryl can add a bit too perhaps. Thanks again. See you Sunday. What time?"

"About ten-thirty suit you?"

"Fine"

Fiona hurried off to the field with the dogs her mind full of the forthcoming dinner, "I'm sorry fellers but you three can't have as long today. I'll make it up to you tomorrow." She would have to organise the meal for Sunday: what a gathering of the clans it would

216

be, ten of them! She would have to do a roast or something for ten; she had never catered for so many for a dinner. Quite excited at the prospect, she hurried back to the cottage and grabbed a pile of cook books. Putting the kettle on the Aga she sat down to leaf through them. S for starters, it would have to be something quick, spectacular, but easy! Pity melons aren't so good now. She couldn't believe it when her mobile rang again, so few people had the number, "Hello is that you Simon?" The phone went dead. "Blast and damnation. It couldn't be, it must be a mistake." Fiona got up to make the coffee, how could someone have got her number. Her mobile rang again and, again, it went dead. Sipping the coffee she punched in Simon's work number, "Hello Simon Philips."

"Simon, it's me. Did you just phone me?"

"No Fee. Why?"

"Then the damned calls have started again."

"Bloody hell, how did they get the number?"

"Good question."

"You OK? Can you cope with it?"

"Yes, I suppose so, I've had a lot of practice. By the way, we have eight coming for Sunday dinner."

"Eight! Who?"

"Tell you when you come home, I'm all behind with the work today and I must go shopping."

Natalie was filling in a schedule for the LKA Championship show. She kept telling herself that it was silly to be so apprehensive about it. It was the first show that she had entered since her marriage to Paul. The time seemed to have flown past what with their trips abroad, and so many other functions, several shows that she had wanted to enter she couldn't, because Paul would be there in some official capacity or another and he insisted that it would look like nepotism, this one, however, he wouldn't be there. Seeing Fiona preparing her dogs for the shows and chatting about them had made her want to show Jamie again. It had been lovely to have him home again and to go for walks with him, she hadn't realised just how much she had missed the dogs, she wished now that she hadn't deferred to Paul's wishes and had kept the others. She liked showing, it was exciting and gave her a framework to plan for the year ahead, she hadn't realised how much she would miss it; she had thought that

217

Paul would fill her every waking moment. She wrote the cheque and put it in the envelope with the form, licking the envelope and putting on the stamp, she pressed it down firmly. Good, I wonder if Fiona is going, I must ask her. She might see Audrey there too. Another thought floated into her mind which made her stop in her tracks, Audrey! Why hadn't she thought of that at the time? She had phoned Audrey to ask if she could help Fiona and Audrey, her friend, had immediately phoned Paul to tell him what she had said to her. Why? What had it got to do with Paul? Did Audrey think that Paul could help more than she could? Surely not. She put the completed schedule on the hall table for posting and, putting her coat on, decided to take Jamie for a walk over the common and post the entry at the same time. It was only when she was enjoying seeing Jamie running around and chasing after a ball that she remembered that she hadn't picked up the schedule.

"What is this Natalie?"
In the kitchen preparing their dinner Natalie called out, "What Paul."
"This schedule for LKA."
"Oh, yes, I thought that, as you wouldn't be there in any official capacity, that I might enter Jamie. I haven't shown him for ages and I do so enjoy it."
"I see, well I don't think that it's a very good idea Natalie."
"Why?"
"No actual reason but.... well, I don't think that he will do very well er... not having shown for a while and, as you are associated with me, it wouldn't look too good not to be placed."
Busy with the dinner preparations, Natalie shook her head, "Paul, I don't know what you are rambling on about."
"Let me put it plainer then Natalie," Paul's voice was getting terse, "You won't get placed very high and that would reflect on my position. If you want to enter a show you should tell me well in advance."
"Because?"
"Because then I could organise things. Surely Natalie I don't have to spell it out, you've seen and heard enough by now to know what I'm talking about."

" Paul, I admit that both he and I may not be up to scratch but I don't think that we'll disgrace you. I'll go to this show and then tell you of the other shows, alright?"

"No, it is not all right. You will not go to this show Natalie, in fact..."

She could hear paper being torn up. Hurrying into the hall she saw Paul throw the torn schedule into a waste bin in the study.

"Paul, what have you done?"

"It's obvious isn't it? I've stopped you from making a fool of yourself and me."

"How dare you behave in such a high-handed and dictatorial manner. If I want to enter that show, or any other, I shall," she marched over to the waste bin and retrieved and smoothed out the torn pieces of paper.

Dinner was served and eaten in complete silence. Natalie's face was still red and angry looking, all appetite gone she just toyed with the food on her plate. Paul realised that, once again he'd overstepped the mark and, at the end of the meal, he offered to make the coffee and left the room. Natalie was still sitting at the table looking angry when he returned, "I've brought the cream and a jug of milk, I wasn't sure which you would prefer my dear."

"I see. It doesn't matter tonight if I eat cream and get fat then. It's my reward for not going to the show is it?"

Paul tried to smile and pass off the remark, "Have you heard from Candida? I thought that we might go over to see them around Christmas time. What do you think?"

Natalie's face lit up, "That would be lovely, I..."

"That's settled then."

Natalie looked across at Paul's smiling face as he stirred his coffee, she felt like a child who had been handed a lolly to stop her crying, did he really have so little regard for her as a person? Part of her wanted to say no, but a greater part of her wanted to see her daughter.

"Yes, it would appear that all is settled wouldn't it. Will you organise the tickets or shall I?"

The next afternoon Natalie went to see Fiona, "Hello, hope it's not inconvenient. Are you busy cooking?"

"No, I'm trying to decide what to have as a starter for Sunday. I've got eight people coming for dinner so that's ten of us in all."

Natalie sat down and together they poured over the various books until they had made their choices, "Great, I went shopping yesterday and I think I've got most of those ingredients and I've got the joint in the freezer so, that only leaves the veg. Thanks Natalie for all your help."

"Well, if you need any help with the cooking just give me a call. By the way, Fiona, I came over to ask if you have entered for LKA yet? It's the last day today."

"No, as a matter of fact, I haven't but I must. Thanks for reminding me."

"Well, I have a hankering to come as well only.... I've lost the schedule. Could you give me the details so that I can enter?"

"Of course I can. Good for you. I'm so glad, you can come with us if you like. I'll get the schedule out now and we'll have a cuppa. I've just heard from Duncan again, apparently Donald is almost a child prodigy as far as he is concerned."

Fiona told a smiling Natalie of Donald's prowess at school.

During their conversation, Fiona mentioned that she had had a couple of the other calls, two of the usual silent ones and one accusing her of ill-treating her dogs.

"He threatened to report me to the 'appropriate authorities'."

"I'm so sorry Fiona, it must be awful for you."

"What's so worrying this time is that it was on my mobile and, as you know, only a few of my closest friends have the number."

"Now that is worrying, do be careful won't you. These sort of people can be quite unpredictable you know."

As Natalie drove home she had a worried look on her face, poor Fiona. Showing was such a wonderful sport, why did some deranged people have to spoil it for others. She felt for the paper in her pocket, good, she had brought the details for LKA, she would fill it in and send it off straight away. She didn't care if she wasn't placed, well she did, but not as much as supporting Fiona at the show and showing Paul that she would not be dictated to like a small child.

The dinner proved to be a great success and Fiona felt very proud as she surveyed the smiling faces round the table. After dinner, while the children went out for a walk, the subject of Michael being head-hunted and the subsequent move to Scotland was discussed. Both Laura and Michael asked and received everyone's personal opinion on the merits of staying where they were or going, several suggestions were advanced and discussed and finally, when it was agreed that, taking into account all the facts, that they should go, Laura and Michael thanked them and said that that was pretty well the decision that they had already come to, it was smiles and nods all round. The one problem left was Tom. He didn't want to move at all because of his 'A' levels. He also didn't want to go to Scotland and leave all his friends. After a lot of further discussion, Tom was called in.

"Tom," said his father, "we know that you don't want to go to Scotland or leave your school and we think that we have come up with a possible solution."

"What's that?"

"If your mother and I, Amanda and the twins go to Scotland, Simon and Fiona have very kindly offered to let you live here until you have completed your exams. It does mean a change of school but you won't have to come to Scotland for a while which would give you more time to think. If you're successful you could apply to go to a University in Scotland perhaps."

"Cool."

"I gather that that means it's all right with you."

"Yeah, that's cool. Thanks Fiona. Thanks Simon."

"Well that's settled, we can't thank you enough but I have to say that I hope you two know what you are letting yourselves in for."

CHAPTER THIRTY- FOUR

"It's always been a mystery to me Simon why there always seems to be so much paint in the brushes when you come to wash them out and yet, when you are painting, you are always having to dip the brush in for more."

They had been giving the walls, in the bedroom that Tom was going to use, a fresh coat of emulsion paint. Fiona had bought some new curtains with a matching duvet cover and bedside lamp, "I'm rather pleased with the effect, I hope that he likes it."

"Sure to."

"I'm really looking forward to his coming in January. I hope that the move doesn't affect his results. He'll need three 'A's if he wants to be a Vet."

"Well, it's up to him isn't it. Move or not, if he doesn't put in the study, he won't do it and then he's looking at another six years work before he can qualify so, we'll see how he gets on."

"Yes, won't it be interesting though. I'm so looking forward to his coming. You really don't mind do you Simon. I was a bit worried that it might recall painful memories."

"No, I'll be all right. How about a cuppa for the workers?"

"OK and while I'm downstairs, I must phone Ruth to arrange times for next Saturday. It's the Ladies Kennel Association show, last Champ show of the year Simon; it seems to have come round so quickly."

"Yeah, it's because you're living with me, I'm so lovely to be with that you don't notice the passing of time," he ducked as a wet cloth was thrown in his direction. It landed on the floor and the two housedogs rushed up barking.

"OK. OK it's nothing to worry about, anyway, what are you doing up here. Clear off before you dirty my masterpiece." Simon picked up the wet cloth and returned it to Fiona, "I just don't know how we'll do under Reggie. At one time I'd have said that we would be well placed at least but; after the year we've had, together with the bad write-ups... I don't know what to expect."

"I do think that's awful. They deliberately say something bad in a critique so that all or most of the future judges immediately put you down, and you have no redress. If you say that it's not true, people still don't believe you. I'd never give any dog a bad critique, it's so unfair."

"Cheer up. Who knows we may have turned the corner and next year will be great, he lifted the hair from her neck and kissed it.

"Hey, don't get paint on my hair."
Simon threatened her with the brush and, calling the dogs, she ran down the stairs. Simon stood there for a moment or two looking at the walls. He didn't believe that next year would be great unless they could find out who was doing this. He must make a few more discreet enquiries, so far he hadn't been able to come up with much. He still had a few more friends to ask, although they didn't like the fact known that they still sympathised with him. He'd see what they could come up with.

On Saturday morning, the rain was coming down in torrents and, as they set off in the dark for LKA, they had the headlights on and the windscreen wipers going continuously. The motorway was a sea of spray and as they drove into the rapidly filling car parks at the NEC it was still not completely light. Fiona shivered as she got out of the warm car, "It's still raining although not so heavily, shall I walk them in? Are we first in the ring?"

"Yeah, we are so I don't think that we'd better walk the young one, I'll cage him; you take Stream, and the bitch." Saffron had improved so much that they had transferred her back into their name and were showing her for the first time but she was still 'the bitch' to Simon.
Fiona set off at a good pace towards the entrances to the NEC while Simon pulled the trolley with Skiddaw in his cage and all their gear and towels on top.
As Fiona made her way to the Cumbrian benches, she saw Natalie settling her dog on the bench, "Natalie, you made it. Great. Did you come on your own?"

"Yes, I did, I know you offered me a lift but, as I wasn't absolutely certain that I could make it today, I popped up in the car. Had to go in the visitors' car park but I'm so pleased and excited to be here that I didn't mind the walk. It's quite like old times isn't it."

"Yes, I'll get these two dried off and come and see you. What class have you entered?"

"Limit."

223

"Right, see you soon," Fiona found her benches as Simon came along with the trolley. Between them they soon dried off the wet dogs and settled all three onto their benches.

"Time for a coffee I think. Want one Fee?"

Simon had bought a catalogue and was grunting as he saw what competition they could expect in their respective classes, "Not too bad for Skiddaw but Stream and the bitch have stiff classes."

Having got Skiddaw prepared, Fiona took him into the ring and managed a fourth place, as she came back to the benches Simon shrugged his shoulders, "We'll see what the other two do."

They were able to see the ring without leaving the dogs so they watched as an obviously nervous Natalie took Jamie into the Limit class, Fiona caught her eye and gave her a thumbs up sign. Natalie smiled and looked a bit happier. She was unplaced at the end of the class but came out smiling, "Hello, am I relieved that's over. I was so nervous that I think I conveyed it to Jamie. Never mind, I shall be better next time."

"That's the spirit Natalie, the point is did you enjoy it?" Simon said.

"Oh yes, I was so proud of him."

Fiona got Stream off the bench, "Wish me luck."

Natalie noticed that Simon was looking rather grim-faced as he watched Fiona go into the ring, "Things aren't any better then Simon."

"Not so that you'd notice. We'll see how this lad does," he'd managed to have a few words with some of his mates but he hadn't been able to get very far. Although the Open class was quite small, Fiona only got a fourth again. Well, his chats had done some good, she hadn't been thrown out although she wouldn't get a mention in the dog papers, so they were still being blacked.

The bitches didn't go in until after lunch so there was plenty of time to wander round and have their sandwiches. A card was being passed around the Cumbrian benches for Harry Benson; an exhibitor who had been in a car crash, everyone was signing it. Here was one of the nice things about dog showing Fiona thought. Fiona was just grooming Saffron who was due to go in the Junior bitch class when she heard a rather loud conversation going on in the next aisle. Looking up she saw Paul standing at Natalie's bench. At first she thought, how nice, he has come to support her but then realised that, although they were standing close together, they were arguing quite fiercely. He grabbed hold of Natalie's arm and she pulled away. Fiona heard her say, "No Paul, no, I will not leave now. I can't leave yet anyway."

Paul muttered something and Natalie said, "I don't care what you can arrange Paul, I'm not leaving now. I want to look round the stalls and I'm going to watch Fiona in the ring with her new bitch."

Paul, now very red in the face, again grabbed her arm and muttered something fiercely in her ear.

"Paul, I may be your wife but, as far as this situation is concerned, I am still able to function on my own and make my own decisions."

Fiona hearing the steward call for the Junior bitch entries, slipped the show lead onto Saffron's neck and made for the ring. Once in the ring she concentrated on keeping the young bitch happy, as long as she was happy she'd walk well and that was all that mattered at the moment. Her turn came to be seen by the judge and Fiona was quite pleased with the way the bitch handled herself. She had just walked back to the line when there was a lot of noise over by the Cumbrian benches, people seemed to be looking at one particular spot and there was some shouting but then, suddenly, it was silent. It wasn't possible to see for the spectators round the ring although even they were looking behind them rather than at the dogs in the ring. Saffron was placed third and Fiona felt so pleased, at last, things were improving. Receiving her card she tried to make her way back to the Cumbrian benches but was impeded by a knot of people all craning their necks in the same direction. Finally, with a deal of pushing, she managed to get back to her bench. There, she realised that everyone seemed to be looking in the next aisle where Natalie was benched.

Fiona stood on the bench to look over and was horrified to see Simon standing there dishevelled and red-faced, "Simon," she called out, "what's the matter."

Simon looked up at her but only shrugged his shoulders in reply. She could see Natalie nearby, her face was white and she appeared to be staring at the floor. Fiona moved to try to see more but her view was blocked. Two show officials then appeared and persuaded people to move along and gradually the crowd began to disperse all still chattering excitedly and gesticulating, some were even laughing.

Fiona climbed down from the bench and asked the people on either side of her what had happened, no-one knew. She asked them if they would keep an eye on her dogs and then made her way towards where Simon was still standing. He was still looking rather shaken and angry but, as she neared him, her attention was drawn to something on the floor. She then realised that the something was Paul Aston. An official was bent over him and Natalie was kneeling on the floor beside him the official was administering to him. As she looked in horrified amazement, Paul stirred and groaned, "Can you hear me sir?" asked the official, "Can you tell me your name sir?"

"Er. Paul, Paul Aston."

"That's good. Now don't try to move for a bit please. A first-aid man is on his way. Just let's see that you are all right before you move."

"What happened? Oh yes, I think I remember now. I want to sit up."

"No Paul, just stay still please, just for a minute or two," Natalie stroked the hair from his face and held his hand, "until we are sure that you are all right. You fell rather heavily."

Simon was still standing there watching this drama being acted out, he looked up as Fiona managed to get to his side, "Simon are you all right? Whatever's happened?"

"It's a long story Fee and right now, I could do with a drink."

"There's some coffee in the flask and...." She could see that his right eye was beginning to close and was looking very swollen and red. "Simon you're hurt."

Simon grinned, " Ouch, I know, but you should see the other fellow."

"Simon, this is not a laughing matter. Come on, let's get back to the bench."

As they started to move away one of the other officials came over to them and said, " Mr?"

"Philips, Simon Philips."

The official wrote down his name and address and asked him to come to the office to make a statement of what had occurred.

It seemed an eternity to Fiona before everything was sorted out and they could leave for home. By now Simon's eye was completely closed and Fiona took over the driving. He hardly said anything in reply to her questions, other than he didn't want to talk about it, so she drove the last part of the journey home in silence wondering again and again what could have caused Simon to do this. She didn't dare think of the possible implications of what had happened. Would it lead to a disciplinary action, would Simon get hauled before a KC committee? Would he be banned from showing? The drive home seemed endless and it was with a great sigh of relief that she saw the cottage and turned into the drive. Ruth, surprised to see them home so early and having looked at Simon's face, was full of questions. Fiona said very little and Ruth tactfully made a quick exit. When Fiona came in from seeing her off, Simon had filled the kettle and put it on the Aga. She felt suddenly drained of energy, cold and frightened, the year hadn't ended yet! Simon, who had gone upstairs, now came down. He had changed into his old jeans and jumper.

"I'll make the tea."

"Thank you Simon, I'm so tired."

"Right, I think we need a drop of whisky in it don't you," he went into the lounge and returned with the bottle. Pouring a good measure into each mug, he sat down at the table and put his head into his hands, "What a bloody mess."

Neither of them felt like eating anything, they just sat on at the kitchen table. After a while Fiona got up, "I must shut the dogs in."

Simon quickly got up as well, "No, let me please. I could do with the fresh air," grabbing his old anorak, he put the hood up and went out into the rain.

Fiona lay there in the darkened bedroom, although she was now warm and comfortable, sleep eluded her. She knew that Simon was laying on his back looking up at the ceiling, he obviously couldn't sleep either, she reached out and, finding his hand, wrapped her fingers around it, "Can't sleep?"

"No."

"Neither can I. Would it help to talk it through?"

"Don't think so, the damage has all been done hasn't it. I'm bloody sorry Fiona. I've buggered everything up now haven't I. We're finished."

"We don't know that."

"We bloody do. You don't go knocking out a member of the KC at a Champ show and get away with it."

"Simon, please tell me exactly what happened."

Simon lifted one arm and putting it around Fiona, settled her head on his chest. He kissed her hair, "Um, smells nice."

After a few moments silence while they lay close to each other, Simon took a deep breath, "Well, I was going to watch you and Saffron in the ring just to get an overall idea of what she looked like and how she performed. I went down the benches away from the ring and round to the next aisle so that she wouldn't see me."

"Yes, go on."

"Well, as I got near Natalie's bench, they seemed to be talking together and suddenly Natalie started walking away, Paul grabbed her arm, she cried out and struggled a bit and I.... Well I went up and told him that he was hurting Natalie. Now I know that you're going to say that I should have minded my own business, but Natalie seemed close to tears and, well I didn't think I just said, "Paul you're hurting Natalie. Leave her alone."

"And."

"Well, that was it, he turned round and said, 'Mind your own business Philips' and I, well I told him that it was not the way to treat a woman, especially when it was his wife. He said.... well it wasn't too nice..." Simon's chest heaved as he took another deep breath, "He said.... that he'd known how to treat you, that you'd never had any complaints or hadn't you told me."

Fiona blushed, "Simon, I'm so sorry. I..."

Simon's arms tightened about her, "Anyway, I grabbed his arm to stop him and he swung round and punched me in the eye with his other arm shouting, "I've owed you that for a long time Philips." He was going to hit me again and I was going to smash his face in when Natalie grabbed his arm and, in trying to shrug her off he must have slipped or something and he went down like a lead weight, bashed his head on the floor and knocked himself out. That was that. I'll be hauled up before a KC committee for bad conduct and very likely barred. I'm sorry Fee. So bloody sorry. I've let you down. The only consolation is that that bastard will go down as well."

They lay together in the darkness for a long while, each thinking of how life must change for them both in consequence. All the years spent thinking of dogs, being with dogs, understanding dogs, showing dogs. All the years and money spent on food, Vets' fees, show fees, cars, tyres, petrol, and all the attendant heartaches and worry, all gone in a few moments of gallantry. Suddenly Fiona pushed herself up in the bed, "I don't care what happens as long as you are with me; last year, when we were apart, wasn't living, not for me. You make me feel alive and I love you. I don't care what the KC does. We can still run the business, we can still breed dogs, we can still go on living here even if it's without shows. Now, I'm going to make a cup of tea. She bent and kissed him on the lips, "My hero. Wished I'd seen you dot him one."

"Don't make me laugh Fee, it bloody hurts."

Natalie and Paul were also laying awake in the darkness but they were neither talking nor cuddling. Paul was not only still very angry and had a terrible headache, but also somewhat concerned about his standing with the KC. He hoped that he would come out of it as the totally injured party and thereby not suffer in consequence. Natalie's thoughts were jumbled and confused. She had seen a side of Paul that she had not hitherto suspected and she didn't like it. She hadn't confronted him that evening, as a former nursing sister, she knew that a blow on the head could result in concussion and she was not going to upset him further but, she would have answers to her questions in the not too distant future. She would know the reasons behind today's behaviour. The first of her questions would be why he was there in the first place? How had he known that she would be there?

CHAPTER THIRTY- FIVE

"Bloomin' miserable news as always," Dennis said to the empty room, he noticed that he had started to talk to himself already and Caroline had only been gone just over a week. He got up and rinsed his plate and mug under the tap and placed them on the draining board. Looking at his watch, he noticed that it was almost time to get ready, he had better find a clean shirt. Going upstairs, he found a clean shirt, he supposed he ought to put a couple in the wash, had a shave, noticed that he needed a haircut and got ready to go out. It was the Christmas dinner of the gardeners' club tonight and they were all going to a pub out in the country that had a reputation for good service. He had debated hard and long whether to go or not, since Caroline had gone to live with this woman Jessica, he had felt too embarrassed and upset to want to go anywhere, he didn't want to face the world, certainly didn't want to tell anyone that she was a..., he couldn't even bring himself to say the word. The memory of that evening when Caroline had explained why she was leaving him was etched indelibly on his mind. For the life of him he still didn't really understand it all. They had been married for years and he'd never had any idea that she gay, if he believed her, neither had she known she was! Part of him expected her to walk in and say that it had all been a silly mistake and that she'd only said those things because she was cross with him about something. Then, part of him wondered if there was something not quite right with him! Then pictures of THAT night surfaced in his mind and he knew, deep down, that there had to be more to it than that. If he was honest with himself, he'd quite enjoyed it! Could it be that they had both made a mistake in the first place by marrying each other?

This morning, George Johns had phoned to ask him if he was going or not because he had to let the pub know the final numbers for tonight. Feeling a bit guilty, he had said yes. Taking a last look in the hall mirror and smoothing his hair down, he really must go to the barbers, he felt in his pocket for the keys, shut the front door and went to the car. Switching on the ignition, he suddenly wished that he had said no, he didn't want people to find out about Caroline. She did come home the other day to see him and to wash and iron his clothes for him as she had promised, but he didn't know if it made it better or worse. It certainly made it damned awkward. He couldn't seem to look at her, he didn't know what to say to her. He certainly didn't want to touch her. Putting the car in gear he set off for the pub.

Quietly slipping into the noisy, crowded room, he made his way to the bar and ordered a pint. He felt less conspicuous with a glass in his hand. Finding a quiet corner he was standing watching the other fellow gardeners when a voice at his elbow said, "Dennis, I'm so glad that you could make it." George was standing there with his wife and a woman he did not recognise.

"Dennis let me introduce you to my sister, Hilary, the one that had your dogs. Hilary, this is one of our newer members, Dennis, and a very good gardener he is, a natural in fact. Dennis, this is Hilary, she has come to stay with us for Christmas."
Dennis smiled and shook her hand without really looking at her, Caroline had done all the arrangements with the dogs, had she told this woman anything?
"Have you lived here long Dennis?"
"No, not very."
"What sort of gardening do you like; flowers? Vegetables? Or perhaps you prefer trees and bushes."
"Flowers and veg."
"I see. Would you rather I left you alone?"
"What? Er.. No, it's just that....um,.....," Dennis could think of nothing to say.
"Well, I hope that you enjoy the evening."
Dennis watched as she walked away from him, he shouldn't have done that, she seemed nice enough; he wanted to know how Patsy and Bonnie had settled in, were they happy? He just felt that he couldn't trust anyone ever again, people weren't what they seemed He noticed that people were moving into the other room so he finished his pint and joined onto the back of the crowd. The tables were marked out with place names and he walked around until he found his name, Hilary was already seated in the next chair to his.

After the first course and a couple of glasses of wine, Dennis summoned up the courage to apologise to Hilary for his rudeness and to ask about the dogs; she accepted his apology with a smile and they started talking. She produced photographs of the dogs from her handbag and gave them to Dennis, "I thought that you might like to see these."

Tears came into his eyes and, for a second or two, Dennis had to swallow very hard or else he would have cried, he'd lost so much! Hilary, sensing that there was some sort of problem continued to chat about the dogs, holidays, gardening, anything until she could see that Dennis appeared to be in control again. After a couple of bottles of French wine and by the time the coffee and mint chocolates appeared they were in a deep discussion on how to preserve an Asparagus bed during the winter months. By the end of the evening he found himself inviting her round to see how he was protecting his Asparagus bed from the frosts. When he went to bed that night, he found that he couldn't sleep. He kept going over the conversation that he had had with her. From the look of the photographs, the dogs seemed to have settled in well and it was obvious that she was very fond of them, she had brought them with her to George's house and he had an invitation to go and see them any time. She was so interesting and certainly knew a lot about gardening. They had talked for ages about the best way to maintain goldfish ponds!

A few days later he rang George's number, "George, this is Dennis, um... sorry to bother you but... is your sister around?"

"No, she and my wife are out doing last minute Christmas shopping. They shouldn't be long now but you know what these ladies are like. Shall I tell her you rang?"

"Yes, please."

"The 'do' was a success don't you think."

"Yes, very good."

"They lived up to their reputation. We'll go there again for our summer get together. I'll tell Hilary that you called."

Dennis made a cup of tea. Well that was that. She wouldn't ring back, why should she. He was just finishing a second cup when the phone rang, he leaped up and hurried into the hall, "Hello, Hello."

"Dennis, this is Hilary. I'm so glad that you rang."

"Yes, well I wondered if you wanted to come over some time to see the greenhouse and the Asparagus beds."

"I'd love to. I'm looking forward to seeing your greenhouse."

"Right, well how about tomorrow?"

"Christmas Eve. Yes, shall I come about ten thirty? Can I bring the dogs?"

Although there was a cold, biting wind, the sun was shining as Dennis proudly showed her around his garden. He had, first of all, made her a cup of coffee and they had sat in the warm conservatory while he played with Patsy and Bonnie who were overjoyed at seeing him.

"I can see that they miss you very much Dennis and you miss them don't you."

"Yes, very much."

Hilary frowned slightly but asked no more questions. He showed her photographs of the garden as it had been when he took it over.

" That's your wife isn't it?"

"Yes."

"Is she not here today?"

"No. We're separated. Look, shall we go and see the garden."

As they walked round and he pointed out various changes that he had made, his tension left him and he felt more and more relaxed in her company. She was a real gardener, understood about muck and fertilisers, pruning and hoeing and she had some damned good ideas too. He opened the door to the greenhouse.

"What a wonderful old sort of greenhouse. They take more looking after but I like them best of all. My granddad had one something like this."

"You're kidding, so did mine."

Time went by, the dogs finished their excited exploration of the garden and still Dennis and Hilary were finding topics of discussion. Dennis suddenly realised that the sun had gone in and a chill wind was blowing and they still hadn't finished the tour of the garden.

"I'm so sorry keeping you out like this, I hope you're not cold."

"That's all right. I've so enjoyed it."

"I've got some ham to make a sandwich, shall I make a bit of lunch?"

"Did you, that's nice. Well, you make a cup of tea and I'll make the sandwich. That is, if you don't mind."

The light had almost gone from the sky as she, Bonnie and Patsy took their leave, by then it had been decided that he should go to

George's house for Christmas dinner and that they would take the dogs for a long walk on Boxing day, weather permitting.

Dennis shut the door and looked around, suddenly Christmas didn't seem so bad after all. He suddenly stopped as he entered the kitchen, he hadn't asked her if she was married.

Beryl and Peter duly arrived on Christmas day and Fiona and Simon put their problems behind them, to make sure that the festivities went well. Fiona had decorated a Christmas tree, they had pulled crackers and laughed at the ghastly jokes over dinner, drank too much wine, watched the Queen's speech and played cards and Monopoly. Both Laura and Duncan had phoned and Fiona was able to forget her problems and enjoy the warmth of friendship.

Towards evening, after Simon and Peter had locked up the dogs, the atmosphere got a little more serious. Peter turned to Simon and Fiona, "Now you two, I hope I'm not speaking out of turn but, now and again, I've thought that you seem to have something on your minds. Is it anything that we can help with?"

"Thanks Peter. I'm sorry, we didn't mean to say anything, don't want to spoil the day."

"So there is something wrong! It's not... you two aren't... no not again."

"No, don't panic. Fee and I are fine. No it's something to do with the dogs."

Simon explained just what had been happening over the past months culminating in the show down at the LKA. He went on to explain what the consequences had meant to them as far as the business was concerned and then what the consequences would be if the KC held a meeting and banned him from shows.

Beryl was amazed, "What. Ban you! But they can't, they don't make the laws. It's not a crime."

"They do though, as far as dog showing is concerned. They are a monopoly and can and do make their own laws as far as what goes on at the shows."

"But who gave them the right? Parliament?"

"Do you know Beryl, I'm not too sure."

The conversation continued to flow but Simon took no more part in it. He sat deep in thought until Fiona suggested that they have some tea. He looked at her and then jumped up from his chair, "I'll make it.

234

How about a game of Scrabble? Where's that big box of chocolates?"

About midnight, long after they had waved goodbye to Beryl and Peter, Fiona was just drifting off to sleep, when Simon sat up in bed and turned the light on again.

"Simon, I love you dearly but I'm ever so tired."

"Well that's better than having a headache. No Fee, I must tell you of an idea I had when we were all talking earlier."

Fiona yawned, "Oh Simon, won't it keep 'til morning."

"No, listen."

He went on to say that, when he had been explaining their position with the KC a thought had struck him. It wasn't really to do with their present situation but, nevertheless, it was interesting.

"Um, interesting. Um."

"No, come on Fee stay awake."

"You know how we all blame the KC for everything that we don't agree with. How we say that they get everything wrong. How they make the wrong choices and decisions and make problems worse not better."

"Um."

"Well, how's this for an idea. They don't have any choice! Well not real choice. They have to do what is best for the big breeders, the syndicates, where the money is or they would lose their revenue and not be able to survive."

"Sorry you've lost me."

"For instance, Open shows! How many times have you heard people say that everything the KC does for Open shows makes them worse and harder to run not better."

"Hundreds."

"Yeah. Well, then more people go to the Champ shows instead. That keeps all the CCs going for the big breeders to make up champions and sell them and the puppies, stallholders and dog food people do better, the big show societies do better and, therefore, the KC does better. How's about that!"

"No, I still like the Open shows, especially for puppies."

"Yeah I know you do, but lots of people don't now just want to make up champions. They want the glamour and the glory. Look how much bigger and grander all the shows have become. Look at Crufts!

Look how people say that it's like a Grand Sunday Market now, it could happily go ahead without the dog showing. You know that's what people say."

"Yes, but they still go don't they Simon. That's the point, they still go! Is that it, can I go to sleep now?" Fiona pulled the duvet up over her ears and turned on her side, "Night Simon, sleep well."

"Yeah, but they are so damned dear now that there's no money left to go to Open shows is there."

"No, there isn't. Night Simon."

Simon turned over but could not sleep, could he be right. Did the KC take their orders from the bigwigs in showing? It was so simple an explanation for so many questionable decisions, could he be right? Why hadn't he thought of it before, why had he always thought the KC was a thing apart? A band of high-minded, well-meaning do-gooders who knew nothing about actual dog showing. He wrestled his pillow and turned over to cuddle Fiona's warm, sleeping body. Whatever happened in the coming months, even if they banned him from showing, he didn't care, he had this girl in his life and that was all that mattered, he cupped her warm breast in his right hand, "I love you Fee. Happy Christmas." Just as his eyes were closing he murmured into her hair, "And Boxing Day, and New Year."

CHAPTER THIRTY-SIX

Natalie had been busy washing some of the pieces of porcelain from the sitting room. Jessie, her cleaner, was getting very slow now and she didn't altogether trust her with some of the more expensive pieces that her first husband, Richard had bought for her from time to time. Paul had argued again this morning that she was silly to keep her on, a young, active woman would get a lot more cleaning done and relieve her of the duty. As he had said, "Why have a dog and bark yourself." Of course, as was often the case, he was absolutely right, but sentiment had to play a part here. She could remember when Richard was so ill and Jessie had been a tower of strength to her, helping in any way she could. Deep in thought about the old days she didn't hear Paul come in, "I thought I told you before Natalie to leave those to Jessie. You said that you wanted to go out today."

"It's really no trouble Paul, and it's done now. I can go out a little later."

"That's not the issue here is it. It's ridiculous to hire someone who can no longer do the job. Sentiment just cannot come into it." Natalie bit her lip hard, she was determined not to start an argument. Several times since the New Year she had found Paul to be somewhat authoritarian, dictating what she should and should not do. She did not like this change of attitude and was inclined to question his decisions. She and Richard had had a very sharing and equal relationship with regard to household and family matters and she found Paul's manner very difficult to deal with. It had certainly not been apparent when they were courting.

As she got ready to go out she recalled the day that, on the spur of the moment, she had decided to call on Fiona and Simon to wish them a belated Happy New Year.
She found them both still sitting at the breakfast table, which was so unlike them that she knew that something was wrong.

"Oh dear, please tell me to go if I have come at a bad time."

"Natalie, how nice to see you. Do come in, sorry about the mess. Would you like a cup of tea? Do you want another one Simon?"

"No, I'll get on with the kennels. Hi Natalie, excuse me," he grabbed his coat and went outside.

"I can see something is dreadfully wrong. Are you sure that you want me to stay. Can I do anything?"

Fiona pushed a letter, which had been lying on the table towards her. Natalie saw immediately that it was on Kennel Club paper. It required Simon to attend a disciplinary hearing with regard to the events that occurred at the LKA. Not wanting to upset Fiona further she had not asked any of the questions that sprang to mind, she wasn't too sure of what this hearing might mean, she had tried to bring the subject up with Paul, after all he was the injured party, but he had refused to speak to her about it, merely saying that it was entirely a matter for the Kennel Club.

Although Paul didn't know it, her outing today was to meet Audrey. She had phoned her yesterday to arrange a meeting and, in view of what had happened before, she told Audrey that, if she informed Paul of this meeting, she would never speak to her again. Audrey had sounded quite worried, "Natalie, I've never known you to be so sharp. What do you want to see me about? It sounds very ominous."

She had arranged the meeting at a country hotel and, as she got out of the car, she could see Audrey's Renault parked nearby, she checked in her handbag before she started to walk towards the hotel entrance, she had written down several pertinent questions to ask Audrey and she was going to get answers this time.

It was beginning to get dark and the lights were being turned on in the hotel as the two old friends came out of the restaurant and stood in the foyer together, "Thank you Audrey, this has been a most interesting afternoon." They both walked toward their respective cars, "Bye Natalie, see you again soon. Do ask Paul about coming to dinner with us won't you," she watched as Audrey got into her car and, with a friendly wave, drove off. Natalie stayed sitting in her car and it was several minutes before she turned the key in the ignition and switched on the lights. Well, she had wanted answers and she had got them, some of the answers had quite shaken her and she had felt very foolish and naive that she hadn't seen some things for herself. Paul was already home when she opened the front door and came hurrying out into the hall, "Hello darling, where have you been? I was getting worried."

"I had lunch with Audrey. We just got chatting and didn't notice the time passing."

"Audrey?"

"Yes, Audrey, she is an old friend of mine you know, is there any reason why I shouldn't have lunch with her?"

"No, no none at all."

Natalie, feeling very tired and distressed after her somewhat revealing conversation with Audrey, suggested that they go out for a meal, "Paul, as it's a bit late to start cooking a meal, shall we go to that Italian restaurant that you enjoy so much."

Paul looked at her keenly, she did look a bit fraught, what had she been talking to Audrey about; he would have to give her a call. "Of course, let's do that. You do look a little tired, I do think that you should consider what I said this morning my dear." Natalie shot a glance at him but refrained from speaking. During the meal, Paul was his usual charming, courteous self and Natalie began to relax a little. He ordered another bottle of wine, "This is very pleasant my dear, good food, good wine but most of all, good company. A lovely ending to the day."

"Thank you Paul. What have you been doing today?"

"Why?"

"No reason, just wondered how your day had gone."

"Quite well."

"Are you busy at work?"

"Yes, fairly. Why?"

"Just wondered, you seem to have so many Championship judging appointments now and committee meetings, I wondered how you were fitting it all in."

"Well you know my dear, I work hard and methodically. I'm not frightened of delegating work to others...."

"No, I'm sure you're not." She paused. " By the way, do you have Fiona's new mobile number?"

"What? Fiona's mobile number? Yes, I suppose so, does that matter?"

"I didn't think that I'd given it to you."

"Didn't you, I don't know, you must have done and forgotten. My dear, you do seem in a funny mood suddenly. Are you all right? What has prompted all these questions? Are you ill or is it something that Audrey has said?"

"Now why should you think that?"

"Because, well because you were perfectly all right this morning and now, since your meeting with Audrey you seem.... odd."

"Do I," Natalie picked up her wine glass and drained it.

Paul frowned and poured her some more wine.

Later that evening, Paul watched as Natalie removed her dress and hung it in the wardrobe, as she removed her bra and her heavy breasts were released, he was roused, as she removed her panties and tights he was even more roused. He had often noticed that she was far more attractive undressed than dressed unlike some women. As she got into bed he turned out his bedside lamp, "Don't feel like reading tonight my dear after that delightful meal." He turned towards Natalie, she was wearing some sort of silky nightdress he noticed as he gently pulled it up around her waist. She lay quite still as his hand started to caress her, normally she responded by taking her nightie off and turning towards him but tonight, she did nothing. He started to kiss her breasts as his hand continued to caress her and she felt annoyance that, in spite of herself, her body started to respond to his moving fingers. He suddenly sat up, removed his pyjamas and then lay on top of her. She could feel that he was very aroused but still, she just lay there.

"Natalie my love, you are beautiful, so beautiful," he said as he pushed her thighs apart.

Paul lay there unable to sleep. Usually, after making love he fell asleep almost straight away but tonight, he couldn't sleep. Natalie had behaved so strangely this evening. All those questions over dinner and then her behaviour tonight. She had never been unresponsive, always grateful and pleased that he had possessed her, making her feel like a woman. Always warm and loving afterwards, stroking his face and praising him until he fell asleep. Tonight, however, she had got out of bed and gone to the bathroom without a word the moment he had left her. When she came back to bed it was to turn away from him, turn the light out and ignore him.

240

Not a word of thanks. What the devil had gone on this afternoon? Blast Audrey Chatsworth and her big mouth. Women just shouldn't be allowed in the higher echelons of the KC. He desperately wanted to get on the phone and speak to her. First thing in the morning, he would have to get to his office quickly and phone the damned woman to find out just what had been said. She was such a blabbermouth, like most women.

Unusually for him, Paul did not wake at his normal time in the morning; he turned over to put an arm around Natalie only to find her side of the bed cold and empty. Looking at the bedside alarm clock he saw that it was already ten past eight. The events of last night flooded into his mind and, flinging himself out of bed, he threw off his pyjamas, grabbed clean underwear from a drawer and made for the shower. Revived by the hot water, he hurried down the stairs calling Natalie's name; there was no reply. Jamie came to greet him his tail wagging, "Get out of the way you damned dog, you should be in your kennel."

"Jessie!" Of course, it was Friday; she didn't come on Friday. Damn. After a quick inspection of the lounge and dining room, the kitchen and the garden, he hurried to the front door and looked out onto the drive. Natalie's car was not there, "Damn, damn, what the devil's going on."

He hurried back into the hall and picked up the phone and dialled Audrey's number, "Audrey, this is Paul Aston, is Natalie with you?"

"Hello Paul this is an early call."

"Don't mess me about Audrey, is Natalie with you."

"No, no she isn't. What's wrong Paul?"

"I don't damned well know, but it's certainly got something to do with you seeing Natalie yesterday. What the blazing hell did you say to her?"

There was silence from the other end of the phone for a minute or two, "Oh dear Paul. I had no idea that Natalie was so naive. I think she was rather surprised about some things."

"What! About me?"

"Well no, not about you specifically, well not really, just general things that we all accept as the norm in the dog world."

"My God. What have you done," Paul slammed the phone down. He had a sinking feeling in his stomach and felt a bit sick. What had that stupid, prattling bitch done. Had she ruined all his efforts, all his plans, this house, the money, the connections, his new standing in the world of dogs. Another thought struck him, of course, that's where she would have gone. He dialled Fiona's number and Simon answered the phone. What the devil was he doing there at this time, he should be at work, "Simon, Paul here. Is Natalie there?"

"Hello Paul, is Natalie here?" looking round at Natalie he could see that she was shaking her head vigorously, "No, I'm afraid she's not. Can I help?"

As soon as he'd heard Simon's voice his temper had risen, now he knew that he was also lying, "Can you help! You! It's all your damned fault, everything is your fault, always has been and always will be until I can get rid of you for good."

"What did you say?"

Realising that he had let his temper get the better of his tongue, Paul slammed the phone down. Pushing his fingers through his hair he looked around at the hall. He was certain that Natalie was at the bloody Philips' house but, he must calm down, he mustn't do anything rash. He'd said too much already. He walked into the dining room and poured a small glass of brandy from the decanter, swilling the liquid around the glass, he walked into the sitting-room and sat down in his armchair. He would deny anything she threw at him; he knew that there was no proof. Nothing could be traced to him because he hadn't had to do a thing himself, there were always crawlers in the dog scene willing to do anything to get on. Everything was done by word of mouth so there was no proof. Sipping his brandy, he continued to sit there and logically bring a degree of calm to his troubled mind. Too much was at stake here, even if he had to back pedal a bit and eat humble pie, for a while anyway, he couldn't afford to lose all this. Revenge would have to wait but it would be even sweeter for the waiting.

Simon had not gone to the office, he had phoned in and said that he would be taking a day from his annual leave. He and Fiona had been woken at six that morning by a hammering on the door. The two house dogs had set up a cacophony of barking and Simon had hurried downstairs. When he looked out of the kitchen window and seen Natalie standing there he had been positive that something dreadful had happened.

242

"Who is it?" A sleepy voice asked behind him.

"It's OK. It's Natalie."

"Natalie. At this time! Let her in quickly, something must be awfully wrong."

"I'm so sorry if I've woken you but I just couldn't wait any longer." Seeing their sleepy but concerned faces looking at her, Natalie had burst into tears and it had been some while and several cups of tea later before they had been able to piece together her jumbled remarks and make sense of them. She had apparently lain awake all night worrying about the things that Paul had done, or rather what she thought that Paul had done. They gradually calmed her down and Fiona and Simon got dressed; after they'd all had a bit of breakfast and more tea, Natalie began to make sense. It was at this moment that Paul had rung.

The upshot of the morning's talking, during which Natalie asked many questions and demanded that Fiona and Simon be honest in their answers, Natalie had a clearer picture of, not only her husband but also the sport of dog showing.

"But why Fiona, why didn't you tell me all these things before."

"Oh Natalie, you were so enjoying your hobby, why spoil it for you. As for Paul, well...."

"I see."

A delivery van drew up outside and Simon excusing himself, went to the door.

"Simon, I'm so sorry. Look, I'll go. I'm holding you two up."

Natalie stayed seated until Simon had gone outside, she then turned to Fiona, "One last question Fiona, and this is the big one."

"Yes."

Looking down at the table Natalie said, "Was Paul in love with you? Is he still?"

Startled for a moment Fiona swallowed hard and said, "Why do you ask that?"

"I have to know for certain."

"Oh Natalie, what do I say."

"The truth please, it's important."

"At one time I did think that he was in love with me..."

Natalie made a sound in her throat and put her hand to her mouth.

"This is awful Natalie, I don't want to upset you."

Natalie took a deep breath and asked her to continue.

"As I said, at one time I thought he was, he suggested marriage and," Fiona stopped speaking, Natalie had put her hands over her eyes.

" And, and I wasn't sure and then he met you and it all stopped." There was silence in the room for several minutes, Natalie got a tissue out of her bag and dried her eyes and blew her nose. "Thank you for being honest. I wish you'd said all this before."

"Natalie, you seemed so happy and I didn't want to spoil it."

"Changing the subject, when I came over to see you last, you told me that the phone calls had started up again on your new mobile phone number. You said that you wondered how the person had got the number because only a very few friends had it."

"Yes, that's right."

Tears came into Natalie's eyes, " I puzzled over that because, I knew that I had given it to no-one and you said that you knew that you could trust all your friends implicitly," she wiped away a tear that was running down her cheek. "I'm pretty certain that Paul has your number and I didn't give it to him. He must have gone through my diary. It's the only explanation."

"Paul. Yes, well we have wondered at times if he could be the one. Simon thought it from the start."

The tears were flowing down Natalie's face as she asked Fiona why Paul should want to do this to them, "Do you think that he still loves you and is jealous?"

"No Natalie no, I'm sure that he does love you."

"Then why?"

"Simon thinks he's just mad but I don't, but equally, I don't know why he would do all this."

"Your affair is over I suppose?"

"Yes!"

"When"

"About the time that he proposed I, " Fiona faltered and sadly raised her eyes to Natalie's, face, she was crumpled in her chair and sobbing. "I thought that he loved me."

"Natalie, I think he does, as much as he can love anyone after himself," crying too, Fiona got up to put an arm around Natalie's shaking shoulders.

Simon, walking in the door, quickly surveyed the scene of the two crying women and, as quickly, walked out again. He had plenty to do outside and he would hear it all from Fee later.

CHAPTER THIRTY- SEVEN

Natalie brought all her professional training as a nursing sister to bear in the next few weeks. No way was Paul to know that her whole world had been turned upside down, apart from the fact that she did not readily kiss him and certainly did not make love to him, she was, to all intents and purposes, her happy, smiling, sensible self. After her devastating conversation with Fiona, she had driven to a quiet spot in the countryside and cried until she could cry no longer. She felt a profound sense of betrayal, even if Paul did genuinely love her as Fiona had insisted that he did, she still was left with this desperate feeling of falseness, of dishonesty and betrayal. She kept remembering happy days and moments of pleasure when she had thought that he adored her and the tears kept coming back into her eyes and running down her cheeks unchecked. She remembered how young and attractive she had felt when they went out for a meal or to the theatre, to a race meeting, on a steam train and, most of all, the nights that he had made love to her. He had rejuvenated her, interested her in so many new things, he had made the world come to life again. She had been feeling so middle-aged and dumpy so dull and settled into a comfortable, middle-aged, unexciting life, the dog showing had certainly stimulated her, had given her something to strive for again but, knowing that Paul loved and wanted her, knowing that her body was still desirable had made her feel.... womanly, yes, sexy, yes, she suddenly had breasts that were desirable, not just a cup size, she had a body which responded to his hands and aroused him, not just a dress size. Suddenly, glamorous underwear and nighties, new make-up, perfume, having a new hair style, plucking her eyebrows had all become important.

It had all been so wonderful, she sighed and wiped her swollen eyes, the holidays with him as well! Everything absolutely everything would be lost if she told him that she knew what he had been doing to Fiona and Simon; not that she had any real proof but, she knew that it had to be him. She stopped reminiscing and wiped her eyes again. Some serious thought and some hard decisions needed to be made now. She shivered as another thought cruelly came into her mind, she didn't even know if he had really been loving her, or the image of Fiona. Supposing that he had been imagining

Fiona's neat, slim body beneath his hands. Natalie closed her eyes and put her hands up to her face, this was just too painful. Perhaps, all along, she had been a stupid, silly middle-aged woman living in a fantasy world. Perhaps he had just wanted the money, the house.... and her friends at the KC. She put a shaky hand to her forehead, she swallowed hard, yes, she had to face facts, that was a distinct possibility. Sitting up straight and wiping her eyes, she opened the car window to let the cold air blow onto her face, "Natalie, get a good grip on yourself. You have got to go home now and put on a brave face. No way is that man going to know anything until you have decided what is best for you," nodding and taking a gulp of fresh air, she wound the window up and started the car and drove home.

As she let herself into the house, its' familiar feeling gave her confidence. Holding up her head she called out, "Paul, where are you? Sorry I'm a bit late, got interested in a book at the library and lost all track of time."

"Hello my dear. I was beginning to wonder where you could be. Had a nice day?"

"Yes, lovely day," she called out as she hurried up the stairs. She didn't want him to see that she had bought nothing and neither did she want him to see that she had been crying. She splashed cold water on her face and eyes and repaired her make-up.

"Paul, as I'm so late, shall we go out for a meal tonight?"

"Yes, if you like. I'm quite happy to do that."

Why does he have to be so nice she thought as they faced each other over the gleaming cutlery on the restaurant table. Knowing what I know, why can't I hate him? Why don't I just tell him to go now. I could just pack all his clothes and put them outside, I could cut all his suits up into shreds, while he was asleep. I could..., her thoughts were interrupted by Paul's voice.

"Natalie! You seem to be deep in thought Natalie, may I ask what you are thinking about. Is it anything I can help with?"

"No Paul it's nothing. I was just wondering about buying new curtains for the bedroom. The trouble is that it would mean redecorating."

"Do you mean our bedroom?"

"Yes."

"I like it as it is, don't you?"

"No, not now. I'd like a change."

Paul frowned and looked a little puzzled, something was still wrong between them, he'd have another word with Audrey. They finished their meal in silence and returned home. Now, thought Natalie, now I must really act my part. She knew that she could, you don't become a nursing sister without being able to hide your feelings.

As she undressed she could feel his eyes upon her, she tried to hurry but, when she had a bit of trouble undoing her bra, Paul, immediately came around the bed, "Here let me do that for you my dear."

As he undid the bra, he slipped his hands round to cup her full breasts and kiss the back of her neck, "Natalie my darling."

She jerked forward releasing her breasts from his hands and grabbed her nightie from the bed, "I'm sorry Paul but, don't you find the room cold? I think I must have a cold coming on. Do you mind if we don't tonight? Perhaps I'll take a couple of Aspirin." As she turned to face him she could see that he was already roused and taut and it gave her a shiver of satisfaction to know that he wanted her body and to know that he wasn't going to have it.

"Of course I mind, I love you and you are looking particularly lovely tonight, I don't know why but, somehow you're different and even more exciting."

"No I'm not, I'm the same Natalie that you fell in love with."

"Indeed you are."

When she came back to the bedroom he was reading. She got into bed and immediately turned out her bedside light.

"Not going to read tonight?"

"No Paul, I'm tired. I think it's this cold coming on."

"Let's hope that the Aspirin help."

Paul read the evening paper for a while and then she heard him turn his light out and settle down. She lay there in the dark for some time formulating her plans until, exhausted, she finally closed her eyes and settled down to a troubled sleep.

The following week, on the day of Simon and Paul's meeting with the KC committee to investigate the reasons for the fight at the LKA, Paul was up very early showering and shaving. He wanted to look his best today, because today he would finish Simon Philips for good.

After his evidence, Philips wouldn't have a leg to stand on. He would see that the KC threw the book at him. He'd be barred from showing again. All that knowledge that he had about dogs, all those good dogs he had bred would all go to pot. Their money would dry up together with the business. Fiona wouldn't want him then, she wouldn't find him so attractive then and serve her right. If he, Paul, hadn't been so slow all those years ago, he could have had Fiona then before Philips got his hands on her. He might have even married her. They wouldn't have put all her money into that damned kennels, he would have invested it for her and got some healthy returns. They would have a good living by now, even a family! He would have been a respected family man with a beautiful wife, a lovely home, in his name of course, Fiona had always been so gullible. He would have still made it in the KC. Not perhaps so fast as he had done with the help of Natalie's friends but.... his thoughts were interrupted, "Would you like a boiled egg for breakfast Paul?"

"No thank you my dear. Just toast. I shall, no doubt, have an excellent lunch at Clarges Street. What are you going to do today my dear?"

"It all depends on the weather. I shall take Jamie for a long walk perhaps."

"Yes, you do that my dear. He smiled, kissed her on the cheek and left the house; it was only as he drove onto the motorway that he realised that she had not wished him luck.

"That's the last one Fee," Simon closed the door to the kennel. It was the day of the hearing at the KC. Neither he nor Fiona had slept too well and, in consequence they had got up earlier than usual. With time on their hands, although Ruth was coming for the day, they had decided to feed the dogs and clean the kennels and runs; it was preferable to sitting around waiting and worrying.

"You know, you don't have to come Fee. You can't come in."

"I know, but as I've said before. I want to be there for when you come out."

They had both showered and changed by the time Ruth turned up, "Hi, you two. It's a nice dry day anyway, not like yesterday." They both looked so tired with dark circles round their eyes. She knew how worrying this was for both of them. It could affect their whole life if it went the wrong way. She smiled cheerfully at them, "Now, what do you want me to do?"

As she waved them off twenty minutes later the smile left her face. They were such nice people, they had always been very good employers and always kind and thoughtful. Fiona never forgot the children's birthdays and they were always given a present at Christmas too. She was a little worried about losing this job but she was more worried for Fiona and Simon, they were good people. Whatever it was that Simon had done, she knew that it would have been fair and honest. Setting the answerphone, she went out to walk the dogs.

.

Fiona wandered around the busy London streets, there was such hustle and bustle, it made the cottage and kennels seem like heaven. Simon had told her to come back in about an hour to an hour and a half and then, if he wasn't waiting for her, to turn her mobile phone on and he would call her. She turned into another busy street and was just looking into a shop window displaying evening wear when the trilling of the phone in her handbag made her jump, "Hi Fee. Are you anywhere near?"

"Simon! I'm not too far away, why?"

"Well, I'm out. Where are you and I'll come and get you."

"That was quick! No don't come to me, everywhere is so crowded; I'll see you at the underground station, that would be better. I'm not far away. How did it go? Are you banned?"

"I'll tell you about it when I see you."

"Oh Simon!"

With a last glance at the stunning dresses displayed in the window, she hurried towards the station. As she approached she could see Simon already standing at the entrance and tried to guess from the look on his face how things had gone.

"Hi Fee. Look, I'm gagging for a drink. Let's find a pub."

"For heavens sake Simon, how did it go?"

"Long story, let's get a drink first."

"Simon, I'll kill you if you don't tell me."

Ordering sandwiches, a pint of bitter and a shandy for Fiona, they found an empty table and sat down, "My God, I needed that."

"For heaven's sake Simon, tell me what happened before I pour this over your head!"

He then proceeded to tell her that there had been quite a lot of discussion, he, Simon had been read the part of the KC rules appertaining to his behaviour, they had then both been asked for their version of events leading up to the fracas. Needless to say, Paul's version had differed quite considerably from Simon's.

"Do you mean that he lied?"

"Well, it wasn't quite lies but equally it wasn't exactly how it happened. They did ask us quite a few questions but you could see though from their faces whose version they believed. I thought that it was curtains for me, they would only have to read out my sentence and it would be all over."

"Oh Simon, you must have felt awful."

"No, just frustrated and bloody angry. After they had read out my sentence, I was going to give them a piece of my mind and tell them that, if they continued to let the tail wag the bloody dog, their days in office would be numbered. The cracks in the show world were already beginning to show."

"I'm glad you didn't."

"Well, I didn't get the bloody chance. It seemed over bar the shouting. I told you, I thought that they were going to condemn me when the door opened and a secretary came in with a sheet of paper. One of the panel excused himself and went out of the door. We all sat around like lemons for about ten minutes; Aston looking bloody smug. The bloke came back into the room and whispered something to all of them. They all read this piece of paper and nodded at the bloke and after a bit of throat clearing he told us that this particular hearing would have to be postponed because there was fresh evidence which conflicted with some of the statements. A new hearing would have to be convened."

"But what was the new evidence?"

"Damned if I know. Paul Aston looked like a bloody thundercloud. He tried to talk to them and say that it should be decided now but they weren't having any of it. Honestly, the silly old duffers went up in my estimation."

"So, do you mean that we've got to wait and wait and then go through all this again?"

"Looks like it."

Fiona sighed, "Simon, I just don't think I can bear it. The 'not knowing' is driving me mad. Do you want this sandwich because I don't; I'm too wound up to be hungry. Let's go home Simon."

Still smarting with frustration and annoyance, Paul let himself into a silent house. Having satisfied himself that Natalie was not in the house, he went into the garden. The new gardener was out there feeding Jamie.

"Do you know where Mrs Aston is?"

"I think she's gone out."

"Yes, yes that's pretty obvious. Do you know where?"

"I'm not sure but I think she said the solicitor's."

"The solicitor's? Why should she tell you that?"

"Don't know."

Paul frowned, Natalie hadn't said anything this morning about going to see her solicitor. Now why was she doing that? And why the hell should she tell the damned gardener! He walked into the dining-room and poured a small amount of brandy into a glass. He needed to think. The proceedings today had surprised him. Whatever was this new evidence they had. He had stayed at the club and endeavoured to find out more but no-one he spoke to knew anything about it. He might phone Audrey and Ian tonight, they might have heard something. Damnation, he thought today would have seen Philips out of the picture altogether. He had been so looking forward to gloating over his defeat. He heard a key in the front door and got up, "Hello Natalie, I'm home."

"How did it go?"

He briefly explained the situation ending with, "So now, we have to wait. I just can't think what this new evidence is but it can't be much. It won't alter the final result; he has flagrantly broken the rules and must pay the price. What have you been doing today?"

Looking at the smug smile on his face Natalie said, "I've been to see Mr Frobisher."

"Yes, I know, the gardener told me. May I ask why? I hope that nothing's wrong."

"No, not now."

She started to go upstairs but then stopped and turned, "Paul, I might as well say this now as later, I no longer wish to live with you, will you kindly pack the rest of your things and get out of my house.

I have already packed quite a lot of your clothes. You will find the suitcases on the landing."

Paul's face first went white and then suffused with red, "Just what the hell are you talking about Natalie. Is this some sort of joke? because, if it is, I think it's in very poor taste."

"No, it's not a joke. I am deadly serious. I wish you to leave my house and not return."

"What do you mean, leave? Why? What's wrong? I don't understand. Do you mean that you want a divorce?"

"Yes."

Paul stared up at her in total disbelief, "But Natalie, what's happened? What's suddenly brought this on? I don't want a divorce, I love you."

"It matters nothing to me whether you file for divorce or not. I have so arranged with the solicitor that you will find it very difficult to get your hands on any of my money or this house."

"What are you talking about? I don't want your money, I want you!"

"As I was saying, I am selling this house and going to live in New Zealand to be near Candida. Everything in time will be gifted to her and the baby. As you have not contributed at all to the upkeep of this house in the short time that we have been married, you are entitled to next to nothing and that is what you'll get. Now, please, take your suitcases and go."

"But... but in heaven's name Natalie, why? What's happened to bring this on? I thought that you loved me, that we were happy! I'm not doing anything or going anywhere until I get an explanation."

"All right, I suppose I owe you that; I see you now for what you really are. I truly think that once, you were a kind and decent man but now.... I know about your affair with Fiona, and doubt that you ever loved me. I know what you have been doing to Simon and Fiona and their business. How could you be so cruel and vindictive?"

"You've got it all wrong. I do love you! As for the other, you haven't got a shred of evidence. Have you been listening to them? They would say that it was me! Philips is just annoyed that I bedded his precious wife and that I've got on in showing and she, well she's just a tart, she'd sleep with any...."

"Please go now Paul, I don't want to hear any more, or do I have to call the police. By the way, just before you go, it was I who wrote to the Kennel Club and told them exactly what did happen at the LKA. I didn't think that I could trust you to tell the truth, I also mentioned what you had been doing to the Philips," she turned and walked up the stairs with Paul's voice calling up to her, "Natalie, Natalie my dear, you've got it all wrong. Please listen to me, I had nothing to do with the Philips business and I only told a few white lies in order to protect us, you and I that is. Natalie! Natalie!"

Natalie continued upstairs, she was shaking so much that she was frightened that her legs would give way and tears were streaming down her face but she straightened her back and walked on, he wasn't going to know that.

As he refused to take his suitcases downstairs and, an hour later, was still trying to remonstrate with her through a locked bedroom door, Natalie opened the window and called to the gardener to come in and carry Mr Aston's suitcases to his car. She heard Paul's voice shouting at the gardener but then, it went quite and Natalie heard Paul's car drive off. Quietly opening the door she saw most of the suitcases still there but his overnight bag was gone.

Still shaking, she went downstairs and Jamie ran up to her and licked her hand, "It's all right Jamie. It's all right." She knew that she must now execute the rest of her plan. Going round the house she started to lock windows and bolt the doors, tomorrow, she would get the locks changed but first, she must drag those damned suitcases down the stairs and put them in the porch.

CHAPTER THIRTY- EIGHT

The shock waves hit Natalie a couple of days after Paul's departure from the house. As she had thought, Paul had tried to come back but her plans had thwarted him. She couldn't understand why she felt so ill, so tired, so devastated, almost more than when Richard had died. She desperately wanted to talk it all out with someone but, as she didn't want to talk to friends and neighbours, especially Fiona and Audrey and she didn't want to upset Candida any further, she finally decided to phone up and arrange a meeting with Richard's old partner, Frank Samuels.

"Hello Frank, it's Natalie Bennett, I mean Aston."

"Hello Natalie, how nice of you to phone."

"It's nice of you to say that after all this time. I haven't spoken to you since.... since my marriage to... Paul," she found difficulty in even speaking his name.

"Well I'm sure that you must have been very busy."

"Yes I have but that's no excuse for losing contact with a valued old friend."

"Never mind that now, it is a pleasure for me these days to hear from old friends. At my age there doesn't seem to be so many of them."

She arranged to meet Frank on the following day for lunch and then, having made a cup of coffee, she took it into the lounge and sat down to make a list of all the points that she wanted to discuss with him. She wanted to get everything, all her plans, in motion as swiftly as possible. Frank would be able to smooth out any wrinkles and to get her organised so that there were no hiccups on the way. The phone rang and as she picked it up she heard Audrey's voice, "Hello, hello, is that you Natalie. Now please don't put the phone down. I have some news for you."

"I don't think that there is anything that you could possibly tell me that I want to hear."

"No, no please listen to what I have to say. I have just come from Clarges Street. There is to be another meeting. Since they received your account of what actually happened at the LKA and the fact that it was Paul who slipped and fell rather than Mr Philips knocking him down and that Mr Philips account of the proceedings is similar in content, they are reviewing the situation. As to the other business with the Philips, there is no actual proof at all that Paul was involved."

"Oh, I'm certain that he was involved all right! As to the other, as long as they exonerate Simon Philips, who was the innocent party in that fight and only stepped in to assist me; I shall be happy. I don't care what they do to Paul."

"My dear girl, I don't pretend to know what's happened between you and Paul, I never interfere between man and wife, but you know Paul is a very useful friend to have, he is such a good liaison officer and organiser, so persuasive when talking to people. He's knowledgeable, generous and kind, look at the things he has bought you and I'm sure that he idolises you."

"I don't want to hear any more Audrey. I know you mean well but thank you for letting me know."

"But Natalie, Paul tells me that you are selling up! Do please think before you do anything drastic, after all dear, we're none of us getting any younger are we and well, it's nice to have a man around, even if it's only as an escort to all the shows and functions that..."

"If that's all Audrey, I must go I have a lot to do, I'm off to see the estate agent now."

"The estate agent! Sop quickly! Oh Natalie surely not."

"Goodbye Audrey."

Her meeting with Frank Samuels the next day, although harrowing, was very helpful and rewarding. He was able to advise her on several matters of which she was unsure and she felt more confident about the decisions that she had made, "Frank, I know now why Richard respected and liked you so much," she took one of his gnarled hands in both of hers, "all through our conversation you have never offered one word of reproach."

"My dear Natalie, when you have lived as long as I have, you realise that life is an extraordinary game and we, the players, are almost helpless to control it."

She waved goodbye to him as he drove away from the hotel and tears formed in her eyes, she knew that she was doing the right thing but it didn't stop it from hurting. The estate agents had been very helpful and keen, it was rare to get such a prestigious and well-maintained property on their books and the partners, without even seeing it, were phoning several people of their acquaintance whom they thought might be interested, before Natalie was out of the building.

Arriving home from her lunch with Frank she found that Fiona had phoned, Mrs Mason had taken the call, "Oh Mrs Bennett," she had never been able to get around to calling her Mrs Aston, it was one of the reasons why Paul had wanted to replace her, "Mrs Bennett, Mrs Philips rang, I told her that you were out and she said that she would ring again later."

"Thank you Jessie."

It was going to be so hard to tell Jessie that she was selling the house, she had been with her since Candida was born. It would be even harder to tell her that she was leaving the country. She decided to tell her tomorrow before the estate agent arrived to measure the rooms. She would make provisions to see that she was adequately provided for. Frank was taking care of all the legal details like that and for selling the house and the car. She had decided that she would leave England as soon as the house was sold. Candida had been wonderful when she had finally plucked up the courage to phone her with the news of her break-up with Paul. She had asked very few questions and had been utterly supportive and very understanding. It had been her suggestion that Natalie came out to live near them, in New Zealand. There were some lovely houses in the countryside nearby. It was an idea which Natalie, at first, had totally disregarded but, later considered and finally accepted. It was a frightening and daunting proposition but she was determined to go through with it, the memory that Richard, just before he died, had suggested that she sold the old house and start afresh helped her to make up her mind.

Candida had expressed a desire to have certain items of furniture and ornaments from the house and she herself wanted to take several things to remind her of her life with Richard including the train set for Candida's future family. She would have to make arrangements for them to be crated and shipped out as soon as possible. Frank had been a mine of information and had reminded her of so many small but significant things that she would have to see to. She could see that it was going to be a very busy time for the next few weeks, which was a good thing, she wouldn't have time to brood. She must also look into the documents required to take Jamie and Juno out to New Zealand with her; she had already collected poor Juno from those people and brought her back home. The poor little thing had been so delighted. At the thought of Jamie and Juno her face crumpled, she had been so happy showing them, having the puppies, getting her life back in fact after Richard. She thought of the chatter at shows, the excitement, the anticipation each time she had filled in a schedule. Her first rosette! The first puppy! She had loved it all until.... Tears, once again, ran unchecked down her face as she took another small sip of sherry. The phone rang but she did not answer it.

"Simon, should I go round there. She's still not answering."

"Fee. After all that's happened, I don't suppose she wants to talk to you, or me for that matter."

"But I've been ringing for more than two weeks."

"I know but.... I suppose you want to tell her about the letter I got today."

"Well yes, I'm sure she'd want to know that the KC have cleared you over that business. Anyway, I want to talk to her, I told you that a 'For Sale' sign went up on her house a week ago, well there's a Sold sign there now. I'm worried about her. What's happening, what's she going to do?"

Simon shrugged his shoulders, he felt very tired today. Now that all his troubles seemed to be resolving themselves and today, realising that their whole future was no longer in jeopardy and that he had nothing to worry about any more, he suddenly felt utterly drained. He now just wanted to get on with his and Fee's life together and enjoy the dogs. Although he felt sorry for Natalie, he couldn't be bothered to be concerned about her at the moment. Finishing his drink, he locked the back door, "Come on Fee. I'm absolutely buggered, let's go to bed," a small grin lightened his features, "I promise not to molest you... well, not tonight anyway. I've got a headache!" He slipped an arm around her waist and drew her close and leered at her, "Of course, tomorrow might be different honey," Fiona laughed and punched him in the ribs, together they went upstairs.

As always, the jungle drums passed on the news of Simon's reprieve and also that someone had been mounting a campaign of lies etc. against the Simfell kennels. Suddenly they were the flavour of the month again, suddenly people were phoning to congratulate them.

People were suggesting that they use their stud dogs in the not too distant future, people were enquiring about puppies.

Fiona put the phone down and went into the kitchen, "Why is everyone so two-faced Simon? That's another enquiry for a puppy. At this rate we shall have sold the entire two litters before they're born. Perhaps we ought to mate up Caroline's bitch as well."

"Won't do any harm. We've a lot of leeway to make up in the financial and popularity stakes. Never mind, we should both get damn good entries when we judge at our next Champ shows. Mine's first isn't it? We shall see."

Fiona looked at his face and smiled, he had been looking so drawn and worried over the past months, it was wonderful to see him happy and enthusiastic again. If only she could settle her differences with Natalie, life would be almost back to normal.

"I'll tell you something Fee."

"What's that?"

"You know I've been thinking that it's not the Kennel Club who really runs dogdom in this country now but the big powerful breeders."

"Yes, I know you think that, I don't. Some people would say that we're big breeders but, as you well know, we've no clout with the Kennel Club."

"No I know that but, there are big breeders and big breeders aren't there. There's the ones like us who have done quite well, have quite a few dogs and breed quite a bit; win quite a bit too. Then there's the one's who've done all that as well but with an eye to power, to controlling things at the top. We've never really set out to do that have we."

"No, we just wanted to be successful at breeding, judging and showing."

"Well, there you are. They're the ones who now, however, call the shots."

"No, I don't agree. What's brought all this up anyway?"

"Well, I had another thought. Look the next logical step would be for the big boys and girls to get complete control."

"And how would they do that?"

"By getting control of all the judging and winning in the Open show world as well."

"Oh yes, and how are they going to do that."

"By getting the KC to devolve responsibility for all shows, both Champ and Open to the committees of the breed clubs."

"And?"

"They'd have complete control then, all secretaries would know that, if they picked a judge that was not approved by the breed committees, they wouldn't get a decent entry. I mean, they know that now with the Champ shows. Everyone in a breed would have to lick the boots of the breed committee or else. Total autocracy!"

"Simon, you make it sound like one of these countries totally ruled by fear."

"Yeah, that's just about it."

Fiona burst out laughing, "Oh really Simon, don't you think that you're being a bit melodramatic this is dog showing we're talking about. I know that we both think that this all goes on in the Champ shows because of all the money to be made and the prestige, but Open shows! No, the Kennel Club would never let that happen."

"They couldn't do anything to stop it. They are totally reliant on the money coming in too. The point to all this Fee is that we must get on as many committees as we can and quickly before this all starts, then, at least we'd stand a chance."

Fiona reached up and kissed him, "I do so love you Simon. Even if you've now entirely lost the plot."

He smiled and kissed her, "You'll see. You'll see my girl."

CHAPTER THIRTY- NINE

Several weeks later, as Fiona was checking on one of the pregnant bitches, a car drove up and an elderly man got out.

"Hello, be with you in a moment," making sure that the kennel door was safely closed, Fiona walked down the path, "Hello, how can I help you."

"You are Mrs Philips. Mrs Fiona Philips?"

"Yes."

"My name is Frank Samuels and I am acting on behalf of Mrs. Bennett.. er.. Mrs Aston."

"Yes I thought that your face was familiar. Didn't we meet at a charity dance? You were with Natalie then."

"Ah, yes. That's right. I've come to give you this letter. It's from Natalie."

"I see. How is she? I've tried and tried to contact her."

Frank Samuels explained that Natalie had already sold her house and would be leaving shortly.

"Leaving here, where is she going?"

"To New Zealand to be with her daughter. I'm sure that, if you read her letter she will have explained everything."

"New Zealand, but she can't go without me seeing her. She can't."

"I'm sorry Mrs Philips but I rather think that Natalie would rather not speak about.... what has happened."

Saying goodbye to Frank Samuels, Fiona took the letter into the kitchen to read it. The two house dogs immediately joined her and lay at her feet. When Simon came home from work, he found her still sitting at the table the letter laid out in front of her, it was obvious that she had been crying, "Hello what's this, what's upset you?"

"It's a letter from Natalie, she's going to New Zealand and doesn't want to see me. She says that it would be too painful for both of us." After he had read it, he pulled Fiona to her feet and hugged her, "Come on Fee cheer up. It was a very nice letter really, she thanks you for introducing her to showing and for your friendship...."

"Yes, and look where that got her."

"She doesn't blame you at all. She says that she will keep in touch. Look Fee. If there is any blame to be apportioned in all of this it's

mine. If I hadn't been such a bloody, jealous fool in the first place and walked out, none of this would have happened. I.."
She stopped him by kissing his mouth, "Sh. It's all water under the bridge now. It's over."

During the months that followed Natalie's departure both Fiona and Simon were kept very busy with the three litters. They only lost one rather small puppy from Saffron's litter. Because of the extra work with the litters, they had taken it in turns to show the dogs and had had several good wins. Even the Glencastles had had a few moderate successes at Open shows and later they would have the pleasure of having a litter from them. Fiona was relaxed and happy, Beryl and Peter had popped over several times to see the litters and Fiona felt that, at last, life was feeling great. Natalie had kept her promise and now she and Fiona were in regular correspondence. Natalie was even thinking of showing her dogs in New Zealand.

Today, Laura had come down to see them and Tom and was staying for a few days. Fiona had been so pleased to see her and to hear all about the new house. She had brought photographs of the twins and Amanda and both Fiona and Simon had exclaimed on how they had all grown. The day passed rapidly with Laura telling Fiona all about their new house in Scotland, their new neighbours; the children's new schools. When Tom suddenly appeared at the door, they were quite taken by surprise. Laura rushed up to him and standing on tiptoes, hugged him and kissed him, "Heavens boy, what have they been feeding you on. You've grown a foot at least."
He had now successfully completed his exams and would be leaving Fiona and Simon and going up to Scotland in a month's time. They would miss Tom, he had fitted in so well and been such good company, especially when things had been so bad, looking after him had helped to take their minds off their problems. He had been an enormous help in the kennels and both Simon and Fiona had become very fond of him; they would miss him very much. The two old friends had a good two days together and when it was time for Laura to depart, Fiona felt quite sad. She had just waved goodbye to her and watched the taxi disappear from sight when she noticed that a police car had stopped in the road and, in fact, was just reversing into the drive. Her heart stopped, what now! Simon, was it Simon or Beryl or Peter or..

A man and woman were walking towards her, "Mrs. Fiona Philips?"

"Yes, what's wrong. Has there been an accident. Who?"

"Please can we go into the house? Perhaps you would like to sit down."

Totally numb with fear, Fiona allowed herself to be led back into the warm kitchen. The female officer suggested that she might like a cup of tea. Fiona rapidly shook her head, "For goodness' sake tell me."

"You are, we understand, the former wife of a Duncan Cameron. Is that right?"

Fiona could only nod her head.

"Did you know that Mr Cameron and his wife and son were holidaying in Switzerland?"

Again, cold and shaken Fiona nodded, "Yes, he told me last week that they were going to stay with friends, they often did. Why what's happened?"

"I am sorry to have to tell you that Mr Cameron's car was in an accident."

"Is he hurt?"

"I'm sorry to tell you Mrs Philips that he was badly injured. He was rushed to hospital, but, I'm afraid, died from his injuries."

Fiona put her hands to her face, oh God, not Duncan, no. She looked up as a thought struck her, "What about Barbara, his wife and Donald, little Donald. Were they in the car?"

"Yes, they were. Mrs Cameron died immediately at the scene of the accident and...."

"Donald, what about Donald?"

"Apart from cuts and bruises. He appears to be all right."

Fiona let out a breath of relief, "Thank God. Where is he now?"

"We understand that he is being kept in hospital for observation for a few days. There was a letter among Mr Cameron's effects giving your name as the contact in the event of an accident"

Laughing and crying at the same time Fiona said, "Yes, that was Duncan, always so efficient. His mother is very frail, not expected to live long and in a nursing home so that's why he would have put my name."

The woman officer handed her a steaming hot cup of tea, "Do try to drink some of this."

Fiona, scrubbed away at her eyes and tried to pick up the cup but her hands were shaking too much, "This has been a terrible shock.

263

Would you do me a favour please and ring my husband, the number is in the address book under 'Simon'." The male police officer left the room.

" He will be home shortly Mrs Philips. Can we contact anyone to come and sit with you?"

"No, no, I'll be all right, honestly. It was just such a shock and thank you for being so kind."

When the police had left, Fiona had another cup of tea and then slowly went upstairs. In the back of her wardrobe she had her old photograph album and her wedding album. Back in the warm kitchen, she put them on the kitchen table, as she leafed through the pages, she smiled through her tears at the photos of her father with Duncan before they were married, and photos of her with Duncan taken in her father's garden. She opened the white wedding album and gently touched the photos of them together on their wedding day, on their honeymoon. There were photos of them in their first flat and later in their house, photos of them on various holidays and photos of Duncan with his mother and father and of Duncan with Sally as a puppy. This last one made the tears flow even more and she was still crying when Simon rushed into the room and quickly took her in his arms, "I'm here Fee. It's alright, I'm here."

It transpired that Duncan had requested in his will that, in the unlikely event of his dying abroad, that he wished to be brought home to England to be buried. Weeks later, after the inquest and all the formalities were over, Fiona and Simon attended the joint funerals of Duncan and Barbara; Laura and Michael came down from Scotland, Beryl and Peter also attended. The partners in his firm, some of Duncan and Barbara's near neighbours and several of Barbara's relatives, but not Donald. It had been decided that he was still not sufficiently recovered from the trauma.

It was some weeks later when all the daffodils were nodding their heads in the wind and their were fleeting glimpses of blue sky and sunshine, that Fiona walked across the field to the woods and sat by Sally's grave, "Sally, I'm so sorry not to have come for a chat sooner but so much has happened and there have been so many things to sort out. I told you didn't I that poor Duncan had been killed and that only Donald survived. I knew that you'd have wanted to know that.

What I didn't tell you, mainly because I had totally forgotten all about it myself, was that several years ago, you know sweetheart, after I lost my baby, Duncan had asked me if I would agree to be Donald's legal guardian in the event of.... Well, to cut a long story short, I said yes, never thinking that I would ever have.... I had been so upset at the time over losing the baby that I had honestly forgotten, so, of course, the big news that I have to tell you is that Donald will be coming to live with us.

Sally, I'm so, so excited, I'm sorry that it had to be like this but, oh Sally! I'll have a little boy at last! After all these years and when I had completely given up hope, I am going to be a Mum, well as good as. Simon has been wonderful and is looking forward to his coming to live with us. He's going to build him a tree house in these woods so you'll see a lot of him. The poor little boy is still very upset and misses his Mummy and Daddy. He still cries at night and has nightmares too but; he has been here for a couple of visits and seemed to like it. When he's better and settled in, I'll bring him up to see you and he can play in the woods. You'll like him. He looks quite serious, just like Duncan! We both love him already. I shall read stories to him, give him parties, take him to school, help him with his homework, Simon is going to teach him how to play football. Oh Sally, my darling Sally, you know what I'm trying to say don't you. You, of all people, know what this means to me. Don't worry Sal I shall never forget you, I'll still come and talk to you. Well, I'll go now, bye Sally. See you soon"

Printed in the United Kingdom
by Lightning Source UK Ltd.
PPZ308C02